Guardians of the Time Stream

Book Three

Music in the Night

Michelle L. Levigne

www.YeOldeDragonBooks.com

Ye Olde Dragon Books
6909 Ackley Rd.
Parma, OH 44129

www.YeOldeDragonBooks.com

2OldeDragons@gmail.com

Copyright © 2016 Michelle L. Levigne

ISBN 13: 978-1-961129-38-2

Published in the United States of America
Publication Date: January 15, 2024

Cover Art © Copyright 2024 Ye Olde Dragon Books

All rights reserved. No portion of this book may be reproduced or transmitted in any form or by any electronic or mechanical means, including photocopying, recording or by any information retrieval and storage system without permission of the publisher.

Ebooks, audiobooks, and print books are *not* transferrable, either in whole or in part. As the purchaser or otherwise *lawful* recipient of this book, you have the right to enjoy the novel on your own computer or other device. Further distribution, copying, sharing, gifting or uploading is illegal and violates United States Copyright laws.
Pirating of books is illegal. Criminal Copyright Infringement, *including* infringement without monetary gain, may be investigated by the Federal Bureau of Investigation and is punishable by up to five years in federal prison and a fine of up to $250,000.

Names, characters and incidents depicted in this book are products of the author's imagination, or are used in a fictitious situation. Any resemblances to actual events, locations, organizations, incidents or persons – living or dead – are coincidental and beyond the intent of the author.

Chapter One

October 1877
Cleveland, Ohio

"Sanctuary has fallen." Randall Endicott stared into the darkness of the underground chamber that had once been part of the cellar of a massive house, overlooking the Cuyahoga River.

For a heartbeat or two, like he always did when his benefactor came to visit, Brogan considered not responding. Endicott wouldn't come into the room, wouldn't raise the candle in his hand and step out of the tunnel that connected the former cellar to the warren underneath the growing port city, until he got a response. When Brogan had been a child, his father teased him that he could see in darkness where cats were blind. If he sat still enough, could he make Endicott think he wasn't here in his office, where darkness soothed the alternating tingling and burning in his mangled face?

He couldn't do that to a man who remembered Brogan Ambrose as he used to be, with a song on his lips and in his heart and dreams of adventure and discovery in service of the Originators. Without Endicott's help and his suggestion of a place where he could hide from the cruel light of day, Brogan suspected he would have taken the coward's way out years ago.

"I think I knew when it happened." Brogan pressed his fingertips against his mangled cheek, remembering the shriek of crystal that had awakened him. "Six weeks ago, on a Friday?"

"Six weeks ago on Friday," Endicott said with a sigh. He put the candle down outside the doorway cut through the rock and took a step into the stygian room. "Are you purposely courting an image of a troll in his lair?"

"I would rather be considered a dragon." Brogan surprised himself with a rasping little laugh. He struck a match and lit the lantern sitting on the front of the long table that served as his desk. When the stink of sulfur faded, he sat back further into the darkness until the chair creaked. Not that it mattered. Endicott knew the ruin of his face.

"Thank you. Some of us can't see in the dark." A soft snort. "Like dragons." Endicott settled into one of the old ladderback chairs facing the desk. "What do you mean, you knew?" He frowned and rested his elbows on his knees, leaning forward. "You felt the reverberation in the crystal?"

"What happened?" He flattened his hand to cover the thickened skin of his cheek, reliving that moment when he woke feeling as if the crystal fragments that had penetrated down to the bone were trying to tear free. And take chunks of his skull with them. The reverberations had shifted through chords, on the edge of music. Visions filled his head in rapid-fire sequence, making him doubt his sanity even more than he usually did. In his mind's eye, he had seen the massive support beams in the foundations of Sanctuary melting and twisting, the tunnels collapsing in on themselves, and felt the shimmering song of thousands of pieces of crystal go sour. As if he had been physically there, for the first time in years. As if he had been picked up and transported across two-thirds of the country.

No, he wouldn't go there with that imagery. Down that road lay madness. And yet, if anything could move the stuff of matter massive distances in the blink of an eye, wouldn't it be crystal, the material the ancestors had brought from the future when they fought to save the history of the known world?

Madness. Don't go there. It's not alive, and it doesn't create doorways around the world. It can't. Not without the lotus. Not without being reassembled more than it has been already. Crystal isn't... it can't... it doesn't...

He wouldn't finish the thought. Yet there were times, since the explosions that killed his family and mangled him, when he fancied that the crystal used by the ancestors to travel through time might be sentient, able to think and reason and choose and act. After the visions and sensations of that night, which Endicott had just confirmed was not another step into madness, Brogan realized he had never pondered the *emotional* factor. The crystal had cried out in terror, and his were the only ears that could hear. His mangled face was proof that crystal could not be destroyed. It could only be reshaped. Unless someone possessed the incredible ability to sing to the crystal, and sing *with* it, then crystal punished all those who attempted to control it. He knew of only a few people who had been able to sing to crystal and coax it into new shapes.

"The simplest explanation is that the Fremonts happened," Endicott said after a long pause. One side of his mouth quirked up in a weary smile. "Odessa reappeared, and we took her to Sanctuary to root out some of that trouble Ernest and Edward were both hunting. She knew where that infernal whistle of Matilda's has been all along. Not only that, she knew the song to play, and the time was right, as Edward feared it would be."

"Ah." Brogan settled back a little more in his chair, trying not to shudder as his imagination filled in what had happened. *If my dream was true, then perhaps I am not quite insane yet? Maybe the doorway isn't all my imagination, either?* He mentally shook himself and focused on the news Endicott had brought.

He was younger than Edward Fremont by a good fifteen years, and had studied with him for a short time. He had been a welcome guest in the Fremonts' home, had met Ulysses a few times and gotten into mischief with him, and knew Odessa when she was a child just starting to display the Fremont brilliance of mind and curiosity. Endicott had kept him informed of events in the family's lives through their tragedies, because he had considered himself a friend.

Then a little more than two months ago, when Brogan expected Endicott for one of his regular visits, a messenger brought a note down saying that incredible events had occurred. He would share the details when he returned to Cleveland. Now with fall turning into winter, Endicott had returned.

"Yes. That is sometimes the most apt reaction when it comes to that infernally brilliant and troublesome family." Endicott chuckled. "Simply put, Ess's memories were blocked even more extensively than we were led to believe. Once the wall fell, many things came together, ending in a trip to South America, to bring Matilda and Ernest and their archeological party forward in time, from the moment of their attack."

"Time travel without the Great Machine? How is that even possible?"

"I don't have the time or the materials to help me explain. However..." Endicott sat back and crossed one leg over the other. "You could always talk with Ernest and Matilda and they could explain all the science and the theories involved."

"Randall..." Brogan refused to go any further in the old argument.

"We need to disrupt your incredible little kingdom. With the fall of Sanctuary, we're going to need a new headquarters. The nice sedate, useful little building we intended to set up somewhere over our heads is fair to becoming the wonder of the New World. Airship docks and access to the railroads and shipping on the Great Lakes, as well as shipping overland by steam-cart. We could make good use of these old slave tunnels and the prehistoric passages your people have found."

"What about my people who have taken shelter here from the injustice above? What about the children who hide down here from the criminals who would enslave them?" Brogan congratulated himself that he didn't howl, half in fear, and he didn't snarl at Endicott in worry for his own safety and the ability to fade into the night.

"They will be protected. Plans are already being made. We will be expanding the Originators. Recruiting. Uly pointed out that we are wasting incredible resources, both in skills and physical prowess, creativity, inventive skills. Your people will be an incredible, valuable resource for us. Not just in making use of this underground kingdom of yours." Endicott gestured to take in the winding tunnels that spread out around them, into the darkness, some carved by water and some by wind. Some were mysteriously smooth as if carved by the futuristic machines the ancestors had once possessed, which no longer existed even in recorded memories and drawings.

"You haven't told anyone..."

"About you? About surviving and vanishing? No. However, I do believe the time has come, Brogan. Come out of hiding, out of your darkness. Time for your people to join the world above ground." He sighed.

"Time to stop licking your wounds, their wounds. Things are coming to a head. The race to find the pieces of the Great Machine is heating up. The best way to defend ourselves is to be part of the army, not the innocent civilians who get trampled in the press of battle."

"For a man who didn't serve in battle--"

"You know what I mean. No sass from you, youngster." He grinned even as he shook a finger at Brogan, where he sat cloaked in darkness just beyond the puddle of lantern light.

"Youngster." Brogan snorted. "I'm not that much younger than you."

"Current events have made me feel entirely ancient." He sat back a little more and sighed. "Time to reveal the miracle of your survival, and the gifts granted you." One corner of his mouth twitched up when Brogan snorted, eloquent response to that statement. "Deny it as you will, the incredible things you have done for the people you shelter and lead make me believe the crystal allows you to see into men's souls."

"Reason enough to loathe all humanity."

"I believe you were spared because you were cloaked in music, practicing your music when the attack occurred and the explosion came."

"Spared?" Brogan sat forward, bracing his hands on the edge of the table, thrusting his mangled face into the light. He felt the warmth of it touching the bubbled, melted flesh and ropey scars running from his left temple, down along his jaw, the twisting sneer in the corner of his mouth. "I was spared, as you put it, because I was too enrapt in my music and didn't know we had visitors." He spat onto the dusty, rough stone floor. "Intruders. Invaders. I wasn't there at my father's side."

"It was the music. Why are you punishing yourself for the miracle, the talent that kept you alive? Would your family grudge you your life? They were proud of your talent. They were sure that you would be the one to make the breakthrough, because they believed, as Edward, Vivian, Ernest and Matilda believed and the children have now proven, that music is the third side of the key to controlling crystal."

"The children." Brogan's thoughts skittered sideways to the street children who had joined the community.

Mouse knew his face because that wily, clever, irrepressible girl was impossible to restrain. While he lingered in the shadows and moved in silence, she followed him and confronted him, and never even blinked when he thought to scare her away by revealing his face. He wouldn't inflict his mangled face on the other children brought down to hide in the tunnels. They had gone through so much already. Orphaned, cast onto the streets, threatened by people who thought Dickens' novels were recommendations rather than condemnation of the downward spiral of society.

"Ess and Uly Fremont," Endicott said.

Then he spent the next half hour astounding Brogan, relating how Ess had first found a canopic jar full of crystal dust and protected it from the

Revisionists, then the experiments she and Uly had performed on it. Brogan thought his cheek burned and buzzed at mention of the word "dust," as if the crystal embedded in his bones rebelled against the idea. The buzzing-burn calmed as Endicott told how the siblings had recreated the visual and audio communication plates of the ancestors, using the crystal dust, locking it to their sole use by blood, and controlling the plates through music. The key, they had discovered, was to use music to persuade crystal to work with them. Not controlling crystal but communicating and creating partnership. Music bridged the gap between the human mind and the energy within the crystal, and the stored information placed there by the ancestors.

Brogan remembered listening to Vivian play her flute, and how the music awakened dreams within him. Matilda had noticed how he grasped esoteric concepts much more easily after listening to the flute with the bits of crystal embedded in it, and recommended he be sent for special training.

Focused on music.

He muffled a sigh as he wondered what he would have accomplished, what he could have learned and regained from the ancestors' knowledge and technology, if he had pursued those special studies. Perhaps he would have been helpful in regaining the communication plates. Perhaps...

"Perhaps I am not quite as mad as I feared," he murmured, startling himself when he realized he spoke aloud.

If crystal and blood and music could awaken such wonders, and if Matilda had seen potential in him, perhaps guessed at hidden gifts, maybe the things he saw in the darkness of the tunnels when the crystal sang to him, making his throat ache to release song... were not so unreal after all?

"Mad?" Endicott shook his head, his smile sympathetic, rather than pitying.

There was a difference, as Brogan had learned over the years since the Revisionist attack that had killed his family and left him a fugitive from light and society. The difference had given him the courage to trust Endicott when the man offered to help him. He had found sanctuary here in Cleveland, in the darkness, where he could help the downtrodden and cheated and abused without fear of terrifying them. He and Endicott had done a great amount of good over the years. His only regrets had been the lack of music in his life, and the suspicion that the silence in his head had brought on madness. First the sensation that the crystal was singing to him, and lately the visions.

What if the visions weren't inside his head, but actually hung there in the darkness where he saw them?

He realized Endicott had continued speaking, but he hadn't heard a word. He stood, picked up the lantern, and held it out to the older man. "I think... I need to show this to you."

Without waiting to see if Endicott followed, he stepped out into the passageway. He didn't need the lantern or the candle. He knew the upward slopes and downward twists of the tunnels. They didn't walk far. Despite the steady increase in population below ground as the weather turned unfriendly with the onset of autumn, leaving the regularly traveled portions of the underground community didn't take long.

"This is new?" Endicott said, when they stopped in a spot where the tunnel widened enough for three to walk side-by-side, and curved just enough that the small oil lanterns set in the intersections of several other tunnels weren't visible.

"Newly discovered, broken through by the explorers." Brogan snorted amusement that had more nervousness than laughter in the sound. It made his throat ache. Or maybe that tension was the subliminal music that always touched him in this bend in the passage. "They refer to themselves as either mole rats or earthworms, depending on their moods. Or how filthy they got that day, and how much Mary scolded them for it. No, this is a tunnel we didn't dig. The odd thing is that we're sure there was no sign of it being here before, with some barrier blocking it off from the other tunnels we've found. I could almost believe the ghost stories some of the rougher characters like telling. Of monsters that slide through solid stone as if it were water, eating granite as if it were candy sticks." He caught his breath as one note in his voice set off a reverberation. The music in his left cheekbone grew louder, the buzz-hum aching for a moment before splitting into a chord that could almost persuade him to sing again.

A spark lit in the open air just beyond where he and Endicott stood. As he watched, the spark expanded, spreading out to fill the tunnel, with a slightly stronger line of light, shimmering through the rainbow where it touched the rock, leaving a faint coruscation of light across the passageway like the filmy walls of a soap bubble. The soft hum of silent music traveled up to his sinuses and down into his lungs. The note continued even when he turned to Endicott and pointed at the light.

"Do you see it?" he whispered, afraid that speaking too loudly would shatter the light.

Endicott looked where Brogan pointed. His eyes widened slightly, but not in the wonder the younger man expected. Needed.

"Something is happening," Endicott whispered, as Brogan's shoulders sagged. The music whispering through his flesh tightened and threatened to go sour, poised to erupt in a moan, because this was more proof he was going mad. "I can't hear it. I can only feel it." He reached in his pocket and brought out a pocket watch. Embedded in the case was a crescent moon-shaped fragment of crystal.

Blue and green shimmered softly up and down the length and seemed to darken at the curved tips of the crescent.

"Your education needs a great deal of catching up," the older man said after a moment. "Music is the key, and with your talent..." He shook his head and slid the pocket watch back into place. "When Ess comes here, after the grand tour with her grandparents and other matters are dealt with, she can work with you and teach you herself. Everyone is being outfitted with bits of crystal, to help cut down on the dissonance that seems to block so many of us from hearing or at least feeling crystal at work. What do you see, that I don't?"

"It's more than seeing." Brogan inhaled, then took a long step, through the soap bubble of light.

He staggered as he emerged into bright sunlight, on a green, wooded mountainside that extended upward and downward for what seemed forever. No matter what time of day or night he encountered the shimmer of light and stepped through, it was always noonday here on the mountain, with the scent of ripening strawberries and apples in the air, and the green smell of lush grass baking in the sunlight. Off to his left, a stream chuckled and bubbled as it cascaded downhill in a silver sparkling ribbon. Brogan's eyes ached from the unaccustomed light, and he closed them as he spread his arms and welcomed the heat soaking into his all-black clothes. Here, he didn't mind stepping into full daylight, because in all his visits to this place hidden beneath the city, he had never encountered any people. No people. No animals other than a few birds, maybe a squirrel or two, some insects. And curiously, no matter how long he stayed and searched, he never found the sun that provided the light. It came from everywhere, bleaching out what shadows were cast from all directions.

Turning, he opened his eyes again, and located the shimmering circle. He almost waited for Endicott to step through after him, then laughed brokenly at himself. Just because Endicott sensed something, that didn't mean the man could find the doorway he obviously couldn't see. Sighing, he stepped back through, his eyes closed to help himself adjust to the darkness and shadows of underground.

"What happened?" Endicott grasped Brogan's arm above his elbow. His eyes grew wider and he leaned back against the curved, uneven wall of the tunnel as Brogan described the scene. He chuckled when the younger man fell silent. "No wonder you thought you were going mad. You did not imagine any of it, because I will vouch that you vanished. I walked right through the spot where you vanished, and I felt... something," he said after a slight pause, and a shrug. "Energy. The crystal in my pocket hummed almost audibly. Whatever talent or gift you possess that lets you see the light, I would wager that is what lets you pass through to this other place." He raised the lantern and peered into Brogan's face.

Brogan tried not to wince, but he knew Endicott studied the mangled side of his face, where the flesh looked like melted wax, rudely shoved into the semblance of a man's face. The intent gaze was almost a palpable touch.

"I would hazard a guess that the crystal embedded in your bones is reacting to some sort of energy present in this one place--"

"There are other places, throughout the tunnels. This is merely the closest," Brogan hurried to say.

"Indeed? Well, I think once again, crystal is the key. You said you feel music more than hear it, when the light is about to appear. Crystal, music... and blood. The three-sided key, as MacDonald so eloquently puts it. I know so very little. When our experts join us, most likely next summer, depending on the progress of our building, then you can discuss this with them."

"Ernest and Matilda?" He liked the idea of turning all this over to them, letting them unravel the mystery and puzzle.

"They are in the amusing position of being students. For now, anyway. No, as Ess observed a short time ago, people are considered experts who merely have the most experience, or the only real knowledge of something. When Ess and Uly come, then you three, I daresay, will accomplish wonders." Endicott raised the lantern again and shone the light at the place where the shimmering circle had been just moments ago. "I shouldn't wonder if this is somehow another variant of what Matilda and Ernest used in South America."

"You will tell me more, especially if this might be linked?"

"I think we've earned some dinner after all this. Please tell me I wasn't mistaken, and I smelled Mary's incredible crayfish stew when I passed the kitchen."

"She knew you were coming, and she knows what you like." He stretched his arm across the passageway. "You are going to tell me about the time bubble, over dinner?"

"Of course. And so much other news." Endicott chuckled when Brogan hesitated a moment, then lowered his arm. "Now, I did tell you that Matilda and Ernest had set up a trap for the traitors among us, didn't I?" he said as they headed back down the passageway.

"No, you did not."

"Ah, then I can see we are going to make a long night of it."

Chapter Two

Late October
Chicago

The autumn wind drove rain in from all directions, or so it seemed as Carmen Mackenzie trudged down the street. One last possibility for work lay ahead of her. If she couldn't persuade the head cook at the Grand Cascade Hotel to take her on, she had only one option left to her. Well, to be honest, two options, but Carmen would rather die than sell her body for money. While the slick men with hard, sharp faces promised her a lifetime of luxury when they approached her, promising with the right clothes she could ask any price she wanted, Carmen knew better. She hadn't been so sheltered when she traveled with her father and the camp meeting team that she didn't know about prostitution and panderers and disease and abuse, and how quickly a young woman aged in that line of work.

No, her only option was to sell her mother's cross. Certainly it would be enough money to get her through the winter, to feed her and pay for the tiny room at the boarding house. In the spring, she could walk out to the farms in northern Illinois and get a job as a field laborer.

The irony was that she had plenty of money, enough to take care of her for the rest of her life, waiting in several safe deposit boxes scattered across the country. However, getting to those boxes without being caught by one of the self-righteous, vindictive people who had destroyed her father's reputation was the challenge. She had gone to Denver, Boston, and Atlanta, attempting to retrieve the family treasures and caches of money. Someone had been looking for her at each place. After all, her father was known and loved in those cities, and it was only logical to expect her to go there for shelter. Chicago had become her destination, spending more of her limited funds than she had liked to spare, simply because no one would look for her here. Since her mother's death, her father had avoided Chicago as if he feared the place.

What Carmen feared was that when she gathered enough money to return to any of those cities, she would discover that her father's former associates had learned of the existence of the safe deposit boxes and obtained legal orders to open them and confiscate the contents.

Why did they insist on taking everything, continuing to punish her father even after his death, after his reputation had been shredded beyond salvaging? Carmen could almost persuade herself she was being hunted for something more than self-righteous vindictiveness and fear.

Right now, all that mattered was surviving until spring, and saving enough money for one more attempt at a safe deposit box. By then, her enemies would have to assume she was dead or at least unable to harm them and give up looking for her. Time and patience and prayers would have to sustain her. Other than her mother's cross, that was all she had left.

Her largest difficulty was that she had tried to sell the cross three times, and each time the shopkeeper wanted the crystal rose that fit into the center of the cross as well. Carmen couldn't bring herself to agree to that. Her imaginary childhood friend, Essie, had showed up in her dreams weeks ago and told her not to sell the rose. While the advice of an imaginary friend couldn't exactly be taken as gospel truth, Carmen wanted to believe her. Just like she had believed with her mother's encouragement that Essie was a real girl when she was a child, she wanted to believe Essie spoke the truth now. She needed to hold onto that crystal rose, and not just because it was the last thing she possessed that had been her mother's.

So she needed to get the job as an assistant cook or dishwasher or whatever was available at the hotel just another block down the street. Mrs. Blomfield, her landlady, knew the right people to find out about jobs opening throughout the great, sprawling city of Chicago. The helpful, somewhat worn old woman had admitted that it would neither hurt nor help to offer her as a reference when Carmen applied for work. Then she had looked up at the sky with the gray, churning clouds moving in from over the lake, and bade her get to the hotel before the rain struck. If she looked like a drowned cat when she asked for work, a recommendation from the First Lady of the United States wouldn't be enough to get her a job.

For luck, Carmen had worn her mother's cross. She hadn't worn it since the dream that helped her make up her mind and flee before she lost everything. Seeing and speaking to Essie in her dream had been the first good thing that had happened to her since her father died. She needed that bit of luck or blessing or whatever one wished to call it.

Clutching the cross through the protective layers of inadequate shawl and jacket and shirtwaist, Carmen stepped under the overhang of a doorway on a side street. She tipped her head back and she closed her eyes and prayed. For good measure, she focused on Essie's face as she had last seen her imaginary friend, and called silently with all her force of will. Perhaps she wasn't being so fanciful, wishing that Essie would turn out to be an angel sent to guard and guide and advise her?

The crystal rose warmed and vibrated through the wet layers of cloth. Carmen gasped and stepped back against the wall. She uncurled her fingers from the cross and tried to catch her breath. No, she was not imagining. The tiny spot where the back of the crystal rose touched her bare skin, under her shirt, was warm. The contrast with the icy rain soaking her clothes was far too clear to be her imagination. She hadn't warmed the cross and rose with her equally cold hand.

Before she could brace herself to clutch the cross and rose again, the vibrations stopped and the warmth faded. The wooden sidewalk rippled like waves under her feet. A more deeply recessed doorway, offering better shelter, was only a dozen steps further down the side street. She needed to sit down, out of the rain, just for a few moments. Hunching her shoulders, Carmen staggered down the sidewalk, aiming for the darkness of the recessed doorway, praying it was dry and deep enough that she could hide from sight while she regained her balance.

A steam-cart trundled down the street from behind her, just as she stepped into the doorway. A whimper of gratitude escaped her clenched teeth. It was deep and wide enough she could have laid down in it, and kept her feet dry. She gratefully sank down into the corner on the right, well out of traffic, if anyone needed to come out of the door. Tugging her skirts down around her ankles, she raised her hand to press against the cross.

The steam-cart came into view, framed in the doorway. It was an open steam-cart, a newer model but without any kind of roof or covering on it. Carmen snorted her disdain for anyone who thought an open vehicle made any sense in Chicago, with its wind and seemingly constant rain. The man who drove it hunched his shoulders, and his eyes were lost in goggles gone white with steam or condensation. The other man in the cart stood up in the passenger section behind him, one hand braced on the seat back, the other on the man's shoulder, and turned his head, surveying the street.

Carmen paused with her hand just above the cross. She couldn't breathe. Just for a heartbeat, the man's gaze seemed to lock with hers. Despite the rain streaming from the flat planes of his chiseled features and darkening his golden hair, slicking it to his head, she recognized him. That flat, hard line of his mouth, she knew very well. It was the last expression she saw on his face before he walked out of her life. Those lips had been as hard as his voice when he castigated her for the choices she had made.

Just a few days before those angry words, he had smiled and spoke only sweet words. Why did she remember his displeasure more clearly?

Richard Boniface. He had wanted to marry her, and when her father said no, he had insisted she should run away with him. Carmen couldn't break her father's heart, even if she had wanted Boniface more than life itself. Her father had raised her to consider every question and choice carefully. Carmen had trusted her father's ability to read people more than her own heart. If he didn't trust Richard as her husband, then neither could she. Richard's fury only confirmed her father's wisdom in saying no. How could she trust her heart to such a changeable man?

When her father fell from grace and his colleagues and superiors chose to believe the vicious rumors that shredded his reputation, peace of mind, and his health, Carmen had thought at first Boniface had been behind those false stories; especially when some of the ugly, unbelievable stories and accusations focused on her. Then he had showed up like an avenging angel, fighting to defend her father, mocking those who chose to believe the lies. Even with the taint of disgrace clinging to Carmen and Reverend Mackenzie, he had still wanted to marry her and take both of them away to a quiet life in a small congregation waiting for him. His anger had been tempered with sorrow when Carmen refused him again.

Now...

Carmen found she could breathe again when Boniface's blue-gray gaze slid off of hers and he turned to study the other side of the street.

"Nothing," he said, his voice colder than the rain.

"Are you sure you heard it?" the driver asked. In a moment, the steam-cart carried them both out of sight.

"You don't hear it, idiot. You feel it. In your bones."

"My bones are frozen."

Whatever Boniface said in response was hidden in the drumming rain, the splashing of the cart's wheels and the rumble-hiss of its engine as they continued down the street.

Carmen brought her knees up to her chest and wrapped her arms around her legs, hiding her face in her knees as she shuddered. For just a moment, even as memories and hurt tumbled through her mind, she had been about to open her mouth and shout for him. What made her think that he could possibly be willing to rescue her?

"You are a fool, Carmen Mackenzie," she whispered. "Just as much a fool as coming here to this great, cruel city in the first place. What ever made you think your answers would be here?"

She knew the answer to that readily enough. When her mother was alive, Chicago had been an adventure. A place of wonders to explore, grand edifices to gawk at, and stores and concert halls and libraries. There was always time for something fascinating after the missionary society business had been attended to. Carmen had felt so sure that when she arrived in Chicago, her memories would guide her to friends of her mother, to people who could help her.

Carmen remembered her mother going on errands in the city, always by herself, and once had asked her father who her mother had visited, what she had done. Reverend Mackenzie had responded that he didn't know. Anna had painful secrets in her past, and he trusted her when she asked him to never ask, because knowing could be dangerous.

Hope had guided Carmen to come here, to awaken memories and follow paths that might lead her to her mother's friends. She knew she looked so much like her mother had in her youth, certainly someone would recognize Anna in her, and reach out in friendship, if not curiosity.

The question was how long she could endure here, with no money to pay for food and shelter. What kind of a fool had she been, to think it wise to come to Chicago in the fall? How much of the city could she cover, showing her face and hoping for recognition, before winter set in?

Three hours later, when she returned to the boarding house, looking even more like a drowned cat and denied the job, Carmen was resolved. She would sell the silver cross *and* crystal rose. After the odd occurrence that afternoon, she didn't think she could bear to wear them again.

Mrs. Blomfield commiserated with her and welcomed Carmen into her kitchen to get a cup of tea and try to warm up before she went to her cubbyhole room. She was uncharacteristically silent, looking a little troubled, and opening her mouth several times as if she was about to say something and then thought better of it. Finally, her landlady admitted that there was one other hotel looking for an assistant cook.

"But you keep your lovely hair covered and your head down and do your best to look older. Hunch your shoulders. Whatever you do, don't attract attention."

"How can I, in a kitchen?" Carmen had asked, resting her hand on the woman's, to try to comfort her. "What's wrong with this place you're going to send me?"

"It's not a good place for pretty young girls. At least, that's the word. But you won't be going to entertain anyone. Nothing wrong with cooking, is there?" Mrs. Blomfield said, more to herself than to Carmen. "Lots of decent folk go there to eat. It's a big place. Good food. They just don't know what goes on in the back rooms and upstairs, do they?"

The next day was sunny and dry, if not any warmer. Carmen wore an old bonnet and tied her hair back severely, and she was still pale from the chill she had taken the day before. She kept her voice soft and hunched her shoulders as Mrs. Blomfield suggested, and the head cook took a liking to her. The hours were long, but she would be indoors in a warm, brightly lit place, her meals provided. While her co-workers were often abrupt during the dinner hour rushes, they were decent folk. Carmen decided before October had ended that she could be very happy there.

February 1878
Chicago

"I declare, if one more person insists that they never believed the official statements that we were presumed dead," Matilda Fremont announced, stepping out of the loading bay of the *Golden Nile*. She paused for a long sigh as the door closed behind her, cutting off the noise of the wind at nearly two hundred feet above the city of Chicago. "Thank you, Uly. I thought for a moment I was going deaf."

Uly bowed to his grandmother, then cocked an eyebrow at Ess, who had led the way across the gangway from the air dock tower.

"Where was I?" Matilda said as their group moved down the passageway to the main lounge area of the airship. They had just returned from a meeting with the local leadership of the Originators.

"More astounded, relieved people declaring they never once gave up on us," Ernest offered, linking his arm with his wife's, and effectively slowing down her pace.

Matilda sighed, narrowing her eyes at him. A moment later, she tipped her head back and laughed. Stepping around their grandparents, Uly bowed to Ess and offered her his arm. The rest of their party joined in the weary laughter and they resumed their walk down the passageway.

Late last summer, the crew of the *Golden Nile* had journeyed to South America and located the site of the Fremonts' archeological camp from nearly eight years before. Using the time key, which had been safe in the custody of Dr. Lockhart, Ess had released the archeological party from the time box that had effectively saved their lives, after traitors within the Originators betrayed them. Since that time, with Athena and Fordyce Chamberlain as their hosts and advisors, the elder Fremonts had made a slow journey across the United States, meeting with the leadership in the loosely scattered cells of the Originators. Their mission was two-fold. First, notify everyone with any authority that they had returned from the dead. Second, finish rooting out the treachery that threatened the mission begun by their ancestors, who had come from Earth's far future to stop the Revisionists from changing Earth's history.

At each stop along the way, not one person had doubted that Matilda and Ernest Fremont were indeed who they said they were. Several traitors had turned themselves in, effectively terrified of the punishments awaiting them. Everyone who could be trusted had been dispatched to spread the news to the smaller cells connected to them. It would take years before the Originators could be completely certain they were secure and free of traitors. Ernest and Matilda were to all intents and purposes the leaders of the organization now. In the spring, they would head across the Atlantic on the *Golden Nile* to contact the cells and field offices in Europe and Asia and Africa. The secrecy and separation that had once protected the Originators had proven to be their undoing. It was time for full and open communication, no more secrets, no more hiding names and connections and locations and progress from each other.

Ess certainly didn't look forward to spring. She and Uly would stay in the United States, but separated as they went out on Originator business. While it was a relief to learn that the blood link in the communication plates created from crystal dust allowed their grandparents to use them, in a way she was disappointed. She wanted an excuse to send either her or Uly on the *Golden Nile* to keep an eye on their grandparents. She still had occasional bad dreams where she went to Matilda's workroom or Ernest's office, and found the rooms empty, no sign that anyone had ever used them.

However, she had made a promise to her friend, Phoebe Stryker, to find Phoebe's three sisters, whom their treacherous uncle had hidden away.

He used the safety of her sisters to keep control over Phoebe and use her to spy in Sanctuary, while he went about the country, disguised as Mr. Judson of the Pinkertons, to further his plans. The details of those plans were still being uncovered. The last Ess had heard from Allistair Fitch, who had the unpleasant task of uncovering Stryker/Judson's activities, he had found two more false identities. The ire of the Pinkerton Agency and their determination to make all things right gave Ess only minimal comfort. She feared that somehow, Allistair might yet uncover the truth of the Originators, and then what would they do if the Pinkertons decided they were a threat to national security?

"She's nattering again," Matilda said, as their delegation entered the lounge and finally began to divest themselves of their winter cloaks and coats and hats and gloves.

"No, Ess is pondering some devious trick or dire punishment for whatever blockade currently resists her," Ford announced, with a grand bow to Ess that earned a chuckle from Athena.

"It's a good thing that rotter, Stryker, is..." Dr. Lockhart chuckled and sank down into the wingback chair that had become his province on board the airship. He settled his mechanical leg and looked around the room. "Well, to be delicate, rotting."

Ess muffled the urge to stick her tongue out at the elderly doctor. She gathered up her outerwear and her grandparents' and trudged down the passageway to deposit their clothes in their respective cabins. It was the least she could do, to make up for her lack of sociability during the dinner party. Why did everyone insist on celebrating with fancy manners and fancy clothes and fancy food, whenever the delegation came down from the *Golden Nile* with their cargo of good and bad and dire and astounding news? By the third city, she had grown exceedingly tired of being told what a heroine she was, how clever she was, how much she looked like her mother, or her father, or Matilda, and how much she took after her parents and her grandparents. As far as she was concerned, they were all wasting time on niceties, when they should be diving into fixing what had gone horribly wrong with the Originators.

The worst part was that her grandparents seemed to enjoy the fuss-and-feathers, as her mother Vivian used to refer to small talk and dancing and fancy clothes.

The errand gave her time to shed her irritation over the time lost that evening and allowed her to shift her thoughts to more pleasant things. The first being that they were now free to leave Chicago and head either east or south, depending on whatever news had caught up with them while they were busy socializing. Perhaps Roscoe had picked up some of the books she was looking for, or a telegram had come with news. She hadn't heard from Agent Sutter regarding the search for Carmen, her last name still unknown, who was the daughter of a Revisionist woman named Anna who had come over to the Originators. Vivian had befriended Anna, and the two women wore matching crystal roses that seemed to promote a mental link between them. Ess had inherited her mother's rose, and it seemed that Anna's daughter had inherited hers, along with sensitivity to crystal. Despite trying nearly every day to re-open the brief connection with Carmen, Ess had had no success beyond those first brief dream-visits. She had given Agent Sutter a sketch she had made of Carmen, as she had appeared in the few dreams, and all the bits and pieces of information that had come through their momentary link. Ess needed to find the other girl, not just for the sake of their mothers' friendship, but because Carmen's sensitivity to the crystal put her in grave danger from the Revisionists.

Theo came around the corner of an intersecting passageway a dozen paces past the doorway of the lounge. He skidded to a stop, rocking back on his heels, then his usually somber, dark face brightened and he held up a piece of paper. It was stiff and square and the dirty snow yellow of telegram sheets.

"Who?" Ess cast her weariness aside and ran down the passageway to meet him.

"Phoebe." Theo chuckled and pretended to flinch as he held out the paper for her to take.

She nearly flung her arms around him. He wouldn't be smiling now if there was bad news in the telegram. Phoebe was working with Allistair to find her sisters, as well as control the damage from whatever Originator or even Revisionist information the search might uncover.

"What is this?" Ess asked, after reading through the sparse message three times, trying to force it to tell her something. She ran her finger under a series of numbers. "They look like coordinates."

"They are." Theo's expression darkened again. "Mixed with code for the designation of that particular location. Basically, Phoebe is telling us that she recognized someone going into a station house that had been declared destroyed four years ago." He tapped the paper above a series of three numbers and two letters. "It doesn't actually say four years ago, but I remember when the report came in because it was so unusual. The location was supposedly surrounded by Revisionists and declared too hot to investigate for the immediate future. Everyone assigned to that station was declared dead."

Chapter Three

"And?" Ess studied the shifting of muscles in his face as he controlled his expression. Theo wasn't the most readable of people, and that was good, considering the kind of work he did for the security of the Originators. However, she thought she had learned a few things after all this time working with him.

"And what, Miss Fremont?" He leaned back against the opposite wall and glanced beyond her to the lounge door.

"I'm guessing the person Phoebe saw is supposed to be dead." She muffled a snort of satisfaction at a slight twitch of the corner of his mouth. "I'll wager Stryker reported the house destroyed, everyone dead, and the situation too dangerous to investigate."

"Someone should investigate if that trinket of yours facilitates the ability to read minds." Theo flicked his forefinger at the crystal rose, temporarily mounted on a satin band around her throat.

"God wouldn't be so unkind as to inflict something like that on me." She shuddered and gestured to the lounge door. Theo really should have delivered the telegram to Athena or Ernest. She appreciated his kindness in letting her see the news first.

"Or the rest of us." He winked and followed her down the passageway.

Ess played with the idea of being able to infiltrate someone's thoughts, then pushed the concept to the back of her mind as the company in the lounge discussed all the implications of the message. They agreed with Theo that Stryker had either suborned the people assigned to that station house or held some sort of power over them, perhaps blackmailing them into silence as he had blackmailed Phoebe. The woman she saw going into the building, Sophia Gruber, was a distant relative on the Stryker side of the family. Sophia's presence increased the chances that the three little girls were there, cared for by a relative.

"Can we assume Captain Astrid has already plotted our course to meet up with our allies?" Athena said.

"As soon as everyone who's been out on errands reports in, we're ready to cast off the mooring lines and head for Detroit." Theo winked at Ess. "I'll wager you're trying to figure out how to add map-reading lessons to everything else you're trying to learn. It irritates you, doesn't it, that you didn't know where those coordinates were?"

"I'm too tired to get into a battle of wits with you right now, thank you very much," Ess retorted. Her face warmed as everyone else chuckled. She joined them a moment later.

Perhaps her hunger to fill in all the education she had missed was amusing. She chose to laugh with her friends, because the alternative was to live in constant vexation over all the gaping holes in her knowledge. Only slightly less irritating was the regular recurrence of headaches and bizarre dreams as more memories emerged and slid into place. She likened her memories to the remains of an ancient Roman villa, with all sorts of gaps and cracks in the mosaic tiled floors and the painted walls. However, in her case, the missing pieces were falling back into place to fill out the image, and the cracks were erasing themselves.

"Where in Detroit?" she asked. "It's such a large and growing city."

"The station house is actually along the river, on the Canadian side. However, it would be wise to stop in at the new station house, which is on the north side of the city." Ford clasped Athena's hand, palm-to-palm, their fingers interlaced.

Ess wasn't sure which to blame for the catch in her chest. The loving gesture, or the somber looks Athena and Ford shared.

"I know the man who heads it. Ash Halverson. The rest of his people, however... well, we can't be too sure who to trust, can we, with the old station house still functioning, but in questionable hands?" He nodded to Ernest. "I feel like we've let you down, everything sliding to Perdition while you were away."

"Nonsense," Ernest said with a rumble in his voice that could have been amusement or deep feelings. "We wouldn't have had to make use of that wretched time box, and chance being lost for all eternity, if things hadn't already been traveling downward too quickly for us to put on the brakes."

"In some ways, your vanishing did help to slam something of an emergency brake into place," Dr. Lockhart offered. "The panic at Sanctuary was thick enough to drown in, for quite some time. Our enemies seemed to be fighting among themselves, as I look back. They were likely accusing each other of jumping the gun or hiding new technology from each other. Then their plans disintegrated and they had no idea where you had hidden all your lovely toys and research."

"Toys," Matilda muttered, with a snort and then a wink for Ess. She patted the corner of the two-seater couch that was her and Ernest's usual perch during the long, interesting nights of talk and reminiscing and plotting in the lounge.

Ess slid over the stool she usually chose and leaned against her grandmother's leg. Sitting just a little lower than Matilda, she could sometimes pretend she was nine or ten years old again. Especially when Matilda stroked her hair. She didn't even mind the occasional teasing from Uly, calling her "kitty."

"I wouldn't doubt your disappearance prompted Stryker to hare off on his own," Dr. Sylvia offered from her usual seat at the table. There, she had enough light to go over the progress reports of her patients and what had been done while she was down on the ground, contributing to what Matilda called the greater emotional and spiritual healing of the Originators. "He never struck me as a very trusting sort, nor much of a follower. If he couldn't trust them to keep any sort of control over their cabal of treachery, then why should he follow any of them? Every man for himself."

"Evidenced by using poor Phoebe to spy on people she liked and respected," Uly offered.

"If you think about it, we're using her to spy on the Pinkertons," Ess said. "Yes, the greater reason for having her work with Allistair and his bloodhounds is to find her sisters, but she's ensuring he doesn't figure things out that we can't afford him to know and warn us if he does. I'm curious how they found the station house."

"I'm sure your Allistair will be only too happy to expound on every step he's taken," Ernest said.

"*My* Allistair?" She barely muffled a squeak of indignation. Uly snorted and his eyes sparkled. "Grandfather, honestly, you as well?"

Their party had returned to the *Golden Nile* shortly after eleven. With the anticipation of having to deal with the new station house and then whatever they found at the old station house, they decided to retire and wake early, when the airship reached Detroit. Theo and his select team of spies and soldiers would accompany Ford to an early morning visit to the station house. If they were lucky, they would catch up with Halverson while he was dealing with morning errands. If necessary, Ford would go in alone and find some excuse to get his friend out of the building for a private discussion, to assess the situation. Theo and the others would keep watch on the other members of the team, in case any of them went running to Stryker's people at the old station house.

Ess added more prayers to her nightly routine, for the success of the morning's first foray, especially that no one would turn out to be a traitor. Stryker could have been lying to everyone, and the people in the station house didn't even know that they had been reported as dead. With the routine secrecy and separation practiced by the Originators, they could believe they had to stay in isolation for the good of the organization.

"Please, blessed Savior," Ess whispered after she had washed her face and brushed her hair and climbed into her bed. "Please, let us have nothing to do but laugh when tomorrow is over. And yes, a little cursing of Stryker's memory, that's expected, but please, no more traitors?"

She stroked the thin crystal panel that controlled the light in her cabin. As the light dimmed and went out, she curled up on her side, and wrapped her fingers around the crystal rose, which now hung on its usual chain around her neck. Closing her eyes, she envisioned Carmen, but tried not to force the tenuous connection between them to awaken. She had learned the hard way, through headaches that lingered all night and halfway through the next day, that banging her metaphorical head against a metaphorical wall resulted in physical repercussions.

Please, Lord, help me to find her. For the sake of the friendship between our mothers, if for nothing else. I can't help feeling she's in terrible trouble, that something dreadful happened to her and she has absolutely no one to turn to. Please, let me talk to her, just long enough to find out her last name and where she is? Would that be too much to ask?

Ess drifted, trying not to think about the fact that she needed to get some sleep. Thinking about what she needed to do was the surest way to ensure she didn't succeed. Uly had likened it to the magician's apprentice who had been warned to try as hard as he could not to think of pink ravens, or he would never learn to perform magic. Naturally, all the poor lad could do was think about pink ravens.

While she pondered who had ever decided that magic had such strange rules as not thinking of something that couldn't exist, Ess fell asleep. Seemingly moments later, she sat up, reaching with one hand and blurting, "Don't. Please. Don't."

Heart racing, she clutched the crystal rose with the other hand. Ess rubbed at her sweaty face. She swung her legs off the side of the bed and leaned forward, feeling as if she had escaped a great fright, but couldn't recall what it was. She opened her hand, stunned to see tiny sparkles of pink and green and silver within the knot of the rose's hair-fine petals. Ess stared, momentarily entranced by the play of light, and let out a sigh as the sparkles faded within just a few heartbeats.

"Don't," she whispered, as a scene unfolded in her mind.

It had to have been a dream. Or could it have been communication between her and Carmen?

For just a moment, she and Carmen stood facing each other in a long, dimly lit, foggy sort of tunnel. Carmen wore all black, just like she had the last time they had communicated through their roses. Her clothes looked worn, and her face looked thinner, paler. She stood with one hand outstretched, the crystal rose embedded in the cross, lying in her palm, the chain hanging off the side of her hand.

She was bracing herself to sell it.

Ess had no idea how she was so certain that was Carmen's plan, other than the sense of grief and fear so thick it was an ashy sort of taste and texture in the air. Images swirled around the crystal rose in those few seconds of contact between their minds. Images of Anna wearing the crystal rose. Carmen's father having the rose put into a cross. Anna putting the cross into Carmen's hands just before she breathed her last.

"I need enough money to be safe, to get away, to eat. To last until I can find a way to make a living," Carmen said. Whether she was speaking to herself or to Ess wasn't clear. Ess couldn't be sure Carmen knew she was there. "I know Father told me to never let go of it, that Mother wanted me to always guard it, but most of my memories bound up in it are bitter, not sweet. Why shouldn't I make a total break and get rid of it? That man offered me two hundred dollars for it."

"Don't," Ess blurted, and reached through the fog that swirled between them. Her heart banged painfully hard against her ribs, as the smiling, deceptively kind face of Alexander O'Keefe, a junior supervisor among the Pinkertons, spilled from Carmen's memories to her mind.

Allistair's investigation had determined that O'Keefe, an associate and recruit of Stryker's, was also suspected of being more than a Pinkerton. He had vanished within days after Stryker's death in San Francisco. If he appeared in Carmen's memories, wanting to buy the cross and crystal rose, then it just reinforced Ess's fear that he was either a traitor or a Revisionist, and Stryker's link to the organization.

"I can't remember what I told her," Ess said, half an hour later as she went over the details of the fragmented dream with Athena and Matilda.

She sat on the couch in the sitting room of her grandparents' suite, in her nightgown and wrapped in a blanket, and hurried to sketch what she could remember from the dream before everything faded away.

"I know what I *wanted* to tell her. The most important thing was not to sell the rose, that it was dangerous to let anyone have it. I think I told her to go to Cleveland, because Mr. Lewis should be there right now, working on the plans for the tower." Her heart seemed to rise in her throat when Athena's lips pressed flat and something flickered in the woman's eyes. "What? What did I forget?"

"Randall is there right now, not Stanton," Athena said.

"Oh, this is so wretched." Ess tried not to toss her sketchpad down on the floor. "There are so many things I know I wanted to tell her, and it makes it hard to remember what I did tell her. I might have even said to go to Mr. Lewis of Endicott, Lewis and MacDonald, but what if I didn't tell her they were lawyers? How is she to find one law office in a massive, growing city like that? Especially if she doesn't know they're lawyers? Oh, why didn't I tell her to come meet us?"

"Besides the fact that you don't know where we'll be two days from now?" Matilda patted her shoulder. "Stop berating yourself, my dear. You did a commendable job with so little, in such a short amount of time. Dreams are tricky, chancy things. Half the time, we don't even know we're dreaming until after we awaken. Then it's too late to do what needs doing." She glanced up as the door opened and Ernest came in, carrying a tray loaded with a coffee pot and cups and a plate of rolls. "Blessed man. How anyone can function without coffee to oil the gears of the mind, I can never understand."

Ess snorted, recognizing hyperbole despite the swirling of her thoughts and the churning of frustration in her belly. She had never known her grandmother to ever require the slightest bit of mental priming of the pump, no matter how early in the morning some emergency had dragged her from her bed. She finished her sketch of O'Keefe while the others filled cups and passed around the rolls. The most frustrating part of feeling the fragments of her dream slipping through her mental fingers was that she couldn't ask her grandfather to hypnotize her, to recall the dream in whole. After the drastic, long-term blocking of her memories, to preserve the secrets of the Originators and find the key to rescue her grandparents and their team, Ess couldn't undergo any more tampering with her mind. She needed years to heal, to regain all her memories and let everything settle. Even a light hypnotic state to recall the dream might do damage. She knew better than to insist that she was willing to take the risk.

Her sketch of Alexander O'Keefe reinforced the impressions she had of Carmen's life before her father's death. The man was costumed like a very prosperous banker, with his hair slicked down and an elaborate neckcloth and a thick watch chain dangling from his pocket. The background showed a large camp meeting tent. The folding chairs and benches extended behind him for some distance, and oil lanterns hung from poles every three or four yards. Whatever traveling preacher or missionary society Carmen and her father had traveled with, they seemed to be most prosperous.

"What are you thinking?" Ernest asked, gently inserting a coffee cup between the sketchpad and Ess's nose. He chuckled when she blinked and shook her head, and took the pad from her hand so she could take the cup.

"I need to make a copy of this for Agent Sutter, as well as Al—for Mr. Fitch." She wrinkled up her nose at Athena, who chuckled softly at how she had corrected herself in the middle of referring to Allistair. "If they can track O'Keefe's route, perhaps they can intersect with the missionary society, and help to identify Carmen's father, even if no one knows where she went." Ess sighed and raised the cup to her lips. "The problem is that they'd have to backtrack him a year, at the very least."

"We are hampered by the fact you couldn't tell him some of the details you know of her," Matilda said. "Certainly a missionary society accusing one of its own of unethical actions, then trying to strip his daughter of everything she possessed would have created some noise. Some backlash among other societies, both those who practice true Christian charity and those who only pretend faith to make money off the faithful. How hard could it be for the Secret Service to track down such an event?"

"Considering our own investigators haven't heard anything along those lines?" Athena said. "Whatever caused them to turn on Carmen's father, and then on her, it must have happened quickly, and was just as quickly hushed." She patted Ess's knee. "I agree with Matilda. You did wonderfully, despite the limitations."

"We are all sunk if she didn't hear me, and she sells the rose." Ess sipped at the coffee. The bitterness seemed to crash through from her tongue to the back of her head. Despite that, she drained the cup. She needed to awaken fully to be ready for the day.

~~~~~

Two hundred miles west, with most of the width of Michigan between the *Golden Nile* and Chicago, Carmen Mackenzie rubbed the condensation of her breath off the window and watched for the sunrise to penetrate the snow-heavy clouds. She prayed as she always did when she woke each morning, asking for guidance, for the miracle of a friendly face, for God's grace to shine upon her once more and prove that the last year had been some horrible dream. She leaned her forehead against the cold glass and tried to believe that the heavy footsteps in the hallway outside the drafty little boarding house room would turn into her father's feet, coming to fetch her for breakfast, and then a long day of walking the streets of the city. They would meander wherever the wind blew, stopping for him to say a few words of encouragement on a street corner or for Carmen to sing a few verses of a hymn, and invite people to come to the camp meeting tent set up outside town in the evening.

The rumble of the train on the tracks on the other side of the boarding house shredded her daydream before she could quite convince herself. No, she was still in Chicago, following the shreds of old memories. After yesterday, that had to end. She should have given up long ago and moved on. Whatever friends her mother had known here, either they had died or moved on, or they lived in a part of town that Carmen never saw.

She had grown comfortable enough with her surroundings and her fellow laborers in the enormous hotel kitchen that she had ventured to sing over her work, peeling and cutting and kneading. She had been happier than she had felt since before her father died. Since before Richard Boniface whispered his sweet, false promises of love. Her co-workers liked her voice and requested songs from her. The last few days, other workers came in during breaks, hoping to hear her sing. They didn't even mind that all the songs she knew were hymns and camp meeting songs. Carmen had thought perhaps she had a chance to plant some spiritual seed, and she had felt that sweet contentment she thought she would never feel again.

A man in a slick black suit, with a red silk vest and a pointed black beard came into the kitchen yesterday, while she sang in rhythm with the potato peelings falling from her knife. He didn't make his presence known until she finished, though she thought she had sensed some change in the comfortably steamy atmosphere thick with the smells of good cooking.

"Very nice," he said, his smile cold when his voice startled a squeak out of her. He came around to stand on the other side of the table from her. "You should be singing upstairs."

"I'm a cook."

"Yes, with those clothes, what else would you be?" His upper lip curled as he looked her over. "I'm Gio Frierri. You know who I am?"

"You're the owner." Carmen set the knife down on the table and wiped her hands on her apron, then kept her hands on her lap, hidden under the table, so he wouldn't see them shaking.

When he asked her to sing again, she hesitated. He rapped out the titles of songs she had never heard of but didn't look upset each time she shook her head and told him she didn't know them.

"That's all right. You'll learn them, and right quick," he said, looking her over again. "Get rid of those widow's weeds and put on some decent clothes."

"These are all I have, and I'm still in mourning," Carmen had said. "Why should it matter what I wear in the kitchen, or what I sing, for that matter? My friends haven't complained about the songs I sing."

"Yeah, but my friends will." He grinned at her, and she shuddered with the momentary illusion that his teeth were pointed. "You're gonna be the new, private entertainment for special guests."

"Thank you, but no." She wished she had held onto the paring knife, even knowing it wouldn't have done her any good. "I'll stay here in the kitchen, if it's all the same with you."

"It's not." He snatched hold of her by her elbow and yanked her up off the stool, kicking aside the bucket with the potato peelings. "You work in the special parlor, or you don't work at all. Understand?"

"Yes, I understand."

He left with a chuckle. Carmen waited until the break after the lunchtime rush, then went to the manager to ask for her pay up through that morning. Frierri must have anticipated she would try to run. The manager, who had always been kind to her, looked afraid when he told her to report to Madame Collette. He whispered that if she was smart, she would leave town tonight.

Madame Collete informed Carmen that her pay was being applied to the dresses Frierri wanted her to wear when she entertained. She smiled warmly enough, but the warmth never reached her eyes. She added that if Carmen did well, she would be offered a room at the hotel, so she wouldn't have any expenses to worry about besides "making pretty." Carmen complied with the fittings for the dresses and tried to calculate how much money she had saved. If only she hadn't bought new boots last week, and a cloak to replace her threadbare shawl. Precious little remained of her pitiful savings, compared to the distance she had to travel to evade Gio Frierri's reach.

Chapter Four

"Cleveland certainly isn't far enough," Carmen whispered now, staring at the condensation on the window.

She stood up straight, frowning. When had the idea of Cleveland come into her head? If anything, she should head west, maybe try to reach her father's friends in Denver.

Carmen shivered, hearing Essie, her make believe friend, insist she had to go to Cleveland. Perhaps her circumstances had become too much for her and she had broken, at long last? She was losing her mind, imagining a friend who came to her in the darkness and shadows and promised help and whispered advice. Yet what if she weren't losing her mind?

Her mother had always told her to pay attention to her dreams, and to never dismiss the impossible when it happened in front of her. Anna had taught her to search for details and patterns and think about the why and how of things. Otherwise, how would she have realized that wonderful, small, helpful things happened when she sang?

Granted, her singing in the kitchen hadn't led to something wonderful, but Carmen had to be honest with herself and admit she had left out an important piece of the pattern. Wonderful things happened when she sang while she wore her mother's crystal rose. She had no idea how, she only knew that when she sang for the children who came to the camp meetings, especially when she held them in her arms, she saw pictures of their fears and dreams, their skinned knees and sore fingers, and knew what to say to encourage them. After she sang to them, pain vanished. Carmen could only attribute the incidents to being used as a vessel of Almighty God's power to do good in the world. A lamp didn't boast over the light it produced. After all, it was only the receptacle of the oil and a resting place for the wick.

She hadn't worn the crystal rose and the cross in months. She hadn't worn it when she worked in the hotel kitchen. Perhaps if she had worn the cross while she sang, God might have worked through her song to protect her, just like the Almighty used her song to help the children. Last night, when she returned to her room from the hotel, Carmen had pulled the cross out of its hiding place in the slot under the windowsill, where the wallboard had rotted away. She had curled up with it and cried herself to sleep, in between praying for answers.

Thinking back, she decided that she hadn't dreamed of Essie, her make believe friend, until she wore the cross again.

Before she fell asleep, she had pondered how much money she needed to go out west, and how much money she could get by selling the cross. If only she could remember the name of the man who offered her so much money for it last year. Then Essie burst from the shadows, begging her not to sell, and most certainly not to him. Whoever he was.

"How do you know who he is, when I can't remember?" She leaned back to study the clear spot on the glass where her forehead had rested. "I wish you could talk to me when I am awake. I've never been much good at remembering dreams once I wake up."

Sighing, she stepped back to sit on the edge of her bed and stared into the sparkles of light and hints of color within the crystal rose.

"Mother, I wish I could remember what you taught me. How can my memories be stored inside the rose? Even if I had a jeweler's tools, I wouldn't be able to write all my thoughts and memories on the petals. Certainly not so they could be read, to remind me." Carmen sighed a bit of laughter at her moment of whimsy.

Common sense would dictate that she pack up her few possessions, find the pawnshop six blocks away, and wait on the front step until it opened. Then she would offer her last few worthwhile possessions until the man in the shop gave her enough money to head west. The wind moaned past her window and she shivered at the chill through the drafty window. Maybe go south? Certainly Texas was warmer than Colorado at this time of the year. Had any of her father's friends gone to Texas? She knew no one in Cleveland.

"Why do I keep thinking of Cleveland?" she murmured, staring into the crystal petals of the rose, trying to follow the play of pink and green and even a few pale blue sparkles.

If only she had been able to remember the people her mother had met when they visited Chicago. Who were her mother's friends? Where were they hiding?

An image of her mother seemed to swirl among the crystal petals of the rose. Carmen saw Anna walking past this very boarding house. That made no sense. She knew she should pull herself out of the images dancing before her eyes, among the sparkles of color and light. Yet she couldn't.

She was twelve years old, and had awakened before dawn, disturbed by the sound of a train whistle howling so mournfully a dozen blocks away from the hotel. She had dressed with the intention of finding the hotel parlor and practicing the new piece of sheet music Reverend Darlington had given her at the society meeting last month. When she stepped out of her room, into the parlor of the suite she shared with her parents, she saw her mother at the door of the suite, swinging her cloak around herself. Without thinking, she had darted back to her room for her own coat and bonnet and hurried to follow Anna.

The morning was rainy and overcast. Carmen lost her mother several times in shadows and walking down alleys between buildings. They had passed the boarding house Carmen stood in now, and walked four more blocks, then turned and walked several more blocks, to a narrow, tall wooden house shoehorned between two other buildings. The door opened immediately after the first knock. Carmen had been afraid to linger and hurried back to the hotel. She had never told her mother what she saw, and never asked what she had done that early, gloomy, cold morning.

Could she remember the way? If she could find the house, would the woman who had answered the door that morning still be there? Would the strong resemblance between Carmen and her mother help her, or hinder?

Hands shaking, Carmen slid the cross down the neck of her dress and blinked rapidly, trying to regain her focus on the present moment and place. Had the vision been an answer to her prayers for help? Despite the losses and betrayals she had endured, Carmen still believed in prayer and the guidance of the Almighty in her life.

"Doesn't really matter, does it?" she whispered, refocused her gaze, and looked around the room. "I need to leave. I need to be gone before he sends someone looking for me. If this doesn't work out, I'll just keep moving." She got up on unsteady legs and gathered up her few possessions.

Mrs. Blomfield didn't seem to know how to smile, but she had a warm heart and looked out for her boarders as well as she could. Carmen regretted not saying goodbye to her landlady, but at least she was paid up for three more days, so Mrs. Blomfield wouldn't suffer while she looked for a new boarder. If Frierri was as much a danger as she feared, telling her landlady she was leaving would just get the old woman in trouble. Carmen left a note in her room, with the bedding pulled off the bed and folded by the door, the room neatened as best she could. She tried to say her thanks and apologize without revealing anything her pursuer could use.

Carmen calculated she had perhaps an hour before her failure to arrive at the hotel sent someone hunting for her. Hopefully, her cooperation yesterday, being fitted for the new dresses, fooled Frierri into thinking she wouldn't run, so he wouldn't have anyone watching the boarding house to ensure she showed up for work. There were plenty of people leaving for work in the darkness before dawn, and she could blend in unnoticed. Snow or sleet would have been welcome, to help her fade from notice.

She remembered the way to the odd, narrow house as if she had walked it many times since she followed her mother here. Carmen shivered whenever her vision doubled and she saw a ghostly image of the streets and buildings as they had been years before, overlaid on the present streets and buildings. Often, the only changes were a touch of shabbiness. Some places, the buildings were painted a different color, or the signs for businesses had changed. The narrow little house was a comfortable brownish-red now instead of the weathered gray with black shutters it wore in her vision.

Walking up to the front door, Carmen's steps slowed. A moment after she knocked, she considered running. She counted her heartbeats as she waited for someone to respond. This was utter madness. Most likely everyone in this house was still asleep in bed. How rude was she, to come at such an early hour? She was a fool to hope—

The door opened, and the same woman, her dark gray hair now completely white, stared at her. She pressed both hands to her generous bosom.

"Child, they told me you were—" She choked on the words.

"I'm Anna's daughter," Carmen hurried to say.

"Ah, the little one." The woman blinked rapidly, as if she fought tears. Then she went up on her toes and looked past Carmen, out onto the street. "Come inside. Quickly now. They likely haven't seen you, but better to be cautious than sorry, yes?"

Carmen let the strong, thin fingers pull her inside. She stepped past the heavyset woman and down the narrow hallway that extended all the way to the back of the building.

"You're in trouble, aren't you?" Gesturing for Carmen to follow, she pushed a door open and led her into the kitchen, just as long as the hallway. They settled at the table that appeared to be anchored to the wall, and the woman poured coffee into battered tin cups.

"Please, I don't even know your name. And no, before you ask, Mother never told me about you. I followed her here on one of our last visits to Chicago. That's how I knew the way." Sighing, she slid her bonnet off the back of her head and let it hang by the strings from around her neck. "And yes, I am in trouble." She cradled the tin cup of coffee, welcoming the heat. "How do you know my mother?"

"When someone is in trouble, and needs to hide and flee, they find us, or we find them." She chuckled. "I'm Harriet. Just Harriet. I worked with the Abolitionists before the war. That's how your mother and I met, and then when she needed help, well..." Harriet spread her hands, as if the explanation didn't need to be spoken.

"I don't understand. Did she need to hide with you? Why did she come here? She came here every time we came to Chicago, didn't she?"

"She had a gift, and she was determined to use it for the right cause." Harriet shrugged and then seemed to deflate a little into her chair. "I think maybe she was trying to atone for the sins of her ancestors. Whenever she found a new piece, she brought it to me and I passed it along to those better suited to deal with it. We always agreed that she couldn't come to see me for at least three, four months, just to make sure that anyone trying to figure out my source wouldn't spot her. I always waited for a month after one of her visits, before I passed it along." A sigh escaped her. "In the end, we weren't nearly clever enough, or careful enough. Not even being married to a preacher-man could provide her enough protection."

"From whom?" Carmen said, her voice dropping close to a whisper.

"If you don't know, child, then Anna didn't pass on her burden or her knowledge to you. If you didn't wear her face, I'd be willing to wager you were safe, but..." Another sigh. "Why hasn't your father told you anything?

Anna told him everything about her past, about her burden and her mission in life. He should have at least given you her journals or told you what she told him. Are you sure you don't know what your mother used to be, the horrible people she escaped?"

"My father is dead. All I was left of my mother's legacy is this." She reached into the collar of her black dress and pulled out the cross. The color fled Harriet's cheeks. "I'm ready to sell this for enough money to go somewhere safe. Except for a cache of books and some mementos and photographs, this is all I have."

"If you have to, sell the cross for the silver, but don't let that rose out of your sight. That is..." Harriet shuddered, her gaze fixed on the cross now lying on the table between them. "Well, if your mother didn't tell you about your heritage, then maybe you don't have a heritage. Doesn't matter six days from Sunday... I could take all the other pieces for Anna, but not this. If the wrong person saw this, they'd know and then wouldn't I have hellfire to explain?" A weak chuckle escaped her. She finally blinked and tore her gaze away from the rose.

"What is so special about the rose?"

"It has a twin. The woman who made both roses befriended your mother when she escaped her terrible heritage. Anna referred to her as her lifeline, a true sister of her soul."

"Can I go to her? Will she help me?"

"I truly wish you could, but she's been dead longer than your mother. Near to tore Anna's heart out. She was that sure Vivian had died protecting her. No, and that's the reason you can't let that rose out of your sight. Or at least, not until you hand it over to the right people," Harriet added, her voice slowing. She nodded once, like a punctuation mark. "Anyone who knew Vivian would recognize that rose. What you need to do is go to someone who was close to Vivian, someone with the connections to protect you and dispose of that tricky little trinket properly. Ah, if only Vivian's in-laws were still... well, it's no use crying over spilled milk, is it?" She thumped both hands flat on the table. "Give me time to think on where you need to go and who you need to talk to. In the meantime, let me feed you good. If you don't mind my saying, you do look more than a little down on your luck."

Harriet scurried around the narrow kitchen with agility that was amazing for her size and put together a breakfast Carmen hadn't seen since the glory days, before her mother died. Her hostess told her a few stories of when she had known her mother, before Anna met Reverend Mackenzie and dedicated her life to God's service. Carmen refused to divulge the heartbreaking way her father's associates had turned on him. She merely said that he had slowed his travels as old age crept up on him. She had lost contact with many of his friends and associates, so when they were robbed, there was no recourse but to sell personal property to pay her father's outstanding debts after his death. Harriet's sympathy and her outrage nearly loosened Carmen's tongue, to spill the reservoir of hurt that sometimes threatened to drown her soul.

She knew better and switched from the topic of her father's last days to how she had fared in the last six months. Dismay made Harriet's face go pale again when Carmen mentioned the name of the hotel where she had been working. Her hostess almost dropped the platter of fried eggs and bacon she was about to put on the table.

"Oh, my dear child, I wouldn't let my worst enemy or her daughters work for that awful man." Harriet swept up the coffee pot and plunked it down on the table, then dropped just as loudly and abruptly into her chair. "Thank the Almighty you're in the kitchen, where he can't set his eyes on you. As thin as you are, in such pitiful clothes, he's a man who can see the diamonds in the dustbin, and he'll snatch you up into a life of depravity so quickly..." Harriet rubbed at her eyes with the corner of her massive apron, then blew her nose in it with a resounding goose honk.

"Well, he did see me." Carmen related how her singing had caught the owner's attention, and her resolve to flee.

"Good for you, and smart, trying to leave before he sets his hounds on your trail. The Almighty sent an angel or two to guide your steps to me. You don't dare go to the train station dressed like that. He'll be looking for you. Where were you planning on going? Did you tell any of your friends in the kitchen about any plans you had, once you got together some money?" Her mouth took on a grim flatness when Carmen confessed that yes, she had mentioned old friends in Colorado. "That settles it, you're going east. And in disguise." She chuckled, a mischievous light glinting in her eyes. "The complete opposite of what you are. A true self-centered little featherhead." With another nod for punctuation, she gestured at the food. "Eat up, child. We have a lot of work to do before you fly."

"Where?"

"Need to think on that. It's useless to run for your life if you're just running any whichaway. You need some place to go *to*, for it to do you any good."

Harriet followed up the overwhelming breakfast with an indulgent hot bath full of perfumed soapsuds. When she finally padded down the hall to the room Harriet had given her, Carmen was astounded at the sight of the jewel-toned clothes waiting for her. Deep purple and sapphire and emerald skirts, snowy blouses and thick, lacy petticoats, and a heavy, dark amethyst woolen cloak trimmed in silk, with a matching bonnet and leather gloves.

"Who have you robbed to outfit me as a lady of substance?" she blurted, when she and Harriet had spent a delightful hour trying on various pieces of clothes. Everything fit perfectly, as if made for her, and proved Harriet had a very good eye for sizes.

"No one at all. I help good people get away from bad trouble. Disguises are part of the parcel. Besides, we want you to look like a lady who is used to being taken care of promptly, not left to sit in a waiting room until her lawyer has time to attend to her. The sooner you talk to my cousin's boy, the better."

"So you've thought of where to send me." Carmen sank down on the end of the bed, among a cloud of petticoats.

"It's only common sense. The question is still *where* to send you, now that I know *who*. My cousin's boy—well, he's not a boy anymore, and he's more the son of a cousin by marriage. No matter, in our line of work, we hold onto family no matter how tenuous the connection. I've met him several times when he had to go through town on business. I even entrusted him with some of the very pieces your mother gave me for disposal and safekeeping."

"Pieces of what?"

"That, of course." Harriet gestured with her chin at Carmen's bodice.

Carmen fought a chill that rose up from her belly, as she glanced down at her cross. No. Not the cross. The crystal rose.

"Now, Stanton is a partner at a law firm deep in the affairs of our organization. As blessed fate would have it, he was also friends with your mother's friend, Vivian, and her husband and his family. Very important people in our organization. I know what you are about to say, child. What organization? Why did your mother bring me pieces of crystal to hide away? I truly believe the less you know, the less danger you will be in. I will entrust Stanton with your education."

"Where is Mr. Stanton's law firm?" she asked, after digesting that bit of mystery and partial information.

"Oh, no, not—" Harriet chuckled. "Stanton is his first name. Stanton Lewis, of the law firm of Endicott, Lewis and MacDonald. Such a powerful law firm, and that's the problem. They have offices in several major cities. New York, Philadelphia, Cleveland, Charleston--"

"Cleveland?" Carmen shivered with that awful certainty of something important just beyond her grasp. Something she was supposed to remember. Then she had it. "Did you say Endicott?"

"Yes, Endicott, Lewis and MacDonald."

"I'm supposed to go to Cleveland. You're going to think me mad, but I've had some most peculiar dreams, giving me advice, telling me to do something, but I can't remember most of it when I wake up."

"Dreams." Harriet's face went very still. "My dear child, listen to those dreams. Your mother spoke of a friend who came to her in her dreams." Her gaze flicked down to the cross. "Well, if the Almighty is blessing us, perhaps you will find Stanton in Cleveland when you get there. At the very least, you can ask his office in Cleveland to contact him and send you on to wherever he happens to be. He goes from one office to another, busy all the time." She chuckled and bent her head over a seam she had already opened, to make a dress fit Carmen better. "His mother is so proud of him."

"What if I can hear people in my dreams?" Carmen had to ask.

"Child... if you know so little about your mother's heritage, the things and the people she fled, then you were kept ignorant to protect you. I am certainly not qualified to be your teacher. However, I do know that if your mother could meet friends in her dreams, then you could have inherited that gift. If the children of Anna's friend inherited that gift, you could be speaking to them." She shook her head. "I need to ask questions, careful questions, and you most certainly cannot be here if I bring trouble down on us both with my questions."

"Harriet, I can't ask you—"

"Oh, yes, you most certainly can. Here is what we will do. I will send you on your way in a few days, and then I will start asking questions. I will try to contact Stanton and have him waiting for you, and I will shake the trees, so to speak, and see what falls out and what I learn." She nodded for punctuation. "Helping people is what the Almighty put me on this world to do, and no piddling little possibility of danger is going to stop me. Understand?" She glared at Carmen, her lower lip sticking out, but enough laughter in her eyes that the girl could only smile and give in.

She vowed she would pray every day, several times a day, for Harriet's safety, until this matter was resolved and they were all safe.

Chapter Five

"Aren't we wasting time?" Phoebe Stryker whispered, as Allistair Fitch crossed to the other side of the massive kitchen in the rented house the Pinkertons were using as a headquarters outside Detroit.

"Absolutely," Ess whispered back. "Uly and his team should have surrounded the old station house by now. The last thing we need is to have a bunch of very observant, suspicious detectives as witnesses if anything unusual happens."

Her friend managed a momentary smile and nodded. She got up and crossed to the icebox to pull out the pitcher of cream before Allistair finished filling his mug with coffee. Ess sat back, watching the silent interaction between them. She liked it. They got along well enough she regretted the need to whisk away Phoebe and her sisters if today's operation succeeded. Her friend had blossomed and had lost her habit of startling whenever someone came up behind her. Living away from the uncertain political alliances of Sanctuary had been good for her.

Ess watched the incoming storm swirl down on the house, the thickening snow obscuring the view of the edge of town, dimming the gaslights that wouldn't go out once daylight came. Uly and Theo and the volunteers from the *Golden Nile* should have descended on the former station house before sunrise, to limit detection and resistance and any resulting injuries. She prayed everything had been handled with calm and quiet and the people inside the station house had cooperated.

Allistair and Phoebe returned to the table, then one of Allistair's men called from the back room and he got up to see what the other agent wanted. The two girls exchanged thin smiles. Ess made a silent wager with herself and started counting just as silently. At thirty-five, Allistair stomped back into the kitchen and came to a stop at the end of the table, gripping the top of the ladderback chair, his scowl deepening.

"When were you going to tell me—"

"That we sent a group of people who are known to those inside that house, to make contact and convince them they are no longer in danger or living in hiding, or whatever false story the unlamented Mr. Judson told them." Ess pushed away her empty mug and stood. She hated the feeling of helplessness when Allistair Fitch towered over her.

"So help me, Odessa, you're a little too bold sometimes. This is a joint operation. You can't keep waving your magic wand of Secret Service connections and keep getting away with blatant rudeness, not to mention taking huge risks."

"It's not my connections," she said, trying not to mirror his stance. She didn't know what to do with her hands. "Which I didn't use, by the way. My brother is heading up the strike force, which we hope will not have to do any striking. It's the secrecy that irks you, isn't it?"

"My uncle betrayed us far more than he betrayed you," Phoebe said, sliding in between them. Ess shifted to one side, but Allistair didn't move over to regain the silent duel of their eyes. "Please, Allistair, I am so very grateful for all the help you and your men have been in unraveling this filthy tangle. You let me contribute to the hunt for my sisters." She rested her small hand on the placket of his shirtfront.

Ess caught her breath, seeing the softening of Allistair's expression, the cooling fire in his eyes. Wonders would never cease. She added a new item to her growing list of dilemmas to resolve, but this would be a pleasant task: ensuring Phoebe Stryker and Allistair Fitch could stay in contact.

"If you haven't already caught on that we have secrets, then you aren't the clever, perceptive man I thought you," she continued.

That earned a snort from Allistair.

"I trust Ess's brother, and the soldiers under his command. The only reason I trust them a little more than your men is because I have known them longer. They know what is at stake, and they know what resources the people inside the station house have at their disposal, for self-defense."

"They are also here," Allistair said, gesturing over her shoulder with a jerk of his chin.

Ess turned to the window. Uly and Theo led the people emerging from the thickening snow. Far more people than had left the *Golden Nile* more than an hour ago. She stood and reached for her coat, lying across the far end of the long kitchen table. Phoebe let out a cry, at the same moment Ess saw the shorter figures walking between Uly and Theo. She tossed Phoebe's coat to her. Neither of them got their coats on before they dashed out the door, into the thickening snow. The tallest of the little girls let out a shriek and raced away from the others, meeting Phoebe on the porch steps. The two sisters clung to each other, lost their footing, and slid down the steps. A moment later, the other two girls caught up with them and the four sisters laughed and cried and hugged. They didn't notice when Allistair, Ess, Uly, and Theo gathered them up and through the door into the kitchen.

"There was no fight at all," Theo reported, as he and Uly settled down at the kitchen table with Allistair less than half an hour later.

Phoebe and her sisters were on their way through the cover of the snowfall to the *Golden Nile*. The rest of the contact team were in the front parlor of the rented house, having their own reunion with old friends and distant relatives who had believed their lives were in danger if they made contact with other station houses.

"Ernest was brilliant, asking among our crew for people who knew the team in the station house," he continued. His gaze strayed to the various papers spread across the table, and he frowned at the sketch of Alexander O'Keefe that Ess had made for Allistair and his people. "Any progress on that path of investigation?"

"Besides confirmation of my general negative impression every time I encountered the man?" Allistair said, his tone sour. His lip twitched, as if he fought not to let it curl. "I don't know if it's any comfort to know Mr. Judson betrayed your organization as much as ours. Speaking of your mysterious organization..." He met their glances in turn. "Phoebe is a lovely girl and very good at keeping secrets while giving us information to get our job done. Up until this morning, at least."

"She didn't know," Ess said.

"You have a bad habit of keeping secrets from your own people. That doesn't do much to lower my irritation at the wall of secrecy between us."

"I will approach the leadership on that very subject," Theo said. "In fact, I may be overstepping my authority, but I hope you are free for dinner this evening. A celebration on several fronts."

"Oh, I'll be there."

~~~~~

By the time Allistair rode the elevator to the top of the docking tower for dinner on the *Golden Nile*, everyone in the station house had been debriefed. Uly confided in Ess that both Sophia Gruber and Ash Halverson, the leaders of the station house, were furious at the deception Stryker had practiced on them for so long. They were astounded to learn they had been declared dead and lost. A number of their people expressed satisfaction in learning Stryker was dead. That satisfaction was tempered by the news that Sanctuary had been destroyed, and centuries of Originator records had been buried, likely inaccessible for years.

Ess hadn't participated in the debriefing. She helped Phoebe settle her sisters and take them through the examination with Dr. Sylvia. Penelope, Portia, and Pearl seemed unharmed by the restricted life they had been living, other than missing their sister. Their uncle hadn't paid them many visits, which Ess imagined contributed to their good spirits. Plus they had been watched over by people who cared about them, living under the same deception. There was no contradiction clouding their relationships, no lies to interfere. Still, she wanted to pummel Stryker, preferably tied up like a calf for branding and hanging upside down.

Phoebe and Ess oversaw the younger girls' baths and dinner in their cabin. They read to them and made plans for a grand adventure of exploring the airship the next day. When the girls were in bed and drowsy enough to ensure they would fall asleep soon, it was time to hurry to their own cabins and dress for dinner. Ess found a note from Matilda on her bed, saying Allistair had arrived and would be busy in a short meeting before dinner. She could only speculate what that meeting entailed.

When Ess reached the lounge, she was not the last to arrive. Allistair sat alone on one of the couches, shoulders hunched and head bowed, lips pursed in deep thought as he stared into his glass of whiskey. Her grandparents stood by the panorama window, their arms around each other's waists, gazing down in silence. They did that often enough, Ess had mentioned the habit to Uly once.

"Perhaps they feel like rulers preparing their next move in a massive game of chess, with the entire world their chessboard," he had responded, his tone sour. Then regret softened his face. "More likely, they're nervous. We've loaded a huge problem on their shoulders, and they have eight years of catching up to do before they can fix what went wrong while they were, in effect, taking a nap."

"Only they weren't able to get any rest whatsoever," Ess said.

"The height and distance makes it a little easier to adjust, I would guess. Looking down with everything so small, that makes it a little easier, gives them some breathing room."

Breathing room was what Ess suspected her grandparents were now giving Allistair. Her former supervisor looked troubled. Judging by the flatness of his mouth, the deep furrows in his brow and around his eyes, and how his shoulders hunched, something threatened to flatten him. Ess guessed what had occurred in that meeting with her grandparents.

Matilda, Ernest, and Athena were of the opinion that Allistair could handle the revelation at the core of the Originators: the Great Machine, the race through time to stop the Revisionists, the advanced science and technology based on the crystal of the dismantled machine, and now the contest between their two groups to retrieve the pieces. Not only that, but he *deserved* to know, after all he had gone through with them, all he had endured, and the help he had been. Ford, Uly, and Theo agreed Allistair perhaps had a right to know what he had landed in but weren't sure he could handle that knowledge. The elder Fremonts had made the revelation here and now, before a dinner party that was meant to be a celebration.

"Would you like a headache powder?" Ess settled on the edge of the cushion next to him. "Or would you prefer I refill your glass?" Less than a finger of amber liquid remained in the bottom of the tumbler.

"You people are insane," Allistair muttered, gazing across the room. A broken chuckle escaped him and his shoulders lost a little of their hunch. He turned to meet her gaze. "I always thought there was something not quite right about you, Miss Fremont. Now I know. Hiding all those bizarre stories in your head and believing they're real. It affects how you deal with the real world."

Ess snorted and was glad to see a twitch in the corner of his mouth. If he could find some humor here, his incredible, analytical mind wasn't about to crack and the world wouldn't lose a brilliant investigative mind. She muffled a chuckle, knowing she would never be able to tell Allistair what she thought of his talents as a detective.

"For the record, Mr. Fitch, a great deal of what my grandparents told you is relatively new to me, too. When they left me behind at that insufferable boarding school, they locked up my memories, to protect me and safeguard our organization. Phoebe's odious uncle and his many names and accomplices are just the tip of a very deep seam of explosive ore. It must be dug out of the ground with extreme caution, and disposed of properly, to ensure the problem never emerges again."

"Locked up your memories. Like mesmerism? Or those strange carnival tricks with magicians and mystics proclaiming they have unlocked the secrets of the ancients?"

"A little of both, and a great deal of science." She held out her hand for his glass, and after a moment of thought, he tipped it back to drain the last mouthful, then handed it to her. "I'm still regaining my childhood, so nearly as regular as clockwork, someone arrives who knows me, but I don't know them until another lock comes undone, another wall falls in my memories." She walked over to the sideboard and poured him another whiskey. "Usually accompanied by a headache or dizziness while I am temporarily snatched back into the past. Everyone here has grown quite used to me suddenly falling silent and staring at nothing for a minute or two."

"Resisting the temptation to pull some childish trick on her while she's mesmerized is pure torture," Uly offered, as he joined her at the sideboard.

"Such as?" Allistair's mouth relaxed a little more.

"Oh, put a silly hat on her, or take away the book or pencil or whatever she's holding." He slid the decanter from Ess's hand and poured himself a tumbler of whiskey while she mixed seltzer and peach syrup in her own glass. He took Allistair's glass back to him.

Knowing how Allistair's mind worked indicated they would need to demonstrate a few bits of crystal-based technology to prove the truth of what now seemed only an insane tale, akin to the work of Mr. Poe or Mr. Verne or Mr. Wells. She would need all her senses clear, as common sense also told her she would be charged with the demonstrations.

Uly stayed standing while she joined Allistair on the couch.

"You're all insane," Allistair repeated, "yet at the same time..." He sighed and put the glass on the floor so he could first knuckle his eyes, then rub at his temples. "At the same time, I do know you, Ess. I trust you. And the reputation of your grandparents, of Miss Latymer—"

"Mrs. Chamberlain," Uly corrected him. He winked at Ess.

"And the Blue Lotus Society," Allistair said, with a nod. "Their reputations are highly respected, logical, intelligent, trustworthy people. Reconciling what I know with this new perspective is taking some time."

"We have some time before dinner," Matilda said, as she and Ernest walked over to join them. She glanced beyond the couch, and Ess turned enough to see Athena and Ford had joined them.

"A demonstration?" Ford said.

They ended up in the cargo bay, for room to set up a target range. Theo dismantled several different sizes of the Zeus guns, to show Allistair their innards, the most important part being the piece of crystal that powered everything. Then he put each one back together. He, Uly and Ford demonstrated the range of each gun and the technique in firing, then let Allistair try his hand with them. He wasn't the least disappointed when he couldn't come anywhere near the various targets with the lightning bolt that came out of each gun.

Theo and Uly then activated several of the mobis, demonstrating what the automatons could do. The Zeus guns had fascinated Allistair, but he laughed aloud when Theo and Ess related what had really happened in the Smithsonian Institution's warehouse, the night the crew of the *Golden Nile* came to search for crystal in the Egyptian artifacts being guarded by the Pinkertons.

Dinner was much more pleasant than Ess anticipated, which she attributed to Allistair's complete turnaround in attitude. He was like a little boy, full of questions, eating without noticing what was on his plate, his eyes wide as the senior members of the group took turns explaining. Phoebe sat next to him, and Ess swore her friend glowed, delighted with Allistair's ability to comprehend the amazing things they told him. The capper for the evening was Uly's astonished frown when he finally caught on to what was building between Allistair and Phoebe. He nearly choked on a mouthful of roast chicken when Allistair laughed at a story Ernest told, and rested his hand on Phoebe's, in the view of everyone. Phoebe blushed prettily, and Ess was pleased when Athena focused on that gesture, raised one eyebrow, then smiled. She turned to meet Ess's gaze and nodded to her.

Well, at least I won't get any more teasing from the two of them about "my" Allistair Fitch.

All in all, the evening was a far greater success than Ess could have hoped.

Even better, there was no need to demonstrate the time box and the time lock for him. Ess had loathed the very idea, because the demonstration would drain so much energy from Matilda, the only one who had been able to activate the time box. Fortunately, Allistair didn't need that demonstration. He was convinced enough to be thoroughly dedicated to protecting the Originators' secrets by rooting out any of Stryker's accomplices who remained within the Pinkerton organization. He understood more fully now what danger they were in, what danger pieces of the Great Machine posed to the course of Human history.

"The task will take some time, but depend on me, I will come up with a cover story sufficient to allow me to use the agency to protect your secrets." Allistair raised his cup of coffee in toast to everyone at the table, as well as sealing his vow. He had switched to coffee after the trip to the bay and had never finished his second tumbler of whiskey. "If my fellow agents ever discovered the truth of what I've learned tonight..." He chuckled, and locked gazes with Phoebe for a moment. "Well, they'll either lock me up in Bedlam, or request cells for themselves."

~~~~~

Ten days after coming to Harriet's door, Carmen boarded a train heading south to the Kentucky and Illinois border. She was dressed, not as the grand lady of means, sure to impress the secretary of a prosperous law firm, but as a timid schoolgirl with a wig of ebony ringlets. She wore pink, which she loathed. A trunk with her next costume change had already been sent ahead, just before a vicious snowstorm paralyzed the city. Harriet had sent a telegram to a friend, whose name Carmen would never know, to pick up the trunk and then meet her at the train station. She would go to the woman's house twenty miles outside the city, stay there a week, change into her next costume and identity as a governess, in a blond wig and dove gray clothes. Then she would travel east by stagecoach to the far eastern edge of Kentucky, where she would take another train to Philadelphia. There, she would stay in a hotel for two weeks, entirely secluded, while she would claim a new trunk and identity, becoming a grand, older lady. From there, she would travel up the eastern seaboard, to spend the spring in Vermont, and from there finally make her way to Cleveland.

After hearing all the details of Carmen's life, and especially the troubles that had dogged her and her father in the last few years, Harriet advised her not to stop in Boston to empty her father's cache there. While the money Reverend Mackenzie had put away would be a great help and buffer if there were any difficulties or delays, she could not risk returning to some place where enemies had been looking for her. Until Carmen was safely in the custody of Mr. Lewis and his allies, all that protected her and Harriet, if something went wrong, were the costume changes and delays in her journey.

Carmen didn't want to think about what could go wrong. She did, however, find some amusement in realizing that she felt no fear whatsoever that Frierri and his minions would track her down before she left Chicago. Some suspicious characters had appeared on Harriet's street just before the snowstorm pounded the city, the first morning she woke up in Harriet's house. They didn't come back, and the boys entrusted with hauling the trunk of clothes to the train station, to send to Carmen's first stop, said that no one had followed them. She didn't meet them, because it would be safer if they never saw her face, but she sat at the top of the stairs and listened to them report on their little mission. They were excited and proud of themselves, and Harriet called them rascals and praised them for their cleverness.

"Thank You, blessed Savior, for memories and friends appearing when I need them the most," she whispered, her breath fogging the window so she couldn't look out at the snowy train station. At this time of the morning, it was nothing but puddles of light amid the darkness before dawn. She had no one to see out there, anyway. Harriet certainly couldn't have come to the station to see her off.

Carmen stifled a yawn and wrapped her cloak around herself. She had a private compartment, but the engine hadn't awakened enough yet to start pumping steam heat from one car to another. A carpetbag, a small bandbox, and a messenger satchel made up her luggage, neatly stowed around her, and adding to the image of a schoolgirl traveling back to school. The satchel held food for the trip. A bottle of iced water with pieces of dried apple in it for flavoring sat on the floor, braced between the carpetbag and the seat. Part of carrying off the disguise was for Carmen not to leave the compartment. She was thin enough to be a schoolgirl, but some people might think her too tall for fifteen. She needed to stay seated and keep her legs tucked up under her skirts.

Her cross was carefully stowed in the carpetbag. Despite Harriet's admonition, Carmen couldn't make herself wear it. So many things Harriet had told her, or only partially explained to her, combined to make her leery of wearing the cross. While the sensation that someone was concerned for her, searching for her, was comforting, the inability to explain what was happening made her more than uneasy.

Carmen wanted to have questions settled, and to have her life a little more secure before she wore the cross with the crystal rose again. Especially if she wasn't hallucinating from hunger and the onset of some illness, and there was indeed some helpful soul trying to contact her through her dreams. Better to wait until she had reached Cleveland and had found Mr. Lewis and the law firm. Better to have friends around her if something should go wrong. At the very least, she could turn to real people for advice before she wore the cross again.

Chapter Six

A thump on the door startled Carmen from her thoughts as the door of the compartment swung open. She wrapped her cloak tighter around herself, ready to start coughing to drive away anyone who tried to share the compartment with her. Instead, her breath caught in her throat as she stared up into the small eyes of Jock Hardy, one of the errand boys for Frierri. His upper lip curled up as he looked her over.

Please, please, just see a little girl, Carmen silently pleaded as his head turned and he looked at the compartment, empty but for herself.

In the back of her mind, she heard his oily voice, saw his lips pull back in a nasty grin, revealing three rotten teeth and two gold ones. Saw him gloat as he made her stop washing dishes to serve him, even though the cook had told him multiple times that she wasn't supposed to have anything to do with dishing up the food. Hardy liked to prove he had the authority to rearrange the world to suit himself.

He looked her over once more and Carmen couldn't make herself look away. The sneer drooped into disappointment and he stepped back and slammed the compartment door closed. She held perfectly still as she listened to his boots stomping to the next compartment. Carmen shivered, releasing a breath she hadn't even realized she was holding, when the man in the next compartment let out a shout, protesting the intrusion.

The whistle blasted three times from the front of the train, warning it was about to pull out of the station. Hardy passed the narrow window of the compartment, heading for the door out of the car. Carmen waited until the long blast of the departure whistle, and then the first jerk of the engine moving forward. Closing her eyes, she sank back into the seat and whispered prayers of thanks.

She thought about writing to Harriet, to tell her about the narrow escape she had, and how well the disguise worked. That letter would have to wait until she reached Cleveland and made contact with Mr. Lewis.

"Thank You, blessed Savior," she whispered, as the train station vanished in billows of smoke and steam and the unfolding of the snowy landscape. "Please watch out for Harriet, that the troubles following me do not land on her."

April
Philadelphia

"Lovely."

The man leaned forward, his gaze focused somewhere between Ess's bodice and chin. He flinched as his gaze shifted upward and met hers. She held her hands still at her side and turned her back on the display of Raphaelite paintings. What she really wanted to do was send him stumbling away with a good right hook to his jaw. Unfortunately, they were not alone in this wing of the art museum that had just opened an exhibition. The same consideration for public displays of violence that stopped her hadn't stopped him from coming entirely too close. He jerked backward a step, nodded, and offered her a crooked, charming grin.

"The bauble. I'm sorry. Very rude of me. I'm a collector of lovely things and that is..."

He flicked the fingers of the gray gloves he held in one hand at the crystal rose hanging around her neck. How had he been able to see it, when her shirtwaist was somewhat opalescent white as well?

"Extraordinary." He held out his other bare hand. "I hope you will forgive me, miss... "

Ess fought not to smile and refused to answer. She rarely played the stickler for social niceties, but sometimes the stuffy rules worked in her favor.

"Please tell me where you bought it?"

"I haven't the foggiest idea, sir, as the piece is a family heirloom."

"An heirloom?" His brows rose at least an inch. "The royal family, I presume?"

She muffled a snort and decided there was more rascal to his rudeness than rogue. That didn't mean she had to give him her real name. When he held out his hand again, with a little bow, she conceded and let him shake her hand. He had the sense not to try something ridiculous, such as kiss it, though she was indeed glad she had remembered to wear gloves.

"Briscoe Harrison," he said, bowing again as he released her hand. "I serve many wealthy, discerning clients in the search for rare pieces of art." He glanced around. "Fortunately, I enjoy what I do. Not to say that anything here is for sale, however... May I ask the name of the forgiving and charming lady who did not shout for the guards?"

"Serenity Winslow." She made the tiniest curtsy she could manage.

"Miss Winslow, please forgive me for interrupting your perusal of these masterpieces, but..." Again, a flick of his gloves at the crystal rose around her neck. "Is there any way of tracking down the history of that piece, perhaps finding where it was obtained?"

"Why is it so important?" She pressed two gloved fingers over the rose and wished she hadn't let the faint humming of the crystal against her bare flesh irritate her enough to bring it out from inside her neckline, to put a layer of cloth between it and her skin. Ess knew she was being ridiculous, wearing the rose constantly. The only time she had a chance of touching minds with Carmen was when they were both asleep, dreaming, but she couldn't take the chance that somehow, entirely by accident, their minds might touch. She had to be ready.

"My wealthy patrons possess exquisite and sometimes eclectic taste. The truly sophisticated enjoy understated and simple elegance."

"And some who consider themselves sophisticated are merely cads in disguise," Ford said, startling them both. "What sort of trouble, sirrah, are you trying to stir up with my little niece?" He tipped his head back just enough to glare at Harrison, then held out his hands for Ess.

"You're not going to threaten the nice man and challenge him to a duel, are you?" She put a little scamper in her step as she crossed to him. A glimpse of Harrison's face, switching from stunned to thoughtful and then back to roguishly charming sent a shiver down her back. Only someone with secrets to hide had the ability or the need to change expressions so easily, hiding their feelings and thoughts with such care.

"Very sorry, sir. No insult intended." Harrison bowed to them.

"What sort of place is this museum, where little girls are accosted by oafs?" Ford growled, tucking Ess's hand into the crook of his elbow. He grumbled something unintelligible as he hurried her down the hall.

"What was that all about?" she demanded, as soon as they had put three doors between them and Briscoe Harrison, and rejoined the other members of their party, Athena and Theo.

Today's trip to the museum had been to retrieve several pieces of crystal, embedded in a crown discovered in a Viking tomb and smuggled across the ocean in a shipment of paintings from a museum in Belgium. While Athena had been examining the crystal to determine which pieces belonged to the Great Machine and which were simple, plain crystal, an odd vibration passed between the crown, the testing rod Athena was using, and the crystal rose. Ess had left to wander about the museum and take the crystal rose out of the field of influence.

"It's the most aggravating thing," Ford said, after explaining what had just happened. Athena shook her head and finished prying the smallest piece of crystal out of the crown. "I know I've seen him somewhere before. Probably on a wanted poster. Then he asked about the crystal. Kept asking, even though she said it was an heirloom. Nothing is an heirloom unless it's been in the family at least three generations."

"I think I should play the concerned older brother and have a talk with Mr. Briscoe Harrison." Theo winked at Ess and headed for the door out of the museum workroom.

When he joined them more than an hour later, he reported no sign of the man. Either Harrison had been frightened off by Ford the protective uncle, or he had finished a legitimate tour of the museum. Ess made a sketch of him and put it into the pile of items and people and questions to investigate when she had time, after the circle of Originator contacts had been made more secure.

New York City

At the end of April, Ess said goodbye to the crew and passengers of the *Golden Nile*. She settled into a hotel suite midway between the harbor and the main docking towers, while the airship headed across the Atlantic. For at least the next six months, Athena and Ford, Matilda and Ernest would be busy contacting the leaders of Originator station houses throughout Europe and Asia, shortening the long threads of the web that had kept small units separate and isolated. Traitors would no longer have the opportunity to tell ten different stories to ten different people and succeed in keeping them from talking to each other. There would no longer be any more manipulation of agents and investigators and scientists for their own profit.

Ess scolded herself for being childish when, the first evening alone, she settled down and had a good cry. Uly was heading to Cleveland, to help with security investigations. Endicott, Lewis and MacDonald were finally procuring the land to build the office building and airship docking tower that would be the new headquarters of the Originators.

Phoebe and her sisters were settling in nicely with Hilda, Tomas, Bridget, Peggety and Waldo. Ess looked forward to going to Cleveland in a few weeks and catching up with them all. She wanted to spend hours in Hilda's kitchen and spend as much time as she could in trousers. The last few months, representing the revised, repaired Originators organization, had been exhausting. She had opted to take a few days off sightseeing in New York once she said goodbye to her family and the *Golden Nile*.

That was a mistake now, she knew. She was a Fremont, and Fremonts weren't designed to be idle. How many libraries and museums and music halls and art galleries could she visit? Especially when her Pinkerton training insisted she analyze the doors and windows and ventilation for security flaws? When she saw a dozen different ways that thieves could circumvent a needlessly complicated security system, and didn't remember anything of the enameled antiques and gewgaws on display, it was time to find something constructive to do.

Unfortunately, she couldn't move on until she had heard from Agent Sutter. She had telegraphed him that she would be at her hotel until the end of the week. Knowing that his response wouldn't come if she stayed at the hotel waiting for it, she decided to play tourist and visit Ellis Island.

Just before the ferry pulled away from the dock, that itching certainty of being watched settled in between her shoulder blades. Her neck positively ached from the struggle not to turn to look around herself. Ess theorized a man-about-town looking for some female companionship. She was visibly alone, a likely target for someone seeking a woman to threaten or frighten or rob. If that were the situation, the hopeful thief would soon regret thinking Odessa Vivian Fremont was helpless. To torment the watcher, she kept her gaze focused on the island ahead of her and moved along the railing of the top deck, staying close to groups of sightseers.

Just before the ferry reached the docks at Ellis Island, Ess reached a somewhat isolated and abandoned section of railing. An opportunist might consider it a good time to approach a hopeful target.

The brisk wind off the water coming from behind her softened, indicating someone had approached close enough to provide a partial windbreak. Then Ess caught the subtle fragrance of sandalwood soap. A man who washed regularly and didn't try to drown his imperfections in hygiene with cologne.

A long-fingered, masculine hand came to rest on the railing to her right and a familiar, baritone chuckle warmed the air.

"I swear you didn't turn around even a few inches, so how did you know I was shadowing you?" Agent Sutter asked.

"I didn't. At least, I didn't know it was you." Ess tipped her head to the left and fluttered her eyelashes at him. That earned a louder chuckle. "How long have you been following me?"

The ferry jolted slightly underneath them as it adjusted to turn around to back into the dock.

"I didn't. I arrived at your hotel about five minutes after you left. The desk clerk informed me you asked for the most scenic route. Wonder of wonders, you actually are relaxing. I got to the ferry and found a seat a good ten minutes before you did."

"And you didn't consider sending out the dogs, fearing I might have been waylaid?"

"I would send out the dogs to pick up the pieces of whoever was foolish enough to accost you." Sutter bent over to rest his crossed arms on the railing as they laughed together. "So, I hear you've given your grandparents permission to go off on another adventure without you."

"They have work to do, and an entire airship full of students and assistants to look out for them. I'm not worried for their safety, if that's what you were hinting at."

"No, rather I should fear for anyone who tries to harm them or even get in their way, while they're abroad. Any international incidents that might arise will be the result of fools coming up against them." He stepped back, nodding at the crowd of people waiting on the dock to board the ferry.

Ess exhaled in some exasperation, seeing the traffic jam about to take place. The people wanting to board and the people wanting to disembark were both trying to take the same gangplank. Common sense said those waiting to board should step aside and let those departing the ferry to leave. Then there would be room on the ferry for them to board. She had seen the same oblivious behavior in public meetings and lecture halls at universities. One class was trying to leave and the incoming class was in such a hurry to get in and find seats that they wouldn't let the outgoing class leave and surrender those seats to them.

She decided to find some amusement in the situation. Agent Sutter didn't speak again while they walked down the plank and wedged their way through the crowd, until they finally reached open space and fresh air. With a sigh and a crooked smile, she accepted the offer of his bent elbow, slipped her hand into it, and they headed down the first gravel pathway to the right, away from the main buildings. During the War Between the States, the island had been a staging ground for the harbor patrols and the Union Navy, and a processing center for boats and ships that were seized for either inadequate paperwork or being in league with Southern forces.

"Are you here to bully me into working for you, now my grandparents have been found and it appears I am not returning to the Pinkertons? Or ..." She fluttered her eyelashes, earning a chuckle and a shake of his head.

"Odessa, I think I prefer you disguised as a dirty boy. Far less dangerous."

"Should I take that as a compliment?"

"An admission of defeat and terror." Sutter patted her hand where it was caught in the crook of his arm. "The 'or' you left hanging refers to our mysterious Carmen. And the answer is yes. We have found her. To some extent."

"You know who she is, you know her history, you know why she fled the organization she belonged to, but you don't know where she is."

"In a nutshell." He snorted. "Have you ever wondered where that phrase came from?"

"Grandfather speculated one time that spies hid messages inside walnuts, to pass them along to the nobility who hired them."

"I should enjoy making better acquaintance with your grandfather." He squeezed her hand and they were silent as they passed a group of people reading the bronze and marble markers, commemorating activities during the war. "Carmen Hope Mackenzie, daughter of the late Reverend Hiram Mackenzie and Anna Shipton Mackenzie, who predeceased her husband by seven years."

"Ah. That could explain some things."

"Such as how she doesn't know to contact your friends?" He sighed, the sound suspiciously like a chuckle, when Ess wouldn't even look at him. "The Reverend Mackenzie was quite a bit older than his wife, who, according to the original members of the Beacon Hill Missionary Society, came out of seemingly nowhere to join their organization. She was a model of propriety and modesty, and the elder members of the leadership came to depend on her to keep the younger volunteers in each town in order. She discouraged all attempts at courtship, and several times tried to leave the

Society when young ministers wouldn't take no for an answer. The general consensus, even recorded in the society archives, is that Reverend Mackenzie offered marriage to shelter her and ensure they wouldn't lose her dedication and organizational skills. All indications are that the Mackenzies were very happy together. She was the perfect minister's wife, serene and confident and always ready to take on one more duty. It was quite a blow to him and the society both when she died."

"How?"

"No one can really say, which makes the circumstances suspicious in my mind." He led her over to a wooden park bench set in the shade of an apple tree that had lost half its blossoms. "The only records say she fell ill during a week-long camp meeting outside of Mercer, Pennsylvania. Just before that, her husband suffered what some at first called cataleptic fits. He would tremble and then go stiff and fall over. Mrs. Mackenzie and her daughter devoted all their time and attention to nursing him. She never left his side. When he seemed to be recovering, she simply collapsed and didn't leave her bed again." He leaned back against the bench and tipped his head up so the sunshine falling through the branches touched his face with shadows and streaks of gold. "What are you thinking?"

"Someone could have tried to poison the whole family, but Carmen's father took the brunt of it, bringing on the fits." Ess shivered, thinking about the crystal rose that was twin to the one she wore.

She had seen Athena use the lotus to heal people and had seen Dr. Sylvia and Dr. Lockhart use fragments of crystal to help the ill and injured guide their own self-healing process. If Anna was as attuned to the crystal as Vivian had been, Ess could easily imagine her purging her husband of whatever poison had struck him, by singing to the crystal. Maybe Revisionists had found her and attacked her husband when they couldn't get to her because of the crowds at the camp meeting.

Her position really had been rather brilliant as a defensive strategy. Anna could live an active life. As the wife of a minister, she would be generally ignored. Yet she would be at the edge of the light constantly focused on him, thus protected. It made too much sense that if Revisionists had found her after all those years, they had to remove her shield, her husband, before they could get to her.

If the whole family had been poisoned, then once Anna drained herself, using the crystal rose to save his life, she became vulnerable. Fatally so. The problem with Ess's theory was that it was just that — theory.

"I'm not going to ask who you think tried to kill him," Sutter said. "There's a saying in the Secret Service that all information is available for the asking, but once I tell you what you want to know, I am duty-bound to kill you to protect it."

"The Blue Lotus Society isn't quite that drastic, but yes, some things are better left hidden in shadows and the dust of the ages. Please continue with your..." She fluttered her lashes, earning a bark of laughter from him. "Story? Or can we call this a report, when it certainly can't be termed official Secret Service business?"

"Let's hope it never does reach that point. Let's see... when Carmen and Reverend Mackenzie returned to the camp meeting circuit, his health wasn't as robust as it once was. People attributed it to his age catching up with him, and grief. He shifted to an advisory and administrative role. Carmen worked with children, organizing activities to keep them occupied while their parents were in the big tents, and moved up from the choir to solo performances."

"Is she talented?" Ess liked the sensation of puzzle pieces fitting together. After all, music was part of the crystal's functioning. She had found records of the dismantling of the Great Machine. One interpretation stated the women who did the job sang the Machine into slumber so it could be spread across the world without attacking those who dismembered it.

"Very. I found mention of trouble with musicians. The musical arts world has quite a nasty side. People remember whatever foolish mistakes you made, and scandals live forever."

"Scandals?" Ess turned to frown at him, uncertain if he was teasing her.

"Carmen Mackenzie caught the attention of a handful of influential people who were determined to put her on stage. For their own profit, of course, as her managers. There was an opera company in New York that pestered Reverend Mackenzie to send Carmen to study with them. In a couple other smaller incidents, people tried to 'rescue' her from the drudgery of saving souls. Meaning, she wasn't getting paid, so they couldn't profit off her golden voice. After a while, she stopped singing solos near big cities with any kind of artistic community. That led to some disagreements with the new leadership of the Beacon Society. Reverend Mackenzie and Carmen were demoted to smaller traveling companies. The ones where raw young preachers got the rough edges sanded off and learned eloquence by suffering in the Lord's army."

Chapter Seven

"You found out a number of unsavory details about the Beacon Society, didn't you?"

"They got too big for their britches, as my granny would say." He paused as voices and the crunching of gravel under shoes grew louder.

Ess looked around and saw what appeared to be a rather large family group approaching, most likely aiming for the other benches scattered around in the shade of the trees. There were at least twenty of them, with several generations visible, many wearing the same beaked nose and angular cheekbones. When Sutter gestured away from their resting place, she nodded and let him tuck her hand back into the crook of his arm. They strolled in silence for several minutes while she digested what he had told her so far.

"The society grew large enough that the people who started it were either nudged to the sidelines, unable to hold the new members to the original vision, or moved entirely out of power?" she suggested.

"They grew old, they grew ill, they grew apart, and I think they grew disillusioned. Some of them handed over the reins to their sons or nephews who had bigger, better, brighter ideas. Or they became too busy to communicate with the others. That's my assessment, based on what I've seen happen in similar situations. Someone wanted power and attacked the old guard. Funds went missing, reports were skewed, people heard all sorts of unkind stories about each other."

"Outsiders joined the society and attacked Carmen's father, didn't they?" Ess said, theorizing aloud.

"Some rumors were odd enough, I'm surprised anyone believed them. All centered on your friend Carmen. I'm inclined to think someone fed the rumors to profit from them."

"Meaning?"

"Carmen stayed off the stage and focused on children. Supposedly she held sick children and healed them by singing to them." Sutter shrugged when Ess turned to meet his eyes, half-hoping she would find him teasing her. "Skinned knees, bloody fingers, black eyes. Then there was a little boy who escaped his house full of scarlet fever. He wanted to hear the lady who sang like an angel and made up songs with the names of all the children who came. He sat on Carmen's lap until the sheriff tracked down the boy and took him home. They say he was healthy as a little horse after that. About the time the rumors grew too odd to believe, an aspiring young unmarried preacher named Boniface joined the team."

"To court Carmen?" Ess could easily envision what had happened.

The Revisionists would have left Carmen alone until she displayed talents like her mother's. What better way to get Carmen away from her father's care than to court her and take her away, believing she was going to be a minister's wife?

"No." Sutter shook his head. "He was focused on the ministry. Supposedly. He made himself a defender for the Mackenzies when the rumors got out of control. Carmen was mobbed regularly. The more she denied the stories, the worse the demands grew."

"Something like that should have appeared in some newspapers, shouldn't they?"

"It happened fast. In retrospect, I can see it must have been guided. Engineered." He gestured at another bench ahead of them on the path that had taken them around the perimeter of the island. "About a month later, Reverend Mackenzie was accused of making a circus act of his daughter. Supposedly, he told people her gift came from ancient civilizations. Most notably, Egypt." Sutter cocked his head, studying Ess from under half-closed eyelids.

"Snake oil salesmen and gypsy peddlers have been claiming to possess the secrets of ancient civilizations for generations," she said, trying to make her tone bored. "I'm guessing no one actually came to the meetings, to listen to him and find out the truth." She sighed when Sutter shook his head. "Too big for their britches, indeed. Too eager for someone else to look bad, so they could get more power."

"That's about the size of it. Some demanded he step down. There were arguments between the old guard and the new leadership. Boniface became the brave knight defending his mentor. He always found proof that each accusation was a lie. Do you find that as suspicious as I do?"

"The best way to have the proof is to be the one who committed the crime."

"You really must consider coming back to work for me, Odessa." He rested his hand on top of hers. "No surprise, Reverend Mackenzie's health crumbled. The fits and seizures returned." Sutter nodded for punctuation as understanding filled Ess. "Boniface offered to rescue them. He had a position at a small country church lined up. Then he professed his undying love for Carmen and asked her to become his wife."

"She didn't believe him, did she?"

"No one is sure. Her father ejected Boniface from the team. He showed up, looking for Carmen, maybe two weeks after her father died. By that time, she had fled, vanished with no clue where she was going. The Beacon Society confiscated everything they owned, claiming Reverend Mackenzie had embezzled Society funds for decades. There is some indication a few of the new members are still hunting for her, to stop her practicing the black arts. I don't blame her for running."

"And all she did was sing to the children," Ess whispered.

"What I find interesting is that the rumors always originated from cities where the teams *hadn't* set up their tents. People who actually saw Carmen sing to the children didn't support the rumors. However, as the rumors grew, fewer people brought their children to the meetings. The numbers of curiosity seekers and troublemakers increased. When Carmen didn't sing, that just made the situation more unpleasant."

"Did anyone have anything to say about the cross she wore?" she asked, and wished she didn't need to ask such a question.

Sutter thought, and then reached into his coat to pull out a small journal where she assumed he had kept notes. She was impressed at this proof that he knew the investigation so well he didn't need to consult his notes up until that point in the recitation.

"Nothing anyone said. Something noteworthy about the cross?"

"It was her mother's, and someone who has been a problem for the Pinkertons tried at one time to buy it from her. It likely has nothing to do with the manufactured scandal, but I thought..." Ess shrugged. "I'm not sure what I thought. It was one of the few leads I had."

"Unfortunately, the tale and the trail both end there. While the vultures gathered, Carmen packed up a few clothes and simply walked away. There was some speculation that she had run off to join Boniface after all. However, he was easy enough to track down, having become personal assistant to the mayor of Cincinnati. When my contact approached him about Carmen, the man feigned shock at hearing her father was dead and she had vanished." Sutter's eyes narrowed. "I felt he asked far too many questions about what we were doing to find her. Last week, my man went back to ask more questions and learned he had quit his position."

"At least we know she didn't go running to him," Ess murmured. All that information was interesting, but not very helpful, and she still had no idea if Carmen had sold the cross and the crystal rose. "Those people took everything her father left her?"

"We're checking to see if the Mackenzies had any sort of property, maybe a home someone else was looking after while they traveled, perhaps a safe deposit box." Sutter shrugged, closed the book and tucked it back in his jacket.

"Where did she go? There has to be someone she trusted, who wouldn't tell the society people."

"Perhaps she was in contact with her mother's people. It is clear Anna Mackenzie was hiding something or hiding from someone."

"Logical, but one rather large problem." Ess flinched as the ferry horn sounded. She assumed it was the signal for imminent departure.

"And that is?"

"My mother was Anna's friend, the only person who kept in contact with her, once she escaped from some dangerous, ruthless people."

"Ah." He nodded and frowned thoughtfully as they picked up their pace, heading toward the dock. "It could be that Carmen will try to go to your mother's last known address, to ask for help, even if she knows your mother died long ago."

"That makes sense. Thank you." She gnawed on her bottom lip. A plan was already solidifying in her head. She needed to return to her grandparents' home, which had finally been restored and repaired. If Carmen knew enough to look for Vivian Fremont, she would go there. Ess refused to tie her head in knots over the possibilities of Carmen being there when she arrived, or more likely having arrived, been frustrated, and then moved on. She would go home first, then start asking questions, and be prepared to follow up on whatever she learned. If fate was kind and the Almighty answered her prayers, Carmen Mackenzie would have left a trail of some kind that Ess, with her Pinkerton training, could follow with ease.

May

At long last, Carmen sat on a train headed for Cleveland. She had shed her governess costume two stops ago and now wore the woman of means outfit that would be her guise until Harriet's Mr. Lewis took over. It was several steps down from the grand lady outfit that Harriet wanted her to wear, but Carmen had finally talked her into seeing common sense. A grand lady would be too memorable, even in a busy, growing port city like Cleveland. Especially if she had no attendants making arrangements for her. A woman of means was more an independent sort, a little easier to overlook until she requested assistance. A woman of means had far less luggage to worry about, and her hotel room would cost half the price of a room a grand lady would expect. Carmen could eat more simply, as well. No one would be scandalized, and remember her, when she walked into a bake shop and bought a meat pie, or purchased a sandwich at a delicatessen, as opposed to sitting down in a respectable restaurant, as a grand lady would.

Most important, in Carmen's point of view, was the simplicity of costume, requiring less fussing as she got on and off the train. She could buy a first class seat, and chances were good she would be left alone, with no one sitting next to her, because first class cars had fewer occupants. People might notice her getting on and off the car, but they wouldn't wonder who she was, and why she was traveling alone.

Saving money and earning respectful treatment, while able to walk through the bustling city without collecting curious looks. That was the way to survive until Mr. Lewis took charge of her and whatever mystery or danger or problem accompanied the crystal rose. There was no guarantee he would be in town when she arrived, and no guarantee he would arrive within a few days. She had to make her funds last for perhaps a month, two at the most, until he returned to his law firm. Harriet had no idea what his schedule was, traveling from one office to another and handling client business. Harriet didn't trust the postal service to protect any messages dealing with Carmen. People were always trying to get into mail addressed to lawyers, either through curiosity or to cause trouble for their clients, according to Harriet. No, it was best for Carmen to hand the letter of introduction to Mr. Lewis himself, and that meant waiting, for however long it took.

"Life would be so much simpler, Mama, if you had told me about our mysterious heritage," Carmen murmured, looking out the window at the late spring landscape. Rolling green meadows stretched to the horizon, only broken by plowed fields covered with straight rows of crops.

The crystal rose and the cross still resided in the secret compartment of her carpetbag. More times than she could count, through the long weeks of traveling, changing her costume, establishing her new identity at a hotel, then boarding another train and changing her costume and identity again, she thought about wearing the cross. More than just the emotional encouragement and comfort, she thought about reestablishing whatever contact might actually exist with her make-believe friend, Essie. Had it been Essie who insisted she should go to Cleveland? If so, shouldn't she try to tell her she was on her way? Carmen had thought long on Harriet's words, her reactions, and fragments of memories of her childhood. She knew the idea touched on the fantastic, the mythical, or perhaps the miraculous. How could wearing the crystal rose let her touch someone else's thoughts? Yet what other explanation was there?

Her months of solitude and leisurely travel had given her time to organize her thoughts and hopefully put the last few years into perspective. The rose had something to do with the odd and amazing and miraculous incidents that her father's detractors had used against him. How could anyone say the miracles that had come through her were evil? Every time she sang and prayed for a child, she lifted up her heart and mind to Heaven, and asked only that the Almighty use her for blessings. The songs were always hymns. She enfolded the child in prayer, and total submission to the will of the Savior. How could the forces of Hell make a tool of her when she tried never to slip out of the grasp of the Savior?

She had had such conversations with her father numerous times over the years, after they realized she was being used as a conduit of Heaven's grace and blessings. Carmen could remember similar conversations between her parents. Her mother had worried about the same thing. Had the Almighty perhaps used Anna for the same purposes? When she wore the crystal rose, had she been able to sing blessings and healing on those she ministered to in their travels?

"Oh, Mama, I surely wish you had trusted me with your secrets," Carmen whispered, and dabbed at her wet eyes with the knuckle of her dove gray gloves.

She froze, remembering her mother's journals. How could she have forgotten her mother's journals all this time? Wouldn't there be some answer, perhaps names, perhaps even a letter to Carmen, explaining things, in the journals?

Carmen could almost laugh at her reflection in the train window, and weep at the same time. She had been so desperate to flee before those greedy, grasping traitors confiscated the three steamer trunks she and her father had hauled from town to town, she hadn't been thinking clearly. Grief and the vague suspicion someone would try to enslave her, to keep her from telling the world what the new leaders of the Beacon Society had done, had muddled her thoughts. Since then, she had been living nearly hand-to-mouth, unable until recently to sit and think at her leisure and remember.

She still mourned her father's library and the rest of the contents of those three steamer trunks that had seen far better days. His gold pocket watch, the sapphire lapel pin, and the gold-embossed slipcase for his Bible, a last gift from her mother. The other items, all of the highest quality, were just things. Possessions. Carmen convinced herself not to care, because she couldn't flee into the night carting a steamer trunk of memories. She still feared that someone might have learned of and gained legal access to her father's three safe deposit boxes. Someday, when she felt truly safe, she would go to each bank and empty the boxes. The truly important possessions, the things that her father refused to risk losing during travel, were safe at those banks. Her parents' wedding rings. Photo portraits of their family, taken at Christmas each year. Ancient books, too precious and fragile to withstand the rigors of constant travel.

Her mother's journals. She had entirely forgotten about Anna's journals until now.

Carmen pounded her fist once into her thigh. Certainly there had to be some answers, some explanations in those pages. Someday soon, she would retrieve the journals. When she had dealt with Harriet's Mr. Lewis, then she might finally have some answers.

"Please, blessed Savior..." Carmen sighed, and caught a smile tugging up the corners of her mouth in her reflection. "I don't know what to pray any longer. Except to ask that this be the last leg of my journey, and soon all my questions will be answered."

Cleveland, Ohio

"I'm sorry, but Mr. Lewis is currently traveling on firm business. His next visit is uncertain, as several concerns of the firm and this office in particular are in fluctuation." The balding gentleman who stood behind the massive desk in the foyer of the law firm did indeed look like he regretted giving Carmen the news. "Would you like to leave a message for him? I could send a telegram to the other offices, in hopes of catching up with him. Or perhaps you would be willing to talk with one of the other partners?"

Carmen resisted the urge to slip her hand into the hidden pocket in the side seam of her dress and feel for the letter from Harriet for Mr. Stanton Lewis. She smiled at the secretary and tipped her head slightly to the right as she thought. Could she trust Mr. Lewis's partners? Yes, Harriet had said it would be safest not to give the letter to anyone except Mr. Lewis, but she had indicated if not said outright that the other partners in the law firm were just as trustworthy and admirable.

"Would Mr. Endicott or Mr. MacDonald happen to be in the office right now?"

"Ah, no, I'm sorry, ma'am. Let me clarify, only junior partners are present right now. All three of the senior partners are occupied with firm business out of town and out of the state. If you would like to leave your name and where you can be contacted?" He picked up an inkwell and a piece of paper and slid them across the massive blotter to her side of the desk.

"Thank you." Carmen took a step back, admitting defeat. Only temporarily, however. "I was instructed to deal with no one but Mr. Lewis. Would it be all right if I stop back in, say, every two or three days, in case you learn he is due to return?"

"That is most gracious of you, ma'am. No bother at all for us. Can I assume you are staying here in town, at a hotel nearby?"

"Actually, my luggage is still at the station, and my next errand is to find a room. The next time I return, perhaps I will leave my contact information."

"Very good, ma'am."

Carmen caught a slight widening of his eyes as she made her farewells and stepped out through the door, which was propped open for ventilation on the warm day. She muffled a chuckle, knowing he was just starting to realize something was wrong. Specifically, she had left without telling him her name.

She stepped out onto Superior Avenue and walked west, crossing Public Square. It was a lovely day, and she had spent so much time seated, hurtling across the countryside, walking felt like a luxury. The ticket for her trunk was safe inside her glove, her carpet bag wasn't heavy at all, so she decided to take a walk. Learning the layout of this bustling, growing port city on the shore of Lake Erie only made sense, if she was going to spend any time here. She needed to let herself adjust to a slower pace and get a feel for the neighborhoods before she chose the hotel where she would stay and wait for Mr. Lewis to return.

Three blocks west of Public Square, she found her way blocked by a group of men filling the sidewalk and spilling out into the street. They milled about, most of their attention focused on the door of one of the narrow, three-story-tall buildings that had been built slap up against each other, ten in a row filling the city block. She drew closer, trying to decide how to go around the crowd without stepping into the street in front of an oncoming line of wagons and carriages. The sign over the door read: Reginald Huckabee, Esq., Attorney at Law. What sort of problem did all these men face, to be waiting for the lawyer inside? As she drew closer, she spied work aprons under coats, a smear of flour on one man's shirtsleeve, a leather apron that indicated perhaps a cobbler or butcher, and other items of clothing that hinted at the trades practiced by these men.

Several men looked around as she drew close enough to have to detour out into the street. One nodded to her and nudged the man next to him. Carmen's face warmed and she nodded her thanks as the men in front of her stepped to one side or another, creating an aisle wide enough for her to pass through. Some of that warmth came from the assessing glances a few men gave her, inspecting her shape or winking. One man even waggled his eyebrows as she met his gaze. The man next to him admonished him silently with an elbow in his ribs. Carmen thanked him with a slow nod and he grinned and tipped his hat. She was barely past the lawyer's door when she caught movement from the corner of her eye and turned to see the door swinging open. A beefy, white-haired man stepped out, holding a sheaf of papers in one hand and polishing his pince-nez on his coat sleeve. The muttering, shifting men grew still, so that Carmen could hear him speaking as she slipped through the remainder of the gauntlet.

"Now, gentlemen, I can understand your concern, but Mr. Winslow has again frightened you for no cause. Or rather, I can't speculate on his cause without being hit with a handful of libel suits."

That earned a few chuckles from some of the men, mutters from others. Curious, Carmen slowed her pace to let her listen.

"So we shouldn't let him negotiate for the things he's got written out there in those papers?" a man called from the crowd.

Chapter Eight

"Oh, you can let him speak for you, and insist that you receive everything he's put in this list of demands, but it's my professional opinion — and I think my long career here has proven that I know what I'm talking about and I've protected the interests of more than half of you here, at one time or another."

That earned a slightly larger and louder ripple of laughter and murmurs from the men. Carmen slowed her steps even more.

"Gentlemen, it's my professional opinion that Mr. Winslow's list of demands is inferior to what you're being offered for your businesses. He's not asking for assistance in transporting your equipment and supplies to a new location. He's not asking for assistance in finding a new location equal to or better than where you are now. He's most certainly not asking for the first month's rent on your new stores and workshops. He's asking for nearly the same price the corporation has offered you. Most curious, he *isn't* telling you what he wants you to pay him for protecting you from the threat of abuse that, in my professional opinion, does not exist."

"He didn't write that down anywhere," a man shouted from the edge of the crowd closest to Carmen. "I read through it five times."

"Yes, Abner, and why did you find it necessary to read any document prepared by Mr. Winslow?" Mr. Huckabee shouted back, a ripple of laughter thickening his voice.

"He's a trickster, that he is. Told you there was always some trap you don't see until it snaps shut on you," another man called. Others in the crowd called out in agreement, a few in disagreement.

Carmen didn't linger any longer. She was nearly to the end of the block and she knew better than to draw any more attention than she already had.

"Gentlemen, common sense says when you work with a lawyer, he's going to charge you fees," Mr. Huckabee said as Carmen turned the corner.

More laughter followed her around the corner. She made a note to ask the hotel clerk, wherever she ended up staying, just what was going on. It sounded like someone was buying up businesses and relocating the proprietors.

By late afternoon, Carmen had made a circuit of the general area, perhaps eight blocks on each side, and found five hotels that looked promising. She also located several grocers and bakeries and a delicatessen where she could obtain the makings of simple meals, so she wouldn't have to pay to eat in a restaurant. Since the secretary at the law firm couldn't predict when Mr. Lewis would return, it was best to be frugal from the start and make her money stretch.

That resolve was enforced a short time later, when she made her choice of hotel and asked for her room for two weeks. She nearly dropped her purse when she calculated just ahead of the clerk what that would cost. Most definitely, she would be wise to take all her meals in her room. The concert hall and other cultural offerings that she had seen listed in shop windows and the community bulletin board outside city hall were beyond her means. Her purse and uncertain future would limit her entertainment to long hours at the library. She hoped to be settled before the free concerts on the city green started.

Back out onto the street, her legs now protested all the walking she had done. Carmen straightened her back and slowed her pace, and tried to calculate how thick the soles of her shoes were, just by the feel. She wouldn't be taking any trolleys or carriages or cabs any time in the near future. A moment of regret almost sent her turning around to cancel her room at the hotel, in favor of one closer to the train station. However, that hotel had struck her as rather unsavory in atmosphere. She couldn't risk people there noticing she was entirely alone, for however long it took for Mr. Lewis to return.

"There's no remedy," she scolded herself. "Do be more careful in the future. Please, Lord, have Mr. Lewis come back to town quickly?"

When she emerged from the train station, her trunk loaded on a handcart to be hauled the four blocks to her hotel, sunset had painted streaks of crimson and peach and lavender across the sky. Carmen wanted nothing more than to hire the one-horse cart sitting in the taxi parking area in front of the train station, to ride back to the hotel. The steam-cart waiting two spaces down from it was entirely out of the question. She took a few deep breaths, pulled her shoulders back, and promised herself something delectable and inexpensive for dinner, to reward all her walking and discomfort and frugality. Then she headed back down the street for the second time today.

The green grocer that appealed to her the most was along the direct route between the train station and the hotel. Carmen wouldn't have to add any extra steps for her weary feet and legs. Right across the street from him was a baker's shop. This late in the day, both should be about to lower their prices, just to get the old wares off the shelves. She could buy quite nice items for tonight's cold dinner and tomorrow's breakfast.

Just as she was about to step up to the front of the green grocer's shop, her attention on the crates of fruits and vegetables attractively displayed out front, Carmen caught a glimpse of two children ducking into the shadows between the stacks of crates and the alley on the other side of the shop. Her only impression was of dusty-grimy clothes and faces, a boy and a girl, small enough to be perhaps nine or ten years old. She had spent enough time with children over the years, she could gauge ages and economic situations from a quick glance, factoring in evidence of inadequate food. She ached, just a moment, for the life she had lost. If she were still part of the camp meeting team, she would approach the children and talk to them. She would buy them something to eat, because why else would they be lingering in the shadows by the grocer's shop? Then she would invite them to the camp meeting and the children's activities outside the main tent. Then, once they trusted her and confessed their situation, she might engage the local pastors or town officials to find help or shelter for them.

Now all Carmen could do was stand a little straighter and pray silently for the children's welfare, that God would send someone quickly to take care of them.

Carmen turned as the grocer in his white apron with his sleeves neatly rolled up out of the way, held in place with black garters, stepped out of the doorway to be of assistance. That last was very nice. The attentiveness of store clerks and people like this gray-haired, walrus-whiskered gentleman had deteriorated in direct proportion to the increasing shabbiness of her clothes. At the beginning of her wandering, Carmen had speculated on the idea that the good Lord had allowed her to slide downward to teach her a few things, so she could better serve Him, and purify her heart and soul.

"Hey there, what have I told you?" the grocer snapped, his polite smile cracking into a frown.

He darted toward the alley, nearly going to his knees as he lunged into the shadows. A shriek like a puppy got its tail stepped on split the air, and a moment later he emerged, holding the little girl by her collar and shoulder. She shut up a moment later, eyes squeezed tight shut, tears rolling down her grimy cheeks.

"Willoughby!" the grocer shouted, as he put the girl down in the doorway and blocked her escape by keeping her between two stacks of crates and his own body. "Beg your pardon, ma'am, but this one and her brother, they've been pilfering from me for going on two weeks now. Willoughby!"

"Hold yer horses," a gravelly bass voice responded.

The child's face went white under the dirt and she opened her mouth to wail. Carmen turned around to find the biggest policeman she had ever seen, trudging down the sidewalk.

"She looks hungry," Carmen offered, sympathizing with the child. Where was the boy who was with her? Why had he fled and left her to fend for herself?

"Oh, most likely. Ordinarily, I don't mind if they help themselves to what I gotta toss at the end of the day," the grocer said. "Why can't they wait until then? Why they gotta take what's good and I could sell? I'm not a charity, am I?"

"That you aren't," Officer Willoughby said, coming to a stop to form a triangle between him, the grocer, and Carmen. He looked down at the child, whose mouth stayed open but no sound came out. A flicker of pain in his big brown eyes gave Carmen a hint at his heart before he schooled his features into sternness.

"Didn't Mr. Gilligan warn you?" he said, bending down to get closer to the child's level. "Didn't I warn you?"

"There ain't nothin' left at the end of the day," the boy declared, sliding between her and Gilligan. He put his arm around the girl. "All the bigger kids get to it first, or they take what we find."

"Is that so?" Willoughby said, taking a step back.

"If the children are eating what they can find, either their father has no employment," Carmen began.

"Got no father. No mother, neither," the boy said, hunching his shoulders.

"Just what I was afraid of," the officer said with a sigh. "Seen them wandering around. Hoped they were newcomers, their parents come looking for work, not settled yet. How'd you get here?"

"Hopped the train." The boy wouldn't meet anyone's eyes, and his shoulders hunched more, as if he was embarrassed at the admission.

"Will you let me cover the damages?" Carmen nearly laughed aloud at the icy thread of horror that shot through her, hearing those words in her voice. Yes, she had more than enough money, but how long would "more than enough" turn into "not nearly enough" and then "none at all" if she stopped to help every pitiful, dirty, hungry, abandoned child she encountered? She was in a large city. The numbers of orphans and destitute widows had to be much larger, just because more people were crammed into fewer square miles.

"Oh, now, ma'am," Gilligan began, his face reddening. He raised his hands in a defensive gesture. Carmen was relieved to see he looked embarrassed rather than angry. "It's not that I don't want to help orphans, you understand. It's just that there are so many more of them lately, you gotta wonder if maybe they're runaways instead of orphans? Or their folks just send them out to steal what they can, because there's nothing in the pot at home. Know what I mean? There's societies like that to take care of folks that can't look after themselves. Am I right, Willoughby?"

"I would hazard a guess that the bigger children get noticed and helped much more often than the little ones," Carmen said, bending down to try to look the boy and then the girl in the eyes. They both stole glances at her through the shaggy hair in their eyes, then down at the sidewalk again.

"Can't go blaming the war anymore," Gilligan continued, his voice taking on a creaking note, as if he had used the words far too often and they were wearing out.

"Unfortunately, we must continue to blame the war. Far too many men came home wounded in their minds and hearts, while their bodies were healed and whole. It has taken years for maladies such as soldier's heart to catch up with them, and then their families suffer along with them." Carmen noted how the boy flinched when she mentioned soldier's heart, and she suspected he had heard the words, perhaps when his father was roughly diagnosed by someone with some authority and experience.

"You talk like you got some experience," Willoughby said.

"I have experience helping children who suffer for the failings of their parents." She took a deep breath and sent up a silent prayer for help, if she had chosen foolishly. "Will you let me intervene and help them?"

The little girl's head slowly rose, her big chocolate eyes glistening and huge with tears. Bewilderment fought with hope. That decided Carmen.

"I don't know," the grocer began. Carmen nearly laughed. Did he think he had some voice in this decision, just because the children had been caught trying to steal from him?

"Look at the options, Gilligan," Willoughby said. "There's the state homes. The good ones are full. You know what'll happen. I'll take them to someone with deciding power and they'll pass the little'uns along and they'll end up at a school that's an army barracks and not half as caring."

"What about Miss Hilda's place?"

Carmen noted how the boy tightened his arm around the girl, who had to be his little sister. She ached for him, guessing he couldn't be more than a malnourished eleven, responsible for perhaps an eight-year-old. How long ago had they lost their parents?

"It's full to bursting, and those busybodies are sticking their noses in just like others are doing with the lawyers' big building. Making up problems where there ain't none and causing delays. If that bunch of sourpusses hadn't raised such a fuss and delayed everything, there'd be plenty of room for these little ones." The officer sighed, his big shoulders drooping. "I could put them in a cell for the night, get them off the streets, away from those gangs gathering up little'uns and..." His face hardened. "Well, best not said what they're doing." He tipped his dusty, sun-faded cap to Carmen. "Jail's no place for children. Most of the time, it's no place for folks who might deserve to go there."

"Then it's settled?" Carmen said. "I know you don't know me. In fact, I just arrived in town. I came to meet with a lawyer, but he's out of town for a few days. He doesn't know me, not yet, otherwise I would use him as a reference." She nodded to the children. "I know you hesitate to entrust the children to a total stranger, but if I promise not to leave town, and if I promise to, say, meet with you on your rounds, so you can see the children are healthy and whole and unharmed, will that suffice?"

"Ma'am, you talk like an educated lady." Gilligan shrugged and offered a grin both relieved and sheepish. "You're not obligated to get involved."

"Oh, I think I am. My father was a minister. I would be betraying him, as well as the Savior I have served all my life, if I did not intervene."

"You could be saying you're a preacher's daughter just to convince us," Willoughby said, "but I got good instincts. You gotta, as a copper. You're about a dozen degrees better than letting these little'uns stay on the streets. What do you say, Gilligan? We let the lady here take charge of these two until a space opens up at Miss Hilda's?"

"Well, my conscience and Mrs. Gilligan would be a lot happier if we at least knew her name. And the lawyer's," the grocer said with another shrug. He grinned when Carmen laughed.

"I'm sorry," she said, holding out her hand to shake his, and then Willoughby's. "My name is Carmen Mackenzie. I'm here on the advice of a friend to seek the help of Mr. Stanton Lewis, of Endicott—"

"Lewis and MacDonald," Willoughby finished for her.

"You know them?"

"Oh, yeah. Everybody in town knows them. Good folks. You know they're good folks, doing good things, when the big brass button movers and shakers either want to be their best friends, or are out to get them." He winked, then went down on one knee and grasped a shoulder of each child. "You two rascals understand what we're talking about? You're gonna go with this nice lady and she'll put a roof over your heads and keep you out of trouble, until we can find a permanent place that'll take care of you. You'll be good for her, won't you?"

Carmen's heart ached for both children when they nodded just a little too quickly, big-eyed and pale under their street grime. She feared some shadows on their faces weren't from dirt, but hunger. She told the officer where she was staying, including her suite number, and then had to laugh when he asked the children's names. Shouldn't she have thought of that first?

They were brother and sister, as she had assumed from the features they shared: chocolate brown eyes and hair, square chins, and high foreheads. Darla and Andrew Pickett, ages eight and eleven.

Mr. Gilligan gave her three slightly shriveled apples, a handful of carrots, and a little straw basket of fresh berries at a steep discount. He wrote a note that he told her to show to the baker on the next street over and the cheese shop next to him, and warned her of four shops to avoid. When Carmen frowned at the mention of the cheese shop, he guessed correctly that she didn't have a knife to deal with cheese in any form, and gave her one. On loan, of course. Officer Willoughby watched all this with a widening grin and a couple waggles of his eyebrows.

The officer escorted Carmen and her new charges to the bakery and cheese shop. When they emerged from the second shop, he was waiting with two candy sticks for the children. Carmen's hotel was outside of his patrol territory, and he truly seemed to regret that, when he tipped his cap, bade them farewell and said he would be on the lookout for when Miss Hilda's place had room for her "ducklings."

His kindness buoyed Carmen through the chilly reception the children received when they followed her into the lobby of the hotel. The front desk clerk lost only a little of his frostiness when Carmen explained that she had taken the children under her wing, temporarily, until there was room at Miss Hilda's. He looked the children over for a third and fourth time, his lip twitching where it wanted to curl up. Obviously Miss Hilda's name was not a magical talisman for everyone. She made a mental note to find out who this woman was, and what made her so special. Then she paid an extra ten cents per night to allow the children to stay in her room with her. The clerk finally relaxed when she asked for a brass tub of hot water, and a cot for Andrew. She and Darla could share her bed. Carmen found it only slightly amusing that the man seemed more concerned about the cleanliness of the children. Did he actually think she would allow them to go to bed in their filthy state?

Finally, she closed and locked the door of her room and lost the feeling that the whole critical world was watching. The children seemed to relax a little, and that pleased her. She had half-feared that their wide-eyed watchfulness came from fear or distrust of her.

"I have several shirts you can wear, for nightshirts and while your clothes are drying and being mended," she announced, turning to her trunk.

"Ain't had a hot bath in forever," Darla whispered, tiptoeing up to the brass tub.

"You can go first." Andrew walked over to the wide window ledge. Not quite deep enough for a proper window seat and cushion, but Carmen looked forward to sitting there to watch the sunrise.

Her heart went out to the boy, so careful of his little sister. She finished digging out the white muslin shirts, meant to go under vests and sweaters and jumpers, and let the trunk lid drop closed. When she turned around, both children were watching her.

"Better hurry while the water's still hot," she said, and got up from her knees to find the thick stack of towels. They had seemed far too many for one person, when she first took the room. Now she was grateful for the little excesses and luxuries.

The children thought it was hilarious to wash their clothes in the bathtub, and very sensible at the same time. They competed to wring out their clothes as much as they could, until Carmen feared the wringing would tear the threadbare cloth. Then they hung up their clean, wet clothes in front of the open window, to catch the warm evening breeze, and ate their dinner, picnic-style, sitting on the carpet. Clean bodies, clean clothes, and good food relaxed the children enough to freely talk.

"Mama prayed," Darla offered, after Carmen offered a blessing over their food before they started eating.

"Did she take you to church?" Carmen asked.

"Before Pa got sick." Andrew ducked his head and seemed suddenly interested in crumbling the crust of the soft roll bigger than Carmen's fist.

"Wasn't sick," Darla countered. "He didn't sneeze or cough or have spots or nothing. He was just mean all the time." She blinked quickly a few times, probably fighting tears. "How come he got mean?"

"Was your father a soldier?" Carmen asked. When both children nodded, she gave in to the longing that had been building over the last hour, and drew the little girl up onto her lap. Darla was so thin, she made a light armful. She grinned and snuggled down in Carmen's lap.

Little by little as they ate, she coaxed details of their lives out of them. Their father had hurt his head in the war, according to their mother and various of their father's relatives who had been "even meaner than Pa" after he died. From what the children had seen and their interpretation of what they heard, an injury to his head four years ago had aggravated the mental and emotional damage from the war. Their father's relatives turned on the widow and her children, evicting them from their cabin on the family farm.

Their mother fell ill after they went into a poorhouse, and lingered for more than a year, then died about four months ago. When Andrew learned that the poorhouse officials were going to separate him from Darla, they ran away and hopped the first train they could find. Since arriving in Cleveland, they had slept in abandoned buildings or in the underbrush along the river. They ate at various soup kitchens and charity shops. Several churches gave them a few things they needed, but Andrew didn't trust any of them enough to ask for a place to stay.

The children relaxed enough to confide in Carmen, and she learned about Miss Hilda. Older boys had warned them to stay away from the woman, despite the food and clothes and education she offered. They claimed Hilda would tie them up and sell them as slaves to another country. Or to the circus. Or cook them for the customers of her restaurant.

Suspicious of people who would warn Andrew and Darla away from someone whom Mr. Gilligan and Officer Willoughby seemed to admire, Carmen asked about these older boys. She wasn't surprised to learn that several had been putting pressure on Andrew to join them. They wanted him to cause distractions, so they could steal from people like Mr. Gilligan. Now their nasty stories made sense. Miss Hilda probably threatened their burgeoning crime organization.

Chapter Nine

Brogan paused, reaching out to the rough, gritty stone wall on his right as the entire tunnel seemed to shift to the right, then the left. He hadn't felt that strange sense of imbalance since the vile bout with the flu that had filled his head to bursting, ruptured both eardrums, and left him on his back for nearly a week. He sniffed deeply, testing for congestion, stopped short by a soft crystal reverberation through his cheekbone. The vibrations turned into a single, sweet note, and he could have sworn he heard a woman's voice singing. Not clear enough to make out the words, but he thought she was a pure, clear alto.

A heartbeat later, the vibrations in his face, the sense of sound poised on the edge of becoming audible, vanished. He swallowed hard and changed direction, heading for the nearest place in the warren of tunnels where he had encountered the light.

He thought he caught a shimmer at the edge of his vision, just before he came around the corner. Something had awakened the crystal in his face. He had thought long enough, noted enough instances when the portal of light opened, he was sure the energy and light were tied into some activity within crystal. When he came around the corner, the light had faded. He could feel it, taste it, sense the shimmer of sound in the air, yet there wasn't enough to create the gate to the noontime mountainside.

What had happened? What had triggered the surge of crystal energy? He stood in the darkness, focusing on the crystal embedded in his face, waiting. His throat ached with the song that tried to slip out from time to time. After a long winter of comparing notes and speculations and exchanging letters with Endicott, he feared his mentor was right, and music had something to do with the gate and the burst of energy and sound-not-sound that drew him here. If he sang, he thought he could open the doorway. He wanted to sing, yet... Brogan feared all the music inside him had been mangled just as brutally as his face. He didn't want to bring it out of the night inside him, into the light of day, to prove he was right.

So that left one more question: What music had awakened the crystal?

~~~~~

Carmen sang the children to sleep. They were worn out, and she suspected the novel sensation of being clean and well fed, with blankets and a mattress and the security of a locked door made them vulnerable to the exhaustion that painted dark smears under their eyes. She perched in the window with moonlight spilling over her shoulder, watched them sleep, and prayed. The sense of satisfaction, of having done something worthwhile, of having returned to her roots of ministry and rescue work, overwhelmed her and threatened to steal her breath.

She had dreamed for years of being a mother, a misty image, idealized and sweet, with no roots in reality. How could she hope to have children of her own when there were very few eligible, young, unmarried men on the camp meeting team? She certainly couldn't believe the blandishments and soulful glances from the young men in the many towns where the team set up their meeting tents. Carmen knew she had been interesting because she was a stranger, and young. She had been warned that local boys who paid more attention to the pretty young singers than they did to the preaching in the tent could only cause her sorrow. She had counseled herself that until her father retired and they settled in one place, she should be wise and discourage suitors.

When Richard Boniface joined the camp meeting team, he broke all the rules and patterns that had guarded and guided Carmen's nomadic life of service. Just seven years her senior, tall, with golden hair and square features. He didn't scorn the heavy work involved in putting up and taking down the tents or hauling equipment from the trains. While most of the men who preached weren't elderly and frail, they were old enough to claim bad backs or injuries from the war to excuse them from the manual labor involved. Richard dug in with gusto. He admitted once to Carmen that he enjoyed the physical work, the straining and sweating, because it made him feel young.

He loved music and made her feel fluttery when he listened to her rehearse, his eyes wide with wonder. Most important, Boniface loved children. Or rather, so he claimed. He often waxed eloquent on how the hope of a bright, beautiful future rested on this generation of children. He loved to discuss ideas to provide superior education for all levels of society, thereby ensuring their country led the world into prosperity. He was utterly charming when he confessed his frustration that he couldn't seem to communicate with the very children he idolized. He came close to rhapsodizing over Carmen's talent with children, and praised the perfect, loving mother she would be someday.

The false accusations against her father and his deteriorating health interrupted the courtship. Boniface revealed his true character when he pressured her to leave with him. He framed his suggestion in the sweetest way, focused on protecting her from the taint of her father's reputation.

She could pound her head against the wall now, looking back, and wonder why it had taken so long to understand Boniface's true concern. He cared about the prestige of the pulpit he would possess someday. Her voice and her skill with children were more important to him than her heart. Carmen had sent him away, and then the vile rumors grew even worse. She had been in a daze of disbelief during the last days of her father's life and had no time to mourn the loss of the man she had considered marrying.

Thinking of those confusing days, culminating in flight, Carmen could almost laugh now. Granted, laughter that could very easily become tears in a heartbeat. She looked at the sleeping children and marveled at the motherhood thrust upon her when she was least able to fulfill the duties. She pressed her hand against her breastbone, over the cross, which she wore only during the day. She hadn't grown brave enough since Harriet's odd words to risk wearing it at night, when it might affect her dreams.

Then again, perhaps she should wear the cross when she slept. The dreams of her make-believe friend would be far more welcome than dreaming of Richard Boniface. She would dream of him, she feared, now that she had thought so long on him for the first time in months.

"You wouldn't like him at all, my ducklings," she whispered, and smiled at the label Officer Willoughby had applied to the children. Indeed, they had followed her back to the hotel like ducklings. "Looking back... He avoided children because he was a cold, arrogant creature at heart, and he knew children would never accept him. He pretended to admire from a distance. I should have known it was a ruse, a masquerade." Carmen sighed. "I am not ashamed to admit, I hope his schemes and his lies have tripped him up. May whatever church he dupes learn the truth before he causes them too much harm."

Her evening prayers were sweeter than they had been in some long time. Perhaps she had only been thinking about herself for too long. Now that she had others to think about and care for and pray for, her own troubles seemed less momentous. She had a ministry and a service again, no matter how small.

~~~~~

In the morning, Carmen let the children sleep as long as they wanted while she mended their clothes. She substituted some of her own stockings for their poor, threadbare remnants. Andrew had given Darla his stockings while he went barefoot inside his shoes. Fortunately, their shoes were still sturdy enough, even if battered. She wouldn't have to worry about replacing those any time soon.

That thought made her pause, and nearly drop the needle she had been threading. Why was she thinking in the long term about taking care of the children? As soon as there was room at Miss Hilda's place, and she could convince the children they were better off there, they would no longer be in her care. By then, Mr. Lewis would have returned to the law firm. She could give him the introductory letter from Harriet and be on her way to a new life as well. Why was she already half-consciously planning and scrimping and budgeting to provide for the ducklings during a long wait?

"Don't be a sentimental fool, Carmen Mackenzie," she whispered, as she studied a long rip in Darla's pinafore, trying to envision how she could repair it as invisibly as possible. The more presentable the children looked, the easier to avoid unfriendly notice. "Thinking about being a mother isn't the same as being one. You can't keep them. They're not kittens rescued from the ash can."

Still, it was a lovely daydream.

When the children woke, she trimmed their hair and had them wash up. Unlike most boys his age, Andrew didn't quibble at having to wash twice in a twenty-four-hour period. Carmen blinked away tears. He and his sister had been on their own, sleeping in alleys and under stairs, long enough to appreciate washing regularly. She wondered how long it would take until good food and sleeping under a roof became mundane and washing became once again a detestable chore.

They ate the remains of yesterday's provisions, then set off in search of the local library. Carmen suspected that the less time she and her ducklings spent in the hotel, the less trouble the front desk clerk could cause her. She certainly didn't want to become memorable or even noticeable. She and the children would spend their days in profitable activity, out of the public eye. She had already determined that while the children knew the alphabet and could add and subtract a little, that was the extent of their education. While they were in her care, she would ensure they put some book learning under their belts.

Her request for directions to the public library earned her some points in the front desk clerk's estimation. Unfortunately, that was the only bit of good news for quite a while. The library lay ten blocks east and six blocks south from the hotel, and the day started out hazy with oppressive humidity. Carmen resisted the temptation to board a trolley a block away from the hotel. Those few pennies made little difference in her pocketbook now, but she had learned to stretch her funds to the point of snapping back at her. Carmen had no assurance her money would last until Mr. Lewis returned or Miss Hilda could take Andrew and Darla. Food and shelter versus using up some shoe leather. No real choice at all.

She consoled herself that the long walk would use up time, and she was quite tired of spending her days sitting. Exercise would do her good.

By the time they found the library, a satisfyingly large, new building that promised weeks of exploration through many different topics, Carmen wondered what had happened to her stamina. She couldn't blame her aching legs and feet and straining lungs entirely on the humidity. Just a year ago, she had been able to get out of bed before the sun rose, organize children's Bible lessons, help with cooking and serving meals for the camp meeting team, distribute leaflets in the nearby town for several hours, to encourage people to attend, and then lead singing in the main tent and the children's tent for hours on end. What had happened to that girl?

She whispered several prayers of thanks through the day: for the shade of the library; for the bottles of cool water and cups set out for patrons to quench their thirst; for the long table tucked back into a far corner where she and the children could conduct their impromptu school without disturbing anyone or being disturbed. Most of all, she was thankful for the comfortable chairs and for the encouraging smiles of the two librarians as they passed during the day. When the two women caught on to what Carmen was doing, they found schoolbooks and offered her the use of several slates and sticks of chalk.

Officer Willoughby was waiting by the checkout desk, when Carmen heeded the ache in her stomach and called a halt to lessons. The children were used to getting by on one meal a day, but she most certainly was not. She could cut back her meals to two a day and increase their meals to two a day, and still protect her funds. Her delight in the children's enjoyment of their lessons shattered when she saw the officer leaning against the front desk, chatting with Mrs. Sullivan, the head librarian. He hadn't come to take the children to Miss Hilda's already, had he?

"Oh, thank you, dear," Mrs. Sullivan said, as Carmen put the stack of slates and chalk on the checkout desk. "What would you think if I put these right here under the counter, so you can just step over and take them when you come back? Tomorrow, yes?"

"Ah—yes—thank you." Carmen looked back and forth between the librarian and the police officer. Had she missed something?

"I think it's a wonderful thing you're doing, tutoring the children. Officer Willoughby didn't say exactly why they aren't in school, but... well..." She shrugged.

Carmen hoped she didn't look too nervous as she urged the children out of the library. Willoughby strolled along beside them, all four silent for nearly a whole block. When he asked what the children had learned, Andrew looked back and forth between the two adults. Darla piped up and chattered easily about their lessons.

"Are we still inside your patrol area?" Carmen asked, once they had walked another three blocks and Darla had run out of lessons to talk about.

"Off duty. Just thought I'd make sure you got back home all right."

"Oh. Thank you."

"My pleasure."

Something shifted inside, releasing the threatened knots in her chest. Carmen wondered how staying out on the street once his shift was over equated to pleasure.

"You weren't worried I'd run away somewhere, taking the children out of the reach of those more suitable to care for them?" She fluttered her eyelashes at him when Willoughby goggled at her a moment. Then he burst out laughing. Peripherally, Carmen saw the children stop and stare at them, then smile.

"Miss Mackenzie, if we had more people who took a personal interest in helping the street children in this town, Cleveland would be the finest town in the entire country. Maybe this half of the world. What you're doing makes a bigger difference than a dozen people throwing wads of money at the problem." He tugged on his cap and nodded for punctuation.

"Well, I'm glad I have your approval."

Carmen learned she had more than his approval. She had his support. At the Weiss delicatessen, Mrs. Weiss scurried out with a package wrapped in butcher paper. She squeezed Carmen's hand as she slipped the bundle into her grasp and hurried back inside. The restaurant across the street from the hotel provided a bottle of cold milk for the children's supper, when Willoughby knocked on the back door. The paper-wrapped bundle turned out to be thick sandwiches of sliced roast beef and chicken, layered with mild white cheese and a spicy, grainy mustard, and another packet of flaky pastries filled with apples and cherries. More than enough for dinner tonight and to set aside for breakfast.

"Thank you. I don't know how we would survive without you looking out for us," Carmen said as they arrived at the hotel's side entrance.

"You should be thanking my granny. She was scolding over my shoulder all day, telling me to check up on you. 'Freddie,' she'd be saying, 'what's the good of being a copper if you aren't a good one? What's the good of hunting down criminals if you ignore the people what be needing real help?' And you know, she'd be right."

"Well, I think your granny should be very proud of you."

Willoughby colored a little. One of the hotel maids came to the door to shake out a rug and gave them a wide-eyed questioning look. He tipped his hat to Carmen and to Darla, then held out his hand to shake with Andrew. The boy stood a little taller and thrust out his chest with a manly sort of swagger as the three of them went around the side of the building to the front door.

That day established a pattern for the next four days. Carmen took the children to the library for lessons. She welcomed other children to their lessons when school let out and Mrs. Sullivan guided a number of them to their corner of the building. It turned out there were quite a few families where both parents worked, either running a shop or in a factory or some kind of manual labor, to cover the rising expenses of daily living. The children had nowhere to go immediately after school, so they went to the library or else, according to Mrs. Sullivan, ran with the gangs of street children. The elderly woman worried that when school let out for the summer, the gangs would swell in numbers, and the problems that came with them.

Officer Willoughby arrived some time just before the library closed for the evening, to walk Carmen and the children back to their hotel. He asked the children about their lessons, and sometimes brought treats for them. A rubber ball for Andrew, a little rag doll for Darla, then some paper-wrapped sweets another time. Each evening, they stopped at a different shop or restaurant to pick up provisions donated by the owner, or a clerk slipped them something without his knowledge. Carmen had the impression from things Mrs. Sullivan had said, there was a general dislike for the street children. She could understand the wariness, if gangs were becoming a problem and threatening to get worse. She could almost hear some people asking why the children weren't in an orphanage. After four days, they hadn't gone back a second time to any place that had provided food. Carmen suspected that once was all they could hope for. She told herself to be grateful.

Maybe if Mr. Lewis arrived soon, and the situation allowed, she would be allowed to take Darla and Andrew with her, wherever the lawyer proposed sending her for safekeeping.

Unfortunately, visiting the law offices of Endicott, Lewis, and MacDonald every other day didn't seem to be doing her any good.

The Fremont Homestead

Ess debated the pros and cons of bad news versus no news at all, until her head ached. While she worked on the final touches of renovations to the family home, she seemed to be the clearinghouse for information among contacts and friends, and the one her brother and others complained to.

First there was all the political backbiting and quibbling in Cleveland to deal with. She read Uly's complaints in long, sloppy, scrawled letters and tried to make humorous comments and helpful suggestions to raise his spirits. Troublemakers were trying every trick in the book to get in the way of obtaining permissions and approvals to erect the combination docking tower and office building proposed by Endicott, Lewis and MacDonald. If someone wasn't bemoaning the change in the character of the neighborhood, someone else was insisting that the engineers and geologists were wrong, and putting a building of that size and weight in that particular location on the bluff overlooking the Cuyahoga River would create massive faults and earthquakes and danger and damage to surrounding buildings. Uly speculated that much of the interference and protests and questions were raised just to create work for inspectors and surveyors and people who measured and took surveys and polls.

Cheats and schemers and con men tried to frighten the owners of the homes and businesses and vacant lots into selling to them, so they could sell at inflated prices to the law firm. Vicious rumors swirled from all directions, some of them mere speculation and some of them specifically created to cause trouble and hard feelings. While Uly's reports were sometimes amusing with his caustic comments and exaggerated sketches of his regular nemeses, they grew to be so repetitive they were tiresome. Still, there was always some progress on making the tower a reality. Knowing she really couldn't be of any help, Ess was glad to be busy elsewhere. She was oddly glad to be off the road for a change. Even though Matilda and Ernest wouldn't be home for at least six months, there was much to get ready for them.

Then there was the curious case of Harriet Angelotti. Matilda and Ernest's attention was piqued last month, when a report finally reached them, sent by steamship, that Harriet had regained contact after years of silence. She had been a valuable asset in helping people evade Revisionists hunting them. She had kept her head down and kept quiet, and at least once a year, someone she wouldn't identify brought her a few stray pieces of crystal. When Harriet lost all contact, common belief was that she had either died or been discovered by Revisionists.

More than three months ago, a letter had reached a former station house, and had taken nearly three weeks for the new owners of the building to pass it on to the former owners, and for them to realize what the letter contained. On the surface, it was a packet of sketches, accompanied by a cheery little note apologizing for not writing sooner. What seemed an amusing little decorative border on the notepaper was a marker indicating what cypher to use to decode the note. The packet had been passed up the line until someone could decode the cypher, which hadn't been used in fifteen years. The writer wanted the note given to Matilda and Ernest Fremont. No one noticed that one of the sketches was of Vivian Fremont's crystal rose necklace until the packet reached the elder Fremonts in Paris.

Harriet Angelotti had resumed contact with the Originators. She had been in contact with a number of people all along, but they were all such low-level people, so cut off from the general news and activities of the organization, they never knew anyone thought Harriet had vanished. She finally learned that Matilda and Ernest had returned seemingly from the dead, and that prompted her to make contact. The truly frustrating part of her message, using invisible ink on the back side of the sketches, was that she hinted broadly while refusing to give helpful information. Even more frustrating was that the sketch of the rose necklace wasn't of Vivian's necklace, but one belonging to an "interesting young lady, the daughter of an old friend, a woman of crystalline reputation who is now dead, who came to me for help not long ago."

Chapter Ten

Matilda had the sketches and messages sent to Ess, knowing instantly Harriet was referring to Anna's daughter. They could only guess that Anna had been the mysterious friend who gave Harriet pieces of crystal to pass on to the Originators. Harriet refused to say anything more until she had made contact with Stanton Lewis. She claimed he knew where to contact her. Unfortunately, Mr. Lewis was on a long trip to Alaska, dealing with a troublesome matter for a client who trusted no one but him to untangle the legal knots in his life.

Ess found some comfort in this proof that when Harriet met Carmen, her childhood friend still had the crystal rose, but the lack of other vital information frustrated her. Where had Harriet sent her? What did Carmen plan to do? Had she received the dream-delivered message to go to Cleveland? If Harriet wanted to contact Lewis, did that mean Carmen had received the message to contact Endicott, Lewis and MacDonald?

The questions threatened to give Ess a headache. If not the questions, then the repeated failed attempts to focus on the crystal rose and force open the communication between their minds. No matter what time of the day or night, Carmen simply wasn't there to make the link. So either she had lost or sold or had been robbed of the crystal rose once she left Harriet. Or, as Ess hoped, Carmen simply wasn't wearing the crystal rose.

Uly's most recent letter was somewhat encouraging, and distracting. He reported the president of a very large railroad company wanted sole rights to run railroad tracks underneath the tower. He had made some proposed changes in the plans, to create a transportation system to go from the river to the first subterranean level, where the train tracks would run, and from that lower level to the street level, and then up a lift system to be installed on the river side of the tower, to carry cargo up to the tracks, and from the tracks to the air docks. The idea of connecting water and ground and air shipping, in one building, excited everyone. Uly teasingly pleaded for Ess to come and help him oversee details and catch the things he missed. He also wanted her to intimidate various members of opposing law firms and city officials.

"I would be eternally in your debt, little sister," he concluded in his letter. "Besides, Mr. Wallace has come back to town, and he is positively moping. You've made another conquest, which is mightily convenient, since you've allowed our tame Pinkerton to slip through your fingers."

Ess snorted as she read that last portion. Phoebe and Allistair were on the verge of betrothal, and he was as devoted to the Originators as if he had been born among them. How could Uly say he had slipped through their fingers? As for Mr. Wallace... she wasn't sure about him, though she had enjoyed all their small encounters over the last few months. When she had time to think of him, she did like knowing that when she went to Cleveland, he would be there.

Arriving in Cleveland, however, would have to be delayed longer than she had originally planned. Uly's letter also contained a list of stops to make. Various scattered members of the Originators were emptying their archives to send up to Cleveland, for safekeeping. Ess would need to hire an entire luggage car on the train, perhaps even two, by the time she reached the shores of Lake Erie. The many side trips and stops to pick up anything from a box of papers to a dozen steamer trunks would change a journey of three days by train into several weeks of travel, depending on how prepared people were at each stop along the way.

Cleveland

Mary reported to Brogan that Hilda wanted to speak with him. Directly, this time. The stern, loving look the elderly woman gave him put a tight feeling in his throat. Partly laughter, partly resignation, and partly that little-boy sense of guilt he missed feeling toward his own mother. Mary ran the kitchen and oversaw the growing number of children living in the underground community, and she didn't like leaving the kitchen, which was in some sense the heart of the community. She was also increasingly the go-between when people had questions for Brogan, and they shied away from facing the man who sat in the shadows.

"Will we lose some of the bounty that she bestows on us?" He supposed he could risk going to the kitchen to check with her early in the morning or late at night, when the children weren't likely to be in the kitchen. For all he owed Mary, starting with her ability to look him in the face and not flinch, from the very first day they met, he could certainly do that much to make her life easier.

"Don't be daft." She snorted. "She trusts me, she trusts our Mr. Endicott, so she trusts you with her children. Especially these girls she needs to send down to us. She just wants to look you in the eye and get the knowing deep in her soul."

"Girls?" He shuddered, knowing what Mary would say, just from the aching, hot look in her eyes.

The growing numbers of street children attracted growing numbers of those who preyed on them, including madams who employed bruisers to ensure the pretty, helpless girls they wanted to add to their stables couldn't say no. He admired Hilda greatly for the work she did, giving children safety and shelter and opportunity. There were always a few who landed on her doorstep who needed more than food and shelter and training. They needed a place to hide.

"Very well, but warn her of the troll in the tunnels."

"Troll." Mary wrinkled up her nose and her mouth moved like she might spit, if she still chewed tobacco. "You're anything but, Brogan. Give the children a chance, and they'll all love you as much as Mouse."

"Mouse is a rascal who needs some frightening in her life, to keep her out of trouble. One of these days, she's going to climb too far, take too big a risk, and end up breaking her clever little head." He sighed. "Maybe those girls can help you keep her under control for a change."

"When pigs fly." She cackled softly as she turned to leave his office and took the lantern with her.

Brogan smiled after her as darkness settled around him. A faint echo of her laughter held a trace of the song that had haunted his dreams this morning, waking him with a sensation that he wanted to sing. He had stayed in his bed, eyes closed, and felt the sunrise come up across the water, stretching through the growing canyon of buildings in the expanding port city, until the sunlight touched the land far over his head. How long had it been since he had gone above ground in the light of day? How long since he had wanted to see a sunrise or sunset? He was truly a creature of the night, only showing his mangled face to the moon and stars.

Endicott assured him that the construction of the tower for the new Originators' headquarters would come nowhere near the tunnels that housed his people. For now. In time, as they dug down and expanded Originator operations, the builders would reach the tunnels. When that day came, he hoped he would be strong enough to show his face to others, perhaps even people who had once known him when music had filled his heart and song filled his mouth.

For now, he would be the troll in the tunnels, the dragon protecting fair young damsels from villains who would destroy their innocence for profit. The laughter of the children, playing in safety, was all the music he needed. Perhaps all he could endure.

Still, the auburn-haired angel who sang in his dreams made him hunger to sing again, so that his throat ached, just as it had this morning.

~~~~~

Carmen's days fell into a pleasant pattern. She woke with the dawn and indulged in half an hour or so of reading in the windowsill. Then she woke the children, and they took turns reading passages from the Bible aloud while they washed and dressed and had their simple breakfast. Usually it was bruised fruit and bakery they had picked up on the way back to the hotel the night before. Every other or every third day, they made a detour on the way to the library to visit the law offices on Superior Avenue, to see if Mr. Lewis had returned. Then they spent the day in the library, reading for several hours, then math lessons, then spelling, then history. The children were astonished to realize that there were countries besides the United States, and each of them had their own history. That guaranteed many hours, weeks and months of simply reading about the history of the world.

Not that Carmen looked forward to spending a year or two plumbing the depths of resources of this lovely, fairly new library. Surely Mr. Lewis had to return to Cleveland soon. When that happened, he would help her place the children in good hands before he revealed the mysterious heritage Harriet had hinted at.

On Sunday, the library wasn't open. Carmen and the children walked along the shores of Lake Erie as far as they could go in one direction until their legs and stomachs protested. Then they found a sheltered spot to sit and eat their simple picnic lunch, biscuits with cheese and some fruit. Carmen read aloud to the children until they fell asleep or they grew restless enough to peel off their shoes and socks and go wading at the water's edge.

Each evening, Officer Willoughby met up with them on their way back to the hotel, to ask about the children's lessons and bring them news of goings-on in the growing city. They always ended up at a shop or restaurant where someone was willing to sell them their dinner and tomorrow's breakfast at a steeply discounted price. Sometimes, when the cook or the store clerk saw the children, they might throw in a treat, or reduce the price still further. Not often enough for Carmen's purse. She finally confided the dilemma of her shrinking resources to Officer Willoughby on their second Sunday evening, heading back to the hotel. He carried Darla papoose-fashion on his back, the little girl's arms limp around his neck and her head drooping against his shoulder. Andrew stumbled from time to time as he walked hand-in-hand with Carmen.

"I'm sorry, miss. It's been kind of nice like this, I just let the time slip away," Willoughby said after a silence just long enough to make her worried he was angry with her. Sometimes it was hard to tell with his square, tanned, solid face, and his eyes that were either bright with interest or hooded and shadowed in thought. "I'll check again at Miss Hilda's tomorrow. In fact..." He frowned at the sidewalk in front of him for a good twenty steps. "In fact, I wouldn't be surprised if Miss Hilda had room for you, too. What with you teaching the children like you've been, I bet she'd want to add you as a teacher. You'd have to be in charge of a whole warehouse full of little'uns. Would you mind?"

"Oh, no, I wouldn't mind at all." Carmen caught her breath when Andrew lifted his head and she got a good look at his face. His eyes were big with fear. "Andrew, so many people say Miss Hilda is a lovely lady who takes very good care of her children. Those boys who claimed she hurts children, you can't really trust them to tell the truth, can you?"

"No," the boy said, his voice pitched so low and sullen, she almost couldn't hear him.

"What's this? Someone's telling lies about Miss Hilda?" Willoughby caught hold of Andrew's shoulder and bent down to the boy's level. "You trust me, don't you, lad?" He waited until Andrew thought a moment and then nodded. "Well then, trust me that Miss Hilda is a good lady. A smart lady. And a dang good cook. You liked those meat pies I brought for all of us the other day, didn't you? She made those. She'll take just as good care of you and your little sister as Miss Carmen has been doing. I swear, on my badge and my nightstick. I swear on my soul." He crossed his heart and held out his hand for the boy to shake.

"Miss Carmen don't want us no more," the boy muttered, ducking his head.

"Oh, Andrew." Carmen went down on one knee and grasped his skinny shoulders. "I don't want to leave you. If there's room, and if Miss Hilda needs my help, I'll come to live with all of you and help take care of you and Darla and many more children. Won't that be nice?"

Grudgingly, the boy nodded.

"Why can't we live with Mr. Willoughby?" Darla asked, her voice clear despite being so soft with weariness. She could barely raise her head to look at them when she spoke.

"Ah -- well -- umm." Willoughby's face turned red so quickly, Carmen had a hard time not laughing. She tried not to look at him as they got walking again. "You see, sweetheart, I live in a boarding house. Just one little room, barely big enough for my bed and my uniforms. Where would I put you? On a shelf? On the windowsill?"

His words earned sleepy giggles from Darla, and even Andrew managed a crooked smile.

"The honest truth is," he confessed, when they reached the front door of the hotel, "I just didn't think how expensive all this is, living in a hotel and taking care of children that aren't your own. I live so simple-like, saving all my money, sending every penny I got back to the family farm in Erie, it just didn't occur to me. I hope you'll forgive me, Miss Carmen."

"Forgive you? Oh, Willoughby." She had the strongest urge to fling her arms around him and hug him like she did Andrew or Darla when they had bad dreams. "You are the sweetest, kindest man. You've been our hero from the first day I set foot in this city."

"Yeah, well, if I'd been smart, I should have thought of the family farm a week ago." He snorted, and his mouth pursed like he might spit. "All my pay goes to the mortgage. We had a couple bad years. What I should have done is pack up all of you and shipped you off to Erie, to help Ma and Sherwood on the farm. Bet the kiddies would love it. Sherwood's raising sheep now, and pigs. Kids like lambs and piglets, don't you?"

"Can we, Miss Carmen?" Andrew said, his face bright just like Darla's.

"Oh, well... the problem is that I'm waiting for word from the lawyer I came here to see." Carmen cringed in anticipation of their disappointment.

"Oh, yeah, sorry. Forgot about that." Willoughby's shoulders seemed to sink just like the children's. "Let's go back to our first plan. I'll check with Miss Hilda tomorrow on my rounds, all right?"

The children agreed, grudgingly. Darla kissed Willoughby goodnight, making the big man blush again. He shook hands with Andrew and then with Carmen, and waited on the pavement until they walked across the lobby of the hotel and stepped into the lift. Then he tipped his hat to them as the door closed.

That night, Carmen pulled the cross out and studied it by moonlight as the children slept.

"You're a fool, Carmen Mackenzie," she whispered, as she tucked the cross under the neck of her nightshirt. Why was she so afraid? Why did she avoid trying to contact Essie in her dreams? Harriet couldn't possibly know everything, could she? What harm could it do to wear the crystal rose, just one night, and hope to meet her childhood friend in her dreams? She certainly needed more guidance, and clarification of those instructions to come to Cleveland.

Whether Essie was waiting in the misty realms of dreams, Carmen never determined. She felt as if she hadn't been asleep more than a few minutes when shouts and the clang of a harsh bell in the hallway tore her awake. She struggled to sit up, feeling dizzy, her throat and eyes burning. Then the taste of smoke filled her lungs and she coughed so hard she slid off the edge of the bed.

The hotel was on fire. That was the fire alarm, out in the hallways. Guests were shouting, their feet pounding as they raced down the halls. Carmen shook the children awake. While they struggled into their clothes, she threw everything she could touch into the carpetbag, sitting on top of her trunk at the foot of the bed. She slid her feet into her shoes without any stockings and flung blankets around herself and hustled all of them out the door and down the hallway to the stairs. The six other guests on their floor were all jammed up in front of the door to the lift, screaming at it to come for them. Her father was right. Fear stole common sense. From all the noise, she supposed those people were still shouting for the lift when she and the children reached the bottom of the stairs and fled the hotel.

She huddled on a bench at the trolley stop across the street from the hotel with the children. A pumper car came and firemen scurried about. Other guests got in the way, trying to get a good view of the fire. It seemed to be coming from the back of the hotel, on the bottom floor. Sitting back so far from all the fuss and excitement gave her a good view when three bedraggled little figures emerged from the alley to the right of the hotel. One of the firemen let out a curse and descended on the children to herd them across the street.

"Lady, are these yours as well?" he demanded, nudging the two boys, who half-supported the little girl between them.

"No, but I'll watch out for them." Carmen caught her breath as the fireman and the children stepped into the puddle of brightness from a gas streetlight and she saw the filthy, ragged condition of the children.

"Hey, Andy," the taller of the boys said. He offered a queasy smile and sank to his knees on the curb.

The fireman scurried back across the street to continue battling the fire. Carmen gathered the children together, and pulled the little girl, even smaller than Darla, onto her lap to soothe her trembling. The grime and wet and soot in the child's clothes didn't matter. Soon she had both girls in her lap, wrapped up in the blanket with her. Andrew made the introductions. The boys were Virgil, age twelve, his cousin Arthur, age nine, and Arthur's sister, Beatrice, age six. The three had been sleeping in the alley behind the hotel, in a nest of discarded mattresses and linens.

They didn't say much after that, everyone fascinated in a horrified way by the battle with the flames and the shouts of the guests and hotel workers. People in surrounding buildings were drawn by the noise. Carmen was startled when she looked around and saw dawn creeping between the buildings. How long had the battle with the fire been going on? The newcomers were all rough-dressed, the people who hauled supplies for restaurants, grocers, butchers, street sweepers and other early morning workers.

The sun became visible between several buildings by the time the firemen packed up their hoses and pumper and peeled out of their oilskin coats and boots. Carmen stayed seated with the children while the hotel manager and the desk clerk and several police officers went into the building. She knew better than to try to get inside right away, and that was confirmed when a growing number of guests got into shouting matches with the police officers who blocked the doorways.

Finally, everyone was allowed back inside the hotel. Carmen picked her way through the rubble in the lobby, with broken glass and shattered wood and water everywhere, glad she had taken the time to put her shoes on. She led the children to the back stairs and was too tired to laugh when she heard the same argument erupt between guests about using the lift.

The hallway leading to her room was wet and full of smoke, with door panels broken open by firemen axes. One end of the hall showed signs of having been on fire, but her end of the hall showed no damage except what the firemen had done. Carmen shuddered when she saw her door smashed to pieces. She hadn't locked it, so why did they need to break it open? Then she let out a cry that threatened to become a sob when she saw the bedraggled mess of her room. What reason could the firemen have to come in here, when the fire was thirty feet away?

There were dirty, wet, huge boot prints on the bed and all over the carpet. Several spots in the wall showed where axes had broken through the plaster to the lathing underneath. Carmen shuddered when she saw black smears that had to be smoke, at the very least. Very well, then, the firemen had been wise to come in here and track down flames that had crept along inside the walls. Still, did they have to make such an awful mess of everything?

Her trunk was tipped over on its side, all her clothes spilled out on the floor, wet and covered with boot prints. Certainly they hadn't thought the fire would erupt among her clothes, did they?

Fortunately, she had gathered up this morning's breakfast along with yesterday's clothes, her father's Bible and a few other precious items and thrust them into the carpetbag as she fled the room. She fed the children first before exploring the rest of the floor. The common restroom was undamaged, and she went in to quickly change her clothes. She would feel more able to handle the stresses of the morning once she was decently dressed.

When she returned less than ten minutes later, the front desk clerk stood in the doorway, glaring at the children, who cowered back against the far wall. Darla and Beatrice clung together, weeping, while the boys visibly wavered between fury and fear.

"May I help you?" She poked the clerk in the arm and he moved aside more easily than she had hoped.

"We're not running an orphanage here, Miss Mackenzie." He gestured at the children. "What is the meaning of this?"

"The children have nowhere to go. I intend to confer with Officer Willoughby when I see him today, to ensure they are given into the care of people who will take good care of them."

"Yes, but where did they come from?"

When he learned the three children had been sleeping in the alley, his face went red and he stomped away, down the hall to the lift, muttering under his breath. Carmen got to work sorting through her bedraggled possessions, trying to repack them neatly, though in their wet, dirty condition that seemed like a waste of time.

Chapter Eleven

By the time the hotel clerk returned with the owner and a police officer, she found her few bits of jewelry had vanished, along with her good shoes, both pairs of silk stockings, several petticoats and other underpinnings, her two shirtwaists, her one good dress, and her shawl, blue silk painted with oriental designs. Either the firemen used the blaze an excuse for theft, or someone had entered the hotel during the inspection to rob the guests. She pressed her hand against the cross, safely hidden under her shirt, and said a prayer of thanks that she had worn it to bed last night.

Carmen stood up from putting the last item in the trunk, turned and saw the desk clerk and the owner approaching, and the police officer behind them. The clerk looked dyspeptic yet gleeful, while the owner and the officer both looked rather grave. She could guess what was about to happen, and chose to strike first.

"I hope you are in possession of insurance for situations like this," she said, approaching the door to keep the three men from crossing the threshold. "A number of my possessions have been stolen. What is even more disturbing is the number of ladies' unmentionables that were stolen. Not only have you permitted thieves to enter your guests' rooms, but they are perverts as well."

"A likely story," the clerk said with a sneer.

"Hodgins," the owner said. He glanced at the officer, who nodded. "I suggest you make the rounds of the other guests and determine if anyone else was robbed."

The clerk gaped like a fish a few times, then with a sniff and a pout, he headed off on his errand. Just as she had feared, Hodgins had run to the owner, accusing the children of starting the fire. Before Carmen could gather her breath to defend the children, the owner assured her that he already had a suspect. A man he had fired two days ago had a temper and wasn't quite right in his head. He had made threats, and still had keys to the hotel basement.

"We don't blame the children, however, there are laws regarding the welfare of children who have no parents." He gestured at the police officer. "You will have to turn them over to the authorities. As Hodgins said, we aren't running an orphanage here."

"All of us?" Andrew stepped up next to Carmen and slipped his hand into hers. "Can't Miss Carmen adopt us?"

"All of you?" He frowned, and all the long hours and the strain of the fire seemed to drop on him, so he looked older and exhausted in his confusion.

Carmen hurried to explain, and soon learned that Officer Willoughby's name was like a magical charm to ease her way. Officer Cooper knew Willoughby. He had asked all the officers who patrolled Miss Hilda's neighborhood to tell him when she could take more children. According to Cooper, half the patrolmen on this side of town knew about Carmen and the children she had taken under her care. That smoothed the way with the hotel owner. The children nearly went limp with relief that they weren't about to be thrown into a paddy wagon and hauled off to jail. Cooper and the hotel owner expected Carmen to hand the children over to Miss Hilda's care that very day. Since that was her and Willoughby's hope, she didn't demur.

Unfortunately, Carmen and her charges couldn't stay in the hotel. There was far too much damage, and even if nearly half the rooms were still livable, the hallways leading to them were a mess, the dining room and the lobby required extensive repairs, and the gas and water had to be turned off because the fire had damaged the pipes. Carmen obtained permission to store her trunk at the hotel until she found a new place to stay. The bellboy who helped her store it gave her a claim ticket. Signaling her to silence, he handed her a canvas bag bulging with items. He whispered that the head housekeeper had thrown together what she could, but Hodgins had an eagle eye. He tipped his battered cap to Carmen and guided her and the children out a side door. Then he gave her directions to the closest public bathhouse, on the edge of a public beach, where people changed their clothes before bathing in the lake.

Carmen wondered about that, until she looked inside the bag. She nearly wept in gratitude, and smiled at the commonsense items she hadn't had time to consider. The head housekeeper no doubt was a mother. The kindly woman had given them several bars of soap, towels and washcloths, a comb, several clean shirts, some mismatched stockings, a block of cheese, nearly a dozen apples, two loaves of bread, two table knives, four tin cups neatly connected by a rawhide thong, and a bag of hard candy.

She gave each child a piece of candy, which improved everyone's mood, and the six of them started down the street, heading for the bathhouse. Before anything else, she would make sure the children were clean and presentable before spending the day in the library. The fewer askance glances they earned, the less trouble they would have from busybodies and critical spirits.

The bathhouse turned out to be more than two miles west. The first pieces of candy were gone and spirits fell as the sun rose higher and threatened a hot day. Carmen cut three apples in half, giving each of them a piece, and that made another half mile of walking more enjoyable. The girls were drooping by the time the rounded roof of the bathhouse came into view. She dreaded the thought of making the children walk all the way back to where they had started, and then trudging the opposite direction to get to the library. They would be hot and sweaty and likely gritty from sand blown up from the beach, thoroughly undoing all the good of washing up.

Would it be so foolish using a few pennies to get them a ride on the trolley, all the way to the library? It would give the children a treat and soothe their spirits more after the fire. If Willoughby was right, they might all be settled at Miss Hilda's by evening, and then she wouldn't have to pinch pennies any longer. Tomorrow was Tuesday. Perhaps she wouldn't be as presentable as usual when she went to the law office to inquire if Mr. Lewis had returned, but the secretary knew her on sight now. Tomorrow, Mr. Lewis would be there, and then everything would be fine.

The children enjoyed themselves tremendously, splashing barefoot through the foam where the waves rushed up across the sand. Carmen scrubbed what clothes of theirs that she could and laughed with them at the sight of her three new charges running around in long, oversized shirts that hung past their knees, with the sleeves rolled up in thick wads above their elbows. Her mending kit hadn't been stolen, though she couldn't understand why. It had an ivory cameo on the clasp of the quilted silk case, and the tiny scissors had gilding. The wealth of pins and needles and various colors of thread made it quite valuable. Perhaps the thieves hadn't seen it when they ransacked her trunk. Carmen said a prayer of thanks and got to work mending their clothes.

For lunch, they each had a thick slice of bread with shavings of cheese on top, another half of an apple, and drank deeply from the pump in front of the bathhouse. Then clean and slightly damp, with a rosy glow from exercise and sun, they walked a few hundred yards to the trolley stop and waited in the shade for the next one to come by. Carmen hoped Mrs. Sullivan wouldn't be worried when they were so far behind their usual schedule.

In point of fact, Mrs. Sullivan was in tears when she saw them come through the library door. She was busy dealing with several people requiring help and gestured for them to go to their usual corner. Carmen had Andrew retrieve their stack of slates and chalk, and they settled down for their lessons. Virgil knew how to read, and Carmen gave him a chapter from a history book to read aloud to the other children when Mrs. Sullivan came looking for them. She expected the explanation of their changed circumstances to take some time, but it turned out Mrs. Sullivan had heard about the fire. She had been waiting on tenterhooks for them to come in, half-afraid they wouldn't, that they had been injured in the fire and taken to the hospital, or worse, killed. She shook her head, and patted Carmen's cheek on learning about the three children added to the ducklings. Then she promised she would find some help for them all by the end of the day.

That help turned out to be a change of clothes for all the children. If not new, they were in much better shape than the mended, patched rags and shoes that were more holes than soles. Carmen was nearly in tears as the children turned and proudly showed off their new clothes. She sniffled a few times when Darla proudly announced that Officer Willoughby wouldn't know them when they met up that evening. Mrs. Sullivan knew people who knew other people who had access to donated clothes and shoes and household goods, stored up for those who went through disasters such as fires and floods. A few notes sent around to the right places had produced the clothes. Mrs. Sullivan proved to have an accurate eye for calculating the children's sizes. Carmen felt in much better spirits, despite the extra walking that day and very little sleep the night before. She led her charges to meet up with Willoughby and tried not to let her imagination paint too blissful a picture of what accommodations would be like at Miss Hilda's. However, an enormous bed took center stage.

Willoughby, however, was nowhere to be found. He wasn't waiting at the usual spot where they met up with him. Carmen kept walking, heading back toward the hotel. He would try to meet up with them there, wouldn't he? Where else would they go, even taking the fire into account? What did common sense say?

Common sense told Carmen to find dinner for the children before all the shops closed, and before the restaurants grew too busy for one of Willoughby's helpful friends to slip out the back door with something still edible but not good enough to put on a customer's plate. She steered the children along a semi-straight course between the regular meeting spot and the hotel, and pressed her forefinger to her lips to silence Andrew when he gave her a questioning look. Of course he would notice before the others that their comfortable, comforting routine had changed.

Movement from the corner of her eye caught her attention as she paused on a street corner, waiting for a long train of wagons to trundle past. Carmen turned and sent up silent thanks when she recognized the young woman coming toward them. She had two large cloth bags in her hands, her shoulders bowed with weariness, but the moment her eyes met Carmen's, she smiled, straightened, and changed her path to meet her.

"How are you and your ducklings?" the women greeted her. Then her eyes widened as she looked over the children. "Did you go and have babies since we met?"

"No, I simply inherited some new responsibilities. Letitia, yes?" Carmen caught the aroma of bread that clung to the other woman like perfume. That made sense, since she worked at a bakery. She sent up another silent prayer, this time aimed at the bags in her hands. "Have you seen Officer Willoughby?"

"Oh. My." Letitia took a step back and looked at the children again. "You haven't heard, have you?"

"Heard what?" Carmen flinched when Darla slipped her little hand into hers, and Beatrice leaned against her on her other side.

"Oh, there was an awful bank robbery, early this morning. Shooting and everything. They even tried to blow a hole in the back wall of the bank. They caught most of the men, but—" Letitia sniffed and blinked, visibly fighting tears. "You can't believe half the things that come through the grapevine, but so many people were hurt. Seems like half the city's police were there. Willoughby was up close to the explosion. He's alive, but nobody's sure..." She glanced over the children and nodded, wide-eyed, obviously trying to convey what she didn't dare say.

"Is Mr. Willoughby gonna die?" Darla whispered.

"We must certainly focus all our prayers on asking God to heal him," Carmen said. The words tasted bitter on her tongue. They were certainly of little comfort to her, and she hated herself for being angry at Willoughby for being injured when she needed his help more than ever.

"We're not gonna eat tonight, are we?" Andrew said.

"Oh." Letitia took another step back, almost flat against the building. "He still hasn't got you settled. Of course. I'm an idiot." Then her contrite expression split into a smile. "But I'm a prepared idiot, at least. These are the leftovers from today's baking. The boss sent me to give this to the City Mission folks. That's a long way to go. You'd be saving me some shoe leather if you took this. And it's going to much better use than down the throats of a bunch of drunks and vagabonds, if you ask me. Not that they don't deserve some pity, but I figure, they made their choices, right?" She handed one bag to Andrew and the other to Virgil. "Ought to feed the lot of you tonight and tomorrow. There's even some sweets down in the bottom for dessert."

"Thank you. So very much." Carmen stretched out her free hand to squeeze Letitia's. "You're an answer to prayer."

"And you're saving me a whole hour of my evening. In fact." She dug into her pocketbook and pulled out a penny. "He gave me this for the trolley fare. It's yours, by rights. Should get you some milk or butter to go with the bread."

"Yes, it will. Thank you again."

Carmen didn't have to urge the children to thank Letitia. The woman smiled as she hurried away, freed for the evening. For a few moments, Carmen could smile, grateful for the miracle of the loaves and fishes performed right in front of her. Granted, there were no fish to add to their meal, but she wasn't going to quibble when the Almighty provided.

While the penny would have indeed provided milk to wash down their bread, there were no shops open to make a purchase. Besides, with Willoughby their protector and provider gone, she needed to be careful of every penny now. Carmen decided to make use of a public water pump on Public Square to quench their thirst and wash down the bread. There was a bench and plenty of grass nearby for sitting, and the weather was pleasant.

The children certainly needed to rest, and she needed some quiet to think, assess their situation, and make some plans and decisions. And pray.

The children ate and Virgil and Andrew took turns running to the pump to fill their tin cups with water for everyone to share. Carmen said a prayer of thanks that she had thrown her purse into the carpetbag when they fled the fire last night. She had some funds, but now she had the hard choice of feeding the children or housing them. She knew better than to expect constant miracles every time she turned around. Her father had taught that while yes, the Almighty provided for those who trusted in Him, He also expected them to be good stewards of possessions and income, to use common sense, and be thrifty. Carmen had sometimes suspected that some people who came to the camp meetings looking for help did so because it was simply easier to expect others to provide for them. Their self-respect and sense of pride had become twisted, so they saw nothing wrong in expecting, even demanding that others provide for their daily needs, instead of working to provide for themselves. Some even considered it their right. She refused to fall into that trap of expecting the good Lord to fill her mouth every time she opened it.

While it would be nice if she walked into the offices of Endicott, Lewis and MacDonald tomorrow and found Mr. Lewis had returned, she knew better than to depend on that. She silently scolded herself when she realized that although she and Officer Willoughby had discussed Miss Hilda's establishment numerous times, he had never told her where to find it. Carmen feared if she asked Andrew to take them there now, he might refuse, or take them on a wild goose chase, until it grew too late and too dark to find the place. Worse, if she stopped an officer to ask for directions, he might take the children from her. Carmen had promised to take care of them. That meant making sure they got to Miss Hilda's, and not trusting anyone else to do it for her.

She remembered Willoughby telling her about some caves found in the steep side of the bluff where it dropped down to the river, where the Cuyahoga wound around the city. Andrew had told her about finding safe places to sleep. Certainly the six of them were a large enough number to ensure some security. Even if they didn't have blankets, they had the shawls and jackets that Mrs. Sullivan's friends had provided, and they could huddle together and keep each other warm. The path down to the water's edge wasn't that far from where they were now. That would take care of them for tonight. They would even have water nearby for washing up in the morning. Tomorrow, she would ask after Mr. Lewis. If he hadn't returned, certainly she had seen enough sympathy in the eyes of Mr. Peterkin, the secretary, she could ask for some advice, maybe an escort to Miss Hilda's. Tomorrow would be the end of their problems. She prayed hard and wasn't ashamed to beg the Almighty for that bit of grace.

Carmen handed out a cookie to each child for dessert, then they gathered up their much-depleted provisions, and headed across Public Square. She decided to tell the children the story of the Children of Israel following Moses across the desert as they walked. It would distract them and hopefully discourage anyone who might question a young woman walking with five children, visibly unrelated to her, so late in the day. If they recognized the story was from the Bible, perhaps they would assume she was a charity worker, dealing with the city's street children. In some sense, she was.

Two blocks away from the visible drop-off, where the street simply ended and there was nothing but sunset-streaked sky and a hazy, distant landscape, their way was blocked. Barricades surrounded a large section of the street where buildings were in the process of being torn down. Windows had been removed, and doors. Signs had been pulled off the fronts of former shops, and the apartments over various shops gaped empty. Carmen looked up, assessing the difference between an abandoned building with no doors or windows, and the uncertain, unknown conditions in a cave. She looked around and saw no one on the street other than the six of them. She made her decision quickly.

Soon, she and the children had settled into the back room of an upstairs apartment that was dry and relatively clean, despite the destruction, and felt warmer than the outside air. They hadn't hesitated for a moment when she announced the change in plans, visibly assessing the options for where to spend the night. This was what their life had been like for months. She shuddered at the prospect of any child having to calculate their safety and fight for the slightest bit of comfort. Carmen scolded herself for quibbling and whining about her own reduced circumstances. Even when she lived in fear of being forced into a degrading position to earn a living, she had never been as destitute or as helpless as these children. Whatever it took, she was not leaving them until they had safe, loving homes again.

She wore the cross, and pressed her fingertips against the crystal rose, begging Essie to come in her dreams. She willingly admitted she needed advice now. To build up their courage, and hers, she sang to the children until they slept. Only later did she think what a foolish thing she had done, risking the wrong kind of attention, with songs coming from a building that should have been empty.

Carmen slept little. She woke at every grumble or whine of the wind through the empty windows, every slip-clatter of loosened masonry falling elsewhere in the no-man's-land of the abandoned buildings, every scrape that could be rats scratching their way through the rubble and inside walls. Or worse, some brute or self-styled Fagan, coming to take advantage of the children and steal them away into a life of criminal slavery.

~~~~~

Brogan stood long in the bend in the tunnel, staring at the circle of light. Song filled his throat. He ached to release it, and ached to hold it in. All his senses stretched out, begging the music to return. This time he had been sure it was a woman's voice, resonating sweetly in the crystal filling his mangled face. He didn't dare sleep. He longed to sleep and find her in his dreams. He feared she would not be there.

"You're a fool," he whispered when the last lingering whispers of song faded from his bones and the rock and damp surrounding him, and the film of light across the passageway faded away.

He could make it return, he had learned in the last several weeks. All he had to do was hum, softly, just a whisper in the back of his throat. Music brought him the doorway to the world of sunlight, yet he proved he was a creature of the night by staying in the darkness and shadows, and silence.

~~~~~

Ess woke, halfway down the stairs of the station house, barefoot, in her nightgown. She closed her eyes and tried to still her thoughts. If the dream that had pulled her from her sleep and her bed, and the voice that had called her returned, force of will would not accomplish it. She needed to surrender to the music that still shimmered with crystalline chimes in her bones.

She waited until the floor grew cold under her feet. Nothing. Then she climbed back up the stairs to her bed. Morning would come sooner than she liked, and there was still an entire wagon to load with boxes and trunks and crates of archives from the station house before they drove twenty miles to town and the train station.

No more dreams came, and she could almost have wept with the certainty that Carmen had been calling her, yet something interfered.

Chapter Twelve

When morning came, Carmen's eyes were crusty and the back of her head ached from lack of sleep. All she had accomplished was to pray half the night away. She supposed that had done her some good, but she would have preferred enough sleep to dream and meet Essie and get some clue what to do next. She castigated herself for cowardice, and tried not to speculate too long on how different her life would be now if she had continued wearing the rose until her childhood friend answered her.

"I wouldn't have my ducklings, however, would I?" she murmured, as she got to her feet and stepped over to the empty window to watch the sunrise. "Please, Heavenly Father... help me find them good homes where they can be raised in the love that I knew. Then I will feel free to pursue my own destiny. Until then..." She slipped the cross off and held it in her hand several long moments.

Her father had had the cross made to enclose and protect the rose. She could get some money for the silver, and the chips of semi-precious stones. All she needed was the rose. While the cross itself was one last memento of her mother, Carmen knew Anna would commend her sacrifice for the sake of the children. If anything, she would laugh a little sadly at how her daughter quibbled over priorities.

Perhaps she wouldn't need to make that sacrifice. Today she would visit the lawyers. She would wash and dress as neatly as circumstances allowed. If Mr. Lewis proved to be in the office today, in just a few hours everything would be settled.

An hour later, her little troop crossed Public Square. When they reached the place where Superior intersected the side street and she saw the building with the law offices, Carmen slowed. The men gathering in the street, with their attention focused on the building, made her reluctant to leave the children on the benches set across the front of the building on either side of the doorway. After a moment of thought, she took them to the far side of Superior, settling them where she could see them from the door of the building. A large section of scraped ground would stand in for a slate. The children made a game of finding straight, strong sticks for drawing in the dirt, and she put them to work practicing their sums and challenging each other with spelling. While she didn't expect that to hold their attention long, they would at least be busy for as long as it took her to go upstairs and inquire about Mr. Lewis. More important, they would be out of earshot of those men with their disgruntled expressions.

She wished she had her hat, but that had been stolen after the fire. Her jacket matched her skirt, but she felt odd carrying her carpetbag. Common sense overrode fashion sense. Someone might take the carpetbag while the children were playing, or even accuse them of stealing it. That bag held all the food and money she had left to take care of her ducklings.

Voices echoed up the stairwell when Carmen stepped out of the lift. The law office was just off the lobby. She hurried to the door.

"Ah, miss, I'm sorry," the muttonchop-whiskered secretary said, looking up as she stepped through the door. "Mr. Lewis isn't here, but I expect him in three, four days at the most. If you'll wait a moment, I'll fetch Mr. MacDonald."

"Why?" Her face heated. "I'm sorry — that wasn't what I intended."

"It's quite all right, miss. Fact is, I've been told that anybody looking for Mr. Lewis is to be detained to speak with the other senior partners."

"Has something happened to Mr. Lewis?"

"Not that I'm aware of."

All along, the suspicion had been growing that Harriet told her to talk to only Mr. Lewis, no one else, because she didn't trust the other partners in the law firm. Maybe they weren't part of the organization he and Harriet belonged to. Part of Carmen wanted to drop onto that bench facing the big desk and weep. She wanted to say yes, she would talk to this Mr. MacDonald, but what if that was the worst possible thing she could do?

"Peterkin," a man called, stumbling through the door. "Warn the partners. The rabble has been stirred up again." He nodded to Carmen and leaned against the desk, breathing heavily. "They're on their way up now."

"I don't suppose there are any police handy?" Mr. Peterkin said. "I'm sorry, miss. You don't want to be here in the next couple minutes. Would it be too much trouble to come back this afternoon, or tomorrow morning?"

"What's going on?" She let him take hold of her hand and lead her through the office, through two connecting rooms to a door that opened out on the hall far down from the lobby.

"Some nasty folk keep stirring up trouble, claiming we're cheating people of their businesses and homes." Peterkin looked down the hall in both directions. "The back stairs are usually used for deliveries, so they aren't lit, but you won't be accosted by brutes. I'm so very sorry." He opened the door to the stairwell for her.

Carmen stammered her thanks and confirmed that yes, she would come back tomorrow, then she was hurrying down the stairs before she quite knew how. She reached the ground floor and paused, trying to decide which door would lead her into the lobby of the building and which would deposit her back on the street. She assumed the stronger door with visible reinforcing and a strong lock was the outside door.

Common sense said the next step was to see what money she could get for her mother's cross, and then figure out how to contact Miss Hilda. If she was as good and trustworthy as Willoughby indicated, then surely Mrs. Sullivan at the library had to know her or someone who knew her.

By the time she returned to the children, she had her plan firmly in mind and felt calm enough to convince them everything was just fine.

The first jeweler she came to, however, gave her a suspicious look and told her to be on her way, he didn't deal with "her kind." Carmen straightened her shoulders and imagined him one of the obstructionist, small-town preachers who never took their sermons from the Bible. She borrowed her mother's most dignified tones as she asked him what exactly he imagined her kind to be. She almost laughed when his eyes widened and he stammered a little. She sailed out of the jeweler's shop before he could explain himself with more genteel euphemisms. She knew what "kind" he thought she was, and she nearly choked on a strange pressure that might be tears and laughter combined, or a furious scream trying to emerge.

That taught her enough to change her inquiry. At the next jeweler's, she mentioned the hotel fire and stated she had lost some of her funds, and hoped he would be so kind as to assist her until she was able to contact friends and replenish her funds, with the hopes of buying back the setting.

"That's not normally something we do, ma'am," the red-faced, balding man said, reaching for the cross while studying her face. Whatever he saw must have at least partially convinced him. He picked up a jeweler's loupe, fitted it into his eye, and examined the cross. "However, times can be precarious, and we have not hesitated to come to the assistance of the leading families of our growing metropolis..."

She heard the unspoken words: she was not known, she was not among the leading families. Still, he was looking at the cross. That was a hopeful sign.

"It would be a pity to take it apart. Anyone can see it was put together by a master craftsman. The chips appear to be diamonds and sapphires and can be used in other settings. The rose, however... ah, that's an amazing thing. I would have to consider quite a while to know what to offer you for that."

"No." Carmen resisted the urge to snatch the whole thing out of his hand. "When I came in, I specifically stated I wanted to sell you the setting. I am not selling the rose."

"Why would that be?" His friendly expression cooled and he closed his hand around the cross.

Carmen snatched it out of his hand just in time, and shuddered at the coolness of his skin, as well as her own temerity.

"The rose is all I have left of my mother. It's a family heirloom. See, here." She pressed on the tiny stud sticking out of the back of the cross and popped the rose and its chain out of the clever slot that held them together with the cross. "It comes out, because my father had the cross made to go around it. And here." She turned it over to show him the inscription on the back of the cross, though she was sure he had seen it during his examination. "His name and hers, and the date of dedication."

"How am I to know you didn't steal this and make up a sentimental story to wring more cash out of me?"

"Do you know Officer Willoughby, who walks the area from East Sixth to West Sixth, from Lakeside to Ontario?"

"Yes, I do. A good man."

"He can vouch for me. He knows my story. He's seen me wearing the cross."

"And I'm just supposed to go lock up my shop and go run him down and ask him if you're a thief or not?" He snorted. "What I should do is call for the police and have you investigated and find out where you got that pretty piece. Might be a reward for getting it back to its rightful owners."

"I am the rightful owner." Carmen blinked quickly, refusing to knuckle her eyes and betray the pressure of tears waiting to burst out. She said a quick prayer.

"Here, you, get out of there," the jeweler snapped, and stepped over to the window, where all five children had lined up and leaned against the glass.

Carmen opened her mouth to scold him not to yell at her children but stopped when she saw a familiar blue uniform strolling down the sidewalk behind them. Other officers knew about Willoughby helping her. Would any of them vouch for her?

"Hey, what are you doing?" the jeweler yelped as Carmen darted to the door, which was propped open.

"Officer? Officer, could you help me for a moment?" Carmen stayed with one foot in the jeweler's shop and waved. "Sir, could you tell me, how is Officer Willoughby? I heard he was hurt in the bank robbery yesterday."

"Excuse me, miss, but I don't know you, and that is kind of personal business," the officer said, tipping his cap to her.

"Mr. Willoughby is our friend," Darla announced, as the children stepped wide around the officer to gather around Carmen. "He helps Miss Carmen take care of us. Is he gonna be all right?"

"Helps Miss Carmen." The officer's incipient scowl softened into a sad smile. "Ah, right. I heard about you, miss. And your ducklings." He winked at Darla. She giggled and pressed closer against Carmen's skirts. "Sorry to say, miss, but Willoughby's being sent home to his family in Erie as soon as he can travel. He's feverish and raving, they say. Talking about putting his children on the windowsill to sleep. He doesn't have any children."

"These children," Carmen said, gesturing at the five. "It was a little joke he made."

"Ah. Right. Sorry. Willoughby's not coming back for a while." His smile flattened into something grim and she heard the unspoken words, saw them in his eyes: Willoughby might never come back.

"So there's nobody to vouch for you?" The jeweler stepped out of the doorway. He nodded at Carmen's closed fist. "Still no proof that belongs to you."

"See here, Fitzwalter," the officer said, "Willoughby's a good judge of people. If he trusts this young lady to look after these children until he can get them to Miss Hilda, then she wouldn't take anything that's not hers. Willoughby even said her father was a preacher."

"Reverend Hiram Mackenzie, formerly of the Beacon Hill Camp Meeting Society," Carmen said.

"See there? I bet even you heard of those good folks."

Fitzwalter the jeweler sniffed and didn't seem to be happy at having to accept her character reference. "Good luck at finding room at Miss Hilda's. Between her association with those lawyers, tearing up half the city, and the trouble moving into her new place, it's a wonder the authorities will let her keep any of the children she's got under her roof now."

"We don't wanna go to Miss Hilda's," Andrew said. "We wanna stay with you, Miss Carmen."

"I would love to keep you with me, sweetheart." Carmen tried to smile, but a thick feeling caught at her throat. "The truth is that we're quite on the ragged edge, as my father used to say. That's why I'm here, to get a little money to feed us until..." She glanced at the jeweler, who seemed far too interested. She also had to think about the officer, who might just report her destitute condition to Willoughby. Worrying about her and the children would only aggravate his condition, perhaps slow his recovery. "Well, until my friends catch up with me and can provide better resources." She gestured for the children to move down the sidewalk. "We need to hurry and get to the library before Mrs. Sullivan starts to worry about us. Thank you for your help, Officer. If you talk to Willoughby before he goes, please tell him that the children and I are praying for his speedy recovery. And thank you, Mr. Fitzwalter."

She nodded to them both and pressed one hand against Darla's back to urge the little girl down the sidewalk. Carmen didn't look back, but she felt the jeweler watching her. That settled it. On the way back across town to the dubious shelter of the abandoned buildings, she would avoid the jeweler's shop. She didn't need him repeating his accusations, or worse, offering her so much money for the crystal rose that she couldn't refuse.

The skies darkened as Carmen and the children hiked the seemingly endless route to the library. She regretted spending money on fare for the trolley yesterday because she feared she would need that money today. While getting soaked to the skin might be an adventure when they had dry clothes and a hot meal waiting for them, being caught in the rain turned into a cascade of problems in their current situation. Last night's shelter might not even be there when she and the children returned tonight.

While she anticipated the problems of feeding the children tonight, and staying dry, why not consider tomorrow's troubles, also? The library closed early on Wednesdays, meaning she and her ducklings would have to occupy themselves without attracting attention or suspicion until businesses closed and traffic dissipated. How much longer could she and the children wander about this part of the city without falling under suspicion? How would she keep her promises to the children and to Willoughby?

Carmen sniffed back a few tears. Fortunately, the boys were loudly discussing the story she had been reading to them, anticipating what would happen in today's chapters. They didn't hear her, and the girls were intent on listening to the boys.

"Please," she whispered. "Blessed Savior, I am trusting in You. Please... keep us dry and help me feed the children. Please take care of Willoughby. And please, please, let me sleep long enough tonight to meet up with Essie. Would it be too much trouble to have her close, to help me right away?"

The rain held off until she and the children stepped into the library, then the skies split apart. The children laughed, then let out little shrieks when lightning answered. They scurried to their corner of the library and settled down where they could watch the storm roll in, safe behind the windows. Carmen greeted Mrs. Sullivan and retrieved their school supplies. With some careful questioning, she discovered their friend didn't know about Willoughby, even though she did hear about the attempted bank robbery and the injured officers. Carmen gave her the sad news and tried not to be too irritated when Mrs. Sullivan didn't ask how she and the children had fared last night. Perhaps she assumed they had found another place that would take them?

Carmen set the children the task of reading to each other, and they had a jolly, cozy time, laughing at their own mistakes and correcting each other. That freed her to consider her options and what she should do next. Mrs. Sullivan lived in a boarding house, she already knew. She couldn't ask her to fit six more people into her little sitting room and bedroom. Tomorrow, she would take the children to the lawyers and settle in and wait until someone with authority could help them. Perhaps it was time to trust and hand Harriet's letter to someone other than Mr. Lewis.

Mrs. Sullivan didn't know Miss Hilda, but she had heard only good things about the woman. She promised to ask her friends to ask their friends and see about finding room for the children. Then she went beyond what Carmen could have hoped for and provided them with a lovely dinner when closing time arrived. Sandwiches big enough for two meals for each of them, fruit tarts, and bottles of milk plugged with corks and wrapped in rope to pad them, safely nestled in a net bag for easy carrying. The milk was more than enough for dinner tonight and for breakfast in the morning. Carmen blinked back tears as she thanked Mrs. Sullivan, and silently apologized for her grudging thoughts earlier.

With the sky looking gray and about to churn with more lowering clouds, she hurried the children back across town to last night's shelter. The risk of getting caught in a downpour was too large to have a picnic dinner in more pleasant surroundings. The workmen were busy putting away their tools and heading home for the night and didn't seem to notice the six of them picking their way through the thickening shadows and rubble.

Last night's shelter had been reduced to half by that day's demolition. The stairs to reach it were completely gone. She and the children settled into the remains of a downstairs room, with the fourth wall missing. They were far back enough in the demolition area that no one walking by would see them, even if the clouds cleared to let the full moon shine. That would have to do.

Thunder rumbled while they set up their dinner and the light visibly waned. The rain returned, and Carmen was grateful that it fell straight down. Her seat was only three or four feet away from the missing wall. Just a little wind would have her soaked, and the children behind her. For now, they were dry and warm and had enough to eat. She would be grateful. Although a little bit of light would be welcome.

As if Heaven heard her, lightning flashed, a long burst that spread out more branches and threatened to shred the sky. Carmen pressed her hand over her heart and tried to laugh for the sake of the children. In that one glimpse of brilliance, they were wide-eyed and solemn, but seemed more intent on filling their bellies. She considered that a blessing.

"Well, we certainly can't read or work puzzles to pass the time," she said. "Shall we sing?"

Last night's singing hadn't brought anyone to chase them away. Tonight, the drumming rain and the thunder booming and crackling overhead muffled all sound. Even if there were a night watchman, no one would come out in this downpour to drive them away. They were safe and relatively comfortable and well fed, and the children fell asleep quickly, exhausted from all their walking.

For Carmen, sleep didn't come so easily. She even found praying difficult. The repetition, the sense of futility, the sense that even the Almighty had to weary of hearing the same petitions again and again wearied her. She had found it hard to sing for the children, and song brought her no comfort.

The storm, both the rain and the events of the past few days, had quite possibly washed all the music out of Carmen Mackenzie's soul.

That bit of fancy brought a brief, stiff smile to her bitten lips. She sighed, took a deep breath, and turned back to the children curled up together like a pile of puppies in the darkness behind her. Her shivers threatened to steal her ability to think of another song to sing, to dredge up some comfort and courage.

Behind her, dust and cold and exhaustion. Before her, a near-solid wall of water. At least the wind had not picked up, so the deluge didn't penetrate their shelter. Singing had often been her best weapon against fear. She refused to let it fail her now, when she needed courage the most.

"When darkness veils His lovely face," she murmured, feeling the rhythm in her soul, hearing the carnival-like, sprightly notes of the old portable organ pounding out the tune in her memory. "I rest on His unchanging grace. In every high and stormy gale, my anchor holds within the veil." It wasn't exactly singing, but closer than she had thought she was capable.

She put her back to the brick wall and tried to adjust her seat on the gritty stone slab. She needed to get a little sleep, to look presentable in the morning. What if she were such an exhausted wreck, her hair and clothes a mess and dark smears under her eyes, that even friendly Mr. Peterkin couldn't recognize her?

"Please, Lord Jesus, we're at our very end," she whispered as she closed her eyes. Dizziness spun through the darkness behind her lids. "We have no other shelter, and no money if I spend it all on a room for just one night. We always manage to get enough food for each day, but sometimes it's so hard to keep trusting that You will continue to provide."

If she sold her last two changes of clothes, that might provide shelter for a night, maybe two. What if the lawyers took one look at her disheveled state and refused to believe her? Perhaps she should forget about Mr. Lewis and the library and seek employment instead. Yet how was she to find a respectable job? Childcare and office work were the most lucrative options. How long until Mrs. Sullivan's friends made the connections for her and she could persuade the children to go to Miss Hilda's care? What if there was no room? What if the children refused to go?

The sense of desperation was the worst part in her situation. Carmen had seen people in desperate straits. She had been glad to bring relief and comfort to others, rescuing the destitute and suffering. Never had she anticipated being on the other side of the assistance.

Chapter Thirteen

All her life had been lived on faith. Through the death of her mother and participating in rescue work, managing soup kitchens and snatching her education from the libraries in each city the team visited, then through her father's disgrace and death. Her faith had brought her here, huddled away from the rain in a half-demolished building, far from the gaslights illuminating the streets of Cleveland, guardian to five street children who trusted her not to turn them over to cold-hearted authorities.

If she could find a place to sing, would that provide for them? Carmen believed in the gold of her voice. Unfortunately, the only establishments looking for singers nowadays seemed to be saloons and the euphemistically labeled gentlemen's clubs, where the clientele were not gentlemen, or looking to spend their evenings with *ladies*.

What about applying for a position as a singer, or perhaps housekeeper on one of the airships that carried passengers across the continent faster than trains? Even if she did get such a position, what would she do with the children if she took a traveling job?

"Please, Lord Jesus, I have believed in miracles all my life. I trust You." She sighed. "Please forgive my impatience, but when will You rescue us?"

Eyes closed, she listened to the thundering of the rain, the counterpoint of water babbling through the remaining gutter pipes down the sides of the buildings, then gurgling through drains not yet clogged with debris. It played a symphony in her head and eased her closer to the edge of sleep.

A child's cry of pain cut through the rain song like a chunk of building stone dropped into the gutters, splashing Carmen back to wakefulness. She sat up, staring out into the wet darkness. Her aching tired body prayed it was a dream, maybe the cry of a bird that had nested in the wreckage.

The cry came again. She muffled a sob, part sympathy and part fury at being disturbed. Carmen looked at the five children huddled together behind her, then out into the deluge. She took a deep breath, aimed herself at the source of the sound, peeled out of her jacket, and stepped out into the drowned darkness.

The sound came again, definitely a child's plea, filled with pain. Carmen shivered from the sound more than the wet that soaked her hair and clothes and added twenty pounds to her, so her tired muscles protested. She muttered a Psalm under her breath and followed the sound.

The crumbled building where the injured child huddled was only a dozen steps away from her shelter. This one had lost most of its roof and two sides. She guessed this child curled into a fetal ball had come here for shelter as well. The child had a small lantern with a stub of a candle sheltered from the wet behind fragments of glass. Just enough light to see by and get into trouble clambering through the rubble of this half-destroyed building. Somehow the lantern had stayed lighted when the child fell.

"Don't know you." She uncurled enough to raise her head and look up at Carmen. The grimy face and ragged boy clothes and cap said boy, but the voice said girl.

"Let me see what's wrong?" Carmen knelt so she could lean over the girl and shelter her a little more from the rain.

She knuckled tears from her eyes. "Done broke it." She clutched her leg with both hands.

"Oh? And you're studying to be a doctor for sure?" she said, dragging up her father's Scottish brogue. That earned a wide-eyed look, then a watery smile from the child. She uncurled enough that Carmen could rest one hand on the thin leg and another hand on the child's head.

Yes, she felt the pain buzzing in her fingertips from the child's flesh, smelled the blood now. For a few seconds, the gift of insight that she thought had deserted her put her inside the child's body. She felt the torn flesh. Hot stabs, deep in the bone.

"Blessed Savior, if there be any grace left for me, move through me now," she whispered, and gently wrapped her fingers around the stick-thin shinbone. The child flinched, and Carmen soothed with soft strokes across the tangled, dirty hair. "Let me be an instrument of Your grace and mercy and healing. Give this child wholeness and strength and health. I pray You."

"You ain't no nun," the child murmured, eyes drooping as warmth filled the drenched, muddy corner where they huddled.

"No, that I am not." Carmen leaned closer over the child, keeping her hand on the limb. Her stiff, aching, exhausted muscles relaxed in the increasing warmth that filled the air. She silently continued to pray and to give thanks for this sign that despite the condemnation of those who thought themselves spiritually superior to her, the One who mattered still counted her worthy of holy service.

When the song came, melting the tightness in her throat, soothing the empty ache in her soul, feeding the starving tension in her muscles, she nearly wept. It took all her strength of will to focus on the child, to will all the heavenly energy to wrap around her, rather than bathe in it herself. If her lips moved, if a song whispered through her throat, she couldn't be sure. All that mattered was that the music came when it was needed.

When the warmth faded, the child had fallen asleep. Carmen gathered her up, careful to shield the bit of candle still burning in the tiny lantern resting on the thin belly and carried her back through the deluge to shelter with her ducklings. Even taking into account starvation and stunted growth common among street children, the girl couldn't have been more than eight years old. Carmen settled her among her five huddled sleepers and arranged herself for sleep again.

The warmth and strength and delicious relaxation that came after being a conduit of healing remained with her, so she fell asleep with a smile on her lips. In her dreams, she stood again on the steps of Canterbury Cathedral and listened to the choir thunder out fragments of Handel's *Messiah*. Though the pressure in her chest and her vocal cords was incredible, she couldn't seem to find the voice to sing along.

~~~~~

"What's got you up so late?" Mary asked, stepping into the kitchen. Her face was lit only by the flicker of flames under the pot of tea kept constantly hot and steeping, day and night.

"I am going mad." Brogan looked back down into the depths of the tea he had been sipping for the last half hour, since the sensation of crystal singing in his bones yanked him out of sleep. He swore whatever had awakened the crystal was directly overhead, again.

"Nothing a walk in some sunshine wouldn't cure," she said with a shrug, and stepped over to the grate to stir up the coals. She glanced over her shoulder, her expression tending toward diabolical in the red flickers of light. One corner of her mouth twitched, resisting a smile.

"As I said." He stretched one leg out, then the other. "I am going mad. If I should collapse, foaming at the mouth, ask Hilda to send for Endicott. If need be, have them bind me and toss me into that pit Dunlevy and his crew found last week."

"They think it's bottomless." She stood up and stomped over to the bench where he slouched against the wall. "What's really ailing you?"

"Hallucinations. Dreams. I can hear a woman singing in the night. Her voice is in my bones." His voice cracked. "I'm mad enough to actually go to the girls' dormitory room, looking for Mouse, to ask her to go check..." He sighed. "She's gone again, by the way. I settled here thinking to catch her sneaking in. One of us should consider applying the rod of correction."

"That one will just laugh at us." Mary settled down next to him and rested her hand on his wrist holding the cup. "You're not going mad. That's just common sense prodding you to stop hiding in the shadows and damp holes in the ground. Time for you to step out and be with people again. The children need a teacher, by the way."

"Eh?" Brogan surprised himself with a weak chuckle. "Where did that come from?"

"We've got a boarding school down here now, with all the children either coming with their parents, or being sent to us for safekeeping. We need to give them some lessons, help them make something of themselves. Just because they can't take their schooling at Hilda's doesn't mean they get short shrift. You're the most book-learned of us all. Share some of that knowledge jammed into that great massive head of yours."

He chuckled a little more. The idea caught his interest, and for a few seconds he played with the idea of teaching the children his love of books, of music, working with the little ones to teach them their sums, so they could find good jobs when they were older. Then the image of a happy schoolroom shifted to the children taking one look at his mangled face and cringing away in fear. Even if they could be persuaded to listen to him teach, how much would they hear, with his face as a distraction?

"If you aren't going back to bed, keep watch for Mouse, would you?" He levered himself to his feet and put the cup of now-cold tea down on the table as he walked out.

"Where are you going?" she asked, when he turned right to go down the passageway outside the kitchen, instead of left.

"To take a walk in the sunshine."

Mary laughed. Brogan smiled and imagined her reaction if he led her down the passageway to the film of light that led to the sunny hillside. He sensed the shimmer was still there, still strong, proving the crystal he had heard singing in his face bones had not been an illusion. That, more than the hunger to go above ground and search through the demolition site for the woman who sang, had kept him awake. Perhaps the energy, the song still humming in the rock ahead of him, was so strong that this time, Mary would see the light.

Then again, maybe she would finally believe him, when he said he was going mad.

~~~~~

A rough hand shook Carmen awake. Terror had her up on her knees, struggling to her feet, instinctively putting herself between the children and the outside world. She blinked hard to get her eyes open.

"What's the world comin' to?" a man said, stepping back. He shook his head and then tipped his cap to rest on the back of it.

The five men standing behind him in the mud and broken bricks of the street did likewise, fists jammed into their hips, shaking their heads. They were all of a type: rough clothes, work boots, with workingmen's kerchiefs around their necks, no jackets, shirts unbuttoned halfway down their chests in anticipation of a hot, muggy day of work. Carmen guessed they were construction workers. How early did construction workers start their workday?

"Couldn't make it to the rescue mission folks?" the man who had shaken her awake asked.

"I didn't know where to look, honestly." Carmen tugged her jacket straight.

"Quite a bunch of ducklings you got with you." Another man gestured with his pipe at the children just starting to uncurl from each other.

A third man stepped up, shaking his head and glancing back and forth between Carmen and the waking children. "You're too young to be the mother of all them kids. Big sister?"

"Not quite—"

He let out an oath that made Carmen jump, leaped in and grabbed hold of the girl she had found last night. He staggered back a few steps, holding her up by her shoulders.

"You're gonna get your skinny neck wrung for you, Mouse. Where you been? He's been tearing the place apart, digging new tunnels belike, wondering about you."

Mouse, obviously the girl's name, hung limply in the big man's hands and grinned sleepily at him.

"Excuse me. You know this child? Does she belong to someone?" Carmen asked.

The man opened his mouth. She could tell he was ready to let out another scorching oath. Then he looked at the other men. She caught him exchanging significant looks with two of them, but couldn't decipher what might have passed between them. The others grumbled and let the two herd them away.

"Don't know that she belongs so much—" the first man began.

"A fine father he is, letting a child climb around in these ruins in such a storm last night," Carmen began.

"Fell from the roof and broke my leg," Mouse reported cheerfully. "The lady came and fixed me up just dandy. Hurt like the billy-ho."

"No language like that from you, young'un," the man scolded, shaking her once before finally putting her on her feet.

Pot calling the kettle black. Carmen knew better than to point out his hypocrisy, though grateful he at least tried to correct the child.

"Where's her father?" she asked.

"Heaven knows." He tipped his hat to Carmen. "She's more errand runner for the Boss."

"The construction boss?"

"Lordy, no!" A rough chuckle broke from him. "Here now, I thought you said your leg was broke." He shook his finger in Mouse's face.

"Was. Ain't no more. Lady fixed it. You know how Preacher talks all the time about angels coming down and helping people? Figure she's an angel." Mouse nodded emphatically and hooked her thumb over her thin shoulder at Carmen.

"I think she bumped her head, and just imagined the severity of her injury," Carmen offered. After all the trouble that had arisen from simply being a conduit of Heaven's mercy, she had learned some tricks for deflecting attention. What mattered most to her was to avoid taking any credit, even by accident, for what had been done through her.

"Don't get all puffed up and proud when Heaven uses you," her father used to preach, with mischief twinkling in his eyes. *"After all, God used Balaam's ass to put the prophet in his place. You're little better than an ass, then, when God works*

through you."

Carmen dearly missed her father right now.

"Severity of her injury, eh?" The man looked Carmen over, head to foot. "I'll tell you about severe injuries, if you and your brood stay around here much longer. This place is even more dangerous than the docks. Or will be, when the foreman gets here. Better get all of you out." He grabbed Mouse by the shoulder of her shirt when the child moved to dart away from him. "You are in a heap of trouble. You go report to him, right now."

He cuffed the back of her head, but Carmen was close enough to see the motion softened into a caress. Mouse grinned as she darted away. Limping, with dark smears on her torn trouser leg that hadn't vanished when her clothes dried.

Sighing, Carmen signaled the children to gather up their bits and pieces. She had the most to carry with the carpetbag. They would find a more comfortable place to have their breakfast. Perhaps they should make the long hike to the bathhouse and make themselves presentable before she tried the lawyers' office once again.

"Are we gonna have breakfast?" Beatrice asked, tugging on Carmen's skirt.

"When we've found some other place to rest." Carmen avoided meeting the gazes of the workmen gathering around again. She cringed as she saw them look over the few possessions among all of them: the canvass sack, the milk bottles tied together, the carpetbag.

"Rescue mission's on Superior, 'long about East twenty-something. It's a hike, but they'll have food for you and the young'uns," a man with a gruff voice offered. He wouldn't meet Carmen's eyes as he gestured east, through the dust and rubble and half-demolished buildings.

"Thank you very kindly." Carmen nodded to the man who had sent Mouse running off and gestured for the children to go on ahead of her. She felt the penetrating gazes of the men as her small party hurried away down the half-demolished street.

"Better find somewhere else to hole up tonight," the man called after her. "We're tearing down buildings every day. Wouldn't want something to come toppling down on you in the middle of the night."

"Why are you destroying so much?" she called, walking backward, and gestured at the street around her.

"They're putting in a huge skyscraper. Gonna be the biggest, tallest building in the entire country," another man called back. Pride showed in his voice and posture. "Gonna have a train station down at the bottom, coming in from all over the country. And at the top, docks for a half-dozen airships. This here tower's gonna put Cleveland on the map."

Progress was all well and good, Carmen reflected as she and her five ducklings trudged away from the demolition area, but there was something very wasteful about destroying perfectly good buildings just to put up something to make a name for the port town. She thought of the Tower of Babel and how the people had such vainglorious plans to create a name for themselves. They hadn't learned anything from Noah's Flood, only a few generations before. God had taught them a lesson that the world shouldn't have forgotten.

Unfortunately, Carmen reflected, Human beings were very adept at forgetting important lessons, and the debts they owed to others.

~~~~~

Brogan lit a candle and set it in the lid of a Mason jar on the plank table. He gestured at a clear spot next to the candle.

"Hop up. Let's see that leg."

"Dontcha believe me?" Mouse shrilled.

He muffled a chuckle at the indignation in the child's voice. No fear there, just fury that her word had been doubted. Everyone else in the world might fear him, even those who turned to him for leadership and protection, but not Mouse. He fancied that she might even say she loved him. The tragedy was that Mouse had most likely never even heard of the word "love," and would scorn the more common definitions if someone tossed them at her.

"There's more to the world than what our hands and eyes and ears show us." Brogan snatched up the child by her collar and deposited her on the rough table. "I know what you say you saw and felt and heard. The day you know everything that happened, all the reasons and causes—that's the day you can take over my job and I'll go find a nice sunny pond and spend my days fishing."

"You? In the sunshine?" Mouse scooted her little bottom around until she could bend her allegedly injured leg, resting her heel on the tabletop. Then she pulled up her torn trouser leg.

Brogan noted the dark, crusty-looking smears on the wrinkled cloth, visible in the candlelight. He had seen enough blood in his lifetime, fresh and day-old and weeks-old stains, to know what he saw now. Mouse hadn't had those stains on her clothes yesterday, when she had come to report to him all the things she had overheard and seen in her daily ramblings about the city. So she *had* injured her leg. Or else fell on top of somebody who was bleeding. Far easier to believe Mouse broke her leg temporarily than that she had tripped over someone she didn't see. The child could see in the dark like a dozen cats and was just as agile.

Brogan leaned forward to see better. He felt some of the candle warmth on the travesty of his face.

Several flat streaks of scarring spread down Mouse's leg, pink and warm to the touch. Brogan knew the girl couldn't have been injured badly enough to produce those scars without being off her feet for weeks. No matter where she had been injured in the city, someone would have heard and brought her to him to tend.

"Tickles." Mouse twitched a little as Brogan stroked the warm scarring one last time and stepped back into the shadows.

Not that he needed to protect her from the ruin of his face. She knew it well enough. Habit kept him in the shadows, little more than a dark, wide-shouldered shape and a voice.

"Watcha think?" She tugged her trouser leg down and swung her legs over the side of the table to hop down.

"I think you need to be more careful in your adventuring."

"Brogan!" She rolled her eyes in exasperation. "About the lady. She talks funny, like Preacher. Real nice. Didn't yell on me for wearing trousers, neither." A giggle escaped her. "Think she's an angel?"

"Hardly." Brogan rubbed his chin, his fingers rasping over the two-day stubble, then catching on the smooth scarring that would never grow a beard again.

Was it possible? Could the surge of crystal energy he felt last night have come from the woman when she sang to Mouse and healed her leg? He had heard of the lotus healing injuries, but the number of people who could work with it decreased with every generation. He had heard stories of women who could sing to crystal and draw out energy for healing, but again, the numbers had dwindled over the centuries.

He almost preferred to think he was going mad, because the possibilities that now beckoned went against the current that he believed directed his life.

Who was this woman who looked too young to be mother to the gaggle of children with her? What was she doing, making camp in the shells of the buildings being torn down to prepare for the foundations of Endicott's tower? She certainly didn't sound like the type of predators who trolled the city streets for orphans and destitute children, to haul them off to durance vile on work farms or in sexual slavery. The presence of crystal didn't guarantee her character. If that were so, the ancestors of the Revisionists never would have succeeded in launching their journey into the past. A do-gooder would have scolded Mouse for injuring herself and then thrown her into the care of the authorities who dealt with street children. A woman looking for children to enslave would have left Mouse lying where she had fallen. Tending the child and healing her would have cut into her profits.

Chapter Fourteen

"Tell me again," Brogan said.

Mouse launched into the tale of falling and the woman who came out of the darkness and rain with her pretty, sad face, to gather her up and hold her furiously aching leg in her thin hands and pray. Then the music came, and the light that came through her shirt. Mouse grinned slyly and admitted that when the lady fell asleep, she had crept close enough to tug open her shirt enough to see a pretty cross with a flower in the center, clear like glass.

Crystal.

A woman who sang to crystal and healed with her music. A woman who sang to the crystal so he felt the energy of it even with yards of rock between them. Maybe with half the city between them, if she had sung the other times he heard and felt the crystal sing.

Brogan had to bring her down here. Not just for his own sake, to seek answers, but because Revisionists could feel the shimmer of crystal at work just as well as he could. She needed protection. She wasn't with Endicott and his people, which meant she wasn't an Originator. She doubly needed protection because she didn't know what she had hanging around her neck. He would bring her down here to protect her.

Would she see the soap bubble film of light down in the tunnels? Would she hear the music? Could she step through the gate to the sun-soaked hillside? Would he finally have proof that he wasn't insane?

A woman who could pray and half-sing over a child's broken leg, making her bones vibrate and her flesh heat and sew itself back together, belonged here in his world of shadows and darkness, tunnels and forgotten cellars, dust and mystery. He was the guardian of mystery, after all.

"Find her. Follow her," he said, and caught up Mouse by the collar to deposit her onto the rough stone floor. "And don't get yourself caught by the coppers, hear me? Takes too much trouble to break you out."

"Coppers don't know how to see me," Mouse retorted with a saucy wink and a wriggle of her backside. Then she scurried out of the room.

"You don't know half the trick of being invisible, my girl," Brogan muttered, and settled further back into the shadows, where the candlelight couldn't touch and warm him. He stroked his fingertips over the ruin of the left side of his face. Damaged nerves tingled and flared.

When Mouse told her story, he had let himself hope, just for a moment, that somehow a miracle had fallen into his dusty, dark, watchful life. He let himself envision, just for a moment, this angel-voiced lady touching his ravaged face, singing over him instead of turning away in disgust, and putting his features back to what they had been a lifetime ago.

"Don't be a fool," Brogan growled, his voice echoing back to him from the rough stone walls. "God turned His face away years ago."

The stone of his chamber threw his voice back at him in soft, subliminal echoes, mocking him. Brogan had too strong evidence that miracles and wonder still existed in this world. The bitterness was that while he was vouchsafed to see and guard the beautifully impossible, and even bask in the magic, it could never touch him, never heal him.

~~~~~

By the time they had walked down the shore to the bathhouse and the children washed up and had their very late breakfast, Carmen decided today would be a day of leisure. What was the use of wearing themselves out, walking in the hot sun at a rapid pace, just to get to the library and sit for two hours before they had to leave? The library closed at noon on Wednesdays. Better to take their time, enjoy the sunny weather, and avoid wasting energy. The few pennies in her purse wouldn't last much longer. Carmen reserved a bun for each child from the bread left from yesterday, to have a mid-afternoon snack. Or, if luck was against them, an early and skimpy dinner. There was plenty of cold, refreshing water from the pump to fill their stomachs.

Mrs. Sullivan would likely assume that Carmen had managed to find Miss Hilda, or another friend of Willoughby's who would help them. She wouldn't worry for a day or two, when she hadn't heard from Carmen. Better to save tomorrow for bad news.

While the children laughed and splashed each other at the water's edge, Carmen sat and thought, weighing her options. Would those angry men still be gathered around the lawyers' office today? Should she take the risk and ask to talk to Mr. Lewis' partners? Look for Miss Hilda?

Perhaps the sensible option would be to go back to Mr. Fitzwalter and take whatever he would give her for the cross. Even more sensible than that, agree to sell him the rose. It might be somewhat defeatist, but if her mother's dangerous, mysterious heritage was tied up in the rose, then being rid of it would benefit her in the long run, wouldn't it? Perhaps she would have enough money to take all of them by train to the safe deposit box in Philadelphia. Then she would have plenty of money to supply their needs. She would take the children west, to settle where land was cheap. The thought of a cabin in a sheltered valley, far from cruel people and street thieves and gossips sounded like bliss. She and the children could farm, get a cow and some chickens and sheep, and supply all their needs themselves.

She pondered her options, discarding them and picking them up again, until her head hurt from the sun's rays splashing directly into her eyes. They couldn't linger at the shore any longer. She gathered up the children and headed back into town. By tonight, Carmen was determined, their lingering and waiting and making do would be over. One way or another.

Carmen prayed hard, silently, in time with her steps as they trudged down the road. She glanced with longing at the trolley that went past them heading for the bathhouse, and then on its return trip, and considered how wasteful it would be to spend a penny to spare them the heat and walking. Did she hesitate through lack of faith, or because a penny seemed like such a ridiculous, frivolous price to pay for a ride of perhaps ten, twenty minutes? Then the trolley passed them and it was too late to flag it down and ask for a ride. She and the children kept walking.

The Old Stone Church on the north side of Public Square offered shade and a respite from the heat and brilliance. Carmen leaned back and studied the tall steeple of the Presbyterian building and admired the structure. Her father had made a hobby of learning about old churches and their histories, to study the building styles that changed through the centuries. She had wanted a closer look on all her trips through the square. The shade was a blessing in the growing heat and stickiness of the morning, with the air so heavy with wet from last night's rain.

"Carmen?" Beatrice tugged on her skirt.

She bit back a rebuke, asking the child not to pull on her clothes like that. How was the girl to understand that she needed her decent clothes to last as long as possible, and that tugging would strain the fabric? She understood just how important appearances were to staying safe, but how could she convey that concept to the children without frightening them? Clean children attracted less suspicious attention, even if they wore secondhand clothes and their shoes were falling apart. Dirty children made people narrow their eyes and grow watchful and prepare to be accosted by pickpockets.

"What is it, sweetheart?"

"It's awful hot."

"I know." Carmen looked at the other four, leaning against the slightly cooler, age-darkened stone of the church. Despite the true purpose of a church, the custodians of beautiful buildings like this wouldn't appreciate a band of children coming inside just to sit and cool off and rest. Still, she had a responsibility to take care of the children, and that meant getting them some shade and respite. Even if they were scolded and run out only a short time later.

"Come along, ducklings." She smiled at their giggles. Anything that would make the children laugh, she welcomed.

Several men sat on the shallow steps up from the street to the doors. None of them turned to watch the party of six but slumped in the sizzling sunshine and stared out at the carriages and trolleys and steam-carts gliding by at a brisk pace. Carmen noticed one man who sat up straight, hands neatly folded on his lap as if in prayer. Sweat plastered his faded black coat to his bony back and his iron-gray hair to his head. He muttered under his breath. A few words were clear, and she caught several in Latin.

Andrew and Virgil hurried ahead to pull open the big iron-bound wooden doors at the front of the church. Carmen held Darla's hand, Beatrice held hers, and Arthur followed close enough to nearly tread on her heels as her small party stepped into the shadows of the foyer. Carmen repressed a sigh of relief at the noticeable drop in temperature. The thick stone structure warded off the heat admirably.

Wooden benches lined two walls, and she directed the children there to sit, with their few possessions tucked underneath. They obeyed, smiling and leaning back against the smooth stone wall. The glory of being in a cool place and out of the blinding sunshine would keep the children quiet, content to sit still for approximately fifteen minutes, twenty at the most. Then someone would get into mischief, even if just getting up to explore. She settled down on the bench in between Arthur and Virgil, the most likely to get restless first.

Someday, she vowed, there would be a place where homeless, hungry children would not only be welcome, but their mischief and laughter and games would be encouraged. Where they could run around to their hearts' content and get dirty and even tear their clothes, and not have to worry about getting new ones, or where they could wash up. Where they didn't have to worry about conserving their energy, because they wouldn't have to go a day or two or three without food. A place where clean, soft beds and plenty of food and wash water waited for them at the end of a long day of simply being children.

Please, Lord Jesus, not for me but for the children You have given to me, send us a champion, a shepherd, a warrior for justice who can shelter us all. Please, let a miracle be waiting for us when we go to the office?

Carmen knew better than to close her eyes as she prayed. Sticklers for ritual would be scandalized, but God had more common sense than most religious folk she had encountered in all her travels. She leaned back so the smooth stone cooled the sweat in her shirt and sent a delicious, short-lived chill across her back.

"Carmen? What's that book say?" Darla gestured at the oversized ledger sitting on an elaborate stone lectern next to the doorway into the sanctuary.

It was on the tip of her tongue to say it was likely a register for guests to the church to sign. She hesitated. At least one child would then insist on signing it, so proud that now they all knew how to spell and write their own names. Another would follow suit and perhaps try to scribble a message, or spatter ink, and tip over the inkwell to boot. In less time than it would take to tie her shoe, there would be a battle around the registry and it would be knocked to the floor. If the custodian or one of the church staff didn't come running to investigate the noise before that happened.

The longer she could keep the children in their seats and quiet, the better for all of them.

"I suppose it's a list of rules for anyone who wants to go into the sanctuary," she said.

At the back of her mind, she heard her father's low, wry chuckle. The Reverend Hiram Mackenzie wouldn't approve of lying, even for a good cause, but he would appreciate the irony of lying to protect the church from the children's mischief, and protect the children from the self-righteous and narrow-minded who sought to protect the church from the very ones who needed its help the most.

"Rules?" The little girl's eyes widened in dismay.

Virgil and Andrew shook their heads, closed their eyes, and slumped a little more against the wall behind them. They wriggled a little. Carmen hoped it was a search for another cool spot on the wall, rather than restlessness.

"Here, now. What's this?" A red-cheeked, stooped old man stepped into the doorway from the shadowed interior of the church. His bushy white eyebrows shot up nearly into his neatly combed and oiled hairline as he glanced from one side of the foyer to the other, studying the six dusty intruders.

"We just stopped to find a little cool and shade, and to sit down for a moment," Carmen said. "The little ones were wilting." She held her breath and prayed the man lived up to his jolly, kind appearance.

"That's all fine and good, but why aren't these children in school?" His eyebrows lowered.

"The library is closed," Beatrice offered, her cheerful little voice the soul of innocence.

"What does that have to do with not being in school?"

"Carmen is our teacher," Darla added.

"Hardly likely." He snorted and looked Carmen over, head to foot and back again. His eyebrows snapped down even lower. The corners of his mouth seemed attached to his eyebrows, dragging his face into wrinkles.

Carmen stood, gesturing for the children. Better to retreat now. If she let him work up to a bluster, he would remember them badly in the future, when she might need to come here to ask for real help.

"Thank you for your Christian hospitality. I'm sure the Lord is pleased that His house provided shelter and a respite from the sun for these least of His flock," she said, and pushed the big door open.

For once, the children hurried out without offering one of their witty, possibly disrespectful observations. The church's guardian shook his head, eyes wide, as if her words had knocked him off balance. Carmen slipped out through the door. She couldn't resist throwing a bit of scripture, in Latin, over her shoulder at the man who was now lost in shadow.

"And if you see your brother hungry and naked and you say to him I wish you well, be fed and warmly clothed and do not stretch out your hand to help him, what good is that to me?" The bony man in black now stood on the curb, looking up at Carmen and the children as they came down the few steps.

Carmen stumbled. He had thrown the scripture she quoted in Latin right back at her in English. Very finely enunciated English, with just a slight accent of someone who might have been educated at the finest seminaries on the East Coast.

"He was a regular old —"

"Andrew! What have I told you about showing respect?" Carmen fought the urge to glance over her shoulder, positive she would find the door of the church open and the man who had been questioning them standing there, glaring and listening.

"I'm hot again, Carmen," Beatrice said, and caught hold of her skirt before leaning against her right leg. "Can't we go back inside and sit?"

"I'm thirsty," Darla added.

"I'm hungry," Arthur said, coming to lean against Carmen's other side.

The bony man's low chuckle surprised her. He spread his arms wide, showing the dark streaks of perspiration plastering his jacket to his body. "Silver and gold have I none, but what I do have, I give to you."

Carmen shivered despite the heat and the renewed sweat sticking her clothes to her skin.

"Come. I know where it's cool and quiet, and there is enough to feed all your hungry mouths." He stepped into the street without checking for oncoming vehicles.

By some miracle, there was no traffic whatsoever. Virgil and Arthur exchanged grins and hurried after him. Darla and Beatrice looked up at Carmen with such pleading in their eyes, she couldn't shake her head or call the boys back. Carmen followed, bringing up the rear with her carpetbag in one hand and Beatrice holding the other. Since Andrew and Arthur were carrying the rest of their few possessions, she couldn't very well stay behind, could she?

To her consternation, the Latin-speaking stranger led them straight across Public Square to the deconstruction area. She held her breath against the dust filling the air and collecting on her sweaty skin. She imagined it turning to cement if it grew any thicker.

At the last moment, their strange guide turned right, heading toward the bridge barely visible against the tops of the big brick buildings and warehouses and the masts and smokestacks of ships traveling the river. He led them around the deconstruction area. Carmen waited until they crossed the next street and decided enough was enough.

"Excuse me," she said, hurrying the twenty steps or so to catch up with their skeletal guide. "Where are you taking us? And who are you?"

"Folks 'round abouts call me Preacher." He gestured as if to tip a nonexistent hat to her.

"Are you?" Arthur grinned cheekily.

"A prophet is known by the accuracy of his words and if what he speaks comes to pass," he intoned, his voice dropping half an octave.

"That isn't what the boy asked you," Carmen said, huffing a little. She shouldn't have picked up her pace in this heat.

"Trust in the Lord with all your heart, and lean not on your own understanding," Preacher said, his voice gentle again. His beatific smile stunned Carmen, so she could only keep walking for another half block, trying to regain her mental balance.

She had seen so very much in her nomadic life with the camp meeting teams. True saints of the Lord, mixed with charlatans who feigned an appearance of righteousness to become rich. They spoke the words of truth and yet never listened to what they taught and exhorted others to believe and do. People with simple, miracle-working faith worked hand-in-hand with the coldly, viciously self-righteous and legalistic.

Was this man sent by God to help them? An angel in human guise? Or a madman, seemingly harmless and slightly odd, who might turn deadly at a moment's notice?

Carmen glanced over her shoulder at the children. She had learned that even when the words and false countenances of men fooled her, children were never fooled. If the children trusted this man, were even slightly amused by him, then perhaps they were safe with him?

Yet what if the children felt safe and comfortable because *she* seemed to trust this man?

Lord, please keep us safe. Bring us unharmed and whole and together, to Your safe pasture.

Carmen wished she could sing. She couldn't count the times her father had bade her sing during difficult, even dangerous times, and the forces of evil had seemingly been driven away by the words of scripture set to music. Her throat felt tight with more than thirst and breathlessness. The weight of their increasingly desperate situation, one disaster and loss after another, quite weighed her down. Perhaps she should call the children back and run away right now.

Please, blessed Lord—

A cooler breath of air brushed across her face. Carmen looked down to see their party stood on the edge of a bluff, above the river. Switchback stairs, carved into the rock in some places, augmented with boards and bricks in others, created a haphazard path halfway down to a wide ledge, perhaps fifty feet wide and ten deep, judging by the men who stood on it.

"Welcome. Be at rest." Preacher bowed slightly, gesturing at the stairway down.

The boys grinned and threw themselves down the steep stairway at breakneck speed. The girls followed suit. Carmen hesitated to follow. Yet what choice did she have? She was responsible for them. She put her left foot on the first step down.

"Ma'am?" Preacher offered his arm, putting himself between her and the open air, so she would have the dirt and rock on her other side as they went down.

"Thank you." Carmen switched her carpetbag to her other hand, tucked her freed hand into his arm, and took a deep breath. "Lord, guard Your sheep," she whispered.

"Amen and amen," he intoned, and started down the stairs.

Carmen knew in her head that the fall wasn't that far to the river below. However, her imagination took over as she let her guide help her down the steps. She saw herself falling and hitting that wide ledge where the children all stood now, looking up at her, and bouncing several times before landing in the river. If she was unconscious or just stunned, what good would her strong swimming ability do her?

What if her guide had brought her down here to give her a push? Yet what reason would he have to do so?

Her imagination showed him suddenly foaming at the mouth, spewing scripture about witches and false prophets before he shoved her off the steps. Her father's detractors had accused her of consorting with dark powers in connection with the few healings of children. With the growing reach of the telegraph, could her father's enemies find her here, on the shores of Lake Erie, and recruit this slightly odd man to hunt her down?

You're doubly a fool, Carmen Mackenzie. When are you going to trust the Almighty?

"And here we are." Preacher bowed and released her arm.

Carmen laughed as she looked around at the bottom of the stairs. She stood securely on the ledge. It was larger than it had looked from above.

"Thank you," she said, and nodded, returning his genteel manners.

"Ain't it grand, Carmen? It's like you were telling us, about Alice and the hole in the ground!" Andrew grasped her arm, turning her a little and pointing at the rock face.

Carmen studied the roughly squared opening through the rock. A cave, or more accurately a tunnel, leading under the city.

Chapter Fifteen

"Alice. Yes." Carmen saw only eagerness and excitement. The children needed distraction. Surely going into that tunnel would give them shade from the merciless sun and distract them from their hunger. For a little while, at least.

If only she couldn't recall so very clearly all the misfortunes Alice encountered, exploring Wonderland. All the decidedly nasty creatures who meant her no good and couldn't care enough about her not to do her any harm in their selfish pursuits.

"Hello again." A grimy-faced man stepped up, touching his cap. "Remember me?"

"You were there this morning," Darla said, stepping up to press herself against Carmen's right leg.

"That's right." He winked at the girl. She loosened her stranglehold of Carmen's leg. "Heard what you did for Mouse. She's a pet of ours."

The boys chuckled and muttered among themselves. Carmen didn't want to know what jokes they had made up from that remark.

"I just found a child lost in the rain and brought her to shelter. Anyone would do that."

"Maybe." He gestured into the cave. "He's got the word out, wants to see you. Thank you."

"He who?"

"Him. The Boss."

"Boss of what?" Carmen glanced upward, in the direction of the deconstruction site. "The foreman?"

"Him?" The man spat and grinned, displaying a missing tooth. "He just thinks he's the boss. Nah, I'm talking about the Boss. The one who makes sure the newcomers are all right and a man down on his luck has a place to lay his head. And those who lost our homes and businesses because of the city's grand plans, we don't get buried and forgotten. Know what I mean?"

Carmen was afraid she did. Movement out of the corner of her eye caught her attention. She turned to see Preacher heading back up the stairs.

"Thank you," she called.

The workman nodded. "Preacher didn't scare you none, did he?"

"My father was a preacher." That didn't answer his question, but she wasn't quite sure what to say.

"Ain't the same. Just spouts a lot of church talk all the time. Kind of crazy, but he's a good enough fellow. Looks out for the little ones. He brought Mouse to him when none of us knew up from down. Guess maybe that was the beginning." He gestured at the cave opening. "Go on inside. Gotta hurry back to work before my lunch hour is over."

"We didn't get any lunch," Beatrice said, shaking her head slowly. "We never get lunch." She caught hold of the edge of Carmen's carpetbag, since Darla had claimed her other side. "Carmen's got no money for lunch for us."

"Ain't she?" The workman nodded to Carmen and winked. "Well, that's no worry. You're where you'll be taken care of, right as rain."

"It rained last night." Arthur leaned against the opening of the cave, looking into the darkness. "That didn't feel right."

The workman burst out laughing, earning some chuckles and grins from the other men moving toward the stairs. If they were all heading back to work, what were she and the children to do? Sit in the dark, cool cave for the afternoon?

That did sound lovely, but she knew her charges. They would grow bored after a while. Andrew and Virgil, at the very least, would want to go swimming. Then they would walk along the ledge, threatening to fall or leap off into the river a dozen times. Carmen knew better than to assume that just because she prayed and sang and opened her soul to Heaven, miraculous healing would take place. She didn't want to have to test the limits of the blessing by begging for the healing of broken bones, broken skulls, and drowning. The water of that river looked none too clean, thanks to the factories and shipping everywhere along its banks. For every airship plying the skies in transportation and shipping, another fifty ships sped down the waterways, powered by steam engines and other wonders of modern technology. The filth from what so many called "progress" wouldn't be washed away from the soil and water for decades to come.

"Come on along with you. You'll understand soon enough." Their new guide gestured and stepped into the cave.

The tunnel had candles positioned at every bend as it descended. After the fifth turn, Carmen wasn't quite sure where she was in relation to the city above them. The candles didn't offer much detail, other than walls that looked like they were mostly rock. She saw very little compacted dirt or clay or roots, and that was comforting. Less chance of cave-ins. Her father had ministered for less than a year among coal miners in Pennsylvania, and Carmen had seen the results of one too many cave-ins, where greed or haste or simple carelessness had created unsafe conditions. The steadiness of the candle flames reassured her that the air was clean and good, no matter how deep underground they went.

"You found 'em!" A small shape hurtled out of the shadows, carrying a lantern. It resolved into the girl, Mouse. Among the dancing shadows cast by the lantern and the candle, Carmen saw they had reached a rounded room, the ceiling perhaps a foot above her head, with several tunnels converging at this point.

"No thanks to you, scamp," the man said. "Can you take them on from here? Gotta get back to work before the foreman decides to dock me."

"What you need work for, anyway?" Mouse pouted, eyes dancing with mischief.

"To get money to bring you candy, what else?" He tousled her tangled curls. "Feed them, first, you hear me?" Then without waiting for an answer from the girl, he tipped his hat to Carmen and headed back the way he had brought them all.

"Feed us what?" Virgil said, challenge in his voice. Carmen suspected he resented having a girl smaller and younger than him in charge.

"Come on." Mouse swung her lantern around and scurried down another tunnel.

Carmen gestured for the children to move, and hurried to follow the child, guided more by panic than trust. She didn't trust herself to bring them all back up to the sunlight and open air. There was no guarantee that just because she didn't see any branches of the tunnel that brought them down, there weren't any. She imagined getting lost here underneath the city of Cleveland, forever immured in darkness and stone.

This is how the early Christians lived during the persecution in Rome, she told herself. *They endured and survived and thrived through the grace of God. So shall I.* Carmen sighed softly as she tried to keep an eye on the shadowy, uneven stone floor under her feet while watching where Mouse led them. *Please, blessed Savior, let us survive and thrive.*

"Here, you." A woman stepped out of a shadowed doorway. "Where are you taking these folks?"

"To see him." Mouse raised her lantern, swinging it a little, so the shadows and streaks of light bounced off the crooked, white-haired woman.

Carmen shuddered a little, noting how no one said a name, but everyone seemed to know who "he" or "him" was.

"And didn't I hear Murphy tell you to make sure these little ones were fed?" She glanced at Andrew, who stood up a little taller. Even in the shadows, Carmen could see the boy was offended at being referred to as a "little one." "And these others with them," she added, winking at the boy.

When Mouse grudgingly agreed that yes, she had been told to feed the visitors, the woman beckoned. All five children immediately looked to Carmen for permission. She rested her hand on Carmen's arm, a gentle touch.

"Do swear on my soul, missy, the children will be safe and fed up good. And if I do say so myself, in this heat, boys need twice as much washing." She winked at Carmen when the boys groaned nearly in chorus.

"Go on," Carmen said, nodding. "Andrew, you're their guardian, remember."

The oldest boy nodded to her, his face solemn. She let the children go because she had no choice. That was the predominant reason, despite the warming sense that the old woman did indeed intend good for them, that she did care.

"Excuse me," she said, as Mouse beckoned for her to follow further down the dark tunnel. "May I ask? What's your name?"

"Goodness, I did forget, didn't I?" The woman chuckled as she stepped up and rested a hand on either of the girls' shoulders, visibly taking them under her wing. "Mary. Most of the little ones we take in, they call me Granny, if they stay with us."

"Thank you, Mary."

"If this one forgets to give you directions, because she thinks everyone else has the map printed on the backs of their eyelids," Mary glared fondly at Mouse, "the blue splotches where tunnels cross always lead to the stores and living area. That's where you'll find food and clothes and fuel and medicine. We'll be in the kitchen."

"Kitchen?" Carmen glanced around the shadowy, damp, stony surroundings. She couldn't imagine a kitchen down here. Unless these tunnels led out into sunshine again, to a house of some kind?

"You'll understand all in good time." Mary patted her shoulder, then nodded at Andrew, tipping her head toward the opening in the rock she had come through. "Lead on, boyo."

Andrew glanced once more at Carmen, then turned and stepped through the opening. In the momentary sweep of candlelight on the wall next to Mary as she passed, Carmen indeed did see a smear of light blue.

"Come on!" Mouse caught at her hand, tugging for a moment. The lantern swung wildly. "Don't never make him wait." She scurried down the tunnel without waiting for Carmen.

"What's his name?" she asked, as she picked up her feet and hurried. It took a few steps before she settled into a stride that kept her carpetbag from banging against her leg and hobbling her. The tunnel was just wide enough for two to walk side-by-side.

"Who?"

"The man you're taking me to see." Carmen wondered if Mouse was dim in the head. She picked up her pace a little more when the child didn't answer. Long ago, when she had some respect because of who her father was, she could afford to refuse to move until someone gave her the necessary information. Carmen glanced at the stone walls that seemed to be moving in closer around her. She would be the biggest kind of fool to try such tactics here. She was a guest, and guests simply did not act that way.

Especially when she had no candles or lanterns or the slightest idea how to get back to the daylight. Or the children. She couldn't, wouldn't leave this place without the children safely in tow.

She stumbled when the tunnel abruptly sloped upward again. The floor felt rougher under her feet. She tried to divide her attention between keeping Mouse in her sights and watching the texture of the floor in the pool of wavering light, so she wouldn't be caught unawares again and trip. To her relief, the walls felt further apart, and the ceiling seemed to be a little higher above her head with every step she took. Carmen took a few deep breaths and the tight, trapped feeling fled. She scolded herself for a fool, without the sense to breathe properly. Mouse stopped abruptly on the threshold of an actual room.

A few squared timbers ran along the ceiling, and definite lines and angles showed where floor met walls met ceiling. A trestle table covered with papers sat near one wall, and several stools and a wooden swivel chair missing two slats in the back formed a rough circle in the center of the room. The walls and floor were still bare stone, but Carmen saw smooth spots where she imagined generations of feet had worn down the rough texture.

A pitcher and several cups sat on a tray on the table amid all the papers and books. Lemon slices floated in the cups of water. How long had it been since she had enjoyed the luxury of lemon slices in water? A sure sign of civilization.

Multiple candles lit the room. Carmen had never appreciated how much light a single candle could cast, until now. Eight candles. In brackets along two walls, in a lantern hung from the center of the ceiling, one fat candle on a little table in the center of the chairs, and two on tall candlesticks on the table, on either side of the pitcher.

One corner was filled with darkness, she realized, as she looked around and resisted the temptation to snatch up a cup of water and drink. She was a guest, after all, and needed to display good manners, despite being ready to collapse from thirst. That corner, she discerned after a moment, held a person.

"Hello." She set down her carpetbag and nodded respectfully, then clasped her hands in front of herself to keep them from shaking. Or reaching rudely for that water.

Silence. She wondered if she imagined the dark figure, if she only thought she sensed the solid form and someone breathing close by. Carmen glanced at Mouse. The little girl frowned, tipping her head to one side, and stared into the corner.

A low, warm, baritone chuckle spread through the room. A part of Carmen that she had learned to tuck away and ignore stretched out eagerly for the sound. Back when her father had been respected, men who laughed like that had been good friends, trusted, benefactors. Men with ideas and dreams and honor.

Since her father's death, Carmen had learned not to trust men who laughed. No matter how rich and warm the sound, that laughter contained an element of power, of superiority. Especially coming from shadows, from someone who hadn't introduced himself to her.

"Welcome," the man said. A hand emerged from the thick shadows, and Carmen realized he wore all black. She suspected he wore a hood, too, because that hand was large and light-skinned. "So you are the lady who sings and heals broken bones."

"I think there's some mistake." Carmen reached up to clasp her hand against her throat. It ached, as if she had forced the music last night. "I prayed over the child, nothing more."

"Hmm, then you are someone God listens to, when He ignores everyone else." That hand gestured at the water. "Please, drink. Have a seat."

Carmen hated how her hand trembled, and how quickly she snatched up the closest cup of water. She took a step back, reaching for the nearest stool, and didn't move it any closer to the table. Distance between her and the speaker would make her feel better.

"I saw the scars on Mouse's leg. Scars that weren't there before yesterday." Another hand appeared from the darkness to rest on the tabletop. "Something happened last night."

"Sir, my father was a minister, and I have seen the grace of God..." Carmen sighed. "I did nothing. If the child's leg was broken, then it was an angel who healed her, not I. Once I thought I might be a vessel of God's power, a channel for His miracles. Not anymore."

"Are you a realist, or bitter?" His voice softened, lowered a few notes. For a moment, she imagined she heard the low notes of a cello in his words. "Forgive me. We have not been introduced. Despite your... reduced circumstances, you talk and hold yourself like an educated, refined young woman. Please forgive my manners. Social graces flee when catastrophe strikes and makes destitute otherwise good men. Will you tell me your name? Please?"

"I am Carmen Mackenzie."

"You don't sound like you hail from the Emerald Isle. Or is that the Scottish Mackenzie?"

"My father's ancestors were Scottish, yes." She sipped at the cup, and wished she could enjoy the taste of lemon in the water more. Was that metallic taste in the cup, or her mouth? "And you are?"

"Ah, as I told you. Social graces. I am Brogan. Simply Brogan. And you are welcome here, Miss Mackenzie. You and your children. Or is that Mrs. Mackenzie?"

"Miss." She flushed, surprised, and almost amused at the flash of insight. Her circumstances had destroyed the luxury of fearing what people thought of her, an unmarried woman with five children hanging on her skirts. "The children are all orphans or abandoned, living in the streets."

"And why did you take them up?" Brogan waited, while Carmen fought through a dozen useless, illogical, and even bitter explanations.

How could she explain that despite fearing God had forsaken her, she felt the children had been given to her as her duty and charge?

"Like those you will meet here in our little anthill, you have learned that the authorities aren't benevolent parents, looking out for the common good. They're evil stepfathers, always ready to think the worst and punish those who have committed no crime."

"Why am I here?" she whispered when she wanted to shout other questions.

"To thank you." He sighed, and the dark shape emerged a little more from the shadows, to reach out and take up a second cup of water. "And maybe I'm bored, sitting here in the darkness. Tell me a story, Miss Mackenzie."

"A story?"

"Tell me about you, how an educated, gently raised young lady ended up on the streets of Cleveland, sleeping in a half-demolished neighborhood, with five children who aren't her own, and talking of God and angels and healing broken bones and then refusing to take any credit for it. An interesting story it must be indeed."

Carmen thought of Sheherezade, telling stories, desperate to amuse the sultan so she wouldn't be beheaded for another woman's crime.

"You need a guardian. Don't hand me that claptrap about God being all the guardian you need," he said, raising a hand to stop her words before she even thought them. "I have half a dozen dimwitted old women under my care who maintained the same thing, but did God watch out for them when they were swindled out of their homes? When all their worldly goods were stolen after strangers moved them to new homes that were little more than crates?"

Despite the bitter grit in his voice, Carmen thought it still beautiful, musical and strong and deep, resonating in her bones, as if the stony walls of the cellar room might ring like chandelier crystals at any moment.

"Some might counter that God used *you* to shelter them. Because that's what you are doing, aren't you?"

"I am the last to ever suggest that God could work through me." A bit of laughter didn't do anything to lighten his tone, and it stung her.

"My father always maintained that God could work through the most impossible tools. He spoke through Balaam's ass, didn't He?"

She braced herself for fury. The silence rang, so she could count her heartbeats through it.

Then Brogan laughed and leaned forward a little into the light so she caught a glimpse of dark hair that glinted with hints of red in the candlelight. A wide forehead and thick brows like iron bars blocked the rest of his face from view and made her wonder what he was hiding. She had half-formed ideas of some monstrosity, mangled by accident or birthmarks, maybe some horrific mask without lips or nose or cheekbones.

Brogan sighed loudly, vibrating with laughter still, and sat back into the darkness of the corner. Her sight must have adjusted to the disparity of candlelight and shadow, because now she could make out the shape of him better, one layer of darkness among the black.

"I don't know whether to keep you among us for amusement or to argue theology. Perhaps more proof I am going mad, because I loathe all exercises of thought that do nothing to deal with the daily needs and worries of the common man." He took a deep breath, sounding put out.

Carmen held onto the memory of that laughter. She liked it, even as the sound stirred up memories of dragons and ogres and other imaginary creatures that had peopled her childhood reading and daydreams. Brogan was a man of power, but whether he would be a friend or enemy remained to be seen. She suspected he was a man to fear even if he was beloved.

"Keep me?" she retorted, and dared to step closer to the table and rest her hands on its uneven top. The boards making up the surface creaked a little. "Do you mean keep us prisoner?"

"Keep as in shelter and tend. Keep a house. Keep a horse. One and the same." He snorted. She had the oddest sensation he was trying to joke. "Have a seat, Miss Mackenzie. Before you join our little community of refugees and outcasts and victims, I need to know all about you."

"Such as?" She paused just long enough before sitting to let him know it was because she chose to do so, and not because he ordered her.

"Where is your father? Why isn't he watching out for you? If he was a man of God, why hasn't the church stepped in to care for your needs? And why doesn't a pretty young lady such as yourself have a husband?"

"I suppose it's a common enough story." She scooted her stool closer to the table and poured herself another cup of water.

Carmen had learned the hard way to be practical. If she and the children were tossed out after this interview, she would at least have her fill of cool, lemony water, even if she didn't get the meal she hoped the children were enjoying that moment.

Chapter Sixteen

"My father was a traveling preacher with a camp meeting society. He had rivals, who accused him of unethical dealings, and lied about him. My father was disgraced, and the betrayal destroyed his health. He had never been strong since the death of my mother. When he died, our former co-workers took everything I had and took me out of the public eye to avoid scandal. Or so they said." She paused to take a gulp of the water. Even this many months later, it still hurt, constricting her throat.

"I'd wager that they considered themselves very charitable," Brogan said, his voice dropping to a low, thoughtful rumble.

"Something like that."

"I suppose in all this, you lost your sweetheart, who cared more about reputation than true love?"

"I have only ever known the love of my parents, and the love of God." Carmen put the cup down and clasped her hands in her lap.

"No beaus at all? I find that hard to believe."

"Several expressed interest in me as a helpmate," she said, stung by the amusement in his tone. "They wanted my talents and training, and my reputation as Reverend Mackenzie's daughter. I refuse to give myself to any man unless he offers me the same love my father gave my mother."

"Ah, yes. A love so strong it destroyed his health, maybe his soul, when he lost her. From where I'm sitting, Miss Mackenzie, that makes love the greatest liability, the cruelest joke, ever to fall from God's hands."

"That is something we will never agree on, so let us agree not to discuss it." She fought the urge to leap from the stool, when Brogan's chair creaked and his shadow grew a little taller among the folds of darkness in the corner. "If we agree to stay here among you, what do you want from me?"

"Ah, a sensible woman. The best kind to deal with. You aren't all high ideals and music." Brogan set his cup of water down on the rough boards with a thud. "We have here orphans and children who have been separated from their parents, or who have come here to hide from danger. We have food and clothes and beds, and men who would give their lives to keep them from harm, but few women able to keep up with them. You'll be in essence a housemother for a dormitory of children at a most unusual boarding school. Can you teach, Miss Mackenzie?"

"If you give me books and slates and a place to sit with the children, where we won't be disturbed." Carmen clenched her fists and fought down the elated, panicky racing of her heart.

"I want these children to be well educated, so they can go anywhere, do anything they want when they're grown. Boys and girls. Are we in agreement on that, Miss Mackenzie?"

"You expect an awful lot from me, when you don't know how far I went in school."

"That's what public libraries are for. Will you take the position?"

"That's all you want? A foster mother and schoolteacher?"

"For now." He sighed and settled back deeper into the shadows, making his chair creak again. "I'm curious. Did no one suggest that you could make quite a good living on your back?"

"Some did, but I know better. While I can manage on very little, the children deserve more. My concern and my prayers have been for them, not myself. I have learned to trust God's provision, even when all seems hopeless. Perhaps that is why we are here now, after testing my faith."

"And if I throw you and your children out onto the streets tomorrow, or the next day?" The amusement had left his voice. Carmen wasn't certain what she heard.

"Then we will have had a day or two of shelter and food, and we will be strengthened for the road ahead of us. Tomorrow, God will move someone else to provide for our needs."

"You always have an answer, don't you?"

"No. Because if I did, I wouldn't be in this situation right now."

Brogan laughed. Carmen heard bitterness, amusement, and something else that made her shiver. When he gestured for her to take one of the candles in a holder and told her to follow the blue markings to the kitchen, she gladly hurried from the room.

The tunnel with the blue splotches branched and re-branched and turned and climbed and dropped as Carmen followed it. She couldn't have guessed where she was in relation to the cave opening above the river, or Public Square or any other landmark aboveground.

"Lord, please grant me eyes to see clearly. Keep my feet on the safe path. Tell me if we are safe here, if we have found shelter among..." She stopped, bemused at the realization she was about to say Philistines, thinking of how David had taken his parents there for shelter during the years he had fled from Saul. Had her mind turned to David because he had pretended to be insane, and because she feared this place was indeed a madhouse, and she had become an inmate?

"Lord, guide me," she whispered. "Lead me to green pastures and sunlight again, still waters and fruit to feed the children you have given to me to..."

That glimmer wasn't a reflection of her candle on some crystalline streak in the stone wall of the tunnel ahead of her. That was light, dancing in the air in the darkness.

She blinked and put down her carpetbag to rub at one eye. Perhaps she was overtired? Had she grown too hot, and the shock of going into the cool and damp had affected her senses? Was that actual light spinning, churning, spreading across the tunnel just a few feet in front of her? Or just an illusion?

Reaching out her hand, Carmen forgot to breathe as the streaks of light wrapped around her fingertips. She held perfectly still as a streak tinged gold and blue and lavender twined like a sentient ribbon between her fingers, tingling and yet feeling as soft and plush as a velvet curtain she had touched once at an opera house.

The light grew brighter, brushing the ceiling of the tunnel. Carmen looked down at the floor and saw the light spreading and aiming for her feet. She hopped up, to avoid tripping. As her feet touched the ground again, she laughed, realizing how foolish she was. How could light be solid enough to make her trip? Her ankles would go right through it.

"Please..." she whispered, blinking rapidly, half-blinded as light exploded around her.

She stood on a grassy hillside with the sun beating down warm on the back of her head. The air was heavy with moisture. She tasted the pungent green of grass and leaves baking in the warmth. Carmen took a deeper breath, to keep from fainting, and tasted the sweet wine tang of ripening apples, coming to her on the soft breeze somewhere to her left. She stood ankle-deep in thick grass of a green so intense that the color itself felt solid, heavy. Ahead, the hillside rose in a gentle slope, climbing for the sky.

No, not a hillside, Carmen decided. A mountain. If she walked for hours, she thought she wouldn't reach the top.

"Savior, help me," she whispered, tipping her head back, trying to see the top of the slope. "This can't be real."

Carmen took a step backward, shuddering, knowing she stood in a dark, damp, stone tunnel somewhere under the growing city of Cleveland. She knew she was hungry and thirsty, sweaty and gritty, and her feet ached. Yet all her senses declared otherwise.

She wanted to ask if she was dead and this was Heaven, but Carmen bit her tongue and swallowed hard, fighting the vibrations in her throat that presaged a shout waiting to explode. She took another step backward. The ground vibrated, buzzing through her thin shoes. She stumbled and turned to catch herself as her knees folded, and hit the cold, damp, grimy stone wall behind her. The candle hit the wall but she managed not to drop it. Carmen sank to her knees, gasping. She smelled the apple-scented air, felt the warm, gentle breeze a moment longer. The scent clung to her clothes. She exhaled, took another deep breath, and the scent of damp stone dominated her senses.

"What was that?" she whispered.

No one answered.

After a few more seconds of listening to her racing heart slow, she picked up her carpetbag and continued down the tunnel. She needed food and rest and to make sure the children were all right.

One more turn took her to a roughly circular room where gaps in the rock let sunlight streak in. She had several moments to look around and take in the makeshift hearths of stone and double-boiler arrangements of enormous cast iron pots full of coals, with smaller cast iron pots and grates suspended over them for cooking. The heartening aroma of chicken soup, baked potatoes, and bread wrapped around her, wiping away the last of her delusion. Carmen saw curtains hanging from what looked like railroad spikes driven into the ceiling, and small rooms behind the makeshift curtains. Beatrice and Darla came running, squealing with delight, to show off the boy clothes that Mary had given them.

"More sensible, down here," Mary said a short time later, as she brought over a bowl of soup and a plate of roasted, salted potatoes with soft, white cheese sprinkled over them. She set them down in front of Carmen on a trestle table and sat on the bench facing her. "Eat up, lovey. Anybody can see you've been starving yourself to look after the little ones. Nobody starves here. He sees to that." She nodded decisively.

Brogan again. Carmen wondered what kind of hold he had on these people. They had to be beholden to him, grateful for his leadership that fed and sheltered them, but what else held them here? Fear? Was it a choice between the inadequate help they might find from charitable organizations tangled in bureaucracy aboveground, and his dictatorship belowground? Or something else? If she hadn't met the man, she might have found it amusing that no one seemed to use his name. Now, Carmen wasn't sure what she felt.

"How long have you been here?" she said instead, as she spooned up the soup. In the lantern light, the broth looked thick with chicken, noodles, celery, and carrots. This was no watery concoction with a few grains of rice in the bottom, some shreds of unidentified vegetables that could turn out to be wood shavings, with only the vaguest perfume of chicken hanging above it. She had endured enough encounters with such fare to identify how long the waterlogged chicken had soaked in the water to give it some flavor.

"Who wants to remember before?" Mary nodded again, her smile widening a little, yet looking grim. "You and your little ones are safe here. That's all that matters. If you'll be part of keeping them all safe, you'll be welcome for as long as you want to stay."

"So I can leave any time I want?"

"Of course. But who'd want to?"

Carmen filled her mouth with a spoon of chicken and deliciously substantial broth, to avoid spilling a long list of reasons to go back aboveground. Sunshine and grass and trees being at the top of that list. She scolded herself to concentrate on her lunch and the warm bath Mary had promised her. She wondered what these people would say when she tried to go back above ground, if she would be allowed to leave the tunnels, to visit the law offices tomorrow. She had to keep trying to talk to Mr. Lewis. Harriet wanted her to be safe. Mr. Lewis could resolve the mystery of her mother's past, her legacy, and the crystal rose.

Besides, if this place turned out to be a lie, she needed some place to flee *to*, when she gathered up the children and escaped. She had learned long ago that it wasn't enough to run away from danger and trouble, she needed a destination, a goal.

The rest of the day, if it could be called "day" when most of the light was provided by lanterns and candles, was spent in settling her and the children. Carmen was amazed and disturbed by the number of children living underground, none of them belonging to the people who followed Brogan. Was the charity system in Cleveland so sparse on the ground, or overwhelmed, that these children had nowhere to go? Or was it that many people who offered them shelter and education, food and clothes, only did it for their own profit?

"Let your charity be done in secret, and say your prayers in a closet, so only your Father in heaven knows of them," she murmured, as she stepped out of the narrow room of the girls' dormitory. Beatrice and Darla had been delighted with their bunks and the older girls who welcomed them with smiles. There were rag dolls enough for everyone, a delightful dollhouse, and a tea set on a miniature table in one corner. The room was large enough for five bunk beds. Seven of the ten bunks had pillows and blankets neatly spread out on them, indicating occupants. Carmen ached for the girls who were endangered so this twilight existence was a haven.

The boys were in a similar situation, but the dormitory room carved out of the rock was twice as long, with twelve sets of bunk beds. Instead of dolls and a tea set, there were blocks and a battered train set and soldiers. The bunks weren't as neatly made as in the girls' dormitory, and Carmen found that encouraging. The children here could be normal children.

Rather, as normal as possible without families and sunshine and fresh air and proper schooling.

Well, she could do something about proper schooling.

Her new room, shared with Mary, had enough room for two bunks, a makeshift stove in the center, to resist the chill and damp of the stone, and a battered wardrobe to store clothes. Once she had been settled, Carmen went to what would be her schoolroom. She was pleased to find a long, horizontal crack in the rock wall, with daylight peering through, obscured by a curtain of leafy vines and grasses. A soft, humid breeze filtered through the curtain. This would be quite comfortable for the summer and fall, but what happened when winter came? Would ice and snow blow in?

She caught her breath, stunned to realize she was indeed thinking seriously about a future here, underground. How could she make such a decision without thinking and praying about it?

Two men brought in a long bench, almost on her and Mary's heels.

Another man was busy pounding spikes into the rock and hanging lanterns. A pile of boards and trestle legs sat in one corner, and Carmen assumed they would soon be assembled into tables.

"What about books? Paper and pencils? Or at least slates and chalk?" she asked, and held her breath, half-afraid Mary would tell her that she would have to scratch her lessons on the walls.

"Books won't be a problem unless you want enough for the children to have their own. Might be a bookstore where we can get some primers. One of ours saw you and your little ones at the library before, so you know about that. Looked like you were holding a class, with more than just yours." The old woman winked. "You can borrow what you need from the library, I suppose. You're not the type to condone stealing for a good cause, are you?"

"Ah... no, I'm not." Carmen almost apologized, but she saw the twinkle in Mary's eye and realized the old woman was teasing her. She let out a sigh and smiled, and soon she and Mary chuckled softly together. Later, she realized at that moment she felt she had made a friend, and her first toehold in establishing a place for herself in this hidden community.

~~~~~

Ess strode down the street at a leisurely pace, to absorb the changes in the center of Cleveland since the last time she had been here. She wished for her trousers and cap, but it was a tossup whether the thickening humidity would have been more bearable in her gingham dress and petticoats, or wearing a jacket to smooth over her figure. Uly had been amused to deliver her the bad news that her stride had changed in the last six months, so she moved more like a girl. She had come close to giving him a black eye. Definitely, she was limited to her boy clothes for nighttime maneuvers. Why did she have to keep growing and changing? It wasn't fair.

Hilda would snort and probably rap her knuckles if Ess dared to voice that complaint. That thought thickened her throat with pending laughter. She paused as she reached an intersection and looked down the street. Just three more intersections before she reached Hilda's... what could she call it? In the last three months, Hilda had added another building to her growing enterprise. Part school, part orphanage, part rescue mission, part cooking school and expanding apprenticeship program. The last time she had heard from Endicott, Hilda faced opposition from people who didn't want her to use yet another building to take more neglected or abandoned children off the street. Political game players now opposed her at every turn. A year ago, she had been praised by anyone who had any kind of power or influence. Now, people who still wouldn't explain why they stood against the law firm's building project had turned against Hilda.

"Miss Winslow!"

That rich tenor voice struck an odd chord of recognition and trepidation, even before Ess remembered that incident at the museum when she had been Miss Winslow.

That settled it. She should have taken to the streets in her boy disguise, despite needing a long jacket to hide her figure.

Briscoe Harrison strode across the street in the wake of a passing steam-cart. His face was alight with pleasure, making his wide, chiseled cheekbones seem wider, his mouth bigger. How did those golden curls stay in place like a wreath around his head, despite the humidity?

"What a distinct pleasure to encounter you here, of all places." He bowed, reaching for her hand. Ess wished she had chosen a more elaborate outfit, to include gloves. At least the kiss he pressed against the back of her hand wasn't wet.

"Why wouldn't I be in Cleveland? It has art, culture, growing industry. It is a major port city, served by railroad, ship, and airship." She tucked her hands behind her back, to rub against her skirt without him seeing.

"Well, when you put it that way..." He chuckled.

"What are you doing here?"

"Business, actually. My employers have asked me to track down several people who are in possession of some rare artifacts. The sad fact is that they most likely don't know what they are holding. They don't realize the value, so of course, they don't act like people entrusted with a great treasure. It makes them..." He shrugged. "It makes them difficult to find."

"Well, then, I shan't keep you from your duties."

"Ah, you know the saying. 'All work and no play...' I refuse to let anyone accuse me of being a dull boy." He offered her his bent arm. The way his eyes widened when she took a step back was almost comical.

"I have business to attend to."

"You must let me accompany you. Especially since your protective uncle seems to be conspicuously missing. A young lady such as yourself, wandering this sprawling city unaccompanied, well, it would violate my vows as a gentleman."

"Mr. Harrison, you go too far."

"Yes, but I'm charming, aren't I?" He chuckled when Ess gave in to a smile she couldn't resist, even as she regretted it. He was amusing more than charming. "You know, I am an expert in finding people who don't want to be found. It is my art, my reason to live. So you might as well agree to let me take you to dinner. I will find you no matter where you go and I will not relent until I have convinced you to take me seriously."

"Believe me, I do take you seriously. If you will allow me to attend to my business today and tomorrow, I will take dinner with you the next evening. Will that satisfy you?"

"Well, it's a start." He bowed again.

While they were exchanging information on their respective hotels, Ess saw a grimy little girl with tangled blonde hair. She stood on the base of a streetlamp, hanging from one arm, and making faces behind Harrison's back. She muffled a grin when she recognized the little girl. One of Hilda's messengers. The woman referred to the truly clever ones as her sparrows. Sparrows with teeth. They were pickpockets and sneak thieves she had taken off the street. Hilda loathed wasting anything, especially the talents her children had picked up for the sake of survival. Ess met the little girl's eyes and winked at her while Harrison was busy jotting her information on a business card with a pencil. The girl crossed her eyes at Harrison, jumped down from the lamp base, and sauntered down the side street.

Ess followed her several minutes later, after Harrison made a show of heading down the street in the opposite direction. So much effort made her suspicious. The child waited in a recessed doorway. She leaned out and looked past Ess and crossed her eyes.

"He's not very good," she said in a sweet voice that belonged to someone wearing lace and smelling of lavender soap.

"How far behind me is he?" Ess took two steps past the doorway, then bent and pretended to pick up something from the pavement. She caught a glimpse of movement ducking back around the corner of the building. "His art, my foot. Why is it that those who are only middling in talent brag, and those who have superior skill find no need to discuss that skill?" She muffled a chuckle when the little girl gave her a puzzled frown. "You're Caroline, aren't you?" Her heart squeezed when the little girl's face lit up and she nodded. "Why don't you like him?"

"He's been poking around our place. Lots. And he's been looking around the lawyers' place. Gotta figure a fancy-dressed man who stops on the door and listens at the keyhole and never goes in, he's not friendly like."

"How long has he been poking around?"

"Four days now."

Chapter Seventeen

Was it entirely coincidence and bad luck that he was here? What was he after, to accost her and lay on the charm so thick? He had to want something, and badly enough to take time away from whatever brought him to Cleveland. It had to do with Endicott, Lewis and MacDonald. It had something to do with Hilda and her children. Otherwise, what made him loiter at both places enough that Caroline noticed him?

Could he be a Revisionist? Had he identified the lawyers and Hilda as Originators? Ess wiped her hands on her skirts, then glanced over her shoulder. She calculated another ten, fifteen seconds before Harrison looked for her again.

"Do you have a bolt hole I can fit through?"

Caroline grinned and held out her hand. She trotted down the street and led Ess through the next doorway, slid a deadbolt home, and led her through the room that ran the length of the building. It looked like a storage room. They went out the other side. Several more such changes, in and out of buildings, took them the rest of the way down the street to Hilda's building. Besides the two entrances on the street, for restaurant customers and deliveries, the back of the building had a fire escape entrance, and then another that connected with several other buildings on either side, via tunnels.

After the destruction of Sanctuary, Ess thought she had had enough of tunnels to last a lifetime. Then again, she had entertained some envious feelings for her grandparents, exploring the ruins of the Old World. Egypt and other civilizations where the time-traveling ancestors had hidden parts of the Great Machine offered many tunnels for exploration.

Finally, she ended up in Hilda's kitchen, the heart of the expanding enterprise focused on rescuing children. Less than half the faces there were familiar. Uly and Endicott had been recruiting the most trustworthy and intelligent of Hilda's rescued waifs, indoctrinating them into the Originators' secrets and mission. After a brief, hard hug, Hilda settled Ess on the sidelines, out of the way, while she and her army of cooks-in-training worked on that evening's menu for the restaurant. They caught each other up on what had happened since the *Golden Nile* had last come through Cleveland. Several of the older children came in and out, bringing notes, which Hilda read and sometimes responded to with more notes. Caroline came in and out twice, and the second time, Hilda frowned after the little girl reported to her on the other side of the room.

"You shouldn't have shaken off that Mr. Fitch so quickly," Hilda said, bustling back over to where Ess had finished her third glass of milk, washed down with enough cookies to make her wretched corset feel tight. The woman sighed and shook her head when Ess just frowned, unsure what she was talking about. "Your newest admirer is back. At least he has the sense to find a new hiding place every time he settles in to stare holes in my walls. Not much of a challenge for my sparrows, though," she added with a sniff and a spattering of chuckles around the room.

"Ah, Mr. Harrison." Ess decided not to even touch the matter of Allistair Fitch. Her last letter from Phoebe indicated he was impatient to formalize their courtship. Not even the mind-stretching wonders of becoming an Originator got in the way of pursuing the young woman who had caught his heart. Ess was glad for them both, even as she entertained the suspicion that she had finally found a flaw in the inestimable Mr. Fitch. He needed a woman who depended on him, who was intelligent and resourceful, and yet not so much that she could rescue herself without any help from him.

"Is that his name now?" Hilda sniffed and bent to check the chickens roasting in five long pans in the main oven.

"Now?"

"Better check in with our lawyer friends as soon as you can. He followed Mr. MacDonald here, so I'm speculating his first target was one of them, and as soon as he heard some of the foolish gossip, he decided we might make a good target, or at least a weak spot."

"No idea what he wants?" Ess sighed and slid off the bench where she had been perched. "I will need a costume change, at the very least."

"You know where everything is."

"What other names is Mr. Harrison using?"

"Hmm, let's see." Hilda closed the oven door and tapped her chin with the dry end of the long spoon she used interchangeably as a baton, a rod of correction, and sometimes for stirring. "Peyton, when he was making a pest of himself among the workmen at the building site. Inspector Hooper, when he was walking around City Hall. And Richards, when he paid his respects to our lawyer friends."

"Interesting. Do you have any sketching paper? I need to spread his face among all our allies, to put them all on the watch for him."

"Riley, you're our artist. Help Miss Odessa."

By the time Ess had picked out the clothes she would wear to walk from Hilda's to the law offices on Superior Avenue, Riley had brought her a full artist's kit, with three sizes of sketching pads, a dozen pencils and two little knives for sharpening them, a watercolor kit, a sealed flask of water and two cups, ten brushes of different sizes and stiffness, and an almost untouched set of colored chalks. He also had a sketchpad of his own work, to show her and prove his skill. It was quite remarkable for a boy of thirteen, and he flushed charmingly when Ess commended him. Then he admitted that he had been apprenticed to be a forger before Miss Hilda boxed the ears of the man who bought him from the institution raising him.

"We shall certainly put your talents to good use. You'll come with me and help me make sketches of this man who can't seem to figure out who he is or what he's really doing in Cleveland."

Harrison hadn't yet budged from his observation post by the front door. Three of Hilda's boys who had left by one of the back entrances circled around behind him and kept watch. He either didn't notice when Ess and Riley left through the delivery entrance, half-hidden behind a wagon of supplies, or he dismissed them as inconsequential. She was almost disappointed when they made it to Superior Avenue with no one paying them any attention. The guard in the lobby did give them a second and then a third look, but didn't stop them when they stepped into the nearest lift.

The door was about to close when Ess heard a semi-familiar voice calling for them to hold the lift. She hit the button that stopped the doors closing, and a moment later Mr. Wallace, the law firm's special investigator, hurried across the lobby. He turned sideways to hurtle through the half-closed doors and nodded to her with a grin.

"Much obliged. Third floor, if you don't mind?" He grinned at Riley, who pressed the floor button, then his smile twitched as he met Ess's eyes.

She fought not to laugh, nodded to him, then tugged her cap lower on her forehead. Wallace looked away, his frown deepening. Then he inhaled and turned back to her.

"Miss Fremont." He tipped his hat to her.

Ess burst out laughing. She was tremendously impressed. Mr. Wallace had most certainly proved his powers of observation. She introduced him to Riley, just before the lift door opened. Wallace held out his hand to shake the boy's, then hurried ahead of them to open the office door. He bowed low. Ess resisted the urge to curtsey and sweep past him as if she wore the skirts she had when she left the hotel three hours ago. Then she saw Mr. Peterkin, the secretary, standing up as if expecting someone important. His dignified smile of welcome faltered.

"Mr. Peterkin, how nice to see you again." Ess swept off her cap and let her hair fall down.

To his credit, Mr. Peterkin immediately smiled and held out a hand to her in welcome. He announced he would fetch "them," and hurried down the longest hallway while Wallace ushered Ess and Riley to his office. Before they could do more than spread the art kit out on the low table, the office door burst open and Uly darted in. He barked laughter and caught Ess up for a tight hug.

"Up to your old tricks, I see," he said, setting her down with a thud. "Ah, and corrupting young Mr. Riley. Boyo, didn't I warn you about my audacious troublemaker of a sister?"

Riley just grinned and settled more comfortably in his armchair.

MacDonald and Endicott were both in Cleveland and expected Lewis in a few days. He had reported success in finding the elusive Harriet Angelotti. Neither of the other two partners were in the office, out dealing with either clients or the detractors who insisted on raising new, useless objections to the tower project. Ess and Uly settled down to talk after Wallace notified Peterkin to send the partners to his office the minute they returned.

Ess related her previous encounter with Harrison, then today's encounter. She was quite gratified by the muted growl from her brother. Before he could insist, she suggested he accompany her to the unavoidable dinner meeting with Harrison. When she related what Hilda and Caroline both reported of the man's multiple names, Wallace stepped down the hall to summon Peterkin. The office secretary only had to glance once at the sketch Ess had made. He confirmed that Harrison had come to the office under another name, and he had also noticed the man loitering around town, dressed in different clothes, looking like a rich man, a city official, and a day laborer, at different times.

"What does he want?" Uly muttered.

"With all the uproar in California last year, my suspicious mind says he's one of the rats who have been driven out of the walls and are looking for a new home," Wallace said.

"I pray not." He shuddered and reached over to catch hold of Ess's hand. "He addressed you by the false name you were using when you first met him. Does that mean he doesn't know who you are? Or he does know who you are and he's playing games with you? But how could he know you were coming here?" He thumped the arm of his chair.

"It could be very bad timing, an unlucky coincidence," Ess offered.

"If it is coincidence..." Wallace slouched a little in his chair and gnawed on his bottom lip. "We could test him, but it might be too big of a risk. Especially if he's a good actor."

"How? With—Oh."

"Oh, what?" Uly demanded, his hand tightening on hers.

"When we meet him for dinner, we tell him who we really are. Depending on his reaction, or lack of reaction, we should have a better idea of who or what he is. Perhaps have a better idea of his purpose."

Uly wanted to refuse. That much was clear on his face, but he saw the necessity of taking such a risk. She and Uly and Wallace caught up on what each other had been doing, the progress on the building project. While they talked, she and Riley made copies of the sketch of Harrison, or whatever his real name might turn out to be. Wallace wanted everyone in the law firm to have a copy, so they could be on the lookout for the man. He also wanted copies for his fellow investigators throughout the city, in case Harrison was in Cleveland for nefarious purposes other than harming Originators.

~~~~~

Next, Carmen had a general tour of the levels of the anthill, as Brogan called it. She learned most of the tunnels were natural, carved out by water erosion and added to over the centuries by the Native Americans who had lived on the shores of Lake Erie and the Cuyahoga River. Some of the workmen who came belowground for dinner, bringing groceries, clothes, dishes, and other useful items they had rescued from the trash bins of the prosperous, gathered around Carmen and the children to welcome them and tell them stories about their new home. McTeague promised to take the boys down to a cavern below the water level of the lake. The community's water supply rose up through the rock there, purified by the filtering action. Carvings and paintings by Indian shamans covered the walls.

"Not all the tunnels were used by the Indians, though," McTeague added, when the boys had expressed eagerness for the adventure. "Don't know how they got here, or," he lowered his voice and hunched his shoulders, as if fearing disapproving ears, "or if they were formed by something unnatural. If you know what I mean."

Carmen repressed a shudder. A glance at all her charges showed they were more fascinated than frightened. The girls were nowhere within earshot. Beatrice and Darla were prone to nightmares. Carmen gave McTeague a questioning look. He winked at her and kept on talking.

"Back when we were first exploring—fell into this place by accident, you might say—some of the digging and exploding aboveground pushed things awry down here. We were exploring, and lo and behold, a solid rock wall we saw on Tuesday was just a pile of rubble on Thursday, and we could feel a chilly, sour-smelling breath of air flowing over the top of the pile. Took us some digging, but those were lean days, with nothing to do with our free time but explore. And hide from those up above who didn't take kindly to honest men with idle hands. If you know what I mean."

He winked again at Carmen. She fought not to laugh at his audacity. The man all but admitted he and his friends were vagrants and thieves. She was relieved to deduce that he had mended his ways and worked above ground at honest, paying work. It occurred to her that the honest paying work obviously didn't pay enough for a room somewhere.

Or was he one of those who worked above to provide for the many who sheltered here underground? Thanks to Mary, she had a general idea of how this community functioned. Despite all they managed to do with the refuse of the city, food scavenged from the backs of groceries, docks, and depots, discarded clothes, dishes, and furniture from more affluent neighborhoods, some things had to be provided with money. McTeague and his friends did that. She admired them.

She wondered how much she would have to do to counteract the influence they were having over the boys now under her care. It was obvious from the admiration in all the boys' eyes that they thought a life on the streets, taking and sneaking, was a glorious adventure.

Such a life might seem so, with a safe, hidden nest to retreat to when the authorities were close on their heels. What about those who stole to live, and had nowhere to hide?

Lord, put the right words in my mouth. Show me early, rather than late, if this is the right place for us to stay. Are we indulging in the riches of Egypt for the sake of food and clothes, and endangering our souls?

"And what do you think we saw when we hauled away enough of the rubble to see into the next room?" McTeague continued. The boys shook their heads. "Tunnels. More tunnels. Smooth as if they'd been drilled and then rubbed with a giant's sandpaper. Curving around and around and down." He nodded for punctuation and sat back against the wall behind his bench, crossing his arms.

"Take us to see it?" Andrew begged.

"One of these days, you bet. But it's not entirely safe. Slippery sometimes. It's under the water level. Erie keeps trying to slip into those tunnels and take over what the stone kept her out of for centuries."

"But you do go down there?" Arthur said.

"Got to. Got some mighty fine veins of salt down there, and salt sells good. We dig it and haul it out in buckets, and then we take it to some friends of ours who purify it and sell it for us." He winked at Carmen. "An honest day's wages for an honest day's work."

Perhaps she had fallen from her high standards, but Carmen found she liked him for his slight mockery of the things she had always considered right and proper and admirable. This was a different world she had entered. She would be an ill-mannered guest to criticize what did not suit her standards before learning why things were the way they were.

~~~~~

Endicott came in late in the afternoon, when they had given their notes to Peterkin to have copies made. Ess ached a little, when she saw how much he had aged in the months since she had last seen him. The relief of having his secret life revealed hadn't been as much benefit as she had hoped. Perhaps she could blame the extra duties resting on him, the tripled workload, since to all intents and purposes, Endicott, Lewis and MacDonald had become the clearinghouse for all communication as the Originators purged and strengthened their ranks. When he asked about her progress in finding Anna's daughter, she hesitated to add to his concerns. She told them what Agent Sutter had found out.

"You said Mackenzie?" For a moment, Endicott seemed to choke. "Can you do a sketch of her?" He got up and stepped out of the room before Ess could respond.

She pulled out the sketchpad, which had been greatly depleted thanks to her and Riley working for several hours on sketches of Harrison. After all this time, doing so many sketches of Carmen from her dreams, it was easy to create a likeness of the elusive young woman with a minimum of strokes. By the time Endicott stepped back into the room with Mr. Peterkin, she had enough of an image sketched out to be identifiable. Ess got a shiver up her back and scalp when Endicott signaled them all to silence, and then gestured for her to complete the sketch. She whisked some color across the pencil sketch, approximating Carmen's hair and eye color. When she finished, she turned it around, and watched Mr. Peterkin.

"Yes, sir. That's the young lady. Miss Mackenzie. She comes in every two or three days, asking to see Mr. Lewis," the secretary said. "I've offered many times for her to talk to you or Mr. MacDonald, but she implied that she had been instructed to only trust Mr. Lewis."

"Do you know where she's staying?" Ess asked, fighting the urge to leap up and shake the man by his muttonchop whiskers.

"I know where she *was* staying, miss." He shook his head. "She let slip the name of her hotel, but it had a fire on Sunday night. I sent one of Miss Hilda's boys over to check, thinking that Mr. Lewis would want me to offer her assistance, and to all intents and purposes, she has disappeared."

"But she is in Cleveland," Ess whispered. She clasped the crystal rose between two fingers, where it was hidden inside the collar of her shirt. "How long has she been in town?"

"Several weeks. I'm sorry, miss. I should have made the connection."

"How could you? I didn't even know her last name until a short while ago." Ess put the sketch down on the table and rubbed at her temples. She didn't much care that her fingers were dirty from the colored chalks. "I have had an impression of... there is a sense of an attempted communication, but someone or something is interfering between us."

"If your link is through Mother's crystal rose, and her mother's crystal rose," Uly said, "could more crystal interfere? Like trying to draw a picture in iron filings, using magnet rods, like Grandfather used to have us do, remember? When a second and third magnet rod were introduced, it made an unholy mess, although it was fascinating seeing the lines of force being drawn by the filings."

"Perhaps a large quantity of crystal lying somewhere between us? Maybe now that I am here in Cleveland, we won't have that interference."

"Perhaps," Endicott said.

"What does that mean?" Uly said with a chuckle.

"There are some things you need to learn about Cleveland, and part of the reason why I insisted on building the tower in that specific spot, despite the resistance we encountered. Later," he said, raising a hand to halt their impending burst of questions. "When we've dealt with this spy. Where I need to take you, the people you need to meet, it's best to wait until there is no chance of enemies following us."

"That delicate and dangerous?" Ess murmured.

"More."

After dinner, Carmen gathered the children together in their new schoolroom to show them where they would spend several hours every day. The girls were more interested than the boys, though several boys were delighted with the books that someone had brought down in the meantime. Carmen only glanced over a few of the mangled spines and covers and decided to return before lessons and rid out the ones not quite suitable for children of their age. There were some classics in the pile, and she wondered at the rich people who could throw out such treasures of literature and education, just because they weren't "pretty" or presentable anymore. She would make regular trips to the library a part of the children's schooling. Mrs. Sullivan would be a big help, perhaps able to provide them with books too damaged for the library to put on the shelves any longer. She would be glad to let the friendly woman know they were all right now. If she could teach the children where to find the means to expand their horizons and fill their minds with learning, then they would be less prone to resort to thievery and their fists and other disreputable means to earn a living.

Just because I've fallen so far doesn't mean that the things my parents taught me to value are a sham, or useless, she decided, as she herded the children down the slightly familiar tunnels, to deposit them in their new quarters and make sure they washed up and went to sleep. *Civilization isn't all trappings and rules and social ladders. It's manners and common courtesy and common sense. Cleanliness, generosity, sharing, and protecting the weak and—*

She shook herself out of that mood before the ache in her chest turned into tears. She scolded herself for being so weak that she missed those days of comfort and gentility and admiration. When she could walk into a room and people knew whose daughter she was. When they listened to her thoughts and concerns. Carmen was proud that she had used her influence to do good for others, but wasn't that type of pride a sin just the same?

God had put her here to take care of these children, and perhaps to teach her something vital for her soul's welfare. It was time she put aside her longings for the past and got on with her life in the present.

Chapter Eighteen

"My granny used to sing me to sleep," Ellie whispered, when Carmen brushed her hair to braid it before she climbed into bed. "Mouse says you sing like an angel. Would you sing to me?"

The other girls paused in their preparations, and Carmen felt as if the underground warren held its breath and listened for her response. Ridiculous, she knew, but there it was all the same. She let out a gasping chuckle, when she realized *she* held her breath, not everyone around her.

"I don't know," she said, and forced her hands to move, to give her brain something to latch onto. She separated the little girl's fine, long hair into three sections. "It's been so long since I've sung."

"You sung to me," Mouse announced from behind her.

Carmen swung around, nearly falling off her perch on the edge of Ellie's bed. The other girl giggled and danced back a step.

"Where did you come from?" Carmen said. If Mouse announced that she had come up through the solid rock floor of the room, she might just believe her. She decided not to scold her for not being with the others on their trek to the schoolroom and back. She had already gathered that the rules for Mouse were slightly different from everyone else's.

"Around." Mouse shrugged and trudged over to the bunk closest to the door. She toed off her ragged shoes and grasped the post at the foot of the bunk, and in a blink of an eye flung herself upward into the top bunk. Grinning, she lay on her back, head hanging over the edge, looking at Carmen from upside down. "You sung my leg un-broken."

"Sang. And no, I didn't. I prayed for your leg, and it wasn't broken. It just felt like it." Carmen shivered, remembering that thrill of energy and sense of divine presence when she held the injured girl. What she wouldn't give to know that assurance again, of being a tool in the hands of God.

Yet... what was so hard about letting go and making herself empty so what moved through her was of Heaven, rather than of Earth?

Everything, she responded deep in her soul. Everything was hard, lately.

"*We were created to be aqueducts of the healing water of Heaven,*" her father had said. "*By necessity, aqueducts must be empty, and allow other forces to fill them and empty them and direct the flow. They cannot act on their own, or they will break and leak and become useless.*"

"Use me, precious Savior," she whispered. "I haven't sung in a very long time. Real singing," she amended when Mouse smirked. "But perhaps it is time to try again. Shall we have a lullaby?"

"Lullabies are for babies," Myrtle said with a snort. She clambered up into her bunk, taking twice as long and with half the grace of Mouse. She was the oldest girl, maybe fourteen. Carmen had wondered why she wasn't working in one of the factories along the river, why she didn't have a job as a seamstress's assistant or as a shop girl or laundress. Perhaps she hid here against pressure to earn a living on her back. She was pretty enough, there had to be considerable pressure to do so. For all Carmen knew, the girl was hiding from people who wouldn't take no for an answer.

"I think it is very comforting to be someone's baby," Carmen retorted, softening her words with a smile. To her relief, the girl smiled back at her. "Very well. Something not for babies." She nodded and turned back to working on Ellie's hair while she thought. "Do you know the song of the turtledove?" she asked after a few moments. The girls were all in their beds now, and everyone shook their heads. "Very well."

She lifted the blanket so Ellie could climb under it and tucked it around her. Carmen stood, took a few deep breaths, straightened her shoulders and posture, and poised herself as if singing for a vast congregation. Her father had taught her to do her very best, no matter the audience. Whether for kings or wildflowers or these ragged girls now in her charge, they deserved her most polished performance, even if it was only an old folk song rather than something by one of the masters.

It surprised her almost speechless when she opened her mouth and smooth, sweet, pure notes spilled out, almost without effort.

Fare thee well my dear, I must be gone
And leave you for a while.
But though I go, I'll come back again,
Though I roam ten thousand miles, my dear.
Though I roam ten thousand miles.

She slid through the other verses, while her voice shimmered back to her from the rough stone walls of the chamber, and even outside in the passageway. Tears filled her eyes, but they didn't scald and they didn't spill down her cheeks.

In the pause between verses, a footstep scraped on the stone outside the doorway of the girls' room. Carmen's voice caught for just a second and she turned to the black blot beyond the spill of candlelight. Who was there? Why didn't he or she come in?

Nonsense, she scolded herself as the last verse faded into the air. There were many people here in this community Brogan had created. Someone was merely checking on the children. They couldn't all be as trusting as the people she had met today, blithely handing the care of these children over to someone who had only joined them today. It only made sense that people would stop and listen and judge if she was a good guardian. She would do the same if their positions were reversed.

A sigh echoed in the passageway. A man's voice. Carmen shivered, sensing pain. Somewhere in there was an emptiness that made her knees go weak.

"Teach me to sing like that," Darla squealed, and sat up in her new bunk, clapping.

The chorus of claps and other exclamations from the girls drove away the sense of a presence in the passageway, and the feeling as if someone had emptied her chest and stolen her breath. Carmen laughed and made the rounds of the room, tucking in blankets, promising to give singing lessons in the afternoon, stroking little heads.

She remembered that sigh, that feeling of being watched, of something tugging at her soul, as she picked up her candle and stepped out into the passageway to go to her own room.

"Savior, like a shepherd lead us," she sang under her breath, and willed the shadows away from before her.

The song wilted on her tongue and her steps slowed. In the quiet and chill and shadows, the doubts that had clung to the edges of her mind like road dust suddenly weighed on her. After all the disappointments of the last few weeks, the disillusionment and betrayals of the long, bitter months before her father's death, how could she accept so easily what these strangers offered? How could she trust them? Was she that hungry for shelter and a resting place, and someone to share the burden of the children?

This underground world Brogan offered was too good to be true in some aspects. People who shared, who took care of each other, who cared, who appreciated what others could give, and especially people who valued children and wanted to shelter them. She had been searching for such a place far longer than a few months.

Yet how could she so blithely take these people at their words, that all was well? Even if this underground shelter was all its inhabitants claimed it to be, how could she consent to live here for months, years, perhaps the rest of her life?

Carmen stopped short, the candleholder bobbing in her grip. The rest of her life?

Yes, she could easily envision staying here, caring for more children over the years as they were rescued from the street. Teaching them, guiding them, feeding and clothing them, singing little girls to sleep, watching them go out into the world above and make their way and find their places.

Yet, how could she commit to living underground, in the cool and damp and shadows, away from sunshine and stars and moonlight and the touch of the wind? Even for the sake of the children.

"Lord," she whispered, barely able to hear herself speak. "Please, what should I do? What work do You have for me now? I believe You gave me the children to care for, but is this the right place to raise them?"

Carmen waited, but nothing stirred in the darkness beyond the soft, flickering pool of candlelight.

Or did it?

She shivered, sensing... something. A presence.

Ahead of her in the curving rock passageway, or behind?

"The crow that's black, my little turtledove," she whisper-sang, and took a step. "Shall change its color white, before I am false to the one that I love." The next few steps came a little easier. She refused to run.

"And the noonday shall be night, my dear," a rich baritone voice declared in soft shimmers of sound from behind her.

"The noonday shall be night," she sang without thought. The voice shifted to harmony, matching her perfectly.

Carmen's heart tripled its pace, and yet she wasn't afraid. She couldn't be quite sure what she felt. Stunned? Intrigued? Excited?

She kept walking.

"Oh yonder doth sit the little turtledove," the baritone sang behind her after a few seconds when she couldn't decide if she should continue or stop and confront the singer. Was he following? She couldn't tell from the echoes and ripples of sound in the passageway.

"He doth sit on yonder high tree," she sang, after two seconds of silence, when her heart jolted and she realized this was her part in the duet she hadn't really agreed to. Or had she?

"A-making a moan for the loss of his love," they sang in unison. His voice vibrated in her cheekbones, and it took all she had not to turn around and look for him just a step behind her.

"As I shall do for thee, my dear," she sang, and her voice caught when she heard only her voice. "As I," she pressed on.

"Shall do for thee," he declaimed, suddenly far down the passageway, dropping into descant.

Carmen reached out her hand to brace against the wall, ready to turn around. And do what? Call for him to come back? She touched wood. Stunned, she looked, and recognized the markings for the room she shared with Mary. Shivering, wrapping her shawl a little tighter around her shoulders, Carmen pressed on the latch, paused to glance down the dark passageway, then went inside.

Mary hadn't come to the room yet, and she was grateful for the solitude to think as she washed and changed into her nightgown. The tune to *Turtledove* returned, bubbling up in her throat until she couldn't resist humming it while she brushed out her hair.

Who had sung with her? What man, among those living underground, reduced to this threadbare yet giving community, had a voice like that? She thought of some of the song leaders of her former acquaintance, who would have spent hours, days on their knees in weeping prayer, asking God to give them such a strong, rich, yet gentle voice. It was a gift from God, and begged the question: why was it down here, in the damp and shadows?

Her thoughts shifted to Brogan. He talked like an educated man, perhaps with the training to know such an old song as *Turtledove*. He talked like a man who had been scorched and betrayed. Perhaps he suffered, paying for some horrendous sin that cast him down from the pinnacle of society, into this place where he was leader and father figure?

She sensed he was like other men she had met, picking at their wounds, mourning the loss of their faith that was once so precious to them, and yet unwilling or even afraid to try again, to take the risk.

In that moment, she decided her choice had been made, her questions answered. At least, answered in part.

She would stay. First for the children, but then for the owner of the beautiful voice. Healing had come through her voice, by God's grace, before this. Perhaps God had sent her here, to this place and this man, to bring healing in new and different ways?

Only time would tell.

A man with a voice like that could only be complete, fulfilled as a tool and vessel of the Almighty. If she weren't reacting like a silly star-struck child, letting her imagination run away with her, and the singer was indeed Brogan, she would repay his kindness by helping him heal and regain the pathway God had chosen for him at birth.

She was still brushing out her hair, humming softly under her breath, when Mary slipped into the room. Carmen felt the soft disturbance in the air and turned, stunned to see the woman's face glistening with tears.

"What's wrong? What happened? The children—"

"The children are fine. Carmen, child, that was you singing before, wasn't it?" Mary sniffed and knuckled away her tears. "It was like an angel descended among us."

"Oh, thank you, but I'm not quite that good."

"Oh, pshaw. Your voice is lovely, yes, but I wasn't talking about..." She sighed and sank down on the bench along the far wall. "We, those of us who have been here since the beginning, we can barely remember hearing Brogan sing."

"I thought it might be him, but I couldn't be sure."

"Ah, yes, it was him, indeed. He used to be full of music, but some great tragedy stole that music. There was only a trickle left when he came here, and he would only sing when he was completely alone, in darkness, in the tunnels. To hear him sing with you." She sighed and wrapped her arms around herself. "Please don't be frightened, but there are some who will never let you leave."

"Is he that greatly feared?" Carmen knew she had misspoken the moment Mary's eyes widened and she sat up straight, as if she had been struck. "Or is he so greatly loved, that people would do anything to please him?" she hurried to say.

"Brogan is a good man who has endured great pain. I don't think anyone here knows the full story, or even the full truth. He could have buried himself in these tunnels, in the darkness, to lick his wounds. Instead, he brought us down here for shelter and healing, sharing his retreat, his hiding place. Yes, he is loved and feared, but it is a good kind of fear."

"So they would keep me prisoner to please him," she murmured.

"Aye, it may seem that way. I hope you won't mind too much. You and the children will be protected and safe, and you'll be part of helping others in the future. It's a good life, however odd it might seem at first."

"My parents would approve. I think that is the deciding factor." She studied her brush a moment, her face warming until she couldn't restrain the words. "Did he—Brogan's voice is so clear and strong. Did he have formal training?"

"You'd think, wouldn't you? I heard that he had music in his soul, and the scars on his heart and soul are far worse than the ones on his face."

Those words stayed with Carmen as she said her prayers and curled up to sleep. A sigh of purely decadent pleasure escaped her. Such luxury: a thick, firm mattress and clean sheets, enjoyed with no guilt because the children were all safe, and sleeping in their own clean beds. Tears prickled in the corners of her eyes, in pure gratitude. She caught the cross with her sleep-loosened fingers and said another prayer of gratitude, for Brogan and the tunnels and Mary and all the new friends she and the children had made today. She had nearly given up; she had wavered on the knife's edge of despair. Behind her prayers lately had been the awful fear that if something did not change soon, she might stop praying.

That hadn't happened. All would be well. Tomorrow, she would go to the law firm again and... Carmen nearly woke up as weary amusement trickled through her. If Mr. Lewis wasn't there, she wouldn't despair. God had provided the safety net she had asked for.

When she dreamed, still clutching her cross, everything was disjointed. The impression of several voices trying to catch her attention was stronger, as if the speakers were closer, yet nothing was any clearer.

Once when she woke, she had to rub at her temples to try to ease an ache building up in her head. She had the oddest sensation that she had been trying to shout and make herself heard by people who were in other rooms, shouting to her. No one would be quiet long enough to hear the others. If her head didn't hurt so much, she might have been amused. She dared to believe—if she weren't quite losing her sanity—that she had announced she was in Cleveland, and she intended to visit her lawyers and go to her hotel to retrieve her trunk in the morning. If anyone could hear her, they were welcome to wait for her at either location.

She couldn't remember if she had given the names of either the lawyers or the hotel.

"I am most definitely losing my mind," Carmen whispered, when she woke and blinked the sleep haze from her eyes to focus on the dim glow of the shielded lantern in the doorway.

Mary's soft breathing in the next bunk was a comforting sound. Odd, how she knew exactly where she was when she woke. Not like the last few nights of waking in confusion and discomfort. Carmen prayed silently and curled up to go back to sleep.

When she woke again, she heard a man's voice, soft and rumbling in the passageway, and Mary responding. Carmen sat up, welcoming the chill of the stone room, bracing and a bit of a shock as she emerged from the warmth of her blankets.

"Ah, good," Mary said, turning from the door. "The boys mentioned you left a trunk at your hotel, and McTeague offered to go take you to fetch it, but you have to hurry, to get back before his shift starts. Do you mind?"

"Oh, no, that's wonderful. Thank you." She stood up and reached for her dress hanging on the rod strung across the end of the room.

In short order, she had washed her face and twisted her hair into a sensible bun high on the back of her head and borrowed a bonnet from Mary. McTeague waited around the bend in the passageway. He pointed out the numbers and colored paint splotches at the intersection of tunnels as they made their way to the surface. They emerged in the cellar of a house that had had its upper two stories removed already, so the floorboards and walls of the first floor were all that came between them and the pre-dawn sky. She had expected to emerge at the cave mouth where they had entered Brogan's domain the day before. Her face must have showed it, because McTeague chuckled.

"Nah, that'd add ten minutes of walking to our trip, and while I'm proud o' me muscles, I don't fancy hauling your trunk down those stairs over the water." He patted his biceps and nimbly led the way up the rickety stairs. "Besides, we need this. The lads didn't say how big the trunk was, and I'm not too proud to ask for help."

He stepped aside at the top of the stairs to reveal a small handcart waiting tucked up inside the wall, where the door used to be. It had one wheel in front, an upright board to keep items from sliding off the front when it tilted, several planks creating a surface maybe two feet by three feet, long handles, and two braces to keep the surface flat when it wasn't being pushed.

"I appreciate this so very much," Carmen said, as they set off down the street. "Getting up early and taking time out of your morning before going to your job."

"Don't think nothin' of it, miss. It's my turn to fetch the morning bread, so I'd be out anyway. Does my heart good, seeing how much the boys think of you. That's the problem with the world nowadays. Boys don't have a mother to think about pleasing and to look after. How can they learn to be gentlemen otherwise?"

"That is... quite wise."

They walked in companionable silence for several blocks, while Carmen tried to decipher what felt different about the neighborhood from the last few journeys through it. She nearly laughed aloud when it struck her that the difference came from the lack of the children. She could pay more attention to her surroundings because she didn't have to keep checking that one of them hadn't wandered off or fallen behind. She no longer feared that someone would snatch one of the children away from her or accuse her of kidnapping. Until now, she hadn't really had the luxury of simply looking at her surroundings for the sake of seeing them. Before, everything had been filtered through the need to protect the children.

The front desk clerk who had given her so much trouble wasn't on duty when Carmen arrived at the hotel. The helpful bellhop was, however, and she didn't even have to produce her claim ticket before he hurried up to greet her. He led her and McTeague around the hotel to the back entrance, where they had easier access to the luggage storage room. From the back, the signs of fire damage and the beginnings of repairs were more visible, and Carmen shivered a little at how close she and the children had come to disaster. She waited outside to guard the handcart while McTeague and the bellhop took the stairs down to bring up the trunk. The two men were talking about the fire and the man who started it as they came up again. She thanked the bellhop and was grateful to have a coin to spare, to tip him. Then they were on their way again. McTeague teased her that the trunk was so light, he could have carried it on one shoulder. Was she sure she had the right trunk?

They stopped at three bakeries to pick up bread that hadn't sold the day before, set aside by folk who were friends of those living in the tunnels. Carmen stayed outside on the street with the trunk and cart while McTeague went in back entrances. The smell of the day's fresh baking filled the air, wrapping her in comfortable warmth against the chill and gloom of dawn. At the second stop, a different chill wrapped around her.

Chapter Nineteen

Carmen couldn't discern the reason for that feeling and tried hard not to be too obvious as she looked in all directions. She could only describe it as the distinct feeling that someone was watching her far too intently for any innocent reason. She had experienced that feeling far too many times when she led the singing at camp meetings. Every time, someone had approached her afterward. Either they wanted to take her away to fame and fortune on the stage—her fame and his fortune—or they had more salacious reasons in mind. She had learned to listen to that feeling, that warning, and ensure she was never alone until the camp meeting team had left that particular town or city.

When she and McTeague stopped at the third bakery, she was grateful that the back door stayed open. Carmen stepped up onto the back step, putting the cart between her and anyone who might try to approach. She prayed she wouldn't have to call for help, or worse, make a problem for McTeague by running into the bakery. He hadn't said in so many words, but she understood that if the baker himself wasn't handing him the unsold bread, then likely the clerk might be in trouble for giving it away.

"Darling?" The rich tenor voice sounded ready to crack from surprise. "It is you, isn't it?" The speaker stepped from the shadows cast by the building next door, into the puddle of sunlight on the side entrance of the bakery. Richard Boniface spread his arms as if he would embrace her, his face brightening with joy.

Carmen took a step back, onto the threshold of the bakery.

"Thank God I finally found you. It's a miracle." He held out his hands as if he would catch hold of her despite the cart being between them. "Do you have any idea how horrified I was, when I heard about your father? And then you simply vanished? Those vicious old hypocrites kept insisting that they had no idea where you would have gone. I came near to tearing apart headquarters, desperate for one clue. And now here you are."

"Yes. Here I am." She wrapped her arms around herself, chilled by memories blaring in her ears.

Boniface pleading with her to run away with him. Criticizing her father while claiming he admired the man. Painting a picture for her of wedded bliss and a simple life in a little church in a farming community.

She also remembered her father's angry words, his suspicions of Boniface growing from a simple uneasy feeling to outright distrust. She heard again the few arguments she had witnessed between the two men,

Boniface's declarations that he loved her more than her father ever could. His vows to take her away to a better life. Her father's declarations that he couldn't be trusted. For some odd reason, her mother had come up. Hiram had declared that Anna would never give her blessing, and Boniface had retorted that Anna had been a fool. How could he say that when he never knew her?

When he left the team, she had thought she had seen the last of him. Yet now he stood there on the street, glowing with delight, dressed as a common laborer. If she didn't know any better, she would have thought he was on his way to the demolition project.

"What are you doing here?" she said.

She wanted to ask why he wasn't in the quaint little white clapboard country church in Kansas he had promised her. Why he was in such rough clothes when he had always been impeccably dressed.

"If I say I have been tearing the country apart, city by city, searching for you, will that earn me a kiss?" He stepped closer, banging his knee against the cart. His frown of consternation might have been amusing, but Carmen sensed the move was calculated, perhaps to charm her.

"Certainly not. I never let you kiss me when we were courting."

"But you are my betrothed. Certainly that grants me some liberties."

"I never agreed—"

"You were about to defy your father and elope with me."

"That was entirely in your imagination."

"But my love, our hearts spoke clearly to each other." He reached for her hand. She stepped further into the bakery doorway. His expression of dismay struck her as calculated. As if he were a player on a stage.

"Miss? You all right?" McTeague stepped up and rested a hand on her shoulder. His other hand clutched a canvas sack, twice the size of the other sacks of bread already resting on the cart.

"I'm fine, thank you. We're running late, aren't we?" She held out her hands for the sack.

McTeague glanced at Boniface, then back to her. One corner of his mouth twitched and he nodded, then slid the sack down from his shoulder. It filled her arms.

"Yes, miss, we're running a little late. Pardon us, mister, but we have a lot of hungry young'uns to feed." He grasped the handles of the cart before Carmen had the new sack firmly settled and turned it to neatly force Boniface to step back.

"Of course. You're working with the destitute. Following your tender heart." Boniface didn't make any attempt to follow them as they headed toward the main street. "You were always a wonder with children. A channel for miracles." His eyes gleamed when she glanced back at him, stung by his choice of words. "I would prefer that you spent your energies and love on our children."

"We have no children, Mr. Boniface. Please excuse us." Carmen turned her back on him and kept up with McTeague. She was grateful for his long strides that forced her to hurry.

"All in good time, my darling. All in good time. I will find you at your mission when you have more time to listen," he called after her as they turned the corner.

"Notice he didn't ask which mission you worked at?" McTeague said, his tone light, after they had gone half a block.

"Notice I didn't correct his false assumption?" She felt immediately better when he chuckled.

"Man must have a powerful strong, stubborn imagination. A blind man could see you weren't happy to see him. And him insisting you felt what you sure didn't."

"I don't dare look behind us, to make sure he isn't following us."

"Don't you worry. Got a couple more bolt holes closer at hand. We can hide your trunk and come back for it later. Kind of hard for a man to follow what he can't see."

"Mr. McTeague, you are my knight in shining armor."

His warm, rumbling chuckles eased away the chill tension that threatened to make her muscles snap. They turned at the next intersection, going opposite of the route they had taken an hour before. She tried not to look, but she saw him glancing back from time to time, taking advantage of their turns. For all she knew, he made those turns to be able to look. They ran down a short, shadowy alley and bumped the cart down a half-flight of steps, through an open door into a cellar. Through another doorway. McTeague closed and barred it behind them. They stood in darkness for a few seconds, until he struck a match and lit an oil lantern, tucked up in the beams perilously close to their heads. A stack of crates hid a rough hole in the bedrock foundation. He had her climb down a ladder and tossed the sacks of bread down to her.

Ten more minutes, and Carmen stepped into the kitchen-cave. She hurried to wash her hands and get to work helping Mary put out breakfast for the residents of the underground community. McTeague snatched a few rolls as soon as they reached the kitchen and hurried off.

Definitely, she wasn't going to risk going above ground to go to the lawyers' office today. She whispered a prayer of thanks that God had brought her into this shelter, with Brogan and his people.

~~~~~

"Something wrong with a man like that, if you ask me," McTeague said, punctuating his words with a sharp nod.

"I trust your judgment implicitly." Brogan turned the undamaged side of his face more into the light, to allow a smile.

McTeague's shoulders drew back and his grim expression brightened, and that voice of disparaging conscience whispered, "Fraud," in Brogan's ear. He hated it when a few words of praise made good, intelligent, hard-working men like McTeague bright with satisfaction. They all looked up to him, depended on him, and refused to show pity or even a flicker of revulsion when he made the mistake of showing the damaged side of his face to the light. Brogan considered them all far better men than he. They didn't hide in shadows and damp tunnels, or fear one more tiny shove would thrust them over the precipice into insanity.

"The boys said she always goes to visit a lawyer's office on Tuesdays and Thursdays," McTeague continued. "Someone she's waiting for to come back to town. They said she was just about in tears the last time, after the fire and taking on three more little'uns."

"Did they say which lawyer?"

"I'll find out."

"Thank you, McTeague. We must protect our Miss Mackenzie at all costs."

"I can ask a couple men to keep an eye on her. Though she seems like a smart one, might notice them following her. Might rile her," he added with a chuckle.

"Yes, I imagine she would notice and be irritated." Brogan sighed and braced himself to stand. Sometimes it seemed he lived in his chair, the center of a growing spider's web of connections and information and gossip. "No, it is my responsibility to express our concern and advise her it might be best to miss today's appointment." He gestured at the door. "I've kept you too long. The foreman is a friend, but it wouldn't do for him to show favoritism, letting you off easy if you're late."

"That it wouldn't." The man tugged on the bill of his cap and turned for the door. He paused with one foot out in the passageway. "Begging your pardon, Boss, but... was that you last night, singing with the miss?"

"Since I didn't feel the foundations of our city crumbling, I will confess."

"Good to hear you singing again. This place needs music. Makes the walls sort of..." McTeague shrugged and stepped through the doorway. "Shiny. Sparkling," he called back, his words punctuated by his boots thumping on the rough stone of the tunnel floor.

"If you only knew," Brogan whispered.

He missed music. It eased the pain in his face, brought warmth to his bones, and somehow made his eyes keener, so he found it easier to walk the tunnels without light. When he first came to this subterranean world, the shelter Endicott had offered him, he had sung often for company, to ease his soul, to seek the healing that his mother claimed came through music. His father had been a guardian of the crystal vaults, and he had spent all his spare time researching the now-indecipherable journals and records of the ancestors. He believed music was the key to understanding, perhaps even communicating with the crystal of the ancestors. Brogan had sung and believed that the crystal embedded in his flesh reacted positively to his music. When the illusions and delusions grew stronger, he had stopped singing.

Until Carmen Mackenzie's voice filled his dark world, both in his dreams and now in reality. Something about her threatened to melt the safeguards he had put around his mind and soul.

How to convince her to trust him, convince her to be willing to spend her days here in shadows and echoes and chill? Like the wild songbirds his parents had brought back from the tropics when he was a child, imprisoning her would first deprive her of her song, and then kill her. Was it arrogance to believe that she would retain her song if she had someone to sing with her?

Brogan kept busy with all the comforting details of administrating the underground community, conferring with Mary and others in charge of their stores. He studied the newspapers sent down by their friends, read scribbled reports on the political maneuvering up top, and found pleasure and satisfaction in mending some of the ripped and waterlogged and otherwise damaged books that the gleaners saved from waste barrels and refuse heaps. He called himself a dozen names for fool as he finished repairs on a book of poetry, sewing up a gash in the fine lavender and gold brocade cover, and anticipating the words to use to present it to Carmen. Shakespeare was a safe poet to create the first bridge of friendship. He knew better than to risk giving her a volume of florid love sonnets.

Finally he had dealt with every task necessary, and still no one brought him word of Carmen preparing to go above. She had asked if someone was going near the library, and if so, could they take a note from her to the head librarian? Then she had settled down for a morning of lessons with the children. Not a word of needing to go above and visit the lawyer. Brogan was pleased that she had the sense to stay hidden while her erstwhile suitor could be roaming the streets overhead, and irked with the man for frightening her as he had. Carmen Mackenzie was a creature of the daylight. Of light, period. Frightening her enough to stay in the shadows was a crime.

The midday meal neared, and certainly she would set the children free from their books soon. Mary had explained the routine to her. The children all had chores to contribute to their community, and they needed some time to play. Brogan had insisted that the children have a chance to play. Soon, she would be free.

He had a vague plan in mind, and an even vaguer idea of the words to say, as he approached the schoolroom.

Laughter rang out to meet him as he made the final turn in the tunnel. Something caught in his chest, as understanding crystalized. He was here to ensure the children could laugh. He was here to provide them shelter and food and protection, and the freedom to laugh. Carmen would give them a chance to expand their minds and learn the skills necessary to climb as high as they dared to dream.

That catching sensation deepened and moved up to the ruined side of his face. Brogan focused on the tingling, buzzing, humming feeling, trying to calm the sensation that hadn't been so strong since the rescuers pulled him from the wreckage of the vault, with the fragments of crystal embedded in the bones of his shattered face.

There was more crystal in his domain, within ten paces of him.

He hadn't felt it this strong when he talked with her yesterday, and he had come close to offering some other plan than having her stay here with the children. Then they had sung together in the darkness, and he feared he could never let her leave. In her song, he felt the pure, sweet, subliminal vibrations of crystal. He had envisioned her as a maiden of the purest crystal, catching and holding and radiating light. This was proof that Mouse hadn't been exaggerating what she described to him, and he hadn't made a foolish mistake, hadn't imagined what he sensed before. Who was Carmen Mackenzie? How could she carry crystal and not be an Originator?

Or had Carmen lied about her background?

A more tricky question: Did she not know her background?

If not, then how did crystal come into her possession?

The sensation grew stronger as he approached the doorway of the classroom. Brogan pressed his palm flat against his vibrating flesh, trying to calculate by the intensity when he would reach that point when the resonance of the crystal in his bone, reacting to the crystal in that room with Carmen, turned from vibration to warmth.

Brogan looked in through the half-open doorway. Carmen was nearly on the other side of the long room. The crystal radiated more energy than he had anticipated. Judging from the resonance strength, it had to be a rod at least two feet long and half a foot in diameter. Where could it be hidden? All Mouse had seen was her necklace, so what form did the rest of the crystal take?

Ringing silence jolted him from his thoughts. Brogan blinked and nearly took his hand down from his face, as he realized every little face had turned to face the doorway.

"Can I help you, Mr. Brogan?" Carmen said, stepping forward and clasping her hands at her waist. She smiled.

There was more fire to Carmen Mackenzie than her hair indicated. She was polite, she didn't like being interrupted, and most important, he didn't frighten her.

"I beg your pardon, Miss Mackenzie. I didn't mean to interrupt. I was drawn by the sounds of children enjoying their lessons. Very pleasant indeed." Brogan took two more steps back into the masking shadows of the passageway, those tight wires drawing up inside him in response to the wide eyes and curious frowns of the children. Those who had never seen him close up, those who had only heard him speak from the shadows.

"You didn't really interrupt. I was just about to release the children. We were discussing the prospect of an outing to the library, and what kinds of stories the children were interested in reading. Or having others read to them." She stepped back and spread her arms. "You are dismissed."

Brogan stepped to the right, keeping the ruined side of his face to the wall as the children scrambled up from their benches and spilled through the door. Mouse grinned cheekily at him, while the others seemed to have forgotten his presence.

"Can I help you?" Carmen wrapped a gray-blue knit shawl around herself and stepped to the doorway.

"I wanted to make sure you were all right after your unpleasant encounter this morning."

Despite the dim lighting, Carmen's blush was clear. He liked that about her.

"I assure you, Mr. Brogan, I am in no danger of reneging on our agreement. The... the person who Mr. McTeague and I encountered this morning was a former associate of my father. I could be considered the perfect minister's wife, trained to the life, and he decided we should marry. My father refused to approve, and perhaps that made him more determined. He insisted we were in love, though I most certainly was not. Obviously, he still labors under his delusion."

Brogan had to laugh. Carmen's mouth flattened and she crossed her arms over her chest. He hoped she fought not to laugh. Otherwise, he would have twice as much work to win her trust and friendship as he had anticipated just half an hour ago.

"Forgive me, Miss Mackenzie. I was not mocking the idea that a man..." He shook his head and took a deep breath to gain a reprieve. Had he actually started to babble? "Well, it is quite understandable that you would be pursued. The flaw is in him for not taking you at your word. Or perhaps blame his mother, for not teaching him that yes, women do know their own minds."

A tiny snort escaped her and one corner of her mouth twitched. The relief he felt nearly drove his mission of discovery from his mind.

"While the children are having their lunch, could I interest you in a guided tour? Perhaps answer any questions you might have about our community. Well," he amended immediately, "some of your questions. While I am the nominal mayor of this twilight village, I cannot claim to know everything."

"Mr. Brogan, you are a man of many interesting layers, not the least of which is quite believable humility."

"I hope we can be friends as well as fellow laborers, Miss Mackenzie. Partnership and friendship are always strongest when laid on a foundation of honesty." He made a half-bow, gesturing back the way he had come.

Oddly, he had a strong desire to offer her his arm. That would have to wait until later. Carmen smiled a little more, then reached back to take a lantern from the shelf next to the door. Either by chance or through tact, she held it in her right hand and walked on his right side, leaving the ruined side of his face in darkness.

"Which would you prefer? To learn the crossroads and escape routes close at hand, or go to the furthest extent of our kingdom and work our way back to the inhabited areas?"

"Tempting. To adventure a little," she added quickly. "Mr. McTeague was telling the boys about digging for salt and finding tunnels that filled with water and then emptied, and a chamber full of crystals inside." She reached up to touch the closure of her collar.

In the shifting light and shadows as the lantern bobbed with the movement of her strides, he saw something sparkle under her collar.

"Indulge my curiosity? Do you have some jewelry?"

"Yes, and thank you for bringing up the subject." She slipped two fingers inside her collar and brought out a silver chain. "I wanted to ask who was best to handle selling something for me, to contribute to the community's resources. You will think me rather foolish, not selling it earlier, to provide for the children, but everything has happened rather quickly."

"That?" Brogan flinched at the feel of his hand pressing against his ruined cheek. He hadn't been conscious of reaching up to touch it. All his attention focused on the shimmer and hint of rainbows in the depths of the crystalline rose resting on two fingertips. "Pardon me, but—"

"Oh, no, not this. This is all I have left of my mother. No, my father had a silver cross fashioned for her, and this rose went into the center of it. He knew how much she treasured it, and the cross was to protect it, making it a little heavier, larger, harder to lose. If the chain had broken she would have felt the cross falling, while she wouldn't have felt the rose sliding away." She frowned down at the flawless sculpture. "Then again, maybe she might have. I am learning so many things lately..."

Chapter Twenty

Carmen sighed and shook her head. "I tried to sell the cross the other day, and the jeweler essentially accused me of theft."

"He should be horsewhipped." He felt as if he could breathe again when a tiny bubble of laughter escaped her. "Most certainly, you shouldn't sell that keepsake of your mother's. What does her family say about it?"

"I don't know who her family is. She came from nowhere and dedicated her life to ministry. I only by chance met a friend of hers, and even she couldn't or wouldn't tell me of her background. Only that she was fleeing danger, and that somewhere out there is a woman with a twin to this rose, and she and my mother were best friends. She was her lifeline. If I find her, perhaps I can find the answers."

"Miss Mackenzie, I promise you, we shall do all we can to someday find those answers." He held out his hand to her, and was delighted when her slim, strong fingers slid easily into his grasp without hesitation.

The shimmer of crystal raced from the place where their palms met, up his arm, to settle into his cheek. He thought he heard the echoes of chimes, just for a moment, and blinked against a momentary soft flash of light.

Did Carmen stare at their joined hands? Did she look as dazed as he momentarily felt? Before he could think of what to say or how to react, she slipped her hand free of his. It trembled, just for a moment, as she reached up to wipe loose strands of hair back into place.

She felt it.

Did he dare test her just a little more?

"This way, I think. We'll try to draw you a complete picture in your mind, linking all the routes you've taken so far. Then I propose we take a walk every day, exploring a little further."

"If that won't waste too much of your time." She smiled easily. Did he dare hope that was eagerness, or was it just his imagination?

"My mother believed that a daily walk, several daily walks, actually, were essential to good health. You will also be assisting me in keeping track of any new tunnels our more adventurous residents have been creating and neglecting to add to the official records."

That amused her, and he was glad.

As they walked down the nearest tunnel, he almost hoped she wouldn't see the film of light and the doorway to the sunlit hillside. There was something vaguely proprietary about the delusion of wide open spaces within his dark labyrinthine sanctuary. He wanted and yet feared to share it. Perhaps he feared madness lingered here in the darkness, some virus hitherto unknown to science. Could delusions be shared among minds, so the sufferers convinced themselves what they saw and felt and heard was real?

Carmen inhaled just abruptly enough he heard it. He glanced at her, saw a sparkle of something in her eyes, and when he turned to look ahead, he nearly stumbled in wonder.

The shimmer spread out from a small spot in midair, reaching to touch the walls of the tunnel. The crystal warmed and hummed in his cheek.

"Do you see it?" he whispered.

Carmen turned to him, her eyes wide, and he saw the same fear and wonder he always experienced when the light opened before him.

"Is it real?" she said. "The mountainside and the sunlight and the warmth and the smell of ripe apples?"

"Unless we are both mad, Occam's Razor says yes, it must be."

She frowned, the merriment in her eyes making a lie of her expression. "Mr. Brogan, that is a false application of the principle of..." Shaking her head, she chuckled.

"Shall we?" He held out his hand. The shimmer of crystal in his blood leaped as she grasped his hand.

In perfect step, they approached the gateway and went through without hesitation. Carmen didn't tug her hand free as she turned to the right and left, head tilted back, gazing in wonder at the hillside that seemed to stretch downward and upward and to either side forever, to be lost in a distant haze. Brogan thought he had never been so happy, simply watching her amazement.

"Have you—" She frowned at the lantern in the hand she gestured with. A giggle escaped her as she bent to put it down on the thick carpet of moss and a groundcover of deep emerald, round leaves the size of his thumb. Regrettably, he had to let go of her hand when she bent down. "Have you eaten the fruit? From the smell, I would hazard it's near harvest. You do provide for the community from what you can access here?"

"I am ashamed to say that no, I have not dared to eat an apple or pick a handful of berries. You can't imagine the hunger to come here with a good book and a blanket, stretch out and read myself sleepy, and bask in the sunshine."

"Why ever not?"

"Because I had convinced myself all this was an illusion. That I was slowly going mad. I didn't want proof, by bringing something with me and having it vanish as soon as I stepped through. Proof that all this was delusion." He spread his arms to encompass the sprawling landscape, the tangles of apple and pear and peach and cherry trees, the pecan and walnut groves, blackberry and raspberry bramble patches larger than some houses, the streams full of fish for the taking, patches of mint and other herbs. He had explored for an hour in every direction, and his senses had grown drunk on the perfumes, the warmth, the brilliance, but he had never tasted.

"Until this moment, until you," he said, answering the questions in her eyes, "no one has been able to see the gateway opening, much less been able to step through with me."

He wanted to sit down with her and tell her about Endicott helping him hide, finding him a safe place, sending people to him who needed his help, giving him a purpose for living. He wanted to tell her about the fascinating discussions they had had during the winter, trying to determine the source of the crystal resonance he felt, and where he had actually gone when Endicott verified he had vanished. They had enjoyed long talks by firelight in the winter, while storms blew in from the lake and blanketed the city with drifts. Speculations on a device of the ancestors that might be hidden somewhere here, perhaps buried by catastrophe, still functioning, opening a doorway through time at random moments. The problem lay in discerning what time that was, past or future. He supposed they would need the help of geologists and massive research to decipher if the mountainside they stood on now had been in Cleveland's past, or its future. However, telling her all that would require hours of explaining the Originators, the Great Machine, the great mystery and wonder of crystal itself, before he could share the theorizing he and Endicott had done since that fateful night he had stepped out in faith and trusted in friendship.

Yet what kind of faith did he have, that even with some assurance he wasn't imagining all this, he still feared he was going mad? Perhaps Carmen had come here to help him regain his faith?

"I have dared to tell one other person, but even though he confirmed that I vanished from in front of his eyes at this very spot...well," he said with a shrug and an answering chuckle from Carmen, "in the spot where we left the tunnels. Even though I vanished for a few moments, he had no proof that I had actually gone somewhere... real. I had no proof that I hadn't hallucinated all this. Tell me everything you see, everything you hear and smell and feel. Please, I beg you," he said, his voice thickening with an urge to bellow laughter to the skies. "Prove I am not a madman."

Carmen did more than describe the colors and scents, the warmth of the breeze, the cool feel of the moss, the rustling of the gently shifting breeze through the trees. She convinced him to get close and explore the trees, to taste the fruit and bend down to a stream and scoop up handfuls of sweet, pure water to drink. They filled her shawl and his coat with apples, pears, plums, walnuts and pecans. She pointed out the multiple stages of growth on all the trees. Different branches indicated different seasons of the year. One branch was full of flowers, heavy with bees pollinating them. Other branches had tiny green buttons indicating the abundance of fruit in the future. More branches had half-ripe fruit, and others had fully ripe fruit.

"It's like in the book of Revelation," she said, as they bent to tie up their impromptu bags. "The trees growing beside the river of life had twelve harvests throughout the year, fruit to feed mankind and leaves for healing their illnesses."

"I would hardly call that the river of life," Brogan said, gesturing at the stream like a liquid diamond meandering across the meadow. It was less than a foot wide at its widest point.

Carmen wrinkled up her nose at him, then laughed with him. He lost his breath a moment later when it suddenly struck him that he had turned the ruined side of his face to her multiple times over the last hour, and she hadn't shied away in revulsion or asked questions or even stared. A quick brushing of his fingertips over his cheek revealed the bubbled, thick, pitted skin and deadened patches hadn't vanished the moment they stepped onto the mountainside. Was the woman blind?

She laughed and dropped to her knees instead of lifting the shawl now that it was neatly tied. Far more neatly tied than the awkward bundle of his coat, with nuts filling the tubes formed from knotting his cuffs.

"What's wrong?" He gathered up the bundle of his coat against his chest, resisting the urge to toss it aside and scoop her up and check her for some heretofore hidden injury.

"I was just about to say, we should be heading back, but... can we go back? How foolish of us, to run around like children at a carnival, without ensuring we could return the way we came."

"The doorway is there, where we came through. As if it is waiting for us to go back before it can close. In fact, I have found that there are gates everywhere here on this eternal noontime hillside of ours. You simply wish for one to open. Pray, I suppose."

"Ask and it will be given, seek and you will find, knock and the door will be opened." Carmen struggled up to her feet, clutching the bundle of shawl to her chest. "How is all this possible?"

"I don't know, but now that there are two of us, perhaps we will find an answer. What I should dearly like to do is to figure out how to bring others with us. Can you imagine the glory of comfort when snow blankets the city, and we can retreat here, with no need of coats, or coal for heat? Eating fresh fruit and freshly caught fish in the winter?"

"How is it we are blessed to have found this gateway? How did we find it?"

"I believe that keepsake of your mother's is the key." He swallowed hard, his throat too thick with a sudden onset of nerves to laugh at that nervousness. He turned his ruined cheek to her. "I can feel the resonance, the energy in the crystal rose calling to the shards of the same crystal embedded here in my face. I theorize that the energy in the crystal reacts to the same energy somewhere in various spots throughout our labyrinth and pulls open the gate to let us through."

"How..." She freed a hand, just for a moment appearing to reach up to touch his cheek. Then she tightened her arms around the shawl. "I'm sorry, it is most likely painful to discuss your accident."

Brogan snorted. "Very charitable of you. Not so much an accident as the results of a battle and an explosion. My father was entrusted with guarding a large quantity of the same crystal as your rose. Shards and dust and chunks as big as your head. We were attacked, the house hit with explosives, powerful enough to destroy the underground vault holding the crystal. My family was killed, and I woke with shards embedded in my flesh and bone. Attempts to remove it only made the scarring worse." He tried to smile. "I wondered if perhaps you had gone blind, or some miracle of biblical proportions had occurred, to heal my face, because you weren't staring as most do. Especially on such short acquaintance."

"That's just it." Carmen shrugged and then gestured with a tip of her head, back the way they had come. He nodded and they headed out of the apple grove, toward the clear space where they had first emerged. "I can only describe the sensation of your presence as... familiar, I suppose. Comfortable. As if we had met regularly for some time now. I can't explain it. As for your scars, well, I have had the double-edged blessing of encountering the most deformed souls behind the most handsome faces. Your deformity, Mr. Brogan, is only outward. While wounded, I believe your soul is a quite handsome one."

"You flatter me, Miss Mackenzie."

"By their fruit ye shall know them. You could have made yourself a tyrant, using your scars and the loss of your family as an excuse for punishing the world and taking all you could get. You could be the head of all the criminal organizations in this city, using your wounds to intimidate and frighten others into obedience. Instead, you look after the lost and unfortunate and you care about the future of children whom others would discard or use for their own profit. Everyone I have met admires you, cares about you. Mary was delighted that we sang together last night."

"You didn't mind? I couldn't resist."

"You have a lovely voice. Did you take training?"

"My mother loved music, we were surrounded by it. Constant exposure to crystal does something to the heart and soul to bring out music."

"Then your pain must have blocked that music, if, as Mary said, you have not sung in years. Not singing must have been painful in itself."

"True. I never considered that I contributed to my problem," he murmured. A shimmer in the air caught his attention. They had returned to the gate. He pushed down a flicker of irritation.

"Can we—" She licked her lips, glancing away.

"Come back soon?" he hazarded. Hoped. Prayed that was what she was about to ask.

"And often?" Carmen's eyes were like the children's. He feared when she looked at him like that, delighted and eager and hopeful, with just a little pleading, he would never be able to deny her anything.

"If you agree to sing with me every night, Miss Mackenzie, then I propose we take a walk every day and explore, until we figure out a way to bring others with us."

"This treasure must be shared."

He had to wonder, a short time later, if there was more than just a gateway to another time and place involved in their journey. There was no sun visible to decipher the time of day or the amount of time they had spent on the hillside, and he didn't wear a pocket watch. Brogan knew they had spent more than an hour there, yet the children were still eating when he and Carmen arrived in the kitchen with their bounty. He discovered another talent in Carmen, easily deflecting Mary's delighted questions by insisting that they had to wash and section some of the pears and apples immediately, to add to the children's meal. Then she proposed an apple and walnut pie for that evening's meal. Did they have enough pans, and flour and sugar and cinnamon?

Brogan emptied his coat of the harvest, much to the delight of the children who went scrambling to pick up the nuts that rolled off the table. Then he bowed to Carmen and Mary and strode out of the kitchen. His chest felt full, almost heavy, with a bubbling kind of contentment and anticipation he hadn't felt since he was a child. The feeling remained, though not as strong, more than two hours later after he had recorded all his thoughts and memories of their excursion and listed all the questions that had been raised. Soon, he would have to send a messenger to Endicott to ask him to come below so they could talk and theorize. Not very soon. Brogan felt most reluctant to share Carmen's existence with anyone above. He feared once Endicott and others started asking questions, trying to track down her mother's identity, who she had been before she came from "nowhere," Carmen might very well be swept away from his world and out of his reach. He wanted to fill his soul with her music, singing in the night, to store away as antidote to the silence that had enshrouded him for so long.

That night, he was ready, braced for the shimmering that started in his chest and warmed his cheek when Carmen sang to the children. He came down the passageway to the children's dormitory rooms and saw her standing in the doorway of the girls' room, holding a single candle. Though he was positive he stayed back in the deepest pool of darkness, she nodded to him. Her smile made something twist and then go light in his chest. Carmen stepped into the room and he couldn't seem to keep his feet from following, to stand in the doorway. He kept careful watch on the puddles of light from the lanterns, to stay out of their reach. Even though most of the girls knew him, he was careful not to give them any foundation for nightmares. Their lives above had been nightmare enough.

Tonight, Carmen sang them a half-dozen little teaching songs from the camp meetings where she had worked with children. Brogan wondered if she chose those songs, and the stories she wove around them, in response to his unspoken doubts of her history. If the crystal rose she wore made her aware of his presence, perhaps she had an inkling, a hint of the doubts in his mind? Did the crystal in his face and the crystal around her neck somehow create wordless communication between them?

He didn't hear the last two songs as his mind swirled through fragments of dreams and impressions. Could they possibly have spoken to each other in their dreams? His dreams had been odd for the last few weeks, coinciding with her arrival in Cleveland. A sense of understanding and recognition just out of his reach. A scent, a taste, a sound, perhaps a voice, just at the edge of his range of hearing.

Carmen finished singing and made her rounds of the girls' bunks, tucking each one in, kissing a forehead here, cupping a cheek there, giving each child a loving benediction. He swallowed hard against a thickness in his throat that threatened his breath and warmed his eyes, remembering his own mother going through such a ritual. She would have liked Carmen very much, if just for her love of music.

His last conversation with his mother, before the attack and explosion, had been a teasing argument. The subject: her wish that he would bring home a nice girl for her to meet and inspect and approve. It was high time he found a life partner, the other half of his soul, as his parents had found each other. She wanted him to be happy, to be complete, while Brogan had chafed at what he considered restrictions, bound to one place with children to look after, and perhaps a wife who didn't share his love of exploration and learning and adventure. If she could see him now, his mother would laugh at him, tears in her eyes, and shake her head in loving exasperation. Wasn't he tied to one place, looking after other people's children?

Yet even here in his shadowy sanctuary, the labyrinth that protected the Minotaur he had become, and protected the world from him, hadn't he found a wonder to explore?

Carmen stepped into the passageway and Brogan nearly grabbed hold of her shoulders, to look into her eyes and blurt what he had discovered. Hadn't she thoroughly enjoyed the adventure they had stepped into that afternoon? She had urged him to explore as he hadn't allowed himself to do. She had seen the possibilities of feeding their community from the trees and the streams. He had never dared consider taking bounty back into the tunnels with him. Didn't that make her a better, wiser, more perceptive person than him?

"Are you all right?" she whispered, as she pulled the door closed behind her.

"My head is still spinning from this afternoon." That was partially the truth, at least. Brogan had the sudden certainty that he wouldn't be able to get away with any lies with Carmen.

"Mary hasn't come to you yet with plans for creating a bakery to create jobs and make use of the abundance, has she?"

"You didn't—" He stopped, clutching at her sleeve. "No, of course you wouldn't." He caught a twitch of her lips. "You're teasing me."

"Partly. She did mention how wonderful it would be, to have a steady stream of fruit and nuts, but not just to improve our menu down here. She said something about her apple strudel being better than 'hers,' whoever 'her' is. I think she was just joking."

"Ah. Yes." He stepped back to let her pass him, and he muffled a sigh as she reached for the door of the boys' dormitory room. Of course, she would treat the children fairly and sing the boys to sleep as well.

Brogan mulled over the idea of creating an industry of sorts, using the produce from the hillside. If they could supply restaurants, maybe even deliver Mary's baked goods to offices and boarding houses, the income they generated could provide necessities and eliminate the burden on the generosity of their friends up above. He liked the idea of being able to return the favor for those who had been so helpful through the years, when the community's friends above ground experienced difficulties and need.

This time he was ready when Carmen emerged from the boys' room. He waited until she pulled the door closed and offered her his arm. She curtsied and that light feeling filled his chest again. They walked in silence down several passageways, taking four turns and branches, until the passageway widened. Carmen raised the shielded lantern, letting the streaks of light from the half-raised shield play over the walls.

"Is that..." She turned to him, her expression clear despite the shadows painting it in shades of lavender and dusky blue and sable.

"Preacher has designated this wider place the chapel. On Sundays, those who have the energy, who have some hunger for spiritual things, bring stools and benches and listen to him ramble." Brogan didn't fight the single shudder that worked through him. "Down here, you can almost believe the Almighty stands around the corner, whispering the message to Preacher. He comes frighteningly close to speaking what is on everyone's heart and mind. When I was a boy, I thought I could feel God under a sky bright with stars, or during a thunderstorm, in wide open spaces. I never thought He would be down here."

"Because we always picture the devil's domain as being underground," Carmen murmured, nodding. "So what does that make your world beyond the gateway of light?"

Chapter Twenty-One

"Our world." Brogan muffled a chuckle when she flinched, her arm still caught in his. "As we are the only two people able to step through that gateway, so far, it rightfully belongs to both of us. Perhaps we should consider it the truth behind 'Paradise Lost'?"

"Misplaced. Waiting to be reclaimed." She smiled up at him and their gazes locked.

The warmth in his ruined cheek increased just to the verge of humming. When her eyes widened just slightly, enough to hint at discomfort, he released her arm.

"Do you know this one, Miss Mackenzie?" He took three steps back and took a deep breath.

*"I know where I'm going
And I know who's going with me.
I know why there's music
On a bright and summer morning."*

With a chuckle, she took three steps back, put the lantern down, and made him laugh softly as she assumed a schoolgirl's recital pose, with her hands clasped, one over the other at her waist.

"I have stockings of silk," she sang, adding teasing vibrato.
*"And shoes of bright green leather.
Combs to buckle my hair.
And a ring for every finger."*

Three verses later, she held onto the final note a few heartbeats longer than him, and then they both held perfectly still, listening to the ripples of echoes, moving out through the tunnels and back to them. Just as he had thought, the wider chamber offered the acoustics of a concert hall, reinforcing and supporting the sound. Brogan flinched as he wondered what others heard throughout the community, and what they thought of the music. He knew Mary approved, and he was touched that the woman cared so much that she would say something to Carmen about last night's impromptu concert. Perhaps he was destroying his image with the people who looked to him for guidance and protection. Perhaps he was forming a better one. Right this moment, he didn't care. All that mattered was dredging up the songs he had loved when he was a young man with dreams and sharing them with Carmen. Every song they held in common was another cable in the bridge he wove between them, and hopefully another stitch in the bonds that would keep her here, with him. After only two days, he didn't want her to ever leave.

~~~~~

The next morning, Brogan stopped in the kitchen to see if any coffee remained from breakfast. Someone had gifted the community with several pounds of roasted beans that had burst from a sack at a grocery store, in front of customers. The grocer couldn't scoop the beans into another sack and try to sell them. Mary declared that there would be no over-indulging, but they would make the treat last. The aroma had drifted down the passageways to his office lair, making him hope some remained.

He found Mary sitting at a table covered with baskets, and Hilda sitting across the table from her, and a sketch of Carmen lying on the table between them. Mary looked up at the sound of his foot scraping on that bump in the floor right in the doorway. She glanced down at the sketch and met his gaze and just slightly shook her head.

Brogan nodded greetings to Hilda, who nodded gravely back to him, her gaze flicking away quickly. He muffled a chuckle that he feared might sound rather hysterical with all the churning inside making him clench his jaw. Mary liked and respected Hilda for the work she was doing, rescuing so many children. At the same time, she held back on true friendship because Hilda was associated with Randall Endicott. She claimed her "second sight" told her he held far too many secrets for a man with that much power. She also had an ingrained distrust of lawyers because of an entire squadron of dishonest ones who harmed her friends and family years ago. Mary wouldn't have said anything to Hilda about Carmen being among them. She would hold her silence until he learned why the woman had a sketch of the young woman and where she had obtained it.

He could have kissed Mary right that moment and swung her about the kitchen in a brief waltz of gratitude. What had he ever done to deserve such loyalty and discretion?

"Blessed woman," he murmured, as he spotted the tall, fire-blackened coffee pot sitting on the front grid over the charcoal fire that was kept burning all day.

He filled his cup and came over to the table to settle down next to Mary, keeping the ruined side of his face turned away from Hilda. The woman saw him so rarely, he supposed she would never get used to the mass of scars and bubbled flesh.

"You bless us with more bounty. Thank you, Miss Hilda." He gestured at the baskets, likely filled with more chalk for the children's slates, food of some kind from her very successful restaurant, maybe some more clothes, odds and ends she could spare from her own work rescuing children, or things she thought they simply needed. He nodded at the sketch of Carmen, because he knew she would suspect something was up if he didn't acknowledge it. "Can we be of any assistance?"

"My girl, I've told you about Odessa, certainly? Well, she's back in town and she's looking for this young lady. Oh, it's all complicated and I'm not certain how it works, except that her mother had a very good friend who she lost touch with, Anna, and as near as we can determine, Anna's daughter looks enough like her to be sisters. My Ess has had information that the daughter, Carmen, has come to Cleveland, and she seems to be in dire straits. There are cruel men hunting for her. My sparrows have the word out, and our friends among the police are getting copies of the sketch as fast as Ess and my boy, Riley, can draw them. If you can ask your people to help look for her, we'd all be grateful."

"What sort of danger?" Mary asked.

"Your Odessa..." Brogan sipped at his coffee while his mind spun through the implications and connections. "She's the Fremonts' granddaughter, yes?" He barely waited for Hilda to nod, tight-lipped. "Then a friend of Vivian's would be... gifted, yes?"

Again a nod from Hilda. Mary had no knowledge of the crystal or the Great Machine or the Originators' mission. At times like this Brogan regretted not trusting her with the knowledge. Having to talk in euphemisms in front of her was bothersome. He had considered educating her from time to time, and flinched away from it because he dreaded losing her good opinion. Despite her claims of having "second sight," she might suspect he wasn't quite right in the head. The irony of that fear, when he had proof he wasn't a madman, made him want to laugh.

"So these men searching for this young lady are enemies of the gifted associates of you and our esteemed Mr. Endicott and the Fremonts." He sighed and glanced at Mary. "These are the same people who caused the explosion that killed my family."

"Ah." Mary rested her hand on his wrist for a moment. "Like as not, we need to send some of our bruisers after them. If we find them on the trail of this girl you're looking for," she hurried to add, nodding to Hilda. Then her eyes narrowed. "So this girl, this Carmen, she's like one of your folk?"

"Most certainly," Brogan whispered. "Can you tell us more about her, the trouble she's in? Why did the mothers lose touch with each other?"

A knot in his gut loosened as Hilda related the same story Carmen had given him, told from another angle, and filled in details. He already knew she hadn't been lying to him, simply because the resonance of the crystal when they sang together was so pure and clear. Brogan appreciated this confirmation. He ached for Carmen, all she had lost, yet he hesitated to take the simple step of telling Hilda yes, they knew where Carmen Mackenzie had taken shelter. Quite simply, he was selfish. Carmen was his new treasure. She had just returned the music to his life. She had proven he wasn't insane. She was custodian with him of the world on the other side of the gateway, and he needed her to explore it with him.

Brogan promised Hilda they would send out word to look for Carmen and thanked her again for all she shared with the tunnel community. He said nothing about Carmen being only a hundred yards down the tunnel to the right, and trusted Mary to give not a hint to Hilda before she left. Though he ached with the need to escort Hilda out personally, he went back to his office and left it to Mary to handle. He needed to plan how to confront Carmen with this news. Certainly she would welcome having more friends, people looking out for her to defend her and teach her how to use the crystal rose. He knew how the future of the Originators rested on the few remaining descendants of the women who had dismantled the Great Machine, and the sensitivity to crystal born in them. She was vital to the Originator cause. Teamed with Vivian Fremont's daughter, what miracles could they perform?

He was selfish, to want to keep her all to himself. He owed her this chance to follow her destiny, to do what the Almighty had planned for her since conception. Somehow, he had to find a way to reveal this news to her while persuading her to stay down here, in the shadows and chill, with him.

~~~~~

Carmen laughed with the children as they swept her along with them on their way to the kitchen for their lunch. She had helped Mary cobble together a stew of chicken, dried peas, green beans, and potatoes that morning, before lessons started. The aromas drifting down the tunnels were tantalizing enough to make her hungry. A plan had been slowly weaving itself together at the back of her mind during lessons. She would take lunch to Brogan's office, and they would eat together while she proposed her ideas. If the crystal she wore and the crystal embedded in his face had somehow helped them find the gateway and step through, and bring back yesterday's harvest, was it possible that if they held hands with others, could they take them through the gateway with them? Could they begin regular excursions of exploration and harvesting? Perhaps that was too ambitious, but they had to start somewhere, didn't they? She liked the idea of the children being able to play in warmth and sunshine when everyone else was housebound on rainy days, and when winter blanketed the city.

Her mind was so caught up in finding the right words to propose her plan, she almost didn't see the woman coming down the passageway, led by Adam. The children called greetings to Adam and several of them hugged the heavyset, white-haired woman, and hurried on to their lunch.

"Hello there," the woman said as they both stopped, stepping to either side of the passageway.

Adam kept walking. Carmen wasn't quite sure yet what was wrong with him, but he shuffled everywhere with hunched shoulders and a vacant stare. Everyone repeated themselves whenever they talked to him.

"You're a new... face," the woman said. She frowned and raised the lantern and stepped a little closer to Carmen.

"And so are you." Carmen offered a smile, realizing as the words left her lips how argumentative they had to be.

"I'm not a regular, though I help out." The woman laughed and held out her free hand. "I'm Hilda. Or rather, everyone calls me Miss Hilda."

"Not the Miss Hilda who takes in all the children? The one having trouble with her new building because of all the politicians?" She clasped the woman's hand and hoped she kept the pleasant smile on her face, and the shock she felt didn't show in her voice.

"Well, you've heard of me, but I certainly haven't heard of you." Hilda laughed, squeezing Carmen's hand a little longer than she thought necessary.

"Well, Officer Willoughby mentioned you — he wanted the children — my children — well, not mine, but I was taking care of them." She tugged her hand free as gently as possible. "Well, that's not necessary now, since we're settled down here. Mr. Brogan has asked me to teach the children living down here."

"Ah. Of course. You're a friend of Willoughby's. Lovely man. Such a tragedy."

"He isn't dead, is he? We heard he was sent home to Erie to recover."

"Yes, that's all I heard. I'm sorry, did you say who you were?"

"Carmen. Mackenzie," she hurried to add. A tiny chuckle caught in her throat, when it occurred to her that everyone around here had a tendency to go only by their first names, as if descending into the tunnels took away all affiliations and family ties.

"Carmen. Well, it's a pleasure to meet you. And of course, if Willoughby wanted your children to come to me, I will most certainly take them as soon as those politicians get out of my way." She flinched as Adam came back into the puddle of light from her lantern and tugged on her sleeve. "I'm sorry, Adam. We must be going. I likely have a huge mess in my kitchen from staying away this long."

An ache in her hands woke Carmen to the fact that she clenched her fists hard enough to cut her palms with her nails. She watched until the light from Hilda's lantern vanished around a bend in the tunnel, then she continued into the kitchen, where the children were waiting for her to lead them in saying grace over their lunch. The stew that had smelled so delicious just moments ago made Carmen feel slightly sick. She discarded her plan to take lunch to Brogan's office and discuss her ideas.

What if Hilda was here to make arrangements to send the children away? She couldn't remember the exact words from just two days ago, when she and the children had first come down here, but she thought, or had it just been implied, that they were being offered shelter as long as they wanted it? Could she be wrong, and Brogan was only taking them until other arrangements could be made? While it was comforting to know that Brogan was friends with the woman Officer Willoughby admired and trusted, somehow the whole idea, the connections, made her want to cry.

~~~~~

A tap on Lewis's office door interrupted the meeting that had barely begun. Ess was closest to the door, so she got up and went to open it. Hilda bustled in, looking flushed and slightly frazzled, and not just from the noonday heat.

"She's here. I'm sure of it. Anna's daughter," she announced, and plopped down into the chair Ess had just vacated.

"Where?" Lewis said, glancing at the elderly woman who had simply been introduced as Harriet.

He had been gone so long because Harriet had been attacked, her station house bombed, and he had needed to find where she was hiding before bringing her to Cleveland. Harriet had indicated that she had indeed sent Carmen to Cleveland by a roundabout method, to keep her from being tracked down. Whoever had been hunting her had followed her as far as Harriet's home in Chicago, and the trail had been months cold by the time they attacked. That was no comfort. Ess, Uly, and Endicott had been about to hear the details of how Carmen had showed up on Harriet's doorstep and the plan they had made, when Hilda entered.

"Here in Cleveland," Uly said. "You're sure?"

"I talked to her not twenty minutes ago in that rabbit warren run by your friend Brogan." Hilda pulled out a handkerchief and mopped at her face. Ess stepped over to the sideboard and filled a glass of lemonade for her, making sure several chunks of ice slid into the glass. "What galls me is that not half an hour before, I told Brogan and Mary about Carmen, left a sketch of her with them, and they said not a word about her. She's there as a teacher for the children." She snatched the glass from Ess and gulped a mouthful down. "I'm sorry, I know you trust the man implicitly, but I have never fully trusted him. Lurking about in the shadows and damp. Like a snake in a den." She shuddered and took a more sedate sip.

"Brogan?" Ess said, turning to Endicott, who frowned down at his clasped hands.

"Brogan Ambrose." He sighed and raised his head and settled back further in his chair, visibly getting comfortable for a long discussion.

"I thought he was dead," Uly said.

"In some aspects, after all he has lost, he is. Some of your grandparents' theories about music being tied to crystal came from the work Brogan and his parents did. He and his mother were incredible musicians. He was mute for months after the attack that destroyed his family. I think he lost or at least forgot the part he played in their research."

"Is this something else that was blocked from my memories?" Ess asked, trying not to let that particular sense of frustration rise up and touch her voice.

"No, investigating the devastation after the attack was one of my first assignments after I got sent away," Uly said. "I vaguely remember him visiting while our parents were alive. I really only know what others said." He nodded to Endicott.

"Sheridan Ambrose," the elder lawyer said after a pause while his eyes darkened with memories, "was a guardian of one of the oldest caches of retrieved crystal. That was mostly because he was also an inventor. Talk to Theo about some of the things he either created from the ancestors' records or re-created. He worships the man's brilliance. Ambrose was making weapons for us and trying to recreate those very communication plates you two recovered. He never thought to use crystal dust," he added with a snort and a brief flicker of a smile.

"Simply put, their station house was attacked. As near as any of the investigators can tell, he tried to use one of his experimental weapons." He took a long breath and Ess reached out to clasp his hand when he shuddered. "He somehow shattered a rod of crystal nearly two feet long. We all pray it was entirely by accident and not on purpose, because that implies someone could find the means to do it again someday. It killed the attackers, shredding them with the shards. However, it also killed Ambrose and his wife and four of their five children. Brogan should have died, but he was on the other side of the house. Even so, the crystal fragments and the dust embedded in his skull—" He paused, a pained smile again touching his face as most of those in the room shuddered in reaction to the mental image.

"The crystal seems to have preserved his life, even as it disfigured him. His entire body was pierced. He suffered delusions for months from the pain, from whatever influence the energy of the crystal had on him as most of the fragments slowly worked out of his system. All except for what is in his face. The rest of his body is unblemished, but his face is massively scarred on one side. I brought him to Cleveland because I was one of the few friends of his parents that he remembered. He trusted me. I tried to give him work to do. I knew about the tunnels under the city, and he explored them and devoted himself to helping the people living in them who had been brought down to nothing. People devastated by financial disasters, families still suffering the damages wrought by the war, people cheated by profiteers. Brogan made himself their champion, their defender." Endicott shrugged. "He is his father's son, after all. Sheridan and Elise would be proud of him."

"These are the same tunnels you want to make part of the tower, use them for Originator business?" Uly said. "Would they make good, secure hiding places for the pieces of the Machine?"

"There are depths and anomalies in the tunnels, used by the natives, dug by water and time and geologic shifting, that even Brogan has not thoroughly explored." He spread his arms in a gesture of helplessness, surrendering to the unknowns, in Ess's opinion, and got up to refill his glass with lemonade.

"Well," Hilda said with a sniff, "that changes some things. A little. Now that I know what he's gone through. Still going through."

"I don't understand why he didn't tell you Carmen was down there with them," Harriet said.

"You said she's there as a teacher?" Endicott paused with the pitcher in one hand and his glass in the other. "That's the key. Brogan would tear this city down to its foundations to protect the children. He takes the ones who aren't safe even under Hilda's care. The ones that the thieves and brothels want. I would imagine that he offered Carmen shelter in return for taking care of the children, and she must be in some kind of trouble to make her willing to accept. He's protecting her, and by doing so he protects the children."

"Something along the lines of the Minotaur protecting Ariadne, instead of threatening her," Ess mused aloud.

Endicott snorted. "He has indeed referred to himself sometimes as the Minotaur in his labyrinth."

"You say he still has crystal in him?" Uly whistled soft and low when the older man nodded. "That could be the problem you've had with touching Carmen in her dreams, Ess. We've verified that the presence of crystal can interfere with using the communication plates. Granny had to move a large cache of crystal to the far end of the *Nile*, and made sure it wasn't physically placed between the plate and us, to clear up communication. What if Brogan has so much crystal in him, it's interfering with the link between both roses?"

"It could be that she isn't wearing it," Ess said.

"Oh, she's wearing it. I saw it around her neck," Hilda said.

"Then I say it's time to stop playing coy and sneaking up on her like we're trying to tame a bird on the windowsill. Will you take me down to the tunnels to meet Brogan and Carmen?" She turned to Harriet. "I think it might be wise to have you with us. She'll be more willing to believe we're on the same side when she sees you."

"Should have given her a sound education on what it means to be on our side," Harriet said. "Wish I had heard from you sooner, that all our sneaking around and keeping secrets had finally stopped."

Chapter Twenty-Two

Bass chords hummed through her skin, like the largest strings on a harp. Carmen turned, nearly stumbling, to see Brogan step through a slit in the air, out onto the mountainside. Though he faced away from her, he immediately turned to look directly at her.

"It's about time," she muttered. Granted, the sense of time passing was difficult to calculate here where it always seemed to be just past noontime. Still, she felt like she had been here for hours.

"You scared me half to death." Brogan hurried down the slope toward where she had been pacing in a circle. "I felt a flare of... I don't know what it was, but I thought the roof was going to collapse and a totally unreasonable tangle of rage and fear shot through me." He pressed his hand against the scarred side of his face. "All I could think was that you were in trouble, but I couldn't find you. Do you have any idea how that feels?"

"Maybe." She tried to hold onto the hot, spiky knot in her chest. "How did you find me? You didn't feel me going through the gate?"

Her face still felt hot, but now she suspected some of it was embarrassment. What idiocy made her think that just because they had gone through the gate together, that somehow he would just know when she went through it by herself? What arrogant delusion made her think he would come running after her?

"When my search brought me to the tunnel and I saw the gate hanging there, glowing, wide open, I guessed." His mouth worked for a moment like he couldn't decide whether to frown or smile. "What's wrong?"

"I met Hilda, the one who takes in all the children." Her inner churning calmed a little when Brogan's mouth dropped open. She swore he lost some color. "Are you trying to get rid of us so soon?"

He muttered something that sounded German and she assumed it was a curse. "More fool me, I thought she was gone before you finished with lessons."

"You didn't want me to meet her?" Carmen shook her head, negating that question. "Then you aren't trying to get rid of us?"

"Merciful Savior, no!" He reached as if he would grasp her shoulders, but instead dropped his arms back to his side, somewhat awkwardly. "You don't want to leave, do you?"

"No, actually."

"Thank God."

"You want us to stay?" She had the oddest feeling she would start giggling like an idiot.

"To be totally honest, Miss Mackenzie..." His grin wiped away twenty years. "The children can all vanish to perdition, because right now all that matters is keeping you here with *me*. If I could," he hurried on, flushing again, "I'd stay here, with you, until the clock of Eternity runs down. You can't imagine the terror I felt, thinking you had been followed down below and kidnapped, maybe hurt, maybe fell down a sinkhole that appeared in a tunnel." He caught hold of one of her hands in both of his. "This is too soon, we've only just met, and I'm a fool, but... you've brought the music back to my life. You are music in flesh and bone."

"Mr. Brogan," she whispered. Carmen knew she should take her hand back, knew she should say something to halt him, knew she shouldn't let this moment continue to where she thought it might end. Yet she didn't want to. All the most beautiful words and longing looks from the most handsome and well-dressed and highly educated and even spiritual men she had ever met couldn't compare to the agony and pleading in his dark eyes. Oddly, even the scarred, bubbled side of his face had become dear to her. "Yes, it is too soon, but... perhaps I'm just as much a fool." The joy that flashed across his face made her heart skip a few beats. "At the very least, I fear we need a chaperon."

Brogan laughed and stepped closer, turning, so he could tuck her hand into the crook of his arm.

"Let me be clear, my dearest Miss Mackenzie. No, I do not want to send away you or the children. Hilda is an associate of the man who brought me here to Cleveland, and who helps to support our community. She brings us children whom she can't help because they are in greater danger than she can handle."

"Such as Ellie," she guessed, as he started them walking back to where the gate shimmered. Carmen wished they could stay and talk and sort things out further, but she did have a trip to the library planned. She needed time to understand what had happened, how her fury and fear of just ten minutes ago could shift into a light, fluttering sensation in her chest, so she quite feared her feet would leave the ground.

"And worse, if that were possible. Growing cities, unfortunately, attract criminal elements. Gangs organize themselves better than an army, because they see the potential for profit and power. They punish those who will not cooperate by attacking their families. Some men have died, standing against such evil, and even though they are dead, their families are still targeted."

"It's a wonder more people aren't living below with us," she murmured.

"Us." He squeezed the hand tucked in his elbow. The richness in his voice made her heart flutter.

Carmen knew her father would express grave doubts about the things she was feeling, the nebulous hopes she didn't dare to even put into words after such a short acquaintance. She didn't care. So much about the situation had to be wrong, but she simply wanted to enjoy the moment, the splendor. Later, she would find a way to make it all right, and if possible, ensure this blissful, completed, hopeful feeling would last forever.

~~~~~

"I'm sorry, but this place reminds me too much of Sanctuary," Ess said, after she, Endicott and Harriet had taken a third turn going downward into the tunnels.

"Why should you be sorry?" a rich, baritone voice asked out of the darkness ahead of them. "I never liked the place myself."

"Hello, Brogan," Endicott said.

"They aren't refugees, are they?"

"No. This lady here is Harriett Angelotti, a friend of Miss Mackenzie. She's anxious to make sure she's all right. This other young lady is... well, she's complicated."

Ess had to laugh. Everything suddenly struck her as entirely too melodramatic.

"This is Odessa Fremont, Edward and Vivian's daughter. We believe that Vivian was a friend of Miss Mackenzie's mother," Endicott went on.

Ess barely stopped herself from clutching at his arm. The rose in the hollow of her throat hummed at the same moment she heard a single footstep scraping against stone, somewhere in the darkness ahead of them. If her and Uly's theory was right, then the rose was reacting to the approach of the crystal embedded in Brogan Ambrose's face. She stepped forward and raised the lantern she held, and with her free hand tugged down her collar to reveal the rose.

"This should be proof enough for you, I think, that I'm a friend of Carmen's." She breathed a soft chuckle. "At least, I believe we will be friends, when she remembers we've met in our dreams."

"No lecture on lying to our esteemed Miss Hilda?" Brogan said, stepping into the light.

Having been warned, Ess tried not to stare at his face, though she found the temptation strong.

"Should I?" Endicott said.

"Will that prevent her berating me the next time she comes below?"

"Hmm. Most probably not," Ess said. "She helped raise me, and she's still slapping my wrist from time to time over disappearing for seven years."

"Disappearing? As in going invisible?" Brogan's smile was nice. Mischievous, inviting her to join in the fun tormenting others into madness.

"More like playing truant," Endicott said. "Could we go somewhere more comfortable to sit and talk? And hopefully have Miss Mackenzie join us?"

"Yes to the first." Brogan turned and gestured for them to follow him down the tunnel. "To the second, Miss Mackenzie is currently on an outing to the library with the children. They're quite excited. She's made them love books very quickly."

"I think I like her," Ess commented.

"Do you like books as well, Miss Fremont?"

"They're far easier to get along with than some people."

That earned a bark of laughter from him.

Shortly, they entered a long room that looked like it had been partially carved by time and erosion, and partly by men digging with pickaxes. Ess marveled at the kitchen that had been assembled here, taking advantage of natural chimneys in the rock, the hearths and makeshift stoves, and the signs that this place took care of feeding dozens of people. Hilda had given her a general idea of this community of tunnels and castoffs who gathered together to take care of each other, but she hadn't imagined something that struck her as actually quite comfortable. The wiry woman working at the hearth turned out to be Mary, who ran the kitchen and oversaw the care of the children, and who everyone seemed answerable to in some way. At least, according to Hilda. Endicott introduced Harriet to her, stressing she had helped Carmen escape danger in Chicago and had sent her to Cleveland looking for help. He explained that Carmen was supposed to meet up with Mr. Lewis of his office, while Lewis had been hunting down Harriet to extricate her from difficulties. Mary shook her head and let out a rasping chuckle.

Ess caught the nod that Mary gave Brogan, and she guessed she and Harriet had passed some sort of test. Brogan suggested Endicott and Ess come with him, while Harriet settled in to wait with Mary until Carmen returned. As he led them deeper underneath downtown Cleveland, Brogan filled in some details of how Carmen had come to them, verifying some things Ess had guessed.

"I theorized that her mother had some strong affiliation or sensitivity to the crystal," he said, as they came to a wider section of the tunnel and he slowed their pace. "Whether by accident or through some talent she doesn't realize she possesses, I am persuaded Carmen has discovered the ability to heal serious injuries. That is what brought her to my attention. One of our children is rather hard to restrain."

Endicott chuckled. "Mouse?"

"I'm positive we could lock her in a safe and chain it and toss it in the Cuyahoga, and she would be on the bank, waiting for us before the ripples settled on the water. She was out exploring the buildings being torn down, at night, in a storm. She fell." His voice caught and Ess decided she liked the man, if the injury to a child bothered him. "Mouse insists her leg was broken. Carmen ventured out in the rain to find her—she and her children were taking shelter in one of the abandoned buildings. She found Mouse and brought her back and sang to her, praying for healing. In the morning,

Mouse walked home."

"You agree her leg was broken?" Endicott said.

"I examined her leg myself. There were healed scars and they were hotter than the rest of her leg."

"Well, more proof of your theory, Odessa. Music controls the crystal."

"Music?" Brogan said. "Do you happen to sing, Miss Fremont?"

"Not really, but I am quite handy with a flute." She considered for a moment. "My brother and I unlocked the secret of the ancestors' instantaneous communication through crystal, using music. I understand your father was working on a similar project."

"Yes, from what I can remember." He glanced at her, frown wrinkles momentarily nesting his eyes. "I have some theories myself. I thought perhaps an affinity for music might be a key, but... well, that piece you're wearing gives me ideas. Here we are," he added, leading them around a bend in the tunnel.

The rose vibrated softly in the hollow of her throat. Brogan stopped, pressing his back against the wall, and lowered his lantern while gesturing for her to go ahead of him. Ess only hesitated for a heartbeat before moving forward. The humming sensation increased.

A speck of light flickered white and blue and green in the air in the center of the passageway. In moments, it grew until it touched floor and walls and ceiling.

"You see it, don't you?" Brogan murmured, his voice coming over her right shoulder.

"See what, exactly?" she asked.

"Do you, or don't you?" Endicott asked.

"I see something." She turned to look at him. His gaze wasn't precisely focused on the film of light. "You don't?"

"What is your theory?" He frowned when Brogan held out his hand to him.

"Carmen sees it, and she has crossed through with me. This is her theory," Brogan said, his voice softening and thoughtful. "Miss Fremont, would you take Randall's other hand?"

She bit back a remark that all the formality was getting tiresome and he should simply call her Ess. That could wait. She held out her hand for Endicott's. He took it, and reached for Brogan's hand, then flinched.

"I see it," he whispered.

"That's one part of her theory. Let's see if the other works." Brogan flashed a fierce grin and nodded at the light. "I call it simply a gateway."

"A gateway to where?" she asked.

"Come and see." He stepped forward. Ess hurried to keep in step, and Endicott leaped to catch up with them.

She was afraid to let go of his hand as sunlight and a warm, sweet, apple-scented breeze surrounded them. Endicott ripped out an oath, smothering it into something unintelligible. Brogan tipped his head back and laughed.

"Where are we?" Endicott asked.

"I have no idea." Brogan let go of his hand.

Ess was glad to see that he had to tug, meaning Endicott wasn't so eager to let go.

"You haven't explored?"

"I suppose we could determine our location by the constellations," she offered.

"There's no night here. No sun." Brogan gestured up at the sky. "I've come here at all hours of the day and night, and the sunlight, the weather, never change."

Ess let go of Endicott's hand and stepped back from them, slowly turning to survey the trees, the silver trickle of water crossing the meadow almost under her feet, the snowy streaks of clouds across the vibrant blue sky. Her mind spun through ideas, sometimes twisting sideways to consider what her grandparents would say, how they would argue with the theory forming like a spider's web spinning itself and tying all the bits and pieces together. Her pulse hammered at her temples, and she nearly laughed to realize she was holding her breath.

"Odessa?" Endicott said, holding out a hand to her, his face creasing in concern.

"It's a time box. A time box that doesn't collapse when you exit. Because somehow, it's self-sustaining. It isn't created at need, it just... is." Ess wrapped her arms hard around herself and kept turning slowly, while her mind spun, casting aside arguments and possibilities.

~~~~~

Carmen shivered despite the afternoon's sticky heat and stopped, her mouth open, about to call for Simon and Roger to hurry and catch up with the rest of the children. She slowed her steps, turning slowly to sweep the long street with her gaze, searching for what bothered her. Would she feel this way every time she came above ground from now on? A tiny snort of amused self-disgust escaped her. She wouldn't really be staying underground day and night, would she? The anticipation of escaping once more to the mountainside brightened her day. Not that she needed any more brilliance. The sun was at just the right angle to evade the rooftops and spear directly into her eyes if she wasn't careful.

No, between singing with Brogan and more trips to explore and bring back fresh food for the community, her life was quite rich now. She hadn't felt this safe, this special, even set aside for blessings and service, since before her mother died.

Her gaze caught on two men, standing on the corner of the next block. Without thinking, before their features registered, she turned the children as they finished crossing the street and took them to the right instead of going straight ahead. Andrew and Virgil slowed their steps and looked up at her, questions clear on their faces. They knew the route to the library.

Richard Boniface and Alexander O'Keefe stood together at the other end of the city block, talking. Both were dressed as prosperous businessmen, down to vests and suitcoats and pocket watches with long chains, and glossy boots. Despite the day's heat. Carmen wished she had elected to wear the boy clothes Mary had given her yesterday, in anticipation of exploration trips in the lower tunnels. Her months of thin living had trimmed down her figure, so she thought she could pass for a tall boy, from a distance. At the very least, Mrs. Sullivan would laugh when she saw her.

More important, she would have had more protection between her and those two men.

Her reaction to seeing Boniface again crystalized. Carmen wasn't at all glad to see him, and could never be glad, but now she was dismayed at his presence. As for O'Keefe, she hadn't liked him from the moment he introduced himself to her before a very important camp meeting. He wouldn't keep his gaze on her face when they talked. It kept sliding downward, so she wanted to step behind the upright piano. Then he inquired about buying her mother's cross, and knowing he had been staring at it, not her bosom, hadn't made her feel any more comfortable. Lust and greed were quite easily the same expressions. She took to wearing the cross tucked inside her shirt, but O'Keefe still stared at her chest during his visits to the camp meetings, as if he knew the cross was there.

Boniface and O'Keefe obviously knew each other. How *long* had they known each other? Could O'Keefe have sent Boniface to join the camp meeting team after he failed to persuade her to sell the cross and rose to him? Her mother's crystal rose was important. Brogan had so much to teach her about it, and Harriet had told her enough to know other people would want it. Had Boniface's courtship been a mere ruse to get hold of the rose?

Carmen wanted to turn the children around right now and take them back to the tunnels, so she could take her speculations to Brogan.

"I am never coming above ground again without—"

Boniface stepped around the corner and planted himself in the center of the sidewalk.

"Darling! What luck. I spied you and your entourage as you turned the corner and I couldn't resist investigating. How relieved I am that you were indeed telling me the truth." He beamed at the children. Andrew, Virgil and Diggory, the oldest of the boys, moved up, creating a wall between him and Carmen.

She clenched her hands to keep from wrapping her arms around all three boys in gratitude.

"Miss Carmen don't lie," Arthur growled, stepping up next to his brother.

"Doesn't." Boniface's upper lip curled as he spared the boy a fleeting glance. "I do have to wonder, my dearest—"

"I am not your dearest, Mr. Boniface. I rejected your marriage proposals. Remember?" she added, when whispers rippled among the children. Amazing, how safe she felt with them all pressed up close to her.

"Bunny face," Beatrice said with a giggle.

"Oh, but my darling Carmen—"

"Miss Mackenzie. I have yet to give you permission to use my Christian name."

When, she wondered, would Brogan use her first name?

"Miss Mackenzie." Boniface gave her a stiff little head-and-shoulders bow. "You told me you were working with children at a rescue mission, and yet when I diligently checked every mission I could find within the entire county, no one heard of you. I thought perhaps you were using a nom de guerre, to separate yourself from the scandal that killed your father, but no one matching your description was working at any of these places, either."

"I never said 'rescue mission.' That was your interpretation. As you can see, I did not lie. The children and I are on our way to the library to augment our lessons. If you will excuse us, we do not wish to be late and worry the very generous librarian who is helping us." Her hands shook just slightly, though she hoped Boniface didn't see, as she gestured for the children to move along.

"Oh, but I don't want to excuse you, darling."

"I think she's lying," a semi-familiar, male voice announced, coming up from behind Carmen. "I don't know you, sir, but I do know this woman, and the horrific scandal that nearly tore apart the missionary society she was once associated with."

Alexander O'Keefe strolled up, parting the children like an ice-breaker on a frozen lake.

So that's the game, is it? They pretend they don't know each other and attack from two sides. At least they don't know that I saw them. Savior, what shall I do?

"Ridiculous." Boniface stepped up next to Carmen and attempted to put his arm around her shoulders. "I am a minister of the Lord, sir, and worked with her esteemed father."

From the corner of her eye, Carmen saw Diggory slap Virgil and two other boys and gesture for them to follow. Her heart sank for two seconds, before she yanked her attention back to the two men.

Chapter Twenty-Three

"My proof," O'Keefe said, as he turned to include several passersby, who had been attracted by the conversation, "is a diamond-encrusted cross that her father tricked a sweet, yet unfortunately witless old widow into giving him. He was supposed to sell the cross for money for Bibles, yet not two days later, this... this... " His lip curled. "This creature was wearing it for everyone to see. They didn't even have the wits to wait until they left the town before they displayed the fruits of their thievery."

"I'm familiar with the cross, sir. My betrothed said it was her mother's," Boniface returned. "She's not wearing it now."

"Oh, she is. Sneak thieves can't resist holding onto pretty sparkling things, can they?" He leaned closer, sneering at Carmen.

She slapped him, realizing too late her hand was a fist. Most certainly, her months of living on the edge had taught her a thing or two. O'Keefe's eyes widened but he didn't move fast enough to evade the solid blow on his cheekbone. He staggered back. The children cheered. At least two men of the growing crowd shouted, "Bravo," and a woman cried, "Serves him right!"

"Search her," he growled, pressing his hand to his cheekbone. "Prove me wrong. I know it's there."

Carmen feared somehow he did know, he could feel the presence of the crystal rose, just like Brogan said the crystal in his face made him sensitive to the presence of the rose. So did that mean O'Keefe carried a piece of crystal?

A whistle blared, coming from behind Carmen and Boniface. She turned and stepped away from him as he continued trying to put his arm around her. A policeman, tall and bony with a bald head and a white walrus-style moustache, stomped down the street. Diggory and the other boys trailed in his wake. The oldest boy grinned broadly at her and hooked his thumbs through his suspenders, very visibly pleased with himself.

"What's going on here?" the officer growled and stepped through the onlookers.

The tunnel children grinned at him and stepped aside, and she distinctly saw him wink at two of them. Carmen caught her breath, near tears with the realization that this man had to be a friend of the underground community. How clever of Diggory to fetch him.

"You're just in time, officer. I've been looking for this little thief for months," O'Keefe announced, pointing melodramatically at Carmen.

"Are you sure of that, laddie?" the officer said, stepping up so he stood slightly ahead of Carmen. "You see, I know the lady. I know the people she works with. I know they wouldn't trust her with teaching these children unless they'd checked her references. I know they wouldn't make a foolish mistake of hiring a thief, like you say she is. So you want to think about what you're saying, and maybe fix any mistakes you made?"

"You have all been deceived," O'Keefe declared, pulling his shoulders straight. "I am going straight to city hall and registering a complaint with the chief of police. I am a man of power and influence, and I do not take kindly to being mocked. I'll have your badge for this."

"Don't think it'll go with yer fancy suit, but if you want it, fine." The officer tugged at his badge, as if that would make it easier to see. He read off the number and announced his precinct. Several of the children and bystanders chuckled. Carmen wondered what the joke was. Several more laughed when he told O'Keefe his name was McTavish. They were still laughing and muttering comments as the man stomped away down the street, the picture of offended dignity.

"Darling, you must let me take you somewhere quiet, to recover from such rude treatment." Boniface reached for her arm again, but Carmen stepped behind Officer McTavish.

"I am perfectly fine, Mr. Boniface."

Several girls joined Beatrice in giggling and whispering, "Bunny face."

"Thank you for your concern, but Officer McTavish knows I am on a rigid schedule. We will soon be late for our scheduled time at the library. Come along, children."

"When will you be done? I'll come for you," Boniface said.

"Four o'clock. I then have to put them on a trolley to the beach, where our mission group will have a picnic dinner waiting." She sighed and pretended to think. "I suppose it will be all right if you join us."

"I look forward to it, my darling." He bowed to her as Carmen spread her arms and gestured for the children to hurry down the sidewalk.

McTavish walked with her, glancing over his shoulder several times as they trotted the length of the block, crossed the street, went another block, and then he turned them right when they should have turned left.

"We're not going to the library, are we, any more than your name is McTavish, is it?" she said, finally daring to look at him.

"No, ma'am." He nodded to her and winked.

"Thank you, so very much, for your rescue. Diggory, all you boys were brilliant." Carmen reached to tap each boy on his shoulder. All of them grinned or shrugged or even blushed a little at the praise.

"Here we go. I figure with that ruckus back there you probably want to get off the street as soon as possible." He directed them into a door at the back of an office building. It led into the cellar, lit by two gaslights, with barrels stacked against one wall and crates scattered across the floor, vanishing into the shadows. "You all just sit and rest. I have a carting company in mind to help get you all home, but you might have to wait until nightfall. You don't mind too much, do you?"

"We could send a few children out at a time," she offered. "Nobody would notice three or four children walking together. Not like they would notice more than twenty in a crowd. Then if someone could come back with a change of clothes for me, a disguise of some kind? I don't mind boy clothes." That made the officer chuckle.

An hour later, the children had left in groups of three and four, until there were only five left with Carmen. She was touched that Andrew and Virgil insisted on staying with her. McTeague showed up with a wagon full of barrels, covered with a tarpaulin, creating a cozy if somewhat fragrant cave for them to hide in, for the ride to the closest access point into the tunnels.

Oddly, Carmen felt a soft humming in the rose where it pressed against her skin, just before the wagon stopped. The humming grew just slightly stronger as they climbed out and went down the cellar steps, and then climbed down into what looked like a cistern. Hands reached out of the darkness before her feet left the bottom rung of the wooden ladder and the crystal rose flared warm as those hands clasped her waist, lifted her, and turned her around.

"Carmen, are you sure you're all right?" Brogan asked, his hands tightening on her waist.

Just for a moment, she thought he would draw her close and hold her tight against his chest. She wanted it, needed it, and a little cry of protest rose up in her throat when the cistern lid dropped shut and he released her. The sound didn't escape as lantern shutters scraped and light spilled out to fill the tunnel.

"I'm fine. Thank you." Her tongue tripped over addressing him as simply Brogan, instead of Mr. Brogan. He used her name, didn't he? That was a good sign. Wasn't it?

Then she gasped as the crystal rose flared warm against her skin again. She turned, and stared, knowing and yet not knowing the dark-haired girl in boy clothes, near her own age, with her sleeves rolled up to her elbows and a cap set back jauntily on her head.

"Hello, Carmen."

"Essie?" she whispered, as the shimmer of energy against her skin grew stronger. "You're—"

"Yes, I'm real. I think that was our problem," Ess said, as they clasped hands. She gasped just as loudly as Carmen when light flared, just for a heartbeat.

"Please tell me you saw that," Brogan said.

"Yes," the older man standing behind Ess said. "That, I saw."

"We didn't believe for so long," Ess said, as they grinned at each other, "and then we never coordinated enough to talk in our dreams, like we used to when we were little."

"Your mother was my mother's friend. Vivian?" Carmen swallowed a sudden need to shriek as all the months of frustration and wondering, and a realization of all the time they had wasted through secrecy and fear, all came crashing down on her.

It's all right, Ess said, her voice a whisper in Carmen's mind. She slid her hand free to tug down the collar of her shirt, and grinned as the crystal rose came into view.

They introduced her to Endicott, Brogan's friend and benefactor, and then settled in the kitchen. Carmen sniffled, fighting tears when she saw Harriet standing by one of the hearths, conferring with Mary over seasoning for a stew for tonight's dinner. Then the big woman saw her and they hugged and the tears turned to laughter as they babbled and talked over each other, asking and answering questions. Carmen sniffled and laughed a little more when Brogan shoved a massive white handkerchief into her hand to dry her face. He sat next to her, and she let herself imagine that if there weren't so many people there, he might have held her hand as she related what had happened.

"Alexander O'Keefe?" Ess and Endicott exchanged sober glances, then she reached into the messenger bag she had set down on the table and pulled out a sketchpad.

Carmen caught her breath, amazed, as Ess sketched O'Keefe's face with a minimum of lines. She confirmed yes, that was one of the men who had accosted her and the children. Endicott and Ess both looked grimmer when she related how the man had tried to buy her mother's rose, and then today accused her of stealing the cross.

"What is worse, when I saw Mr. Boniface with Mr. O'Keefe today, I had an awful idea. Boniface joined the team just a short while after O'Keefe tried to buy the cross."

When Ess asked, she tried to describe Boniface as best she could. Ess didn't start sketching, but instead flipped through the contents of a flat box underneath the sketchbook. Her heart gave a queer little twitch when Ess pulled out a sketch of Boniface.

"I know him as Briscoe Harrison," Ess said.

"Ah," Endicott said, taking the sketch from her after Carmen confirmed that yes, that was Richard Boniface. "That explains much. I'm sorry, Miss Mackenzie, but I would hazard a very certain guess that this man joined your team with the intent of romancing that bit of important crystal away from you."

"Why is it so important?" She didn't even care how her voice reverberated around the kitchen.

"The crystal is how you went through the gateway to that... whatever it is, the mountain that stretches out forever," Ess said. "Yes, we went there, testing your theory."

"It's time to complete your education," Brogan said, taking hold of her hand. "I had my theories of just who you were, what you could do, but didn't even come close." He took a deep breath. "And that picture makes things even more complicated. I need to check with our sentries, but... we have had periodic attempts to invade the tunnels. On one attempt, the sentries took a crystal rod from the man, and I think, from the description, that was the man." He tapped the sketch of Boniface/Harrison with his free hand.

~~~~~

Three hours later, Ess's throat hurt from talking and explaining and filling in the holes in Carmen's education, her heritage, and all the theories and possibilities of what she might be capable of, with the crystal rose. She thought perhaps practice made everything a little easier. Certainly she had been able to anticipate all Carmen's questions and confusion because she had gone through it all herself last year.

Boniface and O'Keefe had likely sensed the presence of the crystal rose and targeted Carmen, just as Boniface had approached Ess when he glimpsed the matching rose around her neck. Tonight's planned dinner with Harrison/Boniface would be another attempt to take the rose, perhaps by force. Brogan sent some of the older boys to watch at the library for Boniface to show up to meet Carmen. After watching for more than an hour, the boys reported that no one matching either sketch had appeared. Chances were good someone had gone into the library before the boys arrived and determined that Carmen and the children never got there. So where were the two conspirators and their allies right now? What would their next step be? Wait at the restaurant for Ess? Or keep hunting for Carmen?

Boniface had likely been tracking the crystal embedded in Brogan's face, using the crystal rod the sentries had confiscated when they found him wandering through the tunnels. That rod most likely was what made O'Keefe so certain when he claimed Carmen was wearing the rose.

Their first priority, therefore, was to take the crystal rod O'Keefe most likely carried now, before he could follow the energy resonance into the tunnels. They could only theorize how much stronger the resonance would become with two roses in close proximity, along with the crystal in Brogan's face.

He offered to send some of his most loyal followers to wait by the restaurant where Ess was to meet Boniface/Harrison tonight. Endicott suggested they send Wallace ahead to examine the restaurant and surroundings and look for any signs of a trap.

"You do realize, we're going to need to let him in on the whole secret of down below," Ess said, as she and Endicott emerged from the entrance hidden in the cellar of yet another building. She had to dress for the dinner appointment trap.

"I trust him implicitly." Endicott gave her a sideways look. Some inexplicable sparkle in his eyes, clear despite the shadows of the cellar, worried her.

"What else are you plotting?"

"Nothing." He raised the lantern until the light reached the half-flight of stairs to the door out.

"However?"

"However," Endicott said, linking his arm with hers as they crossed the floor, "I believe our Mr. Wallace is girding his loins to begin a campaign for your affections."

"What makes you think... that?" Ess's mouth quirked up in a smile, and that stunned her. Maybe she liked the idea? The thought of the firm's investigator romantically interested in her didn't irritate or frighten or generate any other negative reaction in her.

"A thousand little clues." He chuckled as he released her arm so he could open the door for her. "Starting with what feels like a thousand questions, all focused on you, and none of them having anything to do with our duties as Originators."

"I think I will choose to be flattered."

"Very wise. I am depending on his growing interest in you to keep him loyal, when another man might decide we were either insane or in league with the forces of Hell."

Ess stared at him for a moment, then saw one corner of his mouth twitch. She laughed, and he linked their arms again as they reached the alley running behind the building.

"Do you approve? Do you think my grandparents will approve?"

"The more important question is if Hilda will approve. She likes him. She might change her opinion once she learns of his quest."

Ess tried not to act any differently, tried not to watch Wallace when they met up at the law offices and discussed what they had learned about Harrison/Boniface, and any difficulties the man might present. After the massive damage done to the Revisionists in the last few months, thanks to what had been learned in confiscated records, raided lairs, and the information in Stryker's caches, they couldn't be sure exactly what sort of technology their hereditary enemies possessed. They weren't sure even now what technology the Revisionists had stolen from the Originators, what information had been given to them by traitors, if they were ahead, if they were behind, superior or inferior. Wallace had been fascinated by the Zeus gun and learned to handle it quickly. However, carrying it to the restaurant might prove to be a problem if Boniface was carrying a crystal rod, to ascertain if Ess was wearing the rose. If he sensed the sliver of crystal in the Zeus gun, that would negate any benefit of setting a trap for him.

"Is something wrong?" Uly asked, when brother and sister were alone in the lift going down to the lobby. They had to hurry to their hotel to dress for dinner. Wallace had left ten minutes before to go to the restaurant and prepare.

"With what?"

"Between you and Wallace."

"Why would something be wrong?"

"So he still hasn't gotten up the courage to..." His voice faded and his grin flattened. "You don't realize, do you?"

"I found out today, and I'm still not convinced." She pressed the lever to keep the gate for the lift closed when it reached the ground floor. "What do you think?"

"He's one of the few men I know who can keep up with you."

Ess decided it was wise to laugh. "Do you approve?"

"If you didn't care for him already, would you be asking that?"

Her amusement ended with a dropping sensation in her belly.

~~~~~

Carmen was grateful when dinnertime came. She had spent the remainder of the afternoon with the children, making sure they were all right, laughing with them over the adventure they had had, praising them for how well they had evaded detection. Being with them had helped her by delaying the moment she had to face everything she had learned. Having Ess show up in the flesh had been a pleasant surprise. Learning about her mother's past as a fugitive, the history of the two groups called Revisionists and Originators, and still so much to be revealed kept stealing her breath. Yet with the gateway to the mountainside and the demonstrated healing properties of the crystal rose in the past, as proof that such things were real and possible, how could she not believe?

She needed to get away some place where she would be entirely alone, and just sit and think. Or perhaps pace and think would be more accurate. Go to the mountainside? No, she decided against that almost as soon as she had the idea. Brogan would feel it when she went through the gateway. He would be worried and follow her. She needed to get away from him, as well.

Go above? Where, exactly? She didn't dare go to the library, even if it were open late today. Mrs. Sullivan would be concerned for her and ask questions she couldn't answer. She couldn't risk running into Boniface or O'Keefe again. Perhaps she could go to the strip of land along the river, where she and the children had first entered the tunnel community. Yes, the breeze off the river would be pleasant, and no one would think to look down at the end of the workday as they headed home. Yes, she would go to that tunnel entrance and get some fresh air and solitude and thinking time.

If she could remember the way. Carmen nearly laughed aloud as she paused at the first intersection of tunnels she came to and tried to decipher the paint splotches and chisel marks in the rock by the light of her lantern. She caught the rose between two fingers to rub it, as she had taken to doing quite often lately, and that reminded her of that snowy night of thinking and decision back in Chicago, when Frierri's ultimatum hung heavy over her head.

Hadn't the crystal rose helped her to remember other visits to Chicago? Hadn't those memories led her to Harriet, which got her here to Cleveland and Brogan and finally meeting Ess and getting some answers? Ess and Brogan and Mr. Endicott had all agreed that the crystal didn't just help to heal bodies, but stored memories and information. A disturbing thought she didn't want to explore quite yet, thank you very much. So couldn't she somehow ask the crystal to help her remember the path through the tunnels, to the riverside entrance? How exactly could she do that?

Perhaps the rose functioned like the clockwork people she had seen at exhibitions. The automatons could be directed through routine actions with clever metal plates full of punches and ridges, like music box disks. The crystal needed clear, simple directions. Since they said it touched on her mind, and memories were in her mind, perhaps she needed to focus very hard on where she was, and then where she wanted to be? Would the crystal understand?

"Lord, help me, I'm thinking about it as if it were a rational being with a mind and soul," she muttered.

The crystal hummed under her fingertips. Either Brogan was coming to find her, justifiably worried about her, or someone else was coming. Ess? Hadn't they theorized that O'Keefe also had some crystal, and used it to hunt her down? The thought of Brogan hunting for her made her feel warm and somewhat teary-glad, while the thought of O'Keefe made her want to run the opposite direction. Common sense told her Ess was too busy getting ready for the trap they wanted to spring on Boniface.

Now the question remained, which direction should she run?

"Tell me," she whispered, and slipped the chain off her neck, so she could hold the rose in the palm of her hand.

Chapter Twenty-Four

A sound something like a petulant scream caught in her throat when the rose hummed a little stronger, almost a buzz, so she imagined it was like a wasp about to sting, yet nothing significant happened to give her direction. What exactly did she expect it to do? Change in intensity when she waved it to the right or to the left, to indicate direction? Unless it warned about something ahead of her?

"Idiot." She turned and ran the opposite direction. Carmen could almost have laughed as the humming did indeed soften.

If that was Brogan coming after her, then she was foolish to run. Especially as there were no paint splotches to guide her. On the other hand, if that was O'Keefe approaching, wisdom said to get as far and as quickly away from him as she could.

No paint splotches. Blue meant the living areas, and the kitchen. Green meant explored areas, and would eventually take her in a great loop, bringing her back where she started. Red was one long path going under the city, as far as the natural tunnels led. White would take her to the salt mines. Would someone be coming back from the salt tunnels at this time of day? Should she warn them in case Boniface were chasing her?

"At least they have tools as weapons," she thought aloud. Carmen held up the lantern as she came to another intersection. No paint splotches, just gouges in the wall. Arrows, perhaps?

She stepped closer to examine the gouges, praying for paint splotches. Hadn't Mary said to stay in tunnels with paint? Eventually they would lead her back to other people, to help and safety.

The rose hummed stronger in her clenched fist. Carmen caught her breath and turned, looking back down the tunnel the way she had come. She should have gone to the gateway and the hillside for her thinking and solitude, however short-lived it would have been.

"Please, blessed Savior..." she whispered, and slipped the chain around her neck again.

If someone using crystal followed her, should she take off the rose and leave it behind? Yet how would she know if she were still being followed?

Idiot, she silently scolded herself. While she stood and dithered like a featherhead, whoever followed her drew closer. Ess could hear her through the rose. What were the chances so could Brogan?

Please, Brogan, if that is you... please, call out to me? She focused all her energies on the crystal rose and took the tunnel to the right. Until she could be sure who was behind her, the wise choice was to keep moving, even if she had no idea where she was going. Carmen thought about singing, to try to raise some of the energy and magic-but-not-magic of the rose.

No, she couldn't sing, but could she hum, softly, quiet enough no one else could hear? Would that do anything, signal Brogan, perhaps help her figure out what to do?

As soon as she thought it, she hummed the opening stanzas of *Turtledove*, held the rose to her throat, and focused on Brogan's fiercest expression.

Light flared from the rose, illuminating the tunnel ahead of her in stark relief. A harsh buzzing through her flesh momentarily stunned her. Carmen let out a yelp and staggered backward and dropped the rose. The light dimmed as it fell and she muffled a gasp of relief that she still wore it on a chain.

"Well, hello, darling," Boniface said from the darkness of the intersecting tunnel behind her.

Carmen swallowed down a cry and held out the lantern with one shaking hand. Light shimmered softly against the walls at the intersection. Through the hammering of her heart she heard footsteps. Just one set of footsteps?

The light grew stronger. It didn't waver like an oil lantern or a candle. Carmen pressed against the tunnel wall, backing away slowly, and for a moment considered throwing down the lantern and just running in the darkness. Then the rose grew warm through the cloth of her shirt, and the light spilling down the tunnel toward her grew bright enough she nearly needed to shade her eyes.

Boniface stepped into the intersection and turned toward her, holding out a rod maybe as long as his forearm, glowing white as ice, maybe as thick as a gentleman's cane. In his other hand he held a pistol.

Please, Brogan, come to me, Carmen thought with enough force her head hurt, as she clutched the crystal rose tight in her hand.

"Lost?" Boniface gestured back the way they had come. "How convenient that I know the way to the nearest exit. This darkness and damp really aren't good for you. Very bad for your health." He chuckled, a low, throaty sound she equated with bullfrogs and carnivorous animals she had seen in shadowy carnival sideshows. When he gestured with the gun, she complied. At least his hands were full, and he couldn't take hold of her arm or hand.

~~~~~

"Something is wrong." Ess pressed her hand against the rose that buzzed against her skin. It lay between her chemise and her dress, and for a few seconds, she thought an old-fashioned armor-level corset wouldn't have been insulation enough against the flare of energy.

"Very wrong," Wallace said, joining them in the shadowed doorway across the street from the hotel and restaurant where she and Uly were to meet Boniface/Harrison in five more minutes.

"I can guess what's wrong in there," Uly said. "What is that blasted necklace doing now?"

"Carmen is doing something, or something is happening to her." Ess sighed as the sensations faded as quickly as they had erupted. She could only guess that the problem had been dealt with, or the other girl had stopped trying to do whatever she was trying. "What about there?" She gestured with her chin at the restaurant's front door.

"O'Keefe is there," Wallace said, "but Harrison is nowhere to be seen. The head waiter is a friend of mine, and he was very happy to inform me that the gentleman was most upset, to the point of fearing he would draw a gun on him."

"Over what?" Uly said.

"He wanted a private dining room. Then he wanted the staff to tell you that he would be delayed, and you should wait inside. He won't be happy to know you have an escort." He nodded to Uly.

"He's waiting inside, and expects the staff to make Ess think she's walking into an empty room?" Uly grinned and shook his head. "Grandfather is right. Criminals are, in the end, rather stupid."

"This one more than most. Who made the arrangements? Him or Harrison?"

"Harrison. When we encountered each other supposedly by chance," Ess said. "Which it wasn't. Why, what problems did he create?"

"Well, O'Keefe wanted the room reserved all day, so he could make adjustments to the furnishings. Perhaps hide weapons. He expected the private dining room to have an outside entrance and was quite upset to learn only the Macintosh Hotel, two blocks away, has that feature." Wallace leaned back against the wall and looked Ess over. "Pinkertons are masters at hiding an entire arsenal on your persons, when necessary. I hope you're very well armed, Miss Ess."

"I am armed, but I am not getting any closer to that trap than this doorway." She was pleased when her wry response earned a twitch of the lips from Wallace, and nothing more.

"What do you say we leave O'Keefe to stew in his own juices for a while?" Uly offered her his bent elbow.

"He's getting as itchy as a skinnydipper who rolled out of the water straight into a poison ivy patch," Wallace said.

"If only Allistair could have responded and arrived sooner," Ess murmured. "He would have such fun baiting O'Keefe before arresting him."

"You're a cruel young lady, Miss Ess," Wallace said with mocking astonishment. "How would you like to handle this, since our planned trap isn't working out?"

"He's setting up a trap for me. What are the chances he would expect a trap to be set for him?" She turned to her brother. "Does O'Keefe know you?"

Uly's frown slowly shifted to a nasty grin. "Keep him busy? Distract him?"

"Get him so confused, he doesn't realize we're sneaking up on him." She reached into her stiff, unusually large handbag. It was lumpy and clanked a little, the contents settling, as she dug for the one item that she swore was sentient enough to know she was searching for it, and to hide. Then as her fingers closed around the handle of the Zeus gun, Theo's newest and smallest design, she nearly swore. "I am such an idiot."

"What?" Uly almost didn't take the gun when she handed it to him.

"Why isn't Harrison here, if O'Keefe is expecting him?" She looked down the street, trying to remember where the closest tunnel entrance was hidden in one of the surrounding buildings. Brogan had given her a map this afternoon, but she hadn't had time for more than a cursory glance at it.

"Carmen," her brother said. He took a step to head down the street. She caught hold of his arm.

"No, you need to handle O'Keefe."

"I don't suppose you'll let me accompany you?" Wallace said.

"You're known. I need you to convince your friend not to call the police, and to persuade the police not to interfere, if there's a fuss and they do show up. Hurry to catch up." She caught up her skirts and didn't care if she showed too much ankle as she hurried down the street. Why hadn't she listened to instinct and worn trousers underneath her fancy dress?

~~~~~

"You're working with that O'Keefe, aren't you?" Carmen said, when Boniface slowed their progress down the tunnel. There were still no paint splotches on the wall, and she hoped that meant he was lost. "When he couldn't buy my mother's cross, he sent you to romance it away from me."

"More than romance you, darling." He raised the crystal rod higher, examining the chisel marks on the wall ahead of them.

She took some comfort from the muffled oath that escaped his lips. He had stopped smiling with such galling triumph about ten minutes ago. However, he had pocketed his gun and took a tight grip on her wrist at that time. Every time she tried to resist, just the slightest, he yanked hard enough to make her arm ache all the way to her shoulder. If she got the chance to fight free, she was going to need that arm, so she stopped resisting. For now. They moved forward again.

"We wanted you, along with the rose. When you didn't fall into my arms, we resorted to harsher methods. Admittedly, rather amusing. Nothing more entertaining than destroying a bunch of pious do-gooders and making them attack each other in the process."

"You?" Carmen stopped for half a second, and barely felt the yank-twist on her arm as he got her moving again. "You started all the rumors, all the accusations? You destroyed my father's reputation, just for a piece of rock?"

He loosed a vicious, cold chuckle. "The plan was to get you entirely alone, helpless, and destitute enough to sell the rose. Of course, wiser heads wanted Anna's daughter. Even your diluted bloodlines have great potential. Then, as we inflamed rumors, and talked to people who didn't like you, we learned enough to know we had to have you. Re-educate you. If even half the stories we heard are any indication, you have twice the strength and potential your mother did. The filthy traitor." He spat. "We should have known she would go to ground with a bunch of religious idiots, after the way she turned her back on her own people." He glanced at her and chuckled. "Oh, you don't like that, do you? Well, your education is sadly lacking. I'm guessing she hid your heritage from you, including teaching you what crystal could do, what she could do. What a waste." He shook his head.

"Our purpose has always been to wipe out the silly, self-sacrificing, charitable justification for all the time and effort and resources you and your father and his moronic friends have wasted. Our ancestors were right, to try to go back in time and change history. Imagine how much better this world would be if one man hadn't spread the plague of his simpering idealism. Only the strong would survive. The Human race would be much better off. Idiots and defectives wouldn't be allowed to waste food and clothing and shelter and medicine that belong to those more deserving, those who can create a better world, unburdened by the weak and useless."

Carmen shuddered and fought to keep her face stoic. She feared her revulsion would either enrage him so he would be more brutal or amuse him. She was even more proud of her mother, who had turned her back on such cruel selfishness and arrogance. If she could, she would destroy her rose, no matter how precious it was to her, rather than allow it to fall into the possession of such people.

Please, Brogan, hear me! You felt when I went through the gateway. Feel where I am now.

The light coming from the rod rippled, momentarily tinted blue. Boniface stopped short and frowned at it.

"Huh. What are you trying?"

"It's not me." Carmen thought her heart would shudder right out of her chest. She quite lost her breath as an idea came to her, triggered by her desperate call for Brogan. "It's the gateway."

"What are you talking about?" He shook his head and yanked hard on her arm, almost twisting it behind her. "Don't try to be clever this late in the game."

"The ancestors traveled through time, didn't they?" Her words came out strained, but she was proud she didn't give away the ache in her shoulder. "Where do you think they learned to do it?"

Boniface spun her around, shoving her up against the wall. A knob of rock stabbed her low in her spine. He shoved the crystal rod nearly in her face. She imagined him stabbing her in the eye if he didn't like what she had to say next. How much longer could she delay and distract him before he decided he didn't want her after all, ripped the rose from around her neck, and left her lost in the dark? Or worse, killed her before he tried to escape the tunnels?

"Explain," he growled.

"I came here because of an entry I found in my mother's journal. She said there was a place the ancestors had mentioned, the source of the crystal. She knew lots of things that most others didn't know. Using the crystal." Carmen swallowed hard and couldn't take her gaze off the tip of the crystal rod, now only inches from her face. It shone so brightly, she couldn't see Boniface's expression.

"Unfortunately, that's true. She abused her privileges. Turned against us." He muffled a few curses when the rod flickered blue three more times in rapid succession.

Carmen lost her train of thought as the rose buzzed against her skin, in synchrony with the rod.

"Go on." He loosened his grip on her wrist and leaned back a few inches. Maybe he thought she was frightened witless. Carmen wished she were clever enough to play up that assumption, but she could barely think of what to weave into her desperate little story next, let alone dissemble.

"The gateway goes to another place. Another time." She licked her lips. "One single moment in time that doesn't change."

"Where is this gateway?"

"Blue." She tried not to gasp in relief as he released her arm.

He caught hold of her collar and yanked, popping three buttons to reveal the rose. A squeak escaped her as Boniface's fingers brushed against her bare skin and he caught up the rose on two fingers. He was going to take the rose and kill her, just as she had feared.

"Blue what?" He sneered, malice sparkling in his eyes, as he stroked downward with the backs of those two fingers, brushing the top curve of one breast.

"The passageways marked with blue paint. They lead to the tunnel holding the gateway." Carmen caught her breath as the crystal rod's light flickered to blue, but instead of going back to the bright white, the blue deepened.

Boniface frowned at it, and her heart gave a little leap. Could it be he had no idea what it was doing?

Was that a footstep, beyond the thudding of her heart? A single boot scraping on the stone?

Please, Brogan—

I hear you. I'm here. Fight him!

She shrieked at the sound of his voice in her mind and swung her aching arm upward, managing to clip the side of her captor's face. Boniface jerked away, then spun back, swinging the rod up and then slashing down at Carmen's face.

Brogan leaped from the darkness, a sleek black shadow, impacting Boniface square in the back and sending them both tumbling down the tunnel. The crystal rod went flying. Carmen scrambled after it while the two men pummeled and struggled and grunted and cursed in the darkness behind her. The light changed, softening to a warm, golden hue like sunset the moment her fingers closed around the rod. She turned around and hurried back to the fighting.

They were on their feet, punching and staggering and turning each other about so they kept moving down the tunnel, away from her. The light's touch changed them from black, struggling shapes and revealed their features. Brogan delivered a swift undercut to Boniface's ribs, sending him flying into the darkness. He turned to look at her.

"Are you all right?" His face was red with effort, streaked with dirt and blood from his nose and split lip.

"Now I am. Where—"

Three gunshots in rapid succession shattered the air, the echoes deafening. Carmen shrieked and dropped to her knees. Brogan staggered, twisting to the right to slam into the wall. Boniface stepped into the light, pointing the gun at her at the same moment the stink of gunpowder and blood reached her.

Fury burned a clear channel through her. The rose stabbed like a coal through her skin and the rod in her hand lit up bloody red. Whiplashes of flame shot out of the rod. Boniface shrieked, terror turning his face into a carnival mask, and he turned and fled into the darkness. Carmen couldn't unclench her fist as she scrambled forward on her hands and knees to Brogan's side. The light faded to a pale yellow and flickered.

"Please, please, please don't die," she begged as she fumbled one-handed to turn him over and look for his wounds.

"Not yet," Brogan groaned. His eyelids fluttered and he raised his left hand to press against the side of his head where blood spilled from a gash. "Just my shoulder. I swear."

"Just," she sputtered. Carmen swallowed hard against a need to burst into tears and fling herself over him.

She had always despised girls in dramas or novels who gave into hysterics when there were injuries to tend and damage to repair, or breaches in the fortress wall to block before the enemy spilled through. She brought the rod closer to look at his shoulder. The blood made his black coat glisten. She peeled back his coat and vest and then his shirt. She hesitated, her gorge rising, when she saw the bloody, mangled ruin of his upper arm, perilously close to the joint, where the bullet had dug a deep furrow.

"I'm so sorry," she whispered.

"Don't be." Brogan tried to smile. He looked rather greenish. "I've been much worse." He inhaled deeply and pushed with his good arm, trying to sit up. She spotted a shelf-like projection in the rock wall over his head, and put the rod down on it. To her relief, as she helped him sit up, the light didn't go out, though the color did shift from pale yellow to cold white again.

She couldn't understand why her stomach kept twisting as she helped him out of his coat and vest and tore the sleeve off his shirt, to fashion a bandage. All the times she had helped tend the ill and injured and destitute, she had always relied on her strong stomach. Certainly, she had never seen such a bad bullet wound, but why would blood and torn flesh bother her now?

The patient made the difference.

Carmen nearly paused in fashioning a sling with Brogan's vest. The idea reverberated through her head as if it were hollow, and then plummeted down into her chest. Yes, indeed, his injury affected her personally.

"You are the proverbial angel of mercy." Brogan brought his hand, streaked with dried blood, up to rest on hers.

"And you are my guardian angel." She tried to smile and felt like an utter ninny when her voice cracked.

"Fallen angel. Disfigured Prometheus." His smile brought tears to her eyes even as a gasping little laugh escaped her. She finished knotting the ends of the vest and gently slid his injured arm into the makeshift sling. "Perfect. Thank you, Angel."

"We're both fools. Battle shock, perhaps?" She didn't care how it looked, because after all, who was here to see? She cupped his chin and leaned forward to brush a kiss across his cheek, deliberately choosing the disfigured one.

She didn't feel the bubbled, scarred skin under her lips, but a shimmer of something under his skin, a merging of hearing and touch. It filled her head with light. That was the crystal in his flesh and bone.

"Carmen—"

She sat back, delighted he had used her first name again, and looked up to see Boniface slipping the crystal rod off the shelf. His gun was just inches from her face.

"Let's take a walk, shall we?" Even the blood smearing his face, the swelling of his nose and mouth, and the bruise forming around both his eyes couldn't mar the triumph that gleamed there.

Chapter Twenty-Five

Brogan leaned on Carmen, his good arm around her shoulders, his injured shoulder braced by the sling, and his steps increasingly unsteady as they went down the tunnels. Perhaps he was losing his mind, hallucinating from loss of blood, because he had never been so happy in years. He had to be hallucinating, because he could swear every once in a while, he felt the uneven stone flooring through *her* feet, when she half-tripped in dips or over ridges. He felt the ache in *her* back, holding up his weight. He felt the humming of the crystal in his cheek through the top of *her* head, when his head drooped and rested against her hair. The sensation of being somehow bound together with Carmen in mind and spirit wasn't a bad way to spend his last hours, if he were going to die today.

Boniface would definitely kill him. It only made sense. Right now, he used Brogan's weakness to control Carmen. She wouldn't run off and leave him, even if she knew the tunnels well enough to navigate in the dark. The man kept the gun pointed at both of them, forcing her to support him and forcing Brogan to lead them to the gateway.

He thought Carmen was exceedingly clever to come up with that story to distract Boniface, and perhaps even trick him into letting her live a little longer. Until he found out how to get through the gateway, he needed her, and needed Brogan to guide them. Once they were close to an exit, would Boniface need either of them? He supposed the man would shoot him first and brutalize Carmen until she gave him what he wanted. How long could she hold up against such treatment before she succumbed?

You're such a pessimist, Carmen said into his mind. *Can't you think any encouraging thoughts to get us through this?*

You — can hear me?

We need more time to decipher the wonders and mystery of this crystal. While I don't mind hearing your thoughts, because every girl needs some flattery and it's been so long since someone worried about me, well... I wouldn't like other people hearing our thoughts. Especially some of the things you're thinking about me. I think you are hallucinating a little, thinking I smell particularly sweet. How could anyone smell pleasant with all this blood and dirt and damp and...

A tiny chuckling sigh escaped her.

I adore you, Carmen Mackenzie.

Tell me that when we're safe and clean and there are witnesses.

Brogan laughed, only a single bark of sound, because the effort hurt his shoulder.

Boniface shoved the gun into his back, just inches from his bleeding wound. Brogan fancied he heard the wet squelch of metal against blood-soaked cloth.

"How much further?" their captor demanded.

"Almost there." Carmen gestured with her free hand at the blue splotches of paint just above her head on the far wall.

"How does 'almost' translate into time and distance?"

"Just around the next bend," Brogan said.

Light exploded through the back of his head. His knees folded and for half a second he feared Boniface had shot him. Carmen's shriek of fury echoed up and down the tunnel. He pitched forward. No, the man had just clubbed him with the butt of the gun. His forehead smacked against the tunnel wall, creating another flash in his eyes, and he gagged as tearing heat ripped up from his twisted shoulder. Through the thundering of his pulse, he heard footsteps scuffling on the damp stone. Carmen fought as Boniface dragged her away, and he thought he had never loved anyone as much as he did her right that moment.

"Please, Savior, I know we haven't talked much lately, but please... help me save her," he groaned as he reached with his good arm to brace himself and struggle to his feet.

Were those footsteps behind him? He turned, nearly knocking himself off his feet when he was only halfway upright. Everything was blurry, but he could make out a few spots of light. Lanterns. Then he was surrounded by people. McTeague and Ess and Endicott and a dozen other tunnel residents. Endicott steadied him and put an arm around his back to brace him.

"I'm not going back," Brogan insisted, when he could swallow down the nausea enough to speak.

"Wouldn't dream of it." Ess gestured down the tunnel after Boniface and Carmen.

~~~~~

"Amazing," Boniface gasped, his face brightening with wonder. He shoved Carmen hard against the wall so her head slammed against stone and pressed against her, holding her still with the entire weight of his body. Then he gave all his attention to the shimmering ripples of light forming the gateway.

She had half-hoped he wouldn't be able to see it. Most definitely, contact with crystal let people see the doorway. It required no special sensitivity.

"Well, darling, let's see what's on the other side. You said a world where time doesn't pass?" He leaned harder against her, pressing his hips into hers, and chuckled when she gasped in hot, disgusted nausea. "A world outside time. Eternity. Paradise, perhaps?"

"Your kind doesn't believe in paradise," she growled as he stepped back and yanked her away from the wall.

"Every man must make his own paradise. The Moors believe in a paradise where every man has seventy women to satisfy his every need. I could take a paradise like that." Another chuckle as he shook her and shoved her toward the gateway, never letting go of her bruised, aching arm. "Don't be jealous, darling, you'll be my number one wife. If you're a good girl."

Carmen turned as hard as she could and kicked as high as she could. Boniface snarled and backhanded her, so she thought her nose would break and explode through the back of her head. Through her gasps, she heard the pounding of boots and men shouting. Boniface snatched her up, wrapping his arm tight around her waist, and staggered toward the gateway.

She heard people calling her name but everything was a blur, until she heard Brogan's voice. She fought, twisting in Boniface's grip and he lifted her off her feet, swinging her around. She blinked the tears from her eyes, gasping for breath. Then the green-gold light of the gateway flared in front of her eyes.

"How do we get through?" Boniface growled, dropping her on her knees in front of the ring of light. He pulled out his gun and swung it down so the muzzle scraped her cheek.

"You have to hold hands, and hold onto the crystal together," Ess called, as the crowd of people filling the tunnel slid and scrambled to a halt. "Carmen, cooperate, please. Take him through. Hold. On. Tight. Never. *Let. Go.*"

Carmen shook her head, wondering why Ess put such emphasis on those words. Understanding shot through her as Ess spread her fingers wide.

"Take it," Boniface growled, shoving the crystal rod into Carmen's face, so this time she thought it really would go through her eye.

She flinched as she grasped the other half of the rod and the subliminal humming that filled her head turned audible. A hint of discord made the crystal buzz against her palm. It grew louder, shifting into clashing notes in an unhappy chord as Boniface caught his gun hand under her arm and dragged her to her feet. He turned, keeping the gun pointed at her, watching her rescuers standing only ten feet away.

"We'll be right behind you," Brogan said, moving to the front of the group, supported by Endicott. He looked so pale, so grim, Carmen swallowed a sob.

"Listen to the hero," Boniface sneered.

That galvanized her. She let him turn her to face the gateway. Carmen took a deep breath and tightened her grip on the crystal rod and lunged forward with their first step into the light. She twisted, kicking, throwing herself facedown. Boniface cursed, the sound changing to a shriek as she yanked the rod from his grip and her arm slid from his grasp. She landed on her knees in a silver stream of water only a few inches deep.

Alone.

Gasping, fighting sobs, reluctant to think about what she had just done, she dropped the crystal rod, scrambled out of the water, and looked around the hillside. Her heartbeats slowed and the soft whisper of the wind penetrated as her breathing quieted. The perfume of apples and ripening blackberries reached her, and the stream whisper-chuckled over the pebbles as it continued down the hillside.

She was entirely alone. No sign of Boniface. Were the others dealing with him now, or would he be waiting for her, the tunnel strewn with dead bodies, when she came back through?

Brogan and Endicott stepped through in a soft flash of blue-tinted light, tearing a gasp from her. Ess followed, holding hands with McTeague and another man from the work crew. They all drew guns and spread out, looking in every direction. Brogan slid to his knees. His boneless collapse galvanized her into action, nearly leaping the dozen or so yards to reach his side.

Endicott cursed under his breath as he helped Carmen turn Brogan over. She braced him against her and checked the bandage under his coat. It was nearly black with blood.

"You chivalrous idiot," the lawyer muttered.

Brogan smiled. He looked even paler here in the golden light. "Where?" he whispered.

"Boniface?" Carmen lay him down on his back and lifted her skirts to tear bandages from her petticoat. "He's not here."

"He didn't come back." Endicott shuddered.

"What is this place, Boss?" McTeague whispered, staring, turning several times so Carmen thought he might make himself dizzy.

"A gift, a sanctuary." Ess shrugged. "We can figure that out later. We need to get him to a doctor before he bleeds out completely."

"Sing," Brogan said, his voice so soft Carmen thought she was the only one who could hear.

A curse threatened to fill her mouth. What kind of an idiot was she, not to think of that before? Granted, she hadn't had time to think of it with a gun pointed in her face and Boniface dragging her hither and yon. She rubbed at her face and tried to brace herself. Right now, she was perfectly willing to believe the Almighty had used her to heal Mouse's broken leg, that it simply hadn't been cut when the child fell. Could she be a vessel of healing for a man this badly injured?

She didn't have time to question.

"Can you get that?" She pointed at the rod, glinting in the light, sitting on a patch of pale green-gold moss where she had left it. "Brogan... please, blessed Savior, use me. Make me a vessel of Your healing and grace."

Music in the Night

With the smell and sight of blood filling her senses, the first hymn that came to her mind dealt with the blood of Calvary. She held Brogan's hand, took the rod when Ess brought it to her, and sang all the verses. Then went on to another song, while the rod shimmered through red and orange to yellow and then to green and covered Brogan in a soft blanket of color. Peripherally, she was aware of McTeague and the other man taking off their work caps. Endicott knelt on Brogan's other side and held his hand. Ess knelt beside Carmen and gripped her shoulders, and she felt a change in the subliminal humming of the crystal. Perhaps that was Ess's rose joining its energy or power or whatever it contained to the battle. Endicott's lips moved, and during a pause as Carmen searched for another song to sing, she thought she heard him whispering prayers. That brought new tears to her eyes, and she blinked them away, scolding herself for being ridiculous.

Her song faltered when Ess let go of her, but she pressed on. Then Ess shifted around to her other side, to examine Brogan's blood-soaked bandage. Carmen closed her eyes, refusing to falter again. She would if she saw that awful wound. Ess said nothing. Was that a bad sign?

Finally, her throat grew dry and her voice wavered, and she couldn't remember all the songs she sang. She had gone through every song she sang when she tended the injured and ill children at the camp meetings, and sang the song she had sung for Mouse's broken leg three times, just in case there was some healing power in those specific words.

"Carmen." Ess gripped her hand where it held Brogan's, and gently tugged. "It's done. I don't think you can do any more. Best to stop now."

Her protest caught in her aching throat. Carmen opened her eyes and couldn't make a sound as she stared at the dried blood and mangled flesh of Brogan's shoulder. Healing flesh, bright pink with forming scar tissue. No longer bleeding. He was still too pale, but his chest did rise and fall with breaths, and surely if the Almighty had granted healing for his arm, blood would replace what had been lost as well.

Carmen's throat ached with the ragged chuckle that escaped when she couldn't seem to make her fingers open and drop the crystal rod.

~~~~~

By the time Brogan could get out of bed, they had worked out several theories for what the mountainside was, what it could be, and why crystal provided the key to passing through. The ancestors had never recorded the source of the crystal used to build the Great Machine. What if someone was able to locate the crystal in a pocket of time, such as the time box that Matilda and Ernest Fremont had been able to access, and using the technology of the far future, had opened a doorway to remove crystal, thereby creating a key? Those with the most exposure to crystal became attuned to it. There were pockets of crystal scattered all over the planet, as evidenced by the time slips and time "burps," as Uly termed them, that had been documented in other places. Someone in the future had developed the technology to not only find those deposits of crystal, but dig them up, and then form them into the pieces of the Great Machine. Someone had deciphered a way to control the crystal so they could go backward in time, instead of simply stepping outside the stream of time and leaping forward.

"So once we retrieve all the pieces of crystal the ancestors hid when they disassembled the Great Machine," Carmen said, "do we then shift our efforts to finding those deposits of crystal and digging them up to keep them out of the Revisionists' hands, so the ancestors, when they are born in the future, never have a chance to try to change history in the first place?"

"That might be wise, that might be a waste of time." Endicott smiled as he said it and leaned back to gaze up at the sunless sky.

Most of their discussions dealing with crystal and filling in her education about the Originators and Revisionists took place on the other side of the gateway. Usually a large number of them stepped through the gateway with blankets and cushions for comfortable seating, and a picnic lunch. It seemed easier to contemplate the existence of other worlds and the ability to step through time there, in a place that sang softly of possibilities and impossibilities.

"He's referring to the cascade theory," Brogan said, taking hold of Carmen's hand. "We aren't in the original world of our ancestors, so history might not progress as we think it should or will."

"Like the ancients who heard dire prophecies of doom and destruction, and by trying to change the circumstances actually brought about those prophecies," Ess said, "doing nothing might be the best way of preventing the future we don't want to happen." She pressed her fists to her temples and let out a groan. "I'm turning into my grandparents! This actually makes sense to me."

Of course, everyone laughed, and Carmen decided she quite looked forward to getting to know Matilda and Ernest when they returned from Europe. The elder Fremonts and the crew of the *Golden Nile* had been sent for, and she had even had a chance to speak with them through the communication plate, which was a wonder almost strange enough to overwhelm her. Then again, there were times she thought perhaps she had been immersed in so many wonders, nothing could amaze her anymore.

Except for the healing she was sure she saw in Brogan's face. Maybe it was a side effect or residue of the healing of his shoulder, but she could swear the bubbled texture of his scarred cheek had smoothed out. It certainly looked healthier, closer to the skin tones on the other side of his face. She wasn't about to say anything about it because she feared she imagined it, and she didn't want to hurt him. Most especially because sometimes, when the light hit his cheek just right, she thought she saw a sparkle of crystal, just below the surface of his skin. Possibly she was the only one who could see it.

Did it really matter?

Music in the Night

While Brogan had been confined to bed, Ess and Carmen had tested all the Originators within a day's journey of Cleveland to see who could sense the presence of the gateway, who could see the light, and how much crystal they needed in their grasp to awaken the gateway. They applied what Carmen and Brogan had theorized, and what Ess and Uly had learned while recreating the communication plates, and used music as a final test for sensitivity to the gateway. Many who couldn't sense the energy or see the light of the gateway while holding the crystal rod confiscated from Boniface could awaken it when they sang, with just a tiny crystal button clasped in their hands.

Music was the key. Carmen found it quite appropriate, because music had brought light in the darkest moments of her life, and now music awakened light in the perpetual night underground.

Summer rolled across the city, turning steamy despite the cooling breezes off the lake. Carmen welcomed the cooler surroundings underground and settled into her new routine of teaching the children in the morning and studying with Ess and learning about her heritage and her mother in the afternoon. Evenings were for handling the needs of the growing community. They had much work to do to adjust the residential area to accommodate some of the tunnels that would be taken over by the tower to be built above them. Her favorite, most important activity, however, was singing every night with Brogan. He took great pleasure in challenging her with songs he knew but she didn't. When she went out with the children for excursions to the library or to the lake or river, she tried to visit stores that would have sheet music. Sometimes she heard whispers and giggles from the darkness beyond their singing room, with its perfect acoustics. Most of the time, she didn't mind knowing that they had an audience nearly every night. Her parents had taught her that beauty deserved to be shared.

When the audience grew large enough to be distracting, they went to the mountainside to sing. They sometimes lost all track of time passing, so that when they returned to the tunnels, morning light spilled through the cracks in the far walls of the bluff or the ventilation shafts.

They went to the hillside and sang almost until midnight the day that the *Golden Nile* was due to reach Cleveland. Brogan had brought cakes and a bottle of a fruity chilled tea Hilda had created, and they talked. About the airship arriving. The progress on the tower. A new tunnel that the boys had discovered while exploring with McTeague the day before. Explorers armed with chunks of crystal had thoroughly mapped all the places in the tunnels where gateways appeared. After their guests from the *Golden Nile* had arrived, they planned on a series of trips through each gateway, to see where they led. The first three gateways discovered had been tested, and so far they all opened onto the same spot on the hillside.

"What if there is only one moment in time, one spot on the hillside?"

Carmen said. "All gateways lead here."

"Why here, specifically?" Brogan countered, that sparkle she loved filling his eyes. "This place seems to go on forever. How would we know it is the same hillside, just somewhere a mile away, when we come out?"

"We could spend the rest of our lives exploring. Or perhaps there are different places that can only be reached by gateways from other cities, or states, or even countries. The gateways we have found come to the same spot here because they are so close together." Carmen thought she could understand how Ess felt when she proposed theories that should have come out of her brilliant grandparents' mouths.

"We could have a way to travel all over the world, once we learn how far we have to travel from this spot." He caught up her hand. "You did say 'we,' didn't you?"

She nodded, her face warming.

"Until then..." The words she wanted to say caught in her throat. "Well, it just seems wrong that we have this whole enormous place all to ourselves."

"We are sharing it. We harvest food every day, for our own people and to share with the destitute, and to feed Hilda's children. When winter comes, we can come here for outings and sunshine and just to be warm." He sighed and squeezed her hand. Carmen didn't mind if he never let go. "I understand what you mean, though. We take so much from this place already, maybe it just feels as if we should bring something here. In exchange."

Carmen was still thinking about it the next afternoon as she and Ess were putting the finishing touches on the guestroom for Ernest and Matilda. When she mentioned what Brogan had said, Ess laughed.

"Imagine all the things we could store there. The world's largest warehouse. Because it could possibly be an entire world."

"Oh." Carmen dropped the oil lamp she had been about to put on the sideboard. Ess saved her, catching it just in time. "Not just store things. *Hide* things."

"Hide." Ess's gaze locked with hers. One of those rare instances when images leaped between their minds. They smiled and as one person, touched their crystal roses.

The End

Notes on Songs:

"Turtledove" and "I Know Where I'm Going" are folk songs, from the general area of England/Ireland/Scotland, and old enough for a cursory Internet search to reveal multiple variations on the lyrics and no certainty of the original author. In this case, the author used the lyrics as remembered from vocal training class in college. The exact song book is nigh to impossible to trace, because it was borrowed and the class was more than thirty years ago.

"The Solid Rock," by Edward Mote, circa 1834, in the public domain.

"Savior, Like a Shepherd Lead us," by Dorothy A. Thrupp, circa 1836, public domain.

About the Author

On the road to publication, Michelle fell into fandom in college and has 40+ stories in various SF and fantasy universes. She has a bunch of useless degrees in theater, English, film/communication, and writing. Even worse, she has over 100 books and novellas with multiple small presses, in science fiction and fantasy, YA, suspense, women's fiction, and sub-genres of romance.

Her official launch into publishing came with winning first place in the Writers of the Future contest in 1990. She was a finalist in the EPIC Awards competition multiple times, winning with *Lorien* in 2006 and *The Meruk Episodes, I-V*, in 2010, and was a finalist in the Realm Awards competition, in conjunction with the Realm Makers convention.

Her training includes the Institute for Children's Literature; proofreading at an advertising agency; and working at a community newspaper. She is a tea snob and freelance edits for a living (MichelleLevigne@gmail.com for info/rates), but only enough to give her time to write. Her newest crime against the literary world is to be co-managing editor at Mt. Zion Ridge Press and launching the publishing co-op, Ye Olde Dragon Books. Be afraid … be very afraid.

And please check out her newest venture: Ye Olde Dragon's Library, the storytelling podcast. Interspersed between the chapters will be interviews with authors of fantastical fiction. Listen to the podcast on your favorite podcast app or listen on the website: www.YeOldeDragonBooks.com, and click on the Ye Olde Dragon's Library link.

www.Mlevigne.com
www.MichelleLevigne.blogspot.com
www.YeOldeDragonBooks.com
www.MtZionRidgePress.com

NEWSLETTER:
Want to learn about upcoming books, book launch parties, inside information, and cover reveals?
Go to Michelle's website or blog to sign up.

Thanks for reading!
If you enjoyed this book, would you help Michelle by posting a review on Goodreads?

Are you a member of Book Bub? If so, please follow Michelle on Book Bub, and you'll get alerts when new books are coming out.

As a way of saying thanks, Michelle invites you to the Goodies page on her website. It will change regularly, offering you a free short story, a sample audiobook chapter, sneak peeks at new cover art, inside information on discounts and new release dates, etc.

Please go to: Mlevigne.com/good-stuff.html

Also by Michelle L. Levigne

Guardians of the Time Stream: 4-book Steampunk series
The Match Girls: Humorous inspirational romance series starting with **A Match (Not) Made in Heaven**
Sarai's Journey: A 2-book biblical fiction series
Tabor Heights: 18-book inspirational small town romance series.
Quarry Hall: 11-book women's fiction/suspense series
For Sale: Wedding Dress. Never Used: inspirational romance
Crooked Creek: Fun Fables About Critters and Kids: Children's short stories.
Do Yourself a Favor: Tips and Quips on the Writing Life. A book of writing advice.
To Eternity (and beyond): Writing Spec Fic Good for Your Soul. A book defending speculative fiction.
Killing His Alter-Ego: contemporary romance/suspense, taking place in fandom.
The Commonwealth Universe: SF series, 25 books and growing
The Hunt: 5-book YA fantasy series
Faxinor: Fantasy series, 4 books and growing
Wildvine: Fantasy series, 14 books when all released
Neighborlee: Humorous fantasy series
Zygradon: 5-book Arthurian fantasy series
AFV Defender: SF adventure series
Young Defenders: Middle Grade SF series, spin-off of *AFV Defender*
Magic to Spare: Fantasy series
Book & Mug Mysteries: cozy mystery series
Quest for the Crescent Moon: fantasy series starting in 2023

Michelle L. Levigne, Guardians of the Time Stream, Book 3

Steward's World: **fantasy series reboot and expansion**
The Enchanted Castle Archives: **fantasy series**